...d grand romance. Since ...arned degrees in computer science and ...ucation and held various jobs ranging from bookselling to teaching inner-city children to act, but she's never stopped writing.

Visit Jennifer Haymore online:

http://www.jenniferhaymore.com
https://www.facebook.com/JenniferHaymore.Author
https://twitter.com/jenniferhaymore

Praise for Jennifer Haymore:

'Jennifer Haymore's books are sophisticated, deeply sensual and emotionally complex'
Elizabeth Hoyt, *New York Times* bestselling author

'Sweep-you-off-your-feet historical romance! Jennifer Haymore sparkles!'
Liz Carlyle, *New York Times* bestselling author

'[Haymore] perfectly blends a strong plot that twists like a serpent and has unforgettable characters to create a book readers will remember and reread'
RT Book Reviews

The
Rogue's Proposal

Jennifer
HAYMORE

piatkus

PIATKUS

First published in the US in 2013 by Forever, an imprint of Grand Central Publishing,
A division of Hachette Book Group, Inc.
First published in Great Britain as a paperback original in 2013 by Piatkus

A CIP catalogue record for this book
is available from the British Library.

ISBN 978-0-349-40124-9

Printed and bound in Great Britain by
Clays Ltd, St Ives plc

Papers used by Piatkus are from well-managed forests
and other responsible sources.

MIX
Paper from
responsible sources
FSC
www.fsc.org FSC® C104740

Piatkus
An imprint of
Little, Brown Book Group
100 Victoria Embankment
London EC4Y 0DY

An Hachette UK Company
www.hachette.co.uk

www.piatkus.co.uk

For my hero, Lawrence.

Acknowledgments

With heartfelt thanks to:

Selina McLemore and Michele Bidelspach, my brilliant editors,

Kate McKinley, for enduring all my writerly moods,

Cindy Benser, for finding typos no one else in the world can,

My kids, for putting up with such a nutty mom,

My husband, for being such a rock,

And all my readers, who inspire me every day.

Chapter One

Lord Lukas Hawkins wasn't drunk enough. Not yet. He gazed at the glass of ale sitting on the table before him and dragged the pad of his thumb through the drops of condensation on its lip.

He would have preferred something stronger, but the ale was beginning its work. All his sharp edges, those phantom blades that sliced so ruthlessly at him when he was sober, were beginning to dull. The noises of the tavern had faded into an agreeable drone rather than the piercing, headache-inducing racket of when he'd first arrived.

Luke took another generous swallow of the cool amber liquid and leaned back, his eyelids descending to a pleasant half-mast.

He'd asked enough questions for tonight. He'd made no progress in his hunt for Roger Morton, but that didn't surprise him. The villain who'd taken Luke's mother from her home at Ironwood Park was a wily man, slipping through Luke's fingers from Cardiff to Bristol.

Luke wouldn't find Morton here. It was hopeless. What he needed now was to gulp down another three or four tall glasses of ale, unearth some pleasant companionship for the evening, and plummet into a dreamless sleep.

Only to wake up tomorrow and begin the whole fruitless endeavor again.

Taking his ale in two hands, he brought it to his lips, closed his eyes, and tossed back the whole bloody thing.

His eyes reopened as he lowered the empty glass.

Well, well, well.

Straightening his spine, he brought his glass down until it landed with a decided *clunk* on the worn wooden tabletop. His lips curled into a wicked grin. It seemed his pleasant companionship had unearthed itself.

A vision in black and white had seated herself on the other side of the narrow wood-planked table. She was the loveliest thing he'd seen in a very long time. Brown eyes shot through with polished gold gazed at him, their expression inscrutable. Thick, burnished waves of bronze hair escaped the little annoyance of a prim white cap and framed a heart-shaped and pink-cheeked face. Her lips…hell, just edible. Gazing at those lips aroused Luke's senses—the deep red of cherries in the summertime, their sweet scent, the decadent, juicy burst when he bit into one.

Just one glance at those lips was enough to bring Luke's sluggish body to sudden, alert life.

"Well," he said, infusing his voice with a lazy edge of suggestive slyness. He'd perfected the tone over the years, and it had a dual purpose: It told a lady of loose morals exactly what he wanted, while simultaneously warning an innocent maiden to escape while she still had a chance. "It's about time. I've been waiting for you."

To her credit, her only reaction was a slight widening of her eyes. He wouldn't have seen it if he hadn't been looking carefully. Otherwise, she didn't move.

"Have you, now?" she asked.

Lust jolted through him. God, that voice. Potent and smooth, like the finest brandy. It evoked images of the bedroom, mussed sheets, a rough tumble, erotic pleasure.

His body hardened all over. His cock pressed against the falls of his breeches. Between her lovely face, her calm, unperturbed demeanor, and the husky sensuality of her voice, he was done for. He wanted to take her upstairs. Immediately.

But Luke wasn't one to rush things overmuch, especially when he was so intrigued. He possessed some restraint, some patience. Not much, but some.

He cocked his head at her. "What took you so long?"

"Well..." She took a deep breath. The action drew his eyes to her bosom—her full breasts strained at the top edge of her bodice as if they yearned to be set free. He'd be happy to perform that task for her.

"...I was detained," she finished.

"Oh? By what? Or whom?"

The corner of her lip quirked upward. She was playing with him. He was the one who usually toyed with females. But in this case, they were toying with each other. He liked that.

"By ignorance," she said.

Ignorance. Loose women usually didn't use such words, especially not with such inflection. Her throaty voice had spoken the word as only an educated woman would.

Luke settled back in his seat, pushing past his arousal and drunkenness to study her. He'd only noticed her cap before—when he'd wanted to toss it to the floor and push his hand through that bounty of burnished hair. He hadn't noticed the pearl earrings or the fine silk of her dress, white with black velvet trim.

She was no whore. She was a lady.

He stiffened, quickly scanning the area surrounding them. The tavern was crowded with men and women drinking, eating, conversing. The atmosphere was boisterous, and the smells of charred meat and hops and yeast permeated every inch of the place. No one was watching them—at least not overtly. But, hell, ladies like this didn't just waltz into pubs and plunk down across from the first drunkard they encountered. This woman knew something.

None of these revelations made her less appealing. In fact, they fascinated him. She was brazen, lady or not. Luke liked his women brazen. That kind of woman was fearless, more likely to take risks, in bed and out.

He leaned forward, placing his elbows on the smooth surface of the table. The slab of wood was so narrow his face ended up only a few inches from hers. "And now you're no longer ignorant?" he asked her. "Someone has enlightened you?"

She nodded sagely. "Indeed."

She'd probably heard he'd been asking questions about Roger Morton. "So, then, you've information for me?"

"Hmm," she said. Her fingers drummed on the table, drawing his gaze downward. Her brown kid gloves hugged each long, elegant finger as they tapped the wooden surface. "I thought *you* might have information for *me*."

He raised his brows. "Is that so?"

Her brows mirrored his in a haughty reaction. "It is."

He laughed, the rare feeling bubbling up in him and spilling over. His smile widened. This was not how women generally behaved in his presence. They either ran crying to their mamas like abused little kittens or dragged him straight to bed like lionesses on the prowl. This woman was a different kind of creature altogether.

"Therefore, I have a proposal for you, my lord."

Ah, so she knew who he was as well. Or she knew who he spent his life pretending to be.

"And I have a proposal for you. Miss...?"

"Mrs."

"Mrs.," he repeated. But he didn't believe for a second that she was married. No, he possessed the skill of sniffing out married women. And this woman—she smelled of lavender soap, but there was more. Something raw and sensual, something in her gaze that spoke of warm, womanly flesh and dark, languid nights.

No, definitely not married.

So that meant she was lying about her marital status...or she was a widow. She was very young to be a widow, though. He narrowed his eyes at her, trying to see beneath that calm surface, to delve underneath and find some clue that would tell him what this woman was about.

"Mrs. Curtis," she told him.

"Mrs. Curtis," he said, "*I* have a proposal for *you*."

That corner of her lip quirked again. Her eyes sparkled the most fascinating shade of amber.

"Do you?"

He reached up to drag a finger across her lower lip.

Softer than the velvet of her dress ribbons. Plump and red as a ripe, sweet cherry. He wanted a taste.

"Come upstairs with me," he whispered.

She didn't react to his touch, or his words. She was very still. Too still. Then she drew back from his touch and gave the slightest of nods. "Very well, my lord."

Terse and businesslike, she rose. He rose instantly, too, out of long-ingrained habit more than anything else. *Always rise when a lady is standing,* his governess had told him, *or you shall be considered the rudest of gentlemen.*

These days, he *was* considered the rudest of gentlemen, but it still didn't prevent him from rising.

"Please"—Mrs. Curtis gestured in the general direction of the exit—"lead the way."

"Of course." He turned away from the table, seeing his empty ale glass from the corner of his eye. How odd—he'd forgotten to hail the serving girl to ask her to refill it for him. But that seemed unimportant now.

They threaded their way in silence through the crowded pub. No one paid them any mind. They left the large room and walked down a long corridor, ascending the narrow stairs at its end.

Night had descended, and with it came a bitter autumn chill. It was cold in the dimly lit stairwell, and Luke had the urge to draw Mrs. Curtis close to warm her. But he was sober enough to realize that that kind of advance in plain, public view might be unwelcome from such a lady.

On the other hand, he *was* foxed enough to imagine how exuberantly she'd accept his advances behind a closed door.

At the top of the stairs, he paused on the landing to

gain his bearings. It was a large inn, and the corridor branched in three directions from here.

She paused beside him, quirking a bronze-tinted brow at him. "I believe it's this way, my lord."

He followed when she turned to the rightmost corridor and began to walk again. So, he mused, she already knew where his room was located. She grew more intriguing by the second.

She stopped at the very last room. "Here?"

"Yes, Mrs. Curtis. Here."

He withdrew the key from a pocket in his coat and unlocked the door, then stepped inside.

The room was Spartan and cold. Unlike his exalted brother, Simon Hawkins, the Duke of Trent, Luke didn't have the means to set aside entire floors of inns for himself and his party and employ maids and other servants to stoke fires and light braziers to keep them pleasantly warm. Besides, he had no party. There was just him. Always had been, always would be. Especially now that he knew he wasn't a true Hawkins.

He opened the door wider, and she stepped inside behind him. She made to move around him, but he shut the door with a firm *click*, then held up an arm to stop her. She retreated until her back pressed against the door.

He boxed her in, placing a firm arm on either side of her and flattening his palms against the door. "There," he said softly, "now you're my prisoner."

Something flared in her eyes. Heat or fear? Heat, probably. From what he'd seen of her so far, she wasn't a woman who was easily frightened.

He leaned down to whisper in her ear, "You like that idea, don't you? Do you like to be bound, Mrs. Curtis?"

Her reaction was slight—an infinitesimal tremor that ran through her body. It was enough.

He moved his mouth to within a hairsbreadth of hers. The warm wash of her breath fluttered across his cheek. Other than that soft release of air, she didn't move.

His body was an inch from hers. Not touching, but so close he could feel their heat combine and simmer in the narrow gap between them.

Slowly, painstakingly, he touched his mouth to hers in the lightest of kisses. His eyelids sank shut. Her lips were plump and soft, forgiving against his.

He dragged his lips against hers in a back-and-forth motion, a slow, sensual slide. She didn't move, but her flesh yielded beneath his, and he released a low groan. She tasted so good. Sweet. Ripe. He sipped at her unresponsive lips, then touched the tip of his tongue to the corner of her mouth, urging a reaction, but still she didn't move.

God, he wanted this woman. His body screamed at him to haul her against him and take all the wicked pleasure her supple flesh could offer. But he didn't only want her compliance; he wanted her to be an active participant.

He kissed his way from the edge of her lips, across the upper portion of her jaw—such soft, smooth skin—until he nuzzled the tender lobe of her ear.

"Now," he whispered, "are you ready to hear my proposal?"

He feathered his lips over her earlobe, bit down over it gently, then drew back to study her. Her expression didn't change, but her eyelids were lowered. She didn't speak for a long moment.

As she formulated her response, he formulated his own

words in his mind. *I believe you have information for me,
Mrs. Curtis. I believe you might want something from me
in return. But those are things that can be saved for later.
Right here, right now, I want you. I want your lovely body
beneath mine. I want to strip that dress from you and lick
every inch of that delectable skin. I want to make you
scream my name in pleasure again and again until we're
both in such a delirium that there's nothing either of us
can do but to sleep. And then, when we wake—*

"No," she said, finally looking up at him.

"No?"

"I *don't* wish to hear your proposal, my lord."

God, her voice. It scraped his every nerve into a raw,
needy thing that only her touch could soothe.

"I think you do."

"I know I don't," she said. "Because I know the
essence of it."

"And it's not a proposal you believe you'll accept?"

"Absolutely not," she said.

"Why not?"

She looked deliberately down at the arms that caged
her, first his right arm, then his left. Then she turned
her gaze back to his face, her eyes coming to sparkling
golden life, brimming with determination. "Because I've
more important things to do."

He laughed, long and loud. "Trust me, Mrs. Curtis. At
this hour, there is nothing more important than what I intend to suggest."

"There is," she said simply, and the soft curve of her
lips firmed.

He'd humor her, then. "What could it possibly be?"

"The proposition *I* have for *you.*"

He sighed. "Very well. Tell me what it is."

"You've come to Bristol looking for a man named Roger Morton. Is that correct?"

He gazed steadily at her. This didn't surprise him. She knew who he was. She knew the location of his room. Obviously she'd been watching him since he'd ridden into town yesterday and knew exactly why he was here. He hadn't made a secret of it. He was looking for any information that would lead him to the bastard who'd taken his mother.

"Yes, that's true. I am searching for Roger Morton."

"I can help you find him."

His lips curved. "Can you?"

"And that is my proposition. I will give you the information you shall require to find him if you allow me to come with you."

"Allow you to come with me." He repeated her words slowly, tasting them in his mouth as images washed through him. Taking this lovely specimen of womanhood with him in his hunt across England for Roger Morton. Sampling the beds of different country inns. Long nights of feasting on her pale, curvaceous flesh, of vigorous lovemaking...

He studied her face. The color was high on her cheeks now, and her implacable features had hardened, giving her an expression of iron resolve. He stood close enough to her to feel the thrum of purpose under her skin. Whatever this was about, it meant a great deal to her.

"Why would you wish to travel with me? *Alone* with me?" He put emphasis on the word *alone* to remind her of the potential permanent repercussions to her reputation. She was a lady, after all, and ladies simply did not travel alone with gentlemen unless they were married to them.

"Because," she said, her voice throbbing with certainty, "I want to find Roger Morton, too."

He narrowed his eyes at her.

"And then I want to kill him."

* * *

Emma was out of her depth. She knew this. But even though her heart raced, she gazed at Lord Lukas Hawkins steadily, refusing to allow him to intimidate her. He'd come to Bristol now, just in time to save her from an existence certain to drive her mad. She wouldn't let this opportunity pass her by.

He didn't move an inch away from her. He just studied her with those penetrating, devastating icy blue eyes. When she'd come looking for him in the downstairs tavern, she'd no idea he'd be so...compelling.

And...she'd let him kiss her. Good *Lord*.

Do you like to be bound, Mrs. Curtis? Her stomach had clenched hard in response to those words. It hadn't recovered yet.

"You don't seem to be the murdering kind of woman, Mrs. Curtis." He gave her a wolfish grin. "After all, I'm standing here with you, and I'm not in the least afraid for my life."

She simply continued to stare at him, knowing that if her suspicions proved true, she'd gladly kill Roger Morton.

"Very well," he said after a moment, "I'll play. Why do you wish to murder Roger Morton?"

"Vengeance."

His arms tightened at her sides. They were strong arms. Masculine and powerful.

"What for? What did the man do that was so terrible you wish to end his life?"

Where to begin? If she was correct in her suspicions, Morton had destroyed nearly every aspect of her life. But she supposed it was best to start with the worst of his crimes. She closed her eyes and pushed the words out one at a time. "He...*murdered*...my husband."

Silence. Then, "Ah."

Ah? That was all he had to say? She opened her eyes, fury rising. But then he shifted and his hand came to her face, cupping her cheek in his hand, his thumb stroking her cheekbone. It had been so long since a man had touched her...kissed her. And the touches and kisses of her past had been nothing like the ones Lukas Hawkins, a man she'd known for less than an hour, had bestowed upon her. And certainly no one had ever asked her if she liked to be bound.

Heavens. She didn't want to think about any of this right now. She needed to remain focused.

"When?" he asked her softly.

"It's been...a long time." *A lifetime.* "A year ago."

"How long were you married?" he asked. "You're very young."

"We were married for only three months before Henry died. But I'm not so young. I'm twenty-three."

He looked at her with those smoldering, blue-fire eyes, and something within her melted, even as she admitted to herself that Lord Lukas was dangerous. Rogue, rake, scoundrel—however one wished to label this kind of man, he was its epitome.

And she knew about rogues, rakes, and scoundrels. Henry had been of that category as well, with his approachable visage and penchant for drink and gambling…and women. When he died, she'd promised herself that she'd steer clear of those kinds of men in the future.

And now, here was Lord Lukas Hawkins, handsome and dangerous and radiating something so raw and so appealing that a part of her wanted to fall straight into the nearest bed with him.

She'd allowed him to kiss her.

So very, very dangerous.

She steeled her resolve. Danger or not, he was looking for Roger Morton. And, danger or not, she wanted nothing more than to find that man.

"Pretty Mrs. Curtis," Lord Lukas said in that silky voice that seemed to slide down her spine in a wash of smooth heat, "what's your Christian name?"

"Emma," she told him. There was no reason he shouldn't know it, after all.

"May I call you Emma?"

She hesitated. Only her father, sister, and one or two close acquaintances called her Emma these days.

Still, she couldn't seem to bring herself to tell him no, so she responded with her own challenge. "May I call you Lukas, then?"

"Never." His lips curled into a heart-stopping smile. "But you may call me by the name my mother uses: Luke."

"Luke, then." She realized he'd stepped back and was no longer trapping her against the door. A part of her— that stupid part that had fallen for Henry Curtis—felt bereft.

She clasped her hands in front of her. "I heard the Dowager Duchess of Trent had gone missing. I am sorry."

He gave a slight nod of acknowledgment, but the lightness in his eyes vanished. Clearly, his mother's disappearance, though it had occurred months ago, ate at him.

"Do you believe Roger Morton had something to do with her disappearance?"

Luke sighed. Turning away, he ran a hand through his dark blond hair, making it stick up at odd—and somehow endearing—angles. She tamped down the urge to push her hands through his hair to tame those spikes. Instead she kept very still, her back pressed against the door.

"Morton was definitely involved in my mother's disappearance. She was with him the night she left home. He remained with her for at least a month after that."

She nodded. "Roger Morton is evil," she said in a low voice. He'd killed Henry and stolen her father's fortune; she didn't doubt he had done something horrible to the Dowager Duchess of Trent.

Luke slouched against the window frame. Crossing his arms over his chest, he gazed at her across the tiny room. She stared steadily at him, ignoring the little kick in her chest that the sight of his relaxed masculine form gave her. Tall black leather boots clasped his calves like a second skin. He wore dark breeches that hugged strong thighs, a gray-and-black striped waistcoat with the top cloth button open to reveal a simple white cravat and a high-collared black cutaway coat with gray silk lining that emphasized his broad shoulders.

"If Roger Morton is evil, then it wouldn't be very chivalrous of me to allow a lady to join me in my search for him, now, would it?"

She shrugged.

"You'll be happy to hear I've never been accused of chivalry."

"Well, thank God for that."

He didn't smile. "Still, why should I allow you to join me?"

"Because, as I said earlier, I can help you find him."

"How?"

"I am in possession of certain clues that I am positive will lead us straight to him."

"What kinds of clues?"

"Documents."

"Documents of what nature?"

"Receipts and letters."

His lips twisted. "And how did you come to be in possession of those?"

"You ask too many questions. Until we finalize our agreement, I shan't tell you another thing."

"The agreement in which you reveal the location of Morton, then I take you with me to find him. And when we succeed in locating him, you intend to kill him."

"Yes," she said flatly. "But not before you discover everything you can about what happened to the duchess." And not before she discovered what he'd done with her father's money.

"How generous of you, to give me a few moments to question the villain before he suffers a violent death."

"I think so," she said.

Luke laughed. She liked the sound of his laugh—it was low and soft. It made her want to smile and laugh with him. But she didn't. No, the stakes were too high.

She'd known Luke was dangerous from the moment

he'd opened those piercing blue eyes and looked at her over his ale glass. But while he spoke to something intensely carnal within her, Emma had learned her lesson. She wouldn't be dragged into iniquity by the wicked seduction of another man who never saw her beyond her face and the curves of her body. *Never* again, no matter how she reacted to him on a visceral level.

"So, then," she asked, "are we agreed?"

He stared at her for a long moment, assessing her with those fire-and-ice eyes. She felt exposed. Like he systematically removed every stitch of her clothing, burning each seam away so it fell around her in tatters, leaving her stripped bare.

Then his lips curled into that sensual, knowing smile, and a deep flutter spread from her core and through her limbs in response.

His lips had felt so wickedly *good* against hers. She'd wanted—badly—to kiss him back. She ought to have pushed him away. But the angel and devil inside her were engaged in such a furious battle that she hadn't been able to move at all.

"Yes," he said. "We're agreed."

Her muscles suddenly went limp, and she had to battle to keep from sagging to the floor. Only now did she realize how worried she'd been that he'd deny her.

Thank you. Thank you. We'll find him. We'll find Papa's money...and maybe, just maybe, she could save her family.

Slowly, the strength returned to her limbs. She gazed steadily at Luke. "There's just one thing, my lord."

He cocked a brow. "What's that, Emma?"

She swallowed against her suddenly dry mouth. She'd

never spoken so freely to a gentleman before, not even to Henry. But certain things needed to be said.

"If you want my help, I cannot..." She took a deep breath and continued. "I cannot engage in relations—of any kind—with you."

His brow remained firmly nocked upward. "Why not?"

"I'm not the kind of woman who...bestows her favors easily."

He leveled his gaze at her. "You came up here with me. That is evidence contrary to your words. How do you think following me up to my room should be interpreted? By me, and by the people in that tavern downstairs?"

The obvious interpretation of her actions was that she was a loose woman. That she fully intended to offer him any and every favor he chose to ask of her.

It was stupid to have come up here...yet perhaps not so stupid. She didn't care what anyone thought about her anymore. She had nothing to prove to anyone. He hadn't hurt her—something inside her had told her he wasn't a danger, at least not in the most overt sense of the word. She'd been determined to get him to agree to her plan, no matter what it took. And speaking privately with him had seemed like it would offer her an advantage that speaking with him in the noisy tavern wouldn't.

And a part of her, a tiny portion of her mind, had wondered what it would be like to throw away every sense of propriety and responsibility, go upstairs with a man she didn't know, and lose herself to the sensual pleasures that his heated gaze had promised her from across that undersized table.

She spoke carefully. "I don't care what everyone

thought, my lord. But I want you to know that wasn't my intention. I wished to offer you a business proposition. Truly, I cannot help the fact that I am a woman."

His gaze raked her body up and down, leaving trembling gooseflesh in its wake. She was glad her half-mourning dress covered so much of her skin and that he couldn't see how his gaze affected her.

"No," he murmured. "You certainly can't help the fact that you're a beautiful woman."

She swallowed hard. "This is a business proposition. Nothing more. You and I are searching for the same man, and we're assisting each other in that endeavor."

"I don't know," he mused. "What if I require the need for female companionship during the term of this business partnership?"

"Then I shall turn a blind eye," she said automatically. Still, something in her chest clenched at the thought of him seeking out a woman.

His eyes narrowed into slits. "Oh? What if I decide that female ought to be you?"

"I imagine you're capable of controlling yourself."

"Perhaps," he said. "But what if you're not?"

She laughed, but something about it sounded high and false. "I'm entirely capable of controlling myself, too. Not that there shall be anything to control."

His lips twisted, and she didn't blame his disbelief. She made a poor liar.

"You want me, Emma." He studied his fingernails as if something fascinating lurked in the nail beds. "Mark my words, it's only a matter of time before you beg me to take you."

"Oh, I think not, my lord."

He looked back up at her, giving her a wicked smile as he dropped his hands to his sides. "We'll see."

She took a breath, not answering. But her cheeks felt like they were ablaze. *Please*, she thought, *don't let him see that I am blushing.*

But his gaze brushed over her face, and his smile deepened.

"Yes," he continued, "I'll agree to your business proposition. You help me find Roger Morton and you may join me in my search. I will refrain from engaging in... what did you call it? Oh, yes... *relations* with you."

She gave a very businesslike nod, as if they truly were men of trade agreeing on the terms of a deal.

He raised a hand as if to stop her. "But I have a condition of my own."

Her heart sank. "What's that?"

"I can offer you the heights of pleasure, Mrs. Emma Curtis. If, at some point during the term of our agreement, you were to beg... I promise, I'll not deny you."

Chapter Two

Emma woke at the break of dawn the following morning. She'd been up late at the inn with Luke last night, but her nerves were so raw she'd hardly been able to sleep, and when the first gray shadows of light began to creep into her room, she popped out of her bed like a jack-in-the-box and began to pack.

She chose carefully, knowing it would be impractical, and probably annoying to Luke, if she brought too much. So she brought two sets of undergarments, a nightgown, and one other dress, an old but once-beautiful day dress of white muslin sprinkled with pink and green rosebuds and festooned with matching ribbons whose corners were now frayed. After she finished packing her valise, she donned the black-and-white half-mourning dress she'd worn the evening before.

After her husband died, Papa, refusing to blame Henry for any part of the loss of his fortune, had insisted on spending some of the few remaining funds they had to purchase her two stylish mourning dresses. She'd worn them all year long, alternating between the two of them, both black and somber and altogether depressing. They had become frayed and stained, not to mention out of fashion—and since they'd been purchased in autumn, she'd sweltered in them all through summer.

Just last month, Papa and her sister Jane had gifted her with the half-mourning dress. Jane had scrimped and saved so they could afford it. But it was a fashionable dress, and wearing a light color—even with black trim— had made Emma feel alive again. She'd once possessed a closetful of fashionable clothes; now this was the only dress she owned that was presentable in the company of a duke's brother.

A duke's *brother*. Lord Lukas was the famous Duke of Trent's brother. Even now, that fact stunned her. The duke was well known for being a paragon, an absolutely upright gentleman of perfect scruples, respected by everyone in England. But he'd recently caused an enormous scandal by marrying one of his housemaids. The wave of excitement had yet to die down—everyone was still gossiping about the duke and the housemaid.

Even Jane and Emma had huddled together over the newssheets and decided it must have been a love match. Instead of thinking him scandalous, the act only raised their compassion and respect for the man. In the sisters' eyes, the Duke of Trent was a prime example of a powerful man who was honest in his love.

Jane and Emma had been exposed to the *ton*, to some degree. They had been raised as wealthy young ladies, and they had associated with daughters of marquises and earls and viscounts in school every day. But their father was in trade, and he wasn't of the aristocracy. They were nouveau riche, and the aristocratic girls resented their admittance into the prestigious Derbyford School For Girls. They never let Emma and Jane forget their place, which was firmly entrenched in the very lowest rung of the school's social ladder.

So when the highly respected and widely admired Duke of Trent married a commoner, it felt like a victory of sorts to Emma and Jane. A victory for the common folk. To Emma and Jane, not only was he a paragon, but also he was clearly an intrinsically *good* man.

She'd learned tonight that the Duke of Trent's brother was something else altogether. *Good* would not be the first word to come to mind when she thought of Lord Luke. *Wicked* and *arrogant* and *kissable* and *handsome* and *dashing* were five words that came in well ahead.

Taking a deep breath, wiping her memory clear of the way his dark blond hair curled over his ears, Emma snapped her valise shut. It was packed to the brim with her extra dress and underclothes, and, because the days were growing colder, her shabby pelisse, which had once been sky blue but had faded after many washings to a dull slate color.

Straightening, she gazed around her bedchamber for the last time.

Two years ago, a soft Persian carpet had covered the floor. The bed had been of an elaborately feminine design, with whitewashed carved wood and lavender silk bed curtains that matched the curtains on her windows. She'd had a walnut armoire and matching desk and chair, where she used to sit and write letters.

Now it was all gone. Sold to the highest bidder, down

to the yellow silk counterpane that had once lain on the bed.

Maybe someday they'd have it all back. But only if she was successful in her search for Roger Morton...and in finding what that awful man had done with her father's money.

Grabbing her valise, she left the room and traversed the long, empty corridor. Papa had moved them to this enormous modern house on the outskirts of Bristol when she was just three years old and Jane was a babe. Before that, they had lived by the harbor, where her father had owned a ship manufactory. He'd overseen the building of many of the great English sailing ships that dominated the world's oceans.

Downstairs, Emma slipped into his study, which was now, for the most part, used only by her. Papa could hardly leave his bedchamber these days—he was afflicted with the dropsy, but it was more than that. No one could determine exactly what was sapping the strength from his body, though Emma had a firm suspicion that it was a broken heart. When Mama had died, Papa had hardly been able to hold on. Then Henry had been murdered, Roger Morton had stolen everything, and Papa had sunk deep into this miserable sickness that no one seemed able to cure.

Emma couldn't bring Mama back—that was impossible—but her father's money was still out there somewhere. She would do whatever was in her power to return it to him.

Maybe then Papa would at least *try*. They would have the money to find him the best doctors. They'd have the money to refurnish and heat the house for his maximum comfort, to buy the best medicines.

Lowering her valise near the study door, she fetched the key from where it was hidden on the bookshelf between the covers of *A Midsummer Night's Dream* and *Richard III*, two of the books on the single shelf they'd retained. Once, these wall shelves had been brimming with books. Now the shelves were bare, except for this one small row of books.

She went to the desk and used the key to unlock the tiny drawer hidden within a larger one. She removed her father's pistol. The small, deadly weapon lay in its velvet-lined case innocently, as if it weren't capable of cold-blooded murder. She checked its parts carefully before relocking the drawer, then going to the door and locking that as well.

Kneeling on the floor, she removed everything from the valise and repacked it with the gun case at the very bottom. She followed that with the two papers she'd studied ad nauseam for the past year—those that implicated Roger Morton in Henry's death and the crimes against her father—and finally placed her clothes on top.

Then she went to the desk, retrieved the inkpot, a pen, and a used sheet of parchment, which she turned over to write on the blank side, and proceeded to write out detailed instructions to Jane.

Her list included a catalogue of Papa's medicines, reminders about the daily exercises one of the doctors had recommended, and the list of foods he was forbidden to eat as well as those the doctor had said would be beneficial to him. It included information on their dwindling funds and detailed instructions on how to manage bill collectors if they came calling.

She recommended the best and cheapest places for Jane

to purchase food and supplies. Then she listed, in detailed precision, the instructions for the keeping and maintaining of the house and the six acres of land it lay upon.

Finally, she listed her ideas on how to obtain funds should one of the bill collectors lose all patience. It probably wouldn't happen—she'd managed to placate most of them so far, and she intended to be back in Bristol within a few weeks. But just in case, she wrote them in order from first to last to sell:

Papa's bed—he can be relocated to mine.

The remaining books. She winced at that one. She had kept only her favorite books, and to lose them would be like losing a part of her heart.

The desk in the study. The very desk she wrote upon now—one of the last remaining original opulent pieces her father had purchased.

Mama's pearl earrings and her gold ring. It physically hurt her to write that. Those pieces of jewelry were the only pieces of their mother they'd kept. When they'd gone through their mother's possessions and sold them, Emma had decided that she and her sister should each keep something to remind them of Mama. Emma had chosen the earrings and Jane had chosen the ring.

Finally, she listed a few men in Bristol who might be willing to purchase the items in question.

She removed the earrings from her ears and laid them beside the lists she'd written. The near-perfect pearls gleamed against the black shine of the desk, and she stared at them for a long moment.

With a sigh, she rose and returned upstairs, where she slipped into Jane's room, once a lovely haven, now as barren as her own.

Jane was already stirring. An early riser like herself, Emma's twenty-year-old sister was competent and intelligent. Emma had no doubts or worries about leaving Papa in Jane's capable hands.

Jane sat up, rubbing her eyes. "Emma, is something wrong with—" She broke off abruptly, her gaze moving to the valise Emma held firmly in her grip. Then she looked into Emma's eyes, her own widening with alarm.

"Where are you going?" she breathed.

"I'm going with Lord Lukas," Emma told her sister. "We're leaving this morning."

"Em!" Jane gasped, her eyes like saucers.

"It's my only hope to find Roger Morton. Lord Lukas has as much desire to locate him as I do, but not only that, he also has the support of the Duke of Trent—all the resources he'd ever need to bring that bastard to justice."

Jane flinched as she always did when Emma cursed. She frowned and slipped out of the bed, the skirt of her white nightgown falling around her ankles. "But you cannot travel with him alone. Take Marta with you."

Marta was their maid—the only remaining servant, when once they had had a butler and a half-dozen footmen, as well as a housekeeper, housemaids, chambermaids, a cook, scullery maids...

"Absolutely not. You will require her here. You cannot manage this house and take care of Papa all by yourself."

"Are you mad?"

"Are you?"

The sisters stared at each other with challenges in their eyes. But Jane knew when Emma wouldn't retreat.

She lowered her eyes. "People will talk. Do you realize what it will do to your reputation?"

Emma's lips twisted. "What reputation? I am a widow with no money and no prospects. It's not like any gentleman will take a fancy to me now. My reputation is of no consequence, and I'd gladly give it up for a chance to retrieve what is rightfully ours."

Jane sighed. "Oh, I do wish you'd give this some thought first."

"I have. There's no alternative." She took a step forward. "Jane, have *you* thought about what would happen if Papa's fortune was returned to him? About what it would do to Papa?"

"Of course I have. But I wouldn't have you sacrifice yourself for Papa's sake. Is there no solution that will keep you both safe?"

"*This* is the solution," Emma said. "I *am* safe. Lord Lukas is a"—she pushed the word out, because she didn't believe it for a second, despite his pedigree—"gentleman." But then she dealt the winning blow. "Don't forget, he's the Duke of Trent's brother."

Jane sighed wistfully, as she and every other young lady in England were wont to do whenever the Duke of Trent's name was mentioned.

"You're right. I had forgotten." She straightened. "In that case, I'm sure he'll realize that this shall be a sensitive position for you, and he'll do whatever is necessary to protect your reputation in light of the scandalous nature of the situation."

Do you like to be bound, Mrs. Curtis?

A shudder pulsed through her.

"Exactly," Emma lied to her sister. "He will be discreet. I am certain of it."

Jane's brow furrowed. "Oh, Em. I still don't like it."

"There is no choice," Emma said again.

"I wish I could think of something else."

"You can't. I can't. Papa can't. We've all tried."

"Will you say good-bye to him before you go?"

"I don't think I should."

The sisters stood in silence for a few moments, then Jane said, "You're right. You probably shouldn't. He'll try to force you to stay, and I know you. You'll defy him..."

"And I'm not sure if his constitution could withstand such a blow," Emma finished.

"I don't think you should take that risk."

"Nor do I."

Her sister's brown eyes were shining with concern and trepidation. "But what will I tell him?" she whispered.

Emma closed her eyes as all the possible excuses ran through her mind. She went off on holiday with Miss Delacorte, an old school friend. Her grandmother had summoned her to Leeds because she was ill and demanding to see Emma. She wasn't feeling well and was worried she might be contagious—she wouldn't want to further weaken Papa's constitution by making him ill.

"I'll tell him the truth," Jane said. "There's nothing else to tell."

"No," Emma said quietly, "tell him I've gone to Scotland to help a friend in need." In one of their rare moments of camaraderie, Henry had told her that the best way to lie to someone was to remain as close to the truth as possible. "Tell him I'll be back in a few weeks."

"You know he'll ask who took you."

Emma pursed her lips. "Tell him...tell him it is a relation of the Duke of Trent. And if he demands more, then

you must lie." Because if Jane told Papa she'd run off
with a man...No, that wouldn't be good at all. "Tell him
she's a relation of the Duke of Trent."

Jane said nothing. She looked stern but resigned—so
much older than her twenty years. This past spring should
have been her second Season—she'd received five offers
of marriage last year, including one from a baron. She'd
turned them all down.

Of course, they hadn't had the money for a Season
this year. Now that they were poor, she'd told Emma she
would accept any one of the five if given the opportunity.
But, of course, none of those offers still stood. No one
paid attention to either Emma or Jane now.

"Thank you, Jane." After lowering the valise to the
floor, Emma stepped forward to embrace her sister. "Take
care of him."

"I will."

"I'll find a way to get Papa's money back," Emma
promised. "At least, I shall try..."

"I know you will," Jane said. "When you're determined, nothing can stop you."

* * *

Luke blinked hard. His eyes were gritty. He felt like he
hadn't slept more than half an hour, though by the way
daylight blazed through the window, it had to be noon. Or
later.

A slight movement drew his attention, and he blinked
again as the figure of a woman wearing black and white
came into focus. She was seated in the sole chair in the
room, a spindly wooden thing tucked into the corner. She

was gazing at him with an ever-so-patient expression on her lovely face.

"You have clothes on," he said, his voice rasping over his dry throat. "How unacceptable."

Her golden-brown eyes met his, and she raised a brow. "Many people prefer to utilize clothing at this hour of the day. I am one of them."

He closed his dry eyes and fell back against the pillow, his lips attempting to twitch into a smile.

He'd enjoyed her company last night, even though she'd stood stiff when he'd kissed her. She'd still tasted sweet. Then she'd made him a proposition and he hadn't been able to resist—even with her demand that they not engage in "relations."

He chuckled out loud at that memory.

He'd give her time. He wasn't one to force an unwilling woman. But he'd wear her down. Because, even lying here in an uncomfortable bed in a strange inn in Bristol, he wanted her beside him. Naked.

It seemed he'd have plenty of time to work on her resistance. She'd insisted they travel together, after all.

He opened his eyes to find her still gazing at him with that imperturbable expression that wound him in knots and made him want to knock down her wall of defenses, one brick at a time.

"Good morning, Emma," he murmured.

"Good morning, my lord."

"Luke."

She gave him an almost-smile. "Luke. Do you truly prefer that? Surely you are more accustomed to 'my lord'?"

That low and sultry voice washed over him, and he

couldn't prevent his body, already on alert just from her presence in the room, from hardening.

"Mmm," was his only response. He damn well did prefer Luke. That was his real name, given to him by his real mother. Everything else was a sham. And for some reason, while he was usually content to allow his women to call him whatever the hell they liked, he wanted Emma to call him by his true name. Even if he wasn't about to tell her why.

"I think I shall like calling you Luke. Calling the son of a duke by his Christian name—it's such a brazen thing to do. I shall feel as if I'm doing something extremely wicked each and every time I say it."

"Excellent," Luke said. "When the words *wicked* and *brazen* are connected to you, they appeal to me very much."

She shook her head, laughing softly as he stretched and shifted his feet over the edge of the bed. He was wearing only a shirt, but she didn't seem to mind. Obviously she'd seen men dressed only in their shirtsleeves and leaving their beds before.

That thought did not improve his mood.

She was a contradiction. Stoic, then playful. Flirtatious, then frigid. He wondered what thoughts were really going through that pretty little head of hers.

He pulled on his trousers, which had been strewn on the floor beside his feet. He rose and stretched, then used the bellpull to call for some water to wash.

He turned to Emma, who, save for the lack of the little white cap, looked exactly as she had last night. Even her clothes looked the same, with nary a wrinkle. He wondered briefly whether she'd sat there all night, then furrowed his brow. He vaguely remembered her leaving just before he'd removed his clothes and fallen into an exhausted heap on the bed.

He hadn't dreamed at all last night. He'd slept like the dead. Thank God.

"What time is it?"

"A little past noon," she said.

He sighed, rubbing his temple to soothe the headache forming there.

"Can I fetch you something? Something to eat or drink, perhaps?"

"No," he said. He'd rung for a servant. He wasn't about to make a lady like Emma Curtis play serving girl for him. "Thank you," he added belatedly.

He dropped his hand and slanted his gaze toward her. "God knows how long you've been sitting there waiting for me to awaken. I assume you have a plan that I have delayed by my late rising?"

Hell, she looked like a woman with a plan, all tidy and calm. While he was muzzy-headed and had slept half the day away.

She pressed her lips together. Such delectable, plump lips. He wanted another taste of her ripe sweetness.

"Well," she said slowly, "it was no hardship to watch you sleep, I must admit. You look rather innocent and boyish in repose."

Him, innocent? Boyish? He snorted. She ignored it.

"However, I have been thinking of how to proceed," she said, all business now. "I suppose we ought to begin by analyzing the papers that contain the clues as to where we might locate Roger Morton."

He nodded.

"And then we should go."

"Care to tell me where we're going?"

"Scotland."

He raised his brows. "Ah. Perhaps I should see these papers."

"Of course." She rose and knelt down beside the tattered valise that sat beside the chair. She removed a small pile of carefully folded clothes, and Luke realized that was all she planned to bring on their journey. It couldn't have been more than one dress. Not even half the amount of clothing he carted about everywhere.

She removed a file, set it on the small, round table, and then returned the clothing to her bag.

A servant knocked, and Luke opened the door. He ordered water to wash and a light luncheon for both of them, then turned back to her. She'd resumed her seat and was patiently waiting, hands folded in her lap.

He took two steps toward her—it was a damned small room—and held out his hand. "Let me see."

She took the first sheet of parchment from the file and handed it to him.

He looked it over. "It appears to be a receipt for a transfer of funds from the Bank of England."

"Yes, that's exactly what it is. However, that is not my father's signature. It is a forgery."

"You believe Roger Morton forged your father's signature? Then took your father's money and ran?"

"Yes. But before he left Bristol, he killed my husband. Henry was involved somehow—I don't know exactly how. He must have known Morton's intentions, and..." Her voice dwindled.

He looked at her over the top of the wrinkled sheet,

noting the color high on her cheeks. How sickening it must be to discover that your own husband was involved in a scheme to steal your family's money.

"How much did Morton take in total?" he asked in a low voice.

"All of it."

He released a slow breath and glanced at the document. The amount was over five thousand pounds. "Was there more than this?"

"Yes." Her voice was clipped. "Quite a bit more."

"Do you know where the rest of it went?"

She shook her head. "No. That is the only paper that struck me as odd when I was looking through my husband's personal effects after he died. At first, I wondered at the large withdrawal. When I went to my father, he knew nothing about it."

"Why would your husband have this in his possession?"

"He knew Morton. They had an association of some kind." The delicate, pale column of her throat moved as she swallowed and looked away. Her fingers tapped her knee as they had tapped the table down at the tavern last night. "I went to the street in Bristol listed as the location of delivery for the funds. The landlady was very helpful—she told me that a man named Roger Morton boarded there occasionally but hadn't been there for some time—not since"—she took a steadying breath—"since the date of my husband's death."

She suddenly looked vulnerable. Alone. Some unfamiliar instinct urged him to go to her. To take her into his arms and hold her and tell her everything would be all right.

But he couldn't do that. How could he? He wouldn't even know if he'd be lying.

Emma took another shaky breath and continued. "The landlady let me in to search Morton's rooms. It was there that I found an unopened letter." She gestured to the remaining sheet of paper she held in front of her. "When I questioned the landlady later, she told me it had been delivered by the post on the eighteenth of September of last year."

She handed him the sheet of stationery, and he realized then that her evidence consisted of only these two sheets—the money transfer to a home let by Roger Morton and this letter.

He unfolded it and read.

You have taken long enough. Your preoccupation with Curtis does you no credit. End your business with him—the man wastes your time, and mine. If I do not receive the full balance of the amount owed by the first of October, further measures will be required. Don't put my patience to the test.

Please recall I am spending the autumn months at my residence in Scotland. Send the funds directly to me in Duddingston Parish, Edinburgh.

C. Macmillan

Luke read the letter twice, then glanced up at Emma. Today was the seventh of October. Just over a full year after the deadline stated in this letter.

Emma's head was bare, her bonnet hanging from its strings from one of the pegs on the wall behind her.

Sunlight burnished her glorious hair, making it shine in various shades of bronze and mahogany and gold. But it was twisted severely at her nape. So severely that no tendrils curled around her ears as they had last night.

Her body was coiled tight, just like her hair, her only movement that never-ending tapping of her fingers. He wanted her limp and responsive in his arms...in his bed. He wanted to pull out her pins and loosen that glorious, thick fall of russet beauty. He wanted to find the pins that kept her body so tightly coiled and pull those away as well.

And perhaps, if he found this bastard Roger Morton for her, he could do just that.

"When was your husband killed?" he asked quietly.

"Last year on the seventeenth of September."

So, the letter had been delivered to Morton's residence the day after he'd finished his nasty business with Curtis. The letter had never been opened, so clearly Morton had already escaped from Bristol by then.

"I see why you suspect Morton after reading this. This certainly implicates him in the murder of your husband. And it implicates this Macmillan fellow as an accomplice."

"Yes." Her gaze was flat and impenetrable. He wondered if she mourned Curtis. She seemed more angry than heartbroken.

"How was he killed?"

She looked down at the hands clasped in her lap. "Drowned in the Avon. At first, we thought nothing of it. It wasn't the first time he'd been gone all night, and—"

"He'd been gone all night?"

"Well...yes."

"Where to?"

Her chest rose and fell, drawing his eyes to her bosom. *For hell's sake, Luke, focus!*

"I don't know. I thought perhaps one of the taverns on the waterfront. Or maybe one of the gaming hells—"

"How long had you been married?" He'd forgotten what she'd told him last night; he knew only that it had not been long.

"Three months."

He narrowed his eyes. What kind of newlywed man would leave his wife—especially a wife who was as fine a creature as Emma—alone at home while he went off to carouse in a common, dirty tavern or a dishonest gaming hell?

Gazing at her pink cheeks and pale complexion, at those sinful lips, he blew out a breath. "How did you learn about his death?"

"By the following night, I was very worried. He'd never been gone that long. My sister and I alerted the authorities, and they began to search for him. Witnesses told the constable that he had been drunk, that they'd seen him leaving a pub and heading toward the riverfront with another man. Later they found Henry's sodden, ruined coat and then nearby a soiled handkerchief embroidered with the initials R.M. I thought the discovery of the handkerchief was a random occurrence until I discovered Roger Morton's involvement later."

Emma twisted her hands in her lap as the servants arrived with food and a basin of water. There wasn't space for all of it on the tiny table, so Luke directed them to place the items in various locations on the bed and the floor.

She didn't look at him as he washed as best as he could without removing his clothes. Then he moved the table closer to the bed and laid the tray of food on it. He gestured for her to move her chair across the table from him as he used the edge of the bed as his chair. She was still gazing into her lap, her shoulders rising and falling with each deep intake of breath.

"Come, Emma," he said softly. "Eat."

She looked up at him for the first time in several minutes. Then she nodded and dragged the chair a few inches so she could sit on the other side of the table from him.

The meal was simple country fare, but delicious. The smells of gravy and roasted meat wafted through the room. A pigeon pie, roasted vegetables, an apple tart, and weak ale to wash it all down. Luke divided the portions equally between their two plates and didn't pick up his own fork until she had hers in hand and was moving the food around on her plate.

"Sorry," he said softly.

She looked at him in surprise. "About what?"

He shrugged. "Forcing you to relive it all. I can see it is painful for you."

"Yes. Well," she said, but she didn't meet his eyes, instead seeming fascinated by her food. They ate in silence for a long moment. Then she said, "Tell me about the duchess. What happened to her?"

"Ah, my mother. Another dismal topic."

Her lips twisted. "Sorry."

"No," he said. "It's all right." Silence reigned while he ate a savory bite of pigeon pie. "What have you heard about what happened to my mother?"

"Not very much. Just that she went missing this past

spring. I've heard recently that the duke and his family have begun to fear the worst."

Luke scowled down at his food. "Well, all that is true. And unfortunately, even after all these months, we don't have much information. All we have is Roger Morton."

She leaned forward a bit. "How did you link him to her disappearance?"

"When my mother disappeared from Ironwood Park, she took two of her servants with her. The maid—well, she died." He still couldn't banish the image of Binnie's naked body on that table—so cold and stiff and white and pale. He and his brother had caught an anatomist in the midst of his lecture on the viscera just as he had been about to cut Binnie open.

"I'm sorry," Emma said.

He gave her a dismal look, not really knowing how to respond. "It took us months to find the manservant, but when we finally did, he informed us that a man named Roger Morton had taken my mother from Ironwood Park and brought her to Wales, where he kept her at a house in Cardiff. After several weeks, my mother dismissed the servants, so we know nothing more."

Emma frowned, the skin between her eyebrows puckering. "Was Morton involved in a...liaison...with your mother?"

"No." He shrugged. "Well, I don't know for certain. But from the way the servant described it, he deferred to her. As though he were a servant. Not the way my mother usually behaves with her lovers."

Her eyes widened.

"Yes, she has had many lovers," he said dryly. "Although I must give her some credit. I only ever saw a half dozen or so of them, though I know of more. She made an attempt at discretion. A rather weak attempt, but an attempt nonetheless."

"Goodness." She seemed to not know what else to say. They ate in silence for a few minutes. Then Emma asked him, "Did you search for them in Cardiff?"

"I did, but both Morton and my mother were long gone. No one could tell me whether they left town together or separately. All I could find was a man in a pub who knew someone by that name. Described him the same as my mother's servant had—dark hair, dark eyes, nondescript features. Said he used to live in Bristol and frequented the taverns and hells and bawdy houses here. Said there was a good chance I'd find him in Bristol."

"So you came here."

He took some apple tart, chewed, and swallowed the tangy, sweet bite. "So I came here."

"And now...Scotland?" she asked him.

"And now I will find this Macmillan fellow in Scotland to see if he has any further information on Morton's whereabouts," he agreed. Edinburgh was a hell of a long way away—almost four hundred miles. It would take a great deal of time and energy for them to get there. But he'd go. He'd no other choice—this "C. Macmillan" was currently his only clue.

Emma looked down at her plate, poking her fork into a baked apple slice. "I have wanted to go to Edinburgh ever since I found the letter—but I simply couldn't find a way."

Right. A woman, alone. Her husband dead. All her money gone—stolen. It would be nigh impossible for someone like her to travel the distance alone.

Still, it seemed odd she'd turn to Luke—a single man and a complete stranger.

"Don't you have family? Someone who could have helped you?"

"No. My father is ill, and my sister needs to stay to care for him. Other than that, we've only an elderly grandmother who lives in Leeds."

"Servants?"

"Only one left. She must stay as well." She looked up at him with bleak amber eyes. "Jane will need her help."

"You know why I ask, don't you? This will destroy your reputation."

She gave him a tight smile. "I thought you said you wouldn't give a second thought to such matters."

"I wouldn't." He shrugged. "But you might wish to." He met her eyes levelly. "I've been responsible for the ruination of a young woman before. It was highly unpleasant."

"For you, or for the young woman?" she asked.

"For the young woman. I escaped unscathed."

Emma's lips twisted. "I'm sure you did. I must say, I am honored that you are showing such concern, my lord—"

"Luke."

"*Luke*. But, really, my reputation is my concern, not yours."

"Of course," he said mildly. He gave her a carefree grin that said the subject was closed. But something inside him felt tangled and disconcerted. Worried on her behalf.

Really, he shouldn't give a damn about her reputation. He'd never concerned himself with society's perception of the ladies he associated with, and he had no idea why he would start now.

In any case, every bit of him was looking forward to tearing down Emma Curtis's defenses...and making her beg.

Chapter Three

He's joking, Emma thought.

She stood on the curb in front of the inn, staring at a curricle. A *curricle*, not a chaise or a coach, which was what she had expected when Luke had gone off in search of a vehicle that would transport them to Scotland.

Before he'd left, he'd ordered her to wait in the room at the inn. She had been tempted to argue—she knew where to go in Bristol for the best prices on just about anything. But she'd also understood the wisdom in not being seen in town with him. She knew too many people here.

Still, it seemed Lord Lukas was more concerned about her reputation than he cared to admit. That thought gave her a tiny, pleasant flicker inside. A warm, strange glow she'd never felt before.

He gazed down at her from the perch where he held the ribbons. His black coat hugged his shoulders in a way that made her breath quicken. He looked dashing and handsome. Like a man-about-town. A dandy trying to catch the eyes of ladies—and succeeding at it if the two tittering young women casting glances at him and giggling from the other side of the road were any indication.

He looked like a carefree London gentleman. Not like a man who was about to depart on an arduous four-hundred-mile journey across the country.

He grinned that mischievous grin of his, and his blue eyes sparkled in the noontime sunlight. "What do you think?"

Other carriages—more acceptable modes of transportation—traversed the road behind him. The street smelled of the city—Bristol had a salty tang to it, as if it could never quite wash the ocean residue from its streets. People walked in and out of the busy inn, their coats drawn tight like her own pelisse was.

When she didn't answer Luke's question, he stepped down and secured the horses, then came to stand beside her.

"I obtained it for an excellent price." Taking her elbow and steering her around to the back of the spindly thing, he added, "This is a traveling curricle. You see—they added a boot to the area where the tiger is meant to stand."

"Wouldn't you prefer a chaise?" she asked, trying to keep her voice neutral.

He arched a cocky eyebrow at her. "No. Then I'd have to hire a driver."

He was a duke's brother. Surely he was in possession of the funds to hire a driver. She frowned at him.

"I prefer to do the driving myself, Emma. If I'm not to ride my own horse across England, then at least I can drive."

She tried not to flinch at that. She knew her presence

was an inconvenience to him, knew that he'd ridden into town on a lone mount. He wouldn't have needed to secure a carriage at all if she hadn't demanded to join him.

Taking a deep breath, she said, "I understand. But...it seems...*frail*. I have my doubts as to whether it can endure traveling the length of England."

She had visions of hitting a rock in the road and it crashing into splinters. Splinters in the case of the carriage. A mass of bloody, broken limbs for her and Luke's part, as well as the poor horses'.

She looked at them—a slender and lithe gray and a stout black. A mismatched pair if she'd ever seen one.

Luke's blue eyes slid toward her, and he squeezed her elbow gently. "Are you afraid?" he asked softly. "I don't believe this will be a journey for the fearful."

"I'm not afraid of the journey," she said, her shoulders firming. "I'm afraid of this carriage. Do you intend to kill us?"

"Not you," he said.

What did that mean? She didn't know how to respond to that, so instead she continued. "And the weather is changing. What if it rains?"

"There is a hood."

She turned to face him, her brows furrowed in a scowl, and she tried not to grind her teeth too furiously. "Yes. I see the hood." It was a tiny thing that would provide less cover than a flimsy umbrella.

He gazed at her, one eyebrow quirked up, his eyes glowing with bemusement.

She gestured toward the back of the curricle, where the hood had been folded down. "That will keep us dry in a ten-minute drizzle. On a day of hard travel through pouring rain? We'll be soaked through, then catch pneumonia, and"—she snapped her fingers—"just like that we'll be dead."

He chuckled. "In days of heavy rain, then, I propose that we stay ensconced in the warm, dry comfort of the nearest inn. In bed, of course."

Emma gave him a narrow-eyed look, but there was nothing she could do. Beggars couldn't be choosers, and she certainly didn't have the means to obtain a more comfortable mode of transportation herself.

"Very well," she said, sighing. "I shall just pray you're not leading us to our deaths."

* * *

Two hours later, they had left the city of Bristol behind and were heading north on the Bristol Road under a cool, watery blue sky. They would not travel far today, because it was already midafternoon and it grew dark early this time of year.

Consulting one of the books of the two-volume *Paterson's British Itinerary* Luke had laid on the seat, Emma had determined they should stop at a place called the Cambridge Inn near the village of Slimbridge.

"Good," Luke had said. "We will continue on this route to Worcester. We should arrive there tomorrow night, and then we'll stay there an extra day and night before continuing northward."

"Why?" she'd asked him, frowning. Now that they were on their way, the thought of any delay made her squirm. She wished she could simply close her eyes and transport them both to Edinburgh in an instant.

"I've some business to attend to there. Trust me, I'm as eager to find Morton as you are, but this is something I must do."

And that was the only explanation he'd offered. Emma folded her hands in her lap and said nothing. She was wildly curious. But whatever he needed to do in Worcester was technically none of her concern.

She settled back in her seat and watched him. In an instant, he went from being easygoing and relaxed to firm and commanding. His eyes would flash with bright humor and then simmer in darkness.

He was a complicated man. He confused her. Unsettled her. He was nothing like she'd expected him to be. But now she realized her expectations hadn't been fair. He was the Duke of Trent's brother, and she'd pictured him as the embodiment of his brother's stellar reputation. Probably even the Duke of Trent himself wasn't the embodiment of his own reputation.

Ultimately, she was glad Luke wasn't anything like she'd expected. If he had been, he'd never have allowed her to come with him.

And...this man was far more fascinating than she ever could have imagined.

He glanced at her, his blue eyes catching a gleam from the fading sunlight. Something inside her clenched hard. He was so handsome—that was one thing about him she'd predicted. But her reaction to his beauty was far, far more intense than she'd expected.

"You're staring at me," he observed mildly.

"Sorry." She jerked her head away and stared out over the horses' heads. "Does it make you uncomfortable?"

He laughed, that quicksilver joy shining through before it evaporated just as rapidly. "No, Emma." His voice was husky. "Look all you like."

"Very well, I shall." She was feeling mulish and twitchy inside her skin. And it was growing colder, the wind biting through not only her pelisse and dress and undergarments but the blanket on her lap as well. It would probably snow at some point on their journey—and then he'd see what little good that silly hood would do.

She pulled the woolen blanket he'd bought tighter over her lap and shivered. She wished she'd brought a heavier coat—she hadn't predicted she'd be journeying outdoors on an open seat.

Maybe she should stop having expectations at all when it came to this man.

Do you like to be bound, Mrs. Curtis?

She shivered again.

"Are you cold?" he said.

"No," she lied.

"I see." He slanted a glance down at her. "Pull up the blanket to cover your shoulders," he ordered.

She bristled at the rather high-handed command, but she did as she was told, wrapping the blanket over her chest and tucking it behind her shoulders.

"Better?"

"Yes," she admitted.

He turned the horses around a sharp bend in the road. Emma hung on for dear life; every time they turned, it felt like the curricle would flip them to their deaths.

"Oh, it's not that bad," he said, clearly amused.

She glared at him. "This carriage is meant to shoot about on London's perfect roads, not to traverse the ruts and rocks of England's country lanes."

"Ah. I see you've never been to London."

"I *have* been to London," she retorted. "I had two Seasons there."

"Is that where you met your husband?"

"It was. Not at any of the Season's events, mind. I met him in London during my second Season."

"How long was your courtship?"

"Almost a year. When the Season ended, I returned to Bristol with my father and Jane. Henry and I began a correspondence."

"I see. Where did he hail from?" Luke's voice was flat, modulated, so was she imagining the edge to it? But then again, why would he be anything but curious about her murdered husband?

"London."

"So you maintained a correspondence. How did this lead to marriage?"

"He proposed marriage via a letter to my father that winter."

"And your father said yes. You did, too."

She squirmed a little. What a naïve, stupid little girl she'd been. So taken with the handsome and dashing Henry Curtis. He had a curricle like this one, but smaller and even more dangerous. Riding in it had made her feel so reckless and wild, so brazen. The first time he'd taken her riding in Hyde Park and kissed her behind an elm tree, she'd been so breathless and excited she'd nearly swooned.

She wasn't that girl anymore.

"We both said yes," she told Luke now. "We wrote our acceptances in a letter, first my father and then me."

She'd been so certain she was in love, but now she

wasn't so sure. She was in love with the attention he'd given her. She was in love with the way he'd made her laugh. With the way he'd sneaked into her room on a warm London summer evening and kissed her until she couldn't breathe.

She'd been more fascinated by him than by any of the aristocratic gentlemen she'd danced with at the Season's assemblies and soirees. Henry hadn't been a nobleman or an aristocrat, but he was a moneyed gentleman. He'd told her that his parents and sister lived in Yorkshire. When she'd tried to contact them after his death, her letters had been returned unopened.

"Why did you marry him?" Luke asked her now. "Did you love him?"

She stiffened. "That's a rather personal question, don't you think?"

"Yes. So?"

She stared straight ahead, debating whether to answer.

It came down to the fact that Luke had agreed to bring her with him, and she owed him for that. "I loved him," she said in a clipped voice. But then she felt compelled to add, "In some respects."

"I see." He looked at her, his blue eyes serious, a slight crease between his brows. "Did he love you?"

Something inside her recoiled. If she'd thought the last question was too personal, this one surely surpassed all bounds of decency.

They rattled over a rut in the road, giving her a reason to grip the edge of her seat.

She didn't answer for a long while. He didn't press her.

Finally, she said, in a very low, very miserable voice, "I don't think so."

A week after the wedding, she'd started to worry. A month after the wedding, she'd begun to panic. Because as the days went by, it became increasingly clear that Henry possessed no interest in her as a wife, even as another human being. He'd married her for her father's money. He'd married her because she was an heiress with a very generous dowry.

It had had nothing to do with her.

No, he *hadn't* loved her. He'd seduced her and wooed her with everything he had, but once the dowry was in his hands and his future secured with the promise of much more, he'd showed his true colors.

Perhaps he'd even actively disliked her the whole time he'd been telling her how lovely and sweet she was. Perhaps he'd shivered with revulsion when he'd whispered how he wanted nothing more than to take her to his bed.

All the money was gone now. It was her fault. If she hadn't married Henry, he'd have never become involved with Roger Morton. Papa's fortune would still be safe.

Guilt swamped her—a feeling she was accustomed to now. She'd made a foolish choice, and her family had paid dearly for it.

Luke seemed not to have heard her. He was concentrating on negotiating the horses over the bumps and curves in the road.

She was glad he hadn't heard. She didn't want Lord Lukas Hawkins's pity. She just wanted him to help her find Roger Morton so she could get her money back, make Papa well, and see Jane married to someone as good and honest as she was.

She glanced at Luke to find him looking ahead, scowling. "What's wrong?" she asked him.

He was quiet for a long moment, still staring straight ahead, then he said, "I think one of the horses is limping."

She studied the horses. "Which one?"

"The gray."

She stared at the gray mare. "I can't see it."

He stopped the horses, still not looking at her. "I'll check. Wait here." He pressed the reins into her hands.

She held the horses, sitting with the blanket wrapped around her as he stepped off the curricle and then went to check the horse's hooves and legs, running his hand through the dirty-white fur, feeling for injuries in the legs, then coaxing the hooves off the ground one at a time and meticulously inspecting each one. Finally, he returned. She kept her eyes on the gray. "Did you find anything?"

"No. She seems perfectly fine. I was imagining it."

"Well, let's keep an eye on her," she said.

"Yes."

* * *

Luke urged the horses into a trot, pretending to take it slow for the gray's sake. He'd lied. The gray hadn't been limping.

But he'd needed to get off the curricle for a moment. Put some distance between himself and Emma. Because the fact of the matter was, his level of rage was not commensurate to the situation.

He hardly knew Emma Curtis. But damned if he didn't want to wring Henry Curtis's dead, rotting neck right now.

He tightened his hands over the reins and took deep, slow breaths to calm his lingering fury.

The man had hurt her. She sat next to Luke, cold as hell because she couldn't afford to buy herself a decent coat, wrapped up in that woolen blanket. And she looked vulnerable and alone.

He'd seen grieving women before. Women who were so full of regret and sadness they advertised it when they walked down a street. But he'd never felt this way about any of those women. For the most part, he'd ignored them, though he was sickeningly aware of his own selfishness.

More than anything, he wanted Emma to feel better. He wanted to help her. But he had no idea how.

Just keep doing what you're doing.

That was one way to help her. Find Morton, dissuade her from her foolish notion of killing him, and see the man hanged for his crimes against their families.

Still, that wouldn't provide her with physical comfort. It wouldn't make her feel loved. It wouldn't make her believe in her true strength and beauty.

Luke wanted to make her feel that way. He wanted to make her feel like the loveliest, most cherished woman in the world. *He* wanted to be the one to cherish her.

Where in the hell were these thoughts coming from? Good *God.*

He noted that the air of his breaths emerged in little clouds. It was growing colder. And she was correct—if they stayed out in this cold, they would catch their deaths. She would, anyhow, as underdressed as she was.

The first order of business would be to buy her a damned coat.

"I think we're almost there," she said after they went through a turnpike.

"Good," he snapped, realizing belatedly that he still sounded angry. He took a deep breath and modulated his voice. "I grow hungry."

"I should have thought to order some food packed so we could bring it with us," she said.

"No, you shouldn't. We'll dine at the Cambridge Inn at the proper hour."

"Tomorrow, I'll be sure to bring something."

"As you wish." One corner of his lips cocked upward. "However, it's not your responsibility to ensure I'm fed, you know."

She blew out a breath, causing a light cloud of fog that wisped over a curl that had fallen from her bonnet and dangled over her cheek. He tightened his right hand on the rein, resisting the sudden urge to tuck that soft strand of hair behind her ear.

"You're doing all the driving," she pointed out. "You've taken it upon yourself to be responsible for the traveling, so I think I should be responsible for keeping our bellies full, don't you?"

"Very well," he conceded. "If you wish it. Still, I've managed to keep myself alive for many years without someone feeling it necessary to feed me."

She tilted her head at him. "Do you live alone? Not with your family?"

"I live alone in London. I own a town house there. No country houses—alas, those were all bestowed to my brothers."

"So you aren't often in the company of the duke?"

"Sometimes, when I am feeling inordinately blessed with patience and temperance, I will take it upon myself to visit my family at Ironwood Park. I wouldn't say

I go there to visit Trent specifically, but rather my sister and my mother. Sometimes one of my other three brothers."

"Ironwood Park is your brother's seat, is it not? Did you spend your childhood there?"

"Yes, it is his country seat. All six of us spent our childhoods there."

"Do you like it?"

Luke shrugged. "In some ways. But I can never stay there long. It is an enormous house with vast lands, but it has always felt like a prison to me."

"Aren't you your brother's heir? Ironwood Park could be yours someday."

He chuckled. "Highly doubtful. My sister-in-law is increasing already. I predict she'll bear Trent a dozen strapping sons."

"Does that upset you? The fact that you might lose your position as heir?"

"Hell no." He slanted a suspicious look in her direction. "Does it upset *you*, Emma?"

Was that why she seemed so interested in him? Was she angling for a position at his side so that she might someday become a duchess? Women had attempted to play him like that before. It was the worst kind of deception, and when he'd found them out, his reaction hadn't been a kind one.

But she frowned at him. "Why would it matter to me?"

"Think about it," he said.

She did, her brow creased as she studied him, then her eyes widened in horror. "If you believe I have designs on you, that I have some horrid intention to become the next Duchess of Trent, then you don't know me at all."

His lips twitched. "Are you certain?"

"Of course I am!" She shuddered as if in disgust. "Good *Lord*."

Her reaction placated him. "That's a relief."

She looked away, gazing at the landscape rolling by for several moments before she turned to him once again. "I am curious about the home where you grew up—but I assure you, it's not because I intend to be its mistress one day."

He gave a small smile. "Understood."

"It is in the Cotswolds, is it not?"

"It is."

"We shall be traveling near it, then. It can't be far off our course. Shall we visit?"

"It's directly on our course, actually," he said. "But, no. We won't be visiting Ironwood Park."

She seemed to shrink an inch. "Oh. I understand. I shouldn't have mentioned it."

"Why are you using that tone of voice?"

"What tone of voice?"

"The same one you used when you told me your husband didn't love you."

She stiffened, her shoulders straightening. *Good.* He much preferred this Emma over the defeated one.

"I don't know what you're talking about," she said, her tone haughty.

"Oh, yes, you do."

She pulled the blanket tighter around her. She was all wrapped up like a present he wanted to open for Christmas. The most voluptuous, delicious present ever. Too bad she'd made it quite clear it wasn't for him.

Not yet, anyhow.

"It's nothing. Just that I understand why you wouldn't want to bring me to your family."

"What?" Understanding washed over him, and he cast an exasperated look to the heavens. "Oh, good God, woman. You've no idea what you're talking about."

She sat there, rigid as one of the statues in the Stone Room at Ironwood Park, and he sighed. "Listen, my brother and I don't often see eye to eye. I wouldn't want to subject you to our quarrels. That's all. It has nothing to do with you or their perceptions of you. I wouldn't give a damn what Trent thinks about you." He frowned, feeling the furrow deepen between his brows. "Actually, I would. If he judged you—" He broke off, shaking his head.

She didn't move but stared straight ahead. They were passing a copse of trees, the leaves glorious shades of red, orange, and brown. The wind had kicked up, sending swirls of leaves off branches and scattering them across the road.

Finally, she said, "You're an odd man, Lord Luke."

"Just Luke."

"Just Luke," she murmured. She looked at him, her bronze eyes large and soft, her lips curled into a smile. "But...thank you."

"For what?"

"For..." She hesitated, then laughed, the sound a low, throaty chuckle that warmed him to his marrow. "Well, I suppose for having that angry look on your face when you thought about your brother judging me. It made me feel...better."

"If he judged you, I would be less than pleased." An understatement. He reached down to hold her hand where it was tapping her leg. She couldn't return the gesture as her hand was trapped beneath the blanket, but that was all right.

Her fingers stilled beneath his. He kept his hand tight over hers until they reached Slimbridge.

* * *

The Cambridge Inn was a rectangular building made of white brick with uniform rows of square-paned windows on its first floor and a front door flanked by two sash windows on either side. The innkeeper was a burly man who appeared to be in his thirties and more suited to farm labor than to the comparatively sedentary venture of running an inn.

Luke registered them as Mr. and Mrs. Charles Hawkins. Emma didn't say a word about this until they were safely in their room and the servant who'd carried their luggage shut the door, leaving them in privacy.

The room was larger than the room in Bristol had been—nearly twice the size, with a round table and two comfortable-looking chairs on one side of the door and a bed flanked by two small tables on the other.

She gazed for a long moment at the bed, noting it was large enough for the two of them, then looked deliberately at Luke. He smirked at her.

She crossed her arms over her chest. Now where would she sleep? She should probably make him sleep on the floor and take the bed for herself. "Why on *earth* did you do that?"

"My second name is Charles."

"You know that's not what I'm talking about."

He shrugged. "If I'd requested two rooms, what would people have thought? That I am a man attempting to pretend I'm not traveling with my mistress?"

"You could have said we were brother and sister."

"Right," he said in a tone dripping with sarcasm. "We do look *so* much alike."

They looked nothing alike. It would be a stretch of the imagination to believe them to be brother and sister. Him with his blond hair and narrow face and sharp features, her with her dark hair and round face and soft features. Still, not impossible.

She sighed. They should have discussed this beforehand. Agreed upon a suitable course of action.

Turning away from him, she removed her pelisse and hung it over a chair. When she turned back, he leaned over his trunk, busying himself with removing a clean waistcoat, tailcoat, and a simple white cravat. When he closed the trunk, he straightened, unbuttoning the black cloth buttons of his long greatcoat. He looked beautiful, his hair wind-tossed around his face, his eyes a dark, tumultuous blue, his face roughened by his afternoon beard. She could almost imagine how it would feel to run her fingers through his hair or to have the scruff of his beard scratch her skin as he kissed his way softly down her neck—

"I'm going downstairs."

"What?" She fought back a blush as she was quickly jolted from her fantasy. "Why?" Had he forgotten something in the curricle?

His gaze didn't quite meet hers. "I'll take my dinner in the pub."

For a moment, she stared at him, startled by his change

in demeanor. Then, she raised her brows. "I thought you told the servant we'd take dinner here."

"Changed my mind."

Emma steadied herself, but her mind was in a tumult. "Oh. All right, then."

He busied himself with donning the waistcoat and tail-coat, then deftly tied his cravat as he gazed into the small looking glass mounted on the wall beside the table. She watched him in silence.

He swiveled and went to the door, and laying his hand on the door handle, he said, "Lock it behind me."

She just stared at him. Without another word, he opened the door and shut it with a firm click behind him.

Silence.

Then a muffled, "Emma. Lock the damn door."

With a sigh, she went to the door and locked it. He didn't say anything else, but she heard his footsteps as he retreated down the corridor.

She turned back to the empty room to face an evening alone with nothing but the fascinating company of *Paterson's British Itinerary*.

Chapter Four

※

Luke returned to the room after midnight. He'd sat at the table all evening with a glass of ale that kept magically refilling itself. As he ascended the stairs, he tried to remember the serving girl who'd brought him the ale, but for the life of him, he couldn't remember seeing a serving girl at all, after that one who'd removed his empty dinner plate.

Surely there'd been a serving girl. Why in hell couldn't he remember her?

He was still mulling this over when he found himself at the door to the room he was sharing with Emma. *Lovely Emma.*

He searched his pockets but couldn't find a key. He tried the door but it was locked. He smiled slightly. Good girl, his Emma.

Damn. What had he done with the key?

He rattled the door handle as if that would make a key suddenly appear. It didn't work.

But he heard movement on the other side of the door and then the lock turned. The door opened to reveal Emma standing there, decidedly disheveled. And delicious.

Her hair—God, that glorious hair. It was twisted into a thick, decadent braid that trailed down over the front of one shoulder. Its end tickled her luscious breast over her nightgown. He reached out to touch that soft, round curve, but she stepped back.

"My lord." Her tone was frosty. "I trust you had a good *dinner*."

Even in his drunken state, he knew very well the tone of a disgruntled woman.

He tried to remember why she'd be disgruntled. He did remember a pretty woman who'd approached him this evening. He remembered staring at her, thinking she looked something like Emma with her dark hair and generous curves. Thinking that she would have seemed very appealing to him two days ago. That was before he'd met Emma Curtis. Tonight, that woman had done nothing for him. He'd sent her away, feeling vaguely disconcerted about this sudden change in behavior that had seemed to come over him.

"Excellent," he said. "Now that you're with me."

A part of him registered that that had made no sense.

She stepped back, waiting for him to enter the room. So he did. She closed the door behind him. He turned to see her watching him warily in the dimness. The lantern on the table had been lowered so that he could see the expression on her face but not its finer details. Not the velvet-thick lashes on her eyes or the exact shade of the pink of her lips. All those features he'd memorized while he drove the curricle earlier today.

The loveliness of her nightgown snagged his gaze. The bits of lace that adorned its collar and hem and sleeves— he could see those. He could also see the way the white, flowing gown made her look so innocent and virginal.

She isn't a virgin, the sober part of him said. But she might as well be, the way that bastard Curtis had treated her. She'd never been properly loved. All women should be properly loved. Especially this one.

God, how Luke loved women. Especially this one.

"Why are you staring at me like that?" she asked.

"Because I'm drunk, and I can't stop admiring your loveliness," he told her honestly.

Was that his imagination or did the pale pink of her cheeks deepen? He took a step toward her, intent on pinning her to the door as he had last night—was that last night? He couldn't remember. And tasting her again…oh, she'd tasted so…damn…good. But she slipped under his arm and escaped.

"I made a bed for myself, my lord." She gestured to the floor, where she had taken one of the pillows and one of the blankets and folded it to look like it was covering a bed.

Oh, *hell* no.

"You are not sleeping on the floor."

She crossed her arms over her chest. "I am not sleeping with *you*."

A vague part of him remembered the agreement they'd made. "You're not ready for 'relations' yet?"

"No, I am not."

"But you will be soon?" he asked hopefully.

"No."

He sighed dramatically. "Well. Blast," he mumbled.

He fumbled with his coat buttons, finally managed to free them. He stripped down to his shirt, dropping his clothes on the floor, and fell onto the bed.

The bed was comfortable, but damned cold.

Where was Emma?

"Emma?" he called.

No answer.

He struggled to a seated position, panic swarming over him. Where the hell had she gone? "Emma, where are you?"

Her head popped into his vision, and he blinked. Then he realized where she'd appeared from. She'd been lying on the floor and had sat up.

"I'm right here," she told him softly.

"Why aren't you in bed?"

"I told you—"

"I need you here, Emma. No relations." He gave a self-deprecating laugh. "I'm too damned drunk for relations, anyhow. Just sleep. Sleep with me, Emma. It's so cold."

She stared at him for a long moment with one of those unfathomable expressions she seemed to enjoy wearing. Then, with a sigh, she rose, her lovely white nightgown falling to her ankles. Moonlight crept through the thin gauze curtain covering the window behind her, haloing her curvaceous body. She looked like an angel.

She *was* an angel. At that moment, he was sure of it.

She bent down to retrieve the blanket she'd been using and laid it over him. He shivered again.

She fetched her pillow and walked around to the other side of the bed. She stared down at him. "No relations?"

"None," he said in the most reassuring tone he could muster. He'd forgotten what "relations" were, but hell, he just wanted to sleep next to her warm, luscious body.

She hesitated a moment longer, then slipped into bed beside him. Not touching him, she turned her back to him. She hovered on the very edge of the bed. All he had to do was nudge her shoulder and she'd go tumbling off.

He reached out and pulled her against him, feeling her body stiffen in his arms. "Shhh," he said against her warm, soft neck. He breathed in, then shuddered. She smelled so good. Like lavender and flesh and woman. "Shhh," he told her again, stroking her hip as if she were a skittish horse. "Just go to sleep, angel. Go to sleep."

Moments later, he drifted into oblivion, his arms wrapped around the warm, soft, delectable body of Emma Curtis.

* * *

Emma awoke alone in the bed. Luke was nowhere to be seen. Where had that man gone now?

She rose and looked out the window to see that it was a fair day again, with milky blue skies, but when she pressed her palm to the pane, it was ice cold. She checked the door to find herself locked in—this time he'd taken the key. Grumbling to herself, she washed and dressed in her white muslin, casting furtive glances at the door. Thankfully, Luke didn't saunter in to find her half naked.

Fully dressed, she lowered herself into the simple wooden chair at the small armoire tucked into the corner of the room, undid her braid, and pulled a comb through her hair. Memories of last night washed through her.

His behavior...She swallowed hard. He'd called her

"angel." In her entire life, no one had ever called her angel. She'd been called devil, though, and often. Mostly by Mama and the various governesses who had passed through their home. Words like *willful hoyden* and *stubborn hellion* had oft been used to describe Emma. She remembered one of them speaking in low tones to her mother: *It is hopeless, ma'am. No one will ever make a lady out of that one.*

But that woman had been wrong. Emma had gone to boarding school with Jane, and they'd both grown into ladies—though Jane definitely made a more admirable example of a lady than Emma ever had.

Now she'd given up all hope or pretense of ever being a lady again. Further, she no longer felt that burning desire to be a true lady—her days of wanting to please society had vanished along with her father's fortune. All she wanted now was to take care of her family and redeem herself in Papa's and Jane's eyes.

Still, last night, Lord Lukas Hawkins had called her an angel.

Well, one thing was certain, she thought ruefully: the man had been three sheets to the wind.

But she had liked falling asleep in his arms.

No, *liked* wasn't the right word. She'd loved it and hated it and been tortured by it. She had lain there long after his breaths had deepened, signaling that he slept. Her body had felt rigid and pulsing with energy—wide awake and tense and...aroused. Even in sleep, his arms remained clasped firm and strong and masculine around her. He smelled of soap and smooth malt.

The arousal had spread through her like a slow-burning fire. A part of her had wished desperately that he'd forgotten all about their bargain and had tried to take liberties with her. Would she have fought him off?

Her mind—that proud, wary thing inside her—screamed yes, but her body's answer was a definitive no.

She didn't understand him, and she didn't really know him. And there was no question that he bore some of Henry's less savory traits. But she wanted him.

It had taken nearly an hour for her body to cool and for her to relax in the circle of his heavy arms. But finally she did, and when she slept, she'd dreamed of his blue eyes and his kiss, and in her dream, his arms around her had turned into shackles. Even if she'd wanted to, she couldn't have moved. He'd smiled at her with a wicked gleam in those eyes, and he'd said in a gruff voice, "Do you like this, Emma? Do you like to be bound?"

And then he'd lain over her, his body heavy and warm and strong, and in the middle of the night, she'd awakened with a soft moan, trembling through the tail end of a body-clenching orgasm.

She'd lain awake for some time afterward, stiff and terrified that he had awakened, too, but he didn't budge. Finally she let go, forcibly releasing the tension that had built in her muscles. She nuzzled her body against his and, finally warm and relaxed and comfortable, fell into a deep, dreamless sleep.

It seemed she was a bigger fool than she'd originally believed herself to be. She might be able to forgive herself for being seduced by an immoral rake once. But twice? No. Only a complete ninny would make that mistake twice.

He'd obviously risen long before her and had left the

room without waking her. Odd, since she was an early riser to begin with, and he'd probably drunk an entire barrel of ale last night.

Nevertheless, she had to admit, her sleep had been more restful than it had been in a very long time. It was no wonder she'd slept late.

She had twined her hair on her head and was pinning it when she heard the key in the lock, and Luke opened the door and entered, carrying a large parcel.

Holding her hair in place with one hand, she turned to him. "What's that?"

"Good morning to you, too," he said mildly.

"Good morning," she said agreeably. Then, "I'm glad you're feeling better."

He glanced at her with humor in his eyes as he laid the parcel on the bed. "When was I feeling poorly?"

"Last night."

"Ah. That." Straightening, he met her gaze evenly. "I wasn't feeling poorly. I was just cold. You did an excellent job of warming me."

She jammed a pin into her hair, not knowing how to respond. So he remembered. She was glad he hadn't been so drunk he'd forgotten what had happened last night. *You did a fine job of warming me, too, my lord. I was burning. On fire. An inferno… In fact, you had me so hot and wanting you that I came in my sleep.*

Turning back toward the mirror, she gave a self-deprecating laugh into the glass.

He came to her, laid a hand on her shoulder. His touch burned into her, and she froze, staring at him in the little mirror. "Did I scare you last night?"

She pondered the question, then answered him as

truthfully as she could. "Yes. But...perhaps not in the way you imagine."

He took a deep breath, then his fingers tightened over her shoulder. "Know that whatever happens, whatever I say, I would never physically harm you, Emma. Well"—he gave her one of those reckless grins—"unless you asked me to, that is."

What would he do if she asked him to...? Oh, Lord. Something deep inside her clamped down, desire rekindling from last night.

He met her gaze in the mirror, held it for a long moment, his blue eyes simmering with heat, then he turned away. He went to the bed and began to untie the strings of the brown-paper-wrapped package. "Here. I want you to try this on."

Pressing the final pin into her hair, she turned, intrigued. "What is it?"

He pushed the strings aside, tore the paper, and miles of black silk and fur seemed to fall out of it.

Luke held it up for her to see.

It was a hooded cloak of black silk, lined with wool and trimmed with the softest-looking fur she'd ever seen. Ermine, she thought—white fur speckled with black dots. And a matching fur-lined muff.

She gazed at the cloak and the muff for a long moment, unexpected tears prickling at her eyes. "Oh, Luke." She swallowed hard. "I...you...No. They are too much."

"Not at all. I promised I'd try to keep you safe. Yesterday you were chilled to the bone—you could have caught your death out there. These will help."

"I shouldn't accept such a gift."

"Not a gift—a necessity. I can't allow you to freeze to death."

They stared at each other for a long moment, and then Luke stepped forward. "Stand."

She stood, and he laid the cloak over her shoulders. It was exquisitely made, heavy and soft and warm. He tucked the muff over one of her hands, and she obligingly pressed her hand into its other side.

"I've never felt anything so soft," she said.

"Warm enough, do you think?"

"Oh, yes."

He studied her for a long moment, satisfaction in his gaze. Then he removed the cloak from her shoulders and laid it back on the bed. "Breakfast? We have a long drive ahead of us today."

A big part of her wanted to fling her arms around him and kiss him and thank him for such a lovely, thoughtful gesture. But instead she simply said, "Yes. Breakfast."

* * *

It was late morning by the time they left the Cambridge Inn, and it proved to be a long day of driving. They changed horses twice, and now they rode behind two well-matched bay mares, both with star patterns on their noses. Luke and Emma had agreed the two must be sisters, perhaps even twins.

They'd passed the day conversing companionably, stopping for a late luncheon on the banks of the Severn, with a lovely prospect of the Malvern Hills. Having spent his childhood at nearby Ironwood Park, Luke knew this area, and he pointed out its geological features as they ate.

Despite the ease of their companionship, Luke was feeling more and more ill at ease. What would happen tonight? Would he ask her to lie with him again? He wanted to. But he also wanted more...something he'd agreed not to pursue.

The truth was, the more he sat beside Emma, the more he conversed with her and grew to know her, the more he admired her. Her curvaceous and seductive body put wicked images into his head, but her quick, intelligent mind enhanced them. And there was something else, too, something he couldn't define. Something about the two of them just fit. Like they were two pieces of a broken egg whose jagged edges matched perfectly.

Which was a mad thought, really. He'd only known her for two days. But when else did he have a chance to sit beside someone for hours on end with nothing to do but stare at the passing scenery? And talk.

And despite the fact that he wanted her...badly...as he grew to know her better, it became more and more clear that she really was a lady, and although she'd been married for a short time, an extremely innocent one, at that. She hadn't led an easy or uncomplicated existence for the past year, but she remained rather naïve.

As much as his body craved Emma, guilt began to eat at him for being as suggestive as he already had. He shouldn't have kissed her that first night. He'd completely misinterpreted her experience, and her intentions.

He wanted Emma to remain innocent. As much as that devil inside demanded he drag her into the darkness, to utterly and completely debauch and ruin her, he began to realize that he needed to fight it.

It was late afternoon now, and as they made their way

toward the town of Worcester, he mused on how well he felt he understood Emma. Certainly better than he'd understood any other woman. Usually, he didn't sit on a bench and talk to a woman. Usually when he was with women, he had pressing matters to attend to, and those didn't involve talking.

To his surprise, he enjoyed talking to Emma. He liked hearing her interpretations about where they were going and what they were doing. He liked hearing about her past—her antics with her governesses and her mother, and later during her boarding school years; her sister Jane, whom she admired greatly; and her father, who was bedridden with some debilitating ailment of the heart.

He steered well clear of conversations relating to her husband and Roger Morton—because he'd learned yesterday that those subjects did neither of them any good. They deflated her and made him indescribably angry. They were still far from Edinburgh, and they had plenty of time before those topics would need to be broached.

She attempted to draw information from him, too. She seemed especially interested in Trent.

Of course she was interested in Trent, he thought dryly. Wasn't everyone?

"Tell me about your brother," she said as they topped a rise, and the city of Worcester appeared in the distance, the spires of its cathedral peeking over the trees.

"I have four brothers," he told her. "Which one are you referring to?"

She had the grace to blush. "Well, I suppose we could start with the duke."

He sighed. "What do you wish to know?"

"What's he like? Is he similar to you?"

"He's nothing like me." He stared at the road and attempted to contain his sneer.

She looked at him askance. "Well, then. You are close in age, at least, aren't you?"

"Yes. Less than two years apart."

"Describe him to me."

He was accustomed to people asking about Trent, but for some reason, her particular interest in the man suddenly annoyed him. "You do know he's married."

Hell, that had sounded snappish. He was turning into a goddamned shrew.

"Of course," she said mildly. "His marriage has been the talk of England for the past two months."

"Right," he said on a near growl.

Her expression melted into a frown, and she studied him, her bronze-tinted eyes assessing. "Do you dislike him?"

Did he dislike Trent? Hell. That question was far more complicated than she could possibly understand, and, really, there was no answer.

He formulated his response carefully before he spoke. "Trent is my brother. But we usually don't agree. On any topic."

"I see," she said softly. She seemed to mull this over for a while. Then she asked, "Do you know the duchess?"

His first thought was that she was talking about his mother, and he was about to tell her that of course he knew her. But, no. She was talking about Sarah.

This was a query he'd need to answer often in the future. Nevertheless, it was an odd question, because how did one explain how he'd known a woman for much of his life and thought of her fondly as a member of his family—in a servant's capacity? And how to explain the change now that she'd been catapulted into the role of his sister-in-law?

"Yes," he told Emma. "I've known her since I was a boy. Her father is the gardener at Ironwood Park."

"What do you think of her?"

He raised a brow. "She's not a ruthless social climber, if that's what you're thinking."

"No," she said softly, "I never believed that, despite what the scandal sheets have to say about it. If she were such an ambitious sort, I'm sure the duke would have seen through the act."

Something bitter and painful shot through him, but it didn't take long for him to recognize what it was. *Jealousy.* Everyone would always grant Trent the benefit of the doubt. Even Emma.

He blew out a breath through his teeth. They were in Worcester now, turning into High Street and passing the cathedral on their left, an impressive Norman stone structure with a tall central tower and spires.

"I like Sarah," he told Emma. "I have always liked her. She is a good match for Trent, despite what the world may say." Sarah might be the only person in the world who could pull the stick out of Trent's arse, in any case.

She nodded, seemingly content with his answer. "Tell me about your other brothers. And you have a sister, too, correct?"

He glanced at her. She thought she was asking him simple questions, but hell if he knew how to answer them anymore.

He began carefully. With a sibling who was a blood sibling, someone he'd been raised with and who shared his surname. "Samson—Sam is the oldest. He's my half brother on my mother's side."

"I didn't know you had another older brother."

"Yes. He's the product of my mother's liaison with...*someone* before her marriage to the Duke of Trent. She has never said who."

"What's he like?"

"Sam is..." He frowned. How to describe Sam? He was a quiet beast of a man, and it was almost unnerving the way his dark eyes took everything in but how rarely he bothered to voice his opinion. "Taciturn. He has had endured quite a lot. I doubt if he enjoyed growing up in a house in which everyone knew him as the bastard child. The duke ignored him."

The duke had ignored Sam, but had he hated Sam as much as he'd hated Luke? Luke didn't think so.

She flinched. "That sounds difficult indeed. Awful, actually."

"I'm sure it was," Luke said. "As an adult, he hasn't had it any easier. He was a lieutenant in the army, and a few years ago, he was shot in battle and almost died. He's been married twice, but he lost both of his wives—the first in childbed along with their newborn son, and the second on the field with him on the Continent."

Emma wrapped her cloak tighter around her and looked at him with glassy eyes. "Oh, that is awful. The poor man."

Luke nodded. Sam never asked for his pity and Luke never gave it, but still, something inside him burned whenever he thought of all Sam had been through.

They rode in silence for a moment. Then she said, "And the others? Your sister?"

"Esme."

"How old is she?"

"Nineteen."

"What is she like?"

"Quiet."

Luke realized his answers had begun to degenerate to one word. Discussing his family was enough to clench his heart into stone. Even the one-word answers were becoming difficult to spit out. Still, Emma deserved more than this. He took a breath and tried again.

"Esme is quiet. She doesn't do very well in large groups, though my mother and Trent seem to enjoy pushing her into awkward social situations. She's always scribbling away in her journal. My guess is that those pages are the only things in the world that know her true thoughts."

"I imagine it would be difficult, growing up with five older brothers."

Luke smirked. "No doubt. And having a wild mother didn't help her much, either."

They had turned into Broad Street, and he finally reined the horses to a stop in front of the Crown and Unicorn Inn, grateful to be saved from answering any more questions.

He secured a room for them and led Emma upstairs, two servants following behind them with their luggage.

"Well if it ain't my good friend Hawkins," a voice called out from the top of the stairs.

Luke glanced up to see Rupert Smallshaw, one of his carousing partners from London.

Bloody hell.

He plastered a smile on his face. "Small. What a surprise."

Small rolled his eyes heavenward. "I know. Godforsaken place, ain't it, out here in the middle of nowhere?"

Small was a true man of Town. He despised leaving London, where it was easy to find all those decadent pleasures he sought on a daily basis.

Luke reached the top of the stairs, well aware of Emma standing just behind him.

His brain felt scrambled as he attempted to come up with a decent reason to be here with her, heading up to the same room. There was no way for her to escape this with her reputation intact.

"What are you doing so far from Town?" he asked Small as his brain continued to work furiously. Coming up with no decent explanation, panic began to rise in him, a hot, boiling flood.

Calm the hell down, man. She knew this might happen. So did you.

Small shrugged and gave him a look of utmost boredom. "Riding out to Bromyard to check in on the ancestral pile."

Luke raised his brows. "How unlike you."

"I know. Perhaps I'm becoming responsible at last, eh?"

And then Small's gaze lit on Emma. His brown eyes perused her from top to bottom, hovering obviously on her well-endowed bosom.

Luke ground his teeth and stepped in front of her the best he could on the small landing.

"Perhaps I will see you later," he said to Small.

Small's lips curled. "Of course." His gaze, very deliberately, returned to Emma. "I was wondering why you would come to Worcester instead of Ironwood Park. And now I see..." He hesitated, obviously waiting for introductions.

"Small, this is Mrs. Curtis." Immediately, Luke flinched. Why had he given the man her real name?

"Mrs. Curtis, how lovely." Small gave her a gallant bow. "You are the reason Lord Luke felt compelled to visit Worcester. I cannot say I blame him. You're the prettiest bit o' muslin I've seen in some time." His smile turned lascivious. "Do let me know if you'd be willing to accommodate another, love." He winked broadly at Emma. "Perhaps after you're finished with his lordship?"

Luke lunged, his fists clenched. Before he knew it, pain shot up his right arm, and Small crumpled to his knees on the wood floor.

"Luke!" Emma shouted. "Oh, God."

Her hand was on his shoulder, dragging him back as he went for Small again.

"Luke!"

He stopped short. He glanced at Emma, who seemed unscathed, but her eyes were round golden pools. "Stop!" she gasped.

He looked down at Small, who had risen on one elbow and was rubbing his jaw, gazing at Luke with astonishment. "What the devil, Hawkins?"

"I...you...never...don't ever..." His voice emerged as a warbled growl. He couldn't talk. Couldn't think.

"Come," Emma said in his ear. "Let's go to the room."

She led him down the corridor. He stumbled after her, but he barely paid attention to where they were going, instead looking back at Small and hating him. Wanting to wrap his hands around the man's neck and squeeze the life out of his worthless body.

But why? The man was his equal in debauchery. No more, no less. They had shared women before. Small's statement was nothing out of the ordinary.

But it had been directed at Emma.

They stopped at the door. The servants were still back with Small, helping him up, so they waited, since one of them had the key to the door.

Luke took a deep breath, willing himself to calm down. Emma gave him a sideways look. "Are you all right?"

"Are you?" he asked gruffly.

She gave him a tight smile. "Just fine," she said, "but I'd not be fine at all if you were convicted of assault."

One of the servants approached and opened the door. Emma pushed Luke gently into the room, then followed behind the second servant carrying his trunk. When their luggage had been placed inside and the two servants had left, Luke sank into a chair, bending forward with his elbows on his knees and pushing his fingers over his forehead and into his hair.

She came to him, kneeling before him and taking his right hand in her own, studying it and then rubbing it gently in her hands. "You hit him hard."

"Hurt like hell," he mumbled.

"It probably hurt him more than it hurt you."

"Hope so."

Suddenly, she brought his hand to her mouth, closed her eyes, and pressed her lips to his knuckles. She gazed up at him, her eyes bright. "You defended my honor. No one has ever done that for me before. Thank you."

He scowled at her. Why had no one defended her before?

"Are you angry with me?" she whispered.

"No." He wiped the scowl from his face, forcibly relaxing his features. She was still grasping his right hand, so with his left he tenderly tucked a stray curl behind her ear. "No, Emma. I'm not angry."

She looked up at him, her lips spreading into a wide smile.

Luke stared at her, his gut clenching hard. This woman, on her knees before him, smiling up at him with shining eyes, was the most beautiful thing he'd ever seen.

Chapter Five

Dearest Jane,

I hope all is well with you and Papa. Please send all correspondence to Cameron's Hotel in Edinburgh, because although we haven't arrived in Scotland yet, we'll be lodging there.

We are currently in Worcester. The travel has been uneventful, and Lord L____s is behaving the gentleman we knew he'd be. He is so much more than I thought he'd be . . .

Good Lord, thought Emma. Why had she written that? She sighed and stared at the letter for long moments. She couldn't scratch it out—she'd have to start the letter over, and she didn't have another sheet of paper. Chewing on her lip, she continued.

. . . he has such an interesting past and is involved in such interesting pursuits as well.

She chuckled a little at that. Interesting pursuits, indeed. Pursuits of the most rakish variety, for certain. But hopefully that would pacify Jane, who surely wouldn't think of *those* kinds of pursuits. She continued.

The travel has been so lovely; driving up through the Cotswolds, we have seen many of the wonders of the English autumn. I pray that the weather will continue to be as fine as it has been to this point.

She hesitated, wondering whether she should tell Jane about the curricle. No, she decided, definitely not. Emma had no intention of adding to her sister's worries.

We have remained in Worcester for an extra day, for Lord L_____s has some business to attend to...

He'd refrained from sharing any further information about his "business." She'd tried to pry it out of him once more this morning, but he resisted her attempts, just telling her that it had nothing to do with Ironwood Park or Trent or his other family members who resided there.

Her curiosity threatened to run away with her, however. Why would a nobleman rake like Luke feel the need to take care of any kind of business in a place like Worcester— and he said the business would take place outside the city. All sorts of scenarios had run through her mind, but she kept returning to one: It must have something to do with a woman. And perhaps an illegitimate child.

It would make sense, in a place a distance away but still within a few hours' travel from his onetime home, where he could make infrequent visits whenever he was in the area. It would make sense, given his roguish reputation.

The thought of him seeing a woman depressed Emma. Even though she knew she had no right to feel any proprietary feelings over him, she had spent three nights with him now. Two of those nights enclosed in his arms.

Last night had been different from the first. He'd been sober, as she'd asked him—well, if she was honest with herself, she'd *begged* him—not to go down to the tavern for his dinner. Not only did she not want him to get drunk again, but she also didn't want him to risk encountering that awful Mr. Small again.

So they'd slept, but he'd been restless, and she knew he hadn't slept well. In the early morning hours, he'd gasped and sat up straight in the bed, waking her. She'd opened her eyes dazedly and blinked at the sheen of sweat on his brow. It struck her as very odd—it wasn't a warm night.

"What is it?" she'd murmured. "Did you have a nightmare?"

He'd turned to her, clearly shaken and upset. "It's nothing," he'd said in a rasping voice. "Go back to sleep."

He left the bed and sat at the table with his head in his hands while she'd lain there, wondering what to do. Wanting to go to him and comfort him but not knowing how. She'd finally slipped out of bed and gone to him. He looked up, startled, when she put her hand on his shoulder.

"Come back to bed?"

"Can't."

"Why?"

He looked away from her, closing his eyes. "Because I made you a promise. And if I return to that bed right now, that promise will be broken." His bleak gaze met hers. He reached up and stroked her cheek with one knuckle. Then her chin. Then, ever so slowly, he trailed his fingertip over her bottom lip, and a deep shudder resonated through her. "I've broken so many promises, Emma. I don't want to break this one."

Confused, aroused, still clawing through the shroud of sleep that he'd dragged her from with his nightmare, she nodded. "All right," she'd murmured. "Please...come back to bed when you can."

"I will."

She'd stumbled back to the bed and had fallen asleep faster than she'd thought possible, with him still sitting at the table, his head in his hands.

With a sigh, Emma looked back down at her letter to her sister. She dipped her pen into the ink and began to write again.

Tomorrow, we will continue on our journey to Edinburgh. We hope to arrive there in five or six days' time if the weather holds. I pray that it does. I am so eager to come to a resolution with R.M.

I will keep you and Papa in my prayers. My thoughts turn to you constantly. Please write when you can. I so hope I shall find a letter awaiting me in Edinburgh.

> *Your loving sister,*
> *Emma*

Emma folded the letter, then donned her pelisse and buttoned the worn Chinese buttons down the front. She glanced at the silk cloak hanging on a peg by the door, and a smile tugged at her lips as it did every time she laid eyes on Luke's gift, but she would probably be too warm if she wore it.

She tucked the letter into her reticule along with a few coins, then went out of the room, locking the door behind her.

She hurried downstairs and encountered an employee of the inn, a fresh-faced girl whom she asked about the mail to Bristol.

"It goes out at half-eight from the Star and Garter, ma'am."

Good, then her letter to Jane would be on its way tonight. "Where's the Star and Garter?"

"Not far at all." The girl gave her a bright smile. "I'll be happy to deliver it for you, if you'd like."

"No thank you. If it's not far, I'd like to walk. I could use a bit of fresh air." That was the truth. She'd been cooped up inside the room all day.

"Of course, ma'am." The girl directed her to the Star and Garter, and Emma stepped out into the busy street.

"Mrs. Curtis!"

That voice was familiar. Dread curling in her stomach, she turned to see that Small had followed her out of the inn. He was quite the fop, with his black hair shiny with oil and an exact match to his gleaming black shoes and snug buff pantaloons, his dark purple velvet coat and carved walking stick.

She stood tall, trying to look down her nose at him, though he was taller than her.

"Mr. Small."

He chuckled. "It's Mr. Small*shaw*, love. Small's just a nickname."

"My apologies," she said icily. She noticed, with no small measure of satisfaction, that the right side of his jaw had turned quite an ugly shade of green.

"May I accompany you to your destination?"

"No thank you."

She turned and commenced to walk, but the blasted man kept pace beside her. She walked faster, and he sped up, too.

"So, tell me how you became acquainted with Lord Lukas."

She made a scoffing noise and stared straight ahead, as though it took all her focus to negotiate the treacherous terrain of the street. "Not likely."

"No, really, I am ever so curious. You see, Hawkins and I are close friends. *Very* close."

She pretended to ignore him.

"He's never been so protective of a woman before. In fact, he's always been most generous when I've asked him to share. And now he's punching me in the face at the mere suggestion. As I am certain you can imagine, this is a mystery I am *most* eager to solve."

Emma's steps ground to a halt. She gazed up at this man—at his round face with angelic features under all that curly, oily hair—and narrowed her eyes at him.

"Please, Mr. Smallshaw, *please* leave me alone."

"Aw, come now. I'm just trying to be friendly, Mrs. Curtis. I'm quite harmless, really."

She did not like his wheedling tone or his attempting-to-be-disarming grin. In fact, she liked nothing about him.

"Be that as it may," she said, "I'd prefer you to go away."

His brows rose and his lips firmed, his attempt to be

friendly evaporating. She'd known it had been false anyhow. "A set-down from a lightskirt. Now that's a rare thing for a man such as myself."

"A man such as yourself?" she asked. "Meaning a man with neither scruples nor morality?"

"Ah, right," he said, matching her sarcasm tone for tone, "and pray, what sort of man do you believe you're sleeping with? Please refrain from standing there with that high-handed manner, madam, saying that *I* lack scruples and morality."

With a huff, he turned on his heel and strode down the street toward the Crown and Unicorn, his walking stick tapping on the cobbles, not deigning to look back at her.

She continued on to the Star and Garter and delivered the letter to the post, feeling like a heavy cloud had gathered just above her shoulders and was threatening a downpour.

She knew Luke was a rogue. And she knew—at least a part of her did—that he'd engaged in activities and dark pleasures that she could never even conceive of.

But all those women—and those men—who'd seen him drunk and carousing and seemingly with no care in the world...had those people seen him waking from nightmares shaking and covered in sweat? Did they see the anguish in his gaze whenever he talked about his family? Did he call *them* angel? Did he hold on to them at night like he'd never let them go?

It was possible, she conceded. The thought made her sick.

But realistically, she thought not. She remembered that first night in Bristol—his cavalier attitude, his flippant, blatantly carnal behavior. All those were part of who

Luke was. But there was more. He was surprisingly easy to talk to. He was tender, compassionate, and thoughtful. Protective, too. And he possessed a sense of honor he'd never admit to having.

And she still didn't know him. She was certain he kept secrets, secrets that tore him apart but that he felt he could never reveal.

Still, he was a rogue. Her husband had been a rogue, too—but Luke was a different kind of rogue altogether. In spite of his changeable nature, his moods and his secrets, he had proved himself to be different from Henry.

But she couldn't take those little differences he'd showed her as proof that he was any less dangerous to her than Henry had been.

She remembered how he'd said he'd been responsible for the ruination of a girl once, how it had been devastating for her but had hardly affected him.

That girl could be Emma next. Despite what her heart and body were telling her, she couldn't allow herself to forget it.

* * *

It took them five days to reach Edinburgh. Five days of hard driving that sapped the energy straight out of Emma's body. By the time they reached the inns every night, she could do little more than eat a quick dinner, drop into bed, and allow the exhaustion to claim her.

Luke had returned from his mystery "business" in Worcester smiling and flirtatious. He'd sent her fiery looks that evening until, with a sigh, he'd announced he was going downstairs. Each night since then, he'd left her and didn't return until she was fast asleep. He always tucked himself beside her, and at some point in the night she'd wake with his arms around her, and she'd burrow into his shirt and sleep easier.

She wondered if he was seeking out that female companionship he'd told her he might require. She was doing her best to turn a blind eye as she'd promised that first night in Bristol, but it was difficult. When he left her, she felt an odd sort of emptiness inside. A part of her—a part that grew more insistent every day—commanded her to grab him and hold on to him. To refuse to allow him to leave her. To touch any other woman but her.

She didn't want him touching other women. The thought twisted her insides into knots that grew tighter and tighter with every day that passed until she couldn't bear it anymore.

On the final day of their journey to Edinburgh, they stopped for luncheon alongside the Pentland Hills in the southern part of Scotland on the road that would take them into the city that evening. The ground was carpeted by the greenest grass and dotted with darker brush and trees, and the hills rolled into the horizon, smooth and rounded. A brook bubbled nearby, giving the horses a watering place and providing Emma and Luke an opportunity to wash the grime of travel from their hands and faces.

While the horses grazed docilely nearby, they spread the blanket and retrieved their meal from the curricle. She sat across from him, and they ate boiled eggs, salted beef, day-old bread, and hard cheese in companionable silence for a while.

She glanced at him surreptitiously through her lashes,

but he seemed intent on his food. Still, those knots were twisted so tight within her, she couldn't stand it a second longer.

"Luke?"

He glanced at her, his blue eyes clear in the light of the day. Not dark and bloodshot like they were after an evening of imbibing. She sighed.

"Mmm?" he said around a mouthful of food.

"Why do you do it?"

His expression went blank. After he swallowed, he said, "Do what?"

"Leave our rooms at night. Drink...and...and whatever else it is that you do." She swallowed hard.

"Gamble?" he supplied helpfully.

She wrapped her arms across her chest, suppressing a shiver. She was still cold from the road, and thinking about the similarity between her husband's habits and Luke's did nothing to warm her. "Is that what you do? Gamble?"

"I do have a penchant for the pastime," he said in a musing voice. He took a bite of egg.

"Oh, I know how it is." Bitterness limned her tone. "I have learned how quickly a man can bleed money at the gaming tables."

"Ah. Our friend Henry Curtis taught you that lesson, I wager."

"You wager correctly," she said dryly.

He stared down at his half-eaten egg, a frown pulling his brows together. "Truth of it is, I haven't gambled since I was in London last summer." He sighed. "My last wager was a particularly stupid one."

"Care to tell me what it was?"

"It was a foolish bet between gentlemen. Didn't even get a decent card game out of it."

She picked up a bit of beef. "Tell me."

He glanced down, and when he looked up at her again, he appeared very young, almost like he did in sleep. But now, his face held a sheepish expression. "I bet Lord Rutger that it would take between seven and ten days for him to lure Mrs. Wickerly into his bed."

She shook her head. Stupid, indeed. "How long did it actually take him?"

"Five days." He raised his hand, holding his thumb and forefinger an inch apart. "So close."

"And you made this wager sober?"

He released a burst of laughter. "Of course not. I don't even remember making it. All I know is that I was dragged to my club a week later to verify that I had signed my name in the betting book. And, alas, I had."

"Drunken bets are the worst kind."

He immediately sobered. "How would you know that?"

"I was married only three months, but it was a busy three months. Henry made a drunken bet one night and lost five hundred guineas."

Luke's brows rose. "What was the bet?"

She gazed down at her plate, rolling an egg under her finger. "That I'd be with child by the following month."

Luke sucked in a breath.

"Of course, they could not verify whether he had won or lost until several weeks after his death. A man came to me with the wager, written on a piece of paper and signed by Henry, and he demanded either his winnings or proof that I was in a family way." She raised the egg to her mouth and took a bite of it.

"And by then," Luke said softly, "you weren't in possession of the funds to pay him."

"No."

A muscle jerked in Luke's jaw, and he turned away. "I can see why you despise gambling, after that."

"I do despise it." Emma's stomach seemed to close in on itself. He watched the motion of her hand as she laid her boiled egg down, then met her gaze. "So you haven't been gambling," she murmured. "Then what is it you do, Luke? Where do you go?"

"I go down to the taverns. I drink ale."

She couldn't look at him. Instead, she gazed down at her half-eaten food. "Do you...seek out women?" She had to choke out every single word.

"No." His answer was swift—a quick pull of release on all those knots twisting within her, and she couldn't contain her sharp sigh of relief.

He stayed silent for a moment, then he asked in a slightly mocking tone, "Why?"

"I don't like the thought of you lying next to me after having lain with someone else."

"Jealous?" he asked softly.

"Not at all." What a lie. She knew it, and he probably did, too. "I just have no desire to serve as the leavings for a man. I have...I have already served that role, and I won't do it again."

He stared at her, his blue eyes inscrutable, his expression impenetrable. Then he said, quite calmly, "If Henry Curtis were alive, I'd tear him limb from limb."

She frowned at him, then shook her head.

Frustration swelled in his voice. "Emma, as long as you and I lie in the same bed, whether we are having 'relations' or not, I will not touch another woman." He gave her a tight smile. "You and I both know my promises hold little worth, but there it is. As for what I do at night, I drink ale. I sit. That's all."

"That sounds like a very lonely way to spend an evening."

He shrugged.

A part of her believed him, but another part was confused. "Then why do you do it?" she pressed. "Why do you leave every night?"

"You know why," he said.

"No. I don't."

"I told you. After the nightm—after I woke you in the middle of the night."

She shook her head in confusion, and she sighed.

"Because I made a promise not to touch you."

"But you have touched me."

He gave a low, cynical laugh. "Not like I want to."

She closed her eyes against the burning-hot thrill that shuddered through her. He was silent, but she felt the heat of his gaze on her.

"You are a rogue, Luke. I deciphered that within ten seconds of knowing you."

He gave another short laugh, this one with a hint of scorn.

"I promised myself I would never again be taken in by another rogue. Because...well, because Henry was a rogue...and...and that didn't turn out well. At all. And the night I met you, I knew that I must remember that promise. Because you were obviously just like him."

Her heart had started to pound, and her words emerged sounding choppy and breathy.

He tilted his head. "What are you trying to say? Because I know all that, Emma. I know why you are so adverse to intimacy with a man like me. I don't blame you. It's why I am trying to honor the agreement we made."

"I don't like you leaving at night." The words rushed out of her.

His lips parted. He stared at her. Then he shrugged and looked down at his food. His voice took on a cynical quality. "You don't have a choice. *I* don't have a choice."

"Luke," she groaned.

His gaze snapped to hers again, and she couldn't have broken the eye contact even if she'd wanted to. His lips curled in that oh-so-wicked smile he'd used on her that first night. "Remember, I said the only thing that could break our agreement was if you begged for it. Is that what you're going to do? Beg for it?"

A part of her wanted to beg. A very big part of her wanted him to take her to bed and keep her there, and never go down to another pub or tavern again, never drink again, never look at another woman again, never gamble again.

He moved closer, shoving the food out of the way as he advanced. He cupped her cheek in his hand, stroking his thumb over her cheekbone as he spoke. "I want you, Emma. I have since that first night. Every single night, my body is an inferno burning just for you. And every night I deny it. Every night I suffer. Will you beg? Will you relieve my suffering?"

Her throat was dry. She squeezed her eyes shut because she couldn't bear to gaze into the blue fire of his. Soon, that fire would consume her. "I...I don't know."

"Don't do it," he whispered, his breath whispering over her lips. He brushed her lips with his gently as he continued. "I'm not good enough for you. Angels aren't meant for devils."

"I'm no angel," she whispered, "and you're no devil." The declaration surprised her even as it emerged from her lips, but in her heart of hearts, she knew it was true. And in her heart of hearts, she knew with the purest clarity that she wanted him.

He pulled back, his expression growing distant. "I wouldn't be so sure if I were you."

Chapter Six

Luke had never been to Edinburgh, but it was a beautiful, burgeoning city. He grinned at Emma's exuberance as she pointed out the sights to him—Edinburgh Castle and St. Mary's Cathedral and Holyrood Palace.

She navigated him through the streets to Cameron's Hotel—an elegant building with a colonnaded entry and a marble hall adorned with gilded furnishings and crystal chandeliers.

He was weary of country inns. The spoiled-duke's-son part of him longed for a full, linen-lined bath and a five-course meal. A velvet-cushioned sofa and an enormous, comfortable bed with silk curtains.

The hotelier had given Emma a letter, and she clutched the missive in her hand as they entered their room. Neither of them spoke until the servants left them alone.

Emma, of course, was no stranger to opulence. Her father had been rich enough to quit his involvement in trade and spend his golden years enjoying the leisurely life of a gentleman. He'd given his daughters the best educations and Seasons in London.

Luke unbuttoned his coat and laid it over one of the chair backs. She untied her bonnet and hung it, then sank down into one of the gilded armchairs to open the letter.

Alone with Emma. Again. Was there a sweeter torture in the world?

Definitely not, he thought wryly, watching her avid expression as she read her letter. Within a few moments, she glanced up at him.

"From Jane?" he asked.

"Yes."

"How is your father?"

She sighed. "The same. But he seems to lose more interest in the world at large daily."

"I'm sorry." He paused. Then, "Do you think that would change if his fortune was returned to him?"

"I hope so. He did so love his fortune. I think..." She took a deep breath, then continued. "I think it was the only thing he truly loved in this world after my mother died. He was so proud of it, of what doors it had opened for us. And when he lost it, it seemed he also lost every last ounce of joy he'd ever possessed."

He offered her one of the apples from the bowl left on the small sideboard. She folded the letter and laid it on the table, then took the apple with a smile and bit into it with a crisp crunch.

No, there was definitely no sweeter torture than being alone with Emma, Luke decided, watching her lick apple juice from her lips.

He gazed at her, watching her eat, feeling his cock stir—something he'd grown accustomed to these past several days in her company. He was accustomed to it, but it didn't make it any less painful.

She didn't want him downstairs drowning himself in drink, but what the hell choice did he have? Staying with her was far more dangerous.

She looked up at him, oblivious and innocent. He'd never thought a married woman could be so innocent, but he was wrong. Outwardly Emma appeared self-composed and calm, and she was certainly no fool, but she was so naïve.

He shifted his feet, turning away slightly to adjust himself to relieve the pressure against his falls.

"Are you ready for tomorrow?" she asked.

"Of course. Are you?"

She hesitated, then said softly, "In a way, I've been ready for it for a year. In another way I'll never be ready."

He took the seat beside her, grabbing one of the apples for himself. It was shiny and red, and when he bit into it, sweetness burst over his tongue. He looked at the apple in surprise, turning it over in his hand.

"Good, isn't it?"

"Very."

They crunched for a few moments, then he said, "You know, we might find nothing. Macmillan might not be here. He might not even exist..."

"I know," she sighed.

"And if he does, he might not have any information for us, even if he's willing to talk to us."

"He is the only clue we have," she said. "And I truly believe he'll lead us to Morton."

"I hope so. For your family's sake."

"And for yours."

He laid his head on the chair back and gazed up at the ceiling, which was decorated along the edges with fancy plasterwork rosettes. "Most of the time, anymore, I think she's dead."

She was silent. Then a soft, "Oh, Luke."

"She's been missing since April, Em. *April.* How many months is that?"

"Six," she said softly.

"Six months," he said, his voice dull. "Six months without a word from her. How could she not be dead?"

"You can't be sure that she is, though. Not until you have proof."

He released a low groan. He'd been searching for months, following every bit of evidence he could find. Ultimately, he'd achieved nothing. He had no better idea now of where his mother was than he had when she first went missing. As much as he wanted answers, he couldn't quite bring himself to believe that C. Macmillan would be the man to provide them.

She reached out and took his hand, her slender fingers wrapping around his. Words weren't necessary. The squeeze of her hand offered him all the comfort he needed.

They were silent for several minutes, their hands clasped together. Luke finished his apple and set it on the table beside him. Finally she asked in a soft voice, "Was she a good mother?"

"Yes." He gazed at the whorls in the plasterwork, remembering. Once upon a time, before the duke had died and when his life had seemed to consist of one hellish event after another, she had been the only person in the world who'd seemed to understand him. The only one who'd convinced him he was worth anything.

"Though," he continued, "I have hardly seen her in the last several years. First there was Eton"—he'd told her about his antics at Eton during their conversations on the way here—"and then my short-lived education at Cambridge, and then London. I saw her a week here, a week there, but infrequently."

"She is still your mother. She was a good mother, and you miss her."

"Yes. Do you miss your mother, too?"

"Yes, I do."

"Was she like you?"

She gave him a wry look. "I wouldn't say so. My mother was very stern and upright. She insisted Jane and I strive for perfection at every waking moment." She sighed. "I could never please her. The day she died, she reprimanded me for a small tear in the lace of my sleeve. I was so busy being afraid, terrified, mourning her imminent death, I hadn't even noticed."

"How did she die?"

"Consumption."

He released a heavy breath. "I am sorry."

"I tried very hard to please her," Emma continued, "but she always required more. There was a point at which I could only turn to myself to feel pride in my small accomplishments."

"What about your sister?"

Her smile softened. "Yes. Thank God for Jane."

"What of your father? Was he demanding as well?"

"No, not so much." She took a last bite of apple and turned away to discard it. "He was less involved, I suppose you would say. He wanted sons, but he ended up with a pair of daughters. He was mostly indifferent to Jane and me."

"And now that your mother is gone? Have things changed?"

"A little for the worse, a little for the better. He's less indifferent, in any case. But he hates me a little now."

Luke stiffened, sitting up straighter. "Why?"

"Because I am the reason for his poverty. I can't blame him, can I? I *am* the reason."

"For God's sake, Em. You were innocent. You had no idea your husband could have been part of a scheme to ruin your family."

"Yes. I know. But I shouldn't have been so trusting." She gave a heavy sigh, then her eyes slid toward him, their golden flecks glowing in the lamplight. It was already nearly dark outside. The days were growing shorter.

"Will you stay tonight?" she murmured.

He looked at her with hooded eyes. Then, still holding her hand, he rose, pulling her up with him. Slowly, savoring every touch, every slide of the muslin of her dress against the wool of his coat, he pulled her against him.

He held her trapped against his body, his arms wrapped around her, his right palm pressed to the indentation at the small of her back, just above the curve of her buttocks.

She looked up at him, her cheeks flushed, her lips parted.

He stared down at her. She stared up at him. Then, tentatively, her arms stroked his sides in an up-and-down motion.

Just a little taste. He'd take a small taste, then he'd go.

He dragged his fingertips up her spine, feeling the bumps of her cloth-covered buttons. He cupped the back of her head in his hand, then lowered his lips to hers.

Her taste erupted through him, a thousand times sweeter, more compelling, more delicious than he remembered. His cock swelled again. Desire swirled in his gut and circled his spine.

He pulled her tighter against him. His fingers twined in her thick, glorious hair, working the pins and dropping them to the floor one at a time.

Her lips were soft and wet, and this time, they responded to him. Her mouth opened, her mouth tentatively skimming his own. Lust surged through him.

He coaxed her lips to open, wanting to go deeper, wanting to taste her, wanting to claim her, to breathe her in.

She gasped lightly, fueling his desire more. The way her lips moved, the way they stroked him made him mad with wanting.

And then her tongue touched his lower lip, the most tentative of tastes.

His arms tightened. Her hair fell over his hand, a heavy, soft curtain. He grazed her lips with his teeth, swiped his tongue over them. He couldn't get enough. He'd never get enough.

For him, lust was a greedy, demanding thing, but it was something he could usually control. With Emma, though, it was more greedy and more demanding than it had ever been before. And right now, it was demanding he push her to her knees, open his trousers, and feed her his cock.

Guilt at the coarse thought washed over him, as effective as a barrel of ice-cold water. He groaned as he dropped his hands and took a step back. Forcing himself away from her felt like he was tearing the skin from his flesh. It burned. It ached. It bloody *hurt*.

He was breathing hard. So was she—more beautiful than ever with that hair in waves around her heart-shaped face and gazing at him in glazed-eyed confusion.

"No," he whispered harshly. "No." As if he'd convince himself.

He couldn't look at her anymore. He tore his gaze away.

"Bloody hell. Damn it," he cursed. "Bugger it. To the devil—"

"Stop, Luke." Her low, husky voice was surprisingly strong. At odds with the bewildered look that had resided on her face seconds ago. "It's all right."

He whipped around to face her again. Now she was calm, composed, but her eyes still glimmered with some emotion he couldn't define.

All right? What about this was all right? What about any of this was all right?

Jesus Christ.

"I'm going," he croaked out. "I have to go."

He turned and left the room, grabbing his coat from the chair on his way out.

He stumbled downstairs and into the opulent dining room. They wouldn't call the damned thing a pub or a tavern here.

The place was too snobbish. It reminded him of Ironwood Park, its patrons just like his brother looking down their noses at him.

He left that place and stepped out into the street. A blast of cold shot through his coat and arrowed straight into the marrow of his bones.

He strode along the street, the evening air burning his lungs.

He had made a fine hell of a mess of things today, first over their luncheon in the field and then just now. If she never forgave him, he wouldn't blame her.

He pushed his hand through his hair and realized he'd forgotten his hat.

In Bristol, he'd been determined to seduce her, to bring her to the point of begging so that he could have his wicked way with her. A big part of him still wanted that, and wanted it with a thousand times more urgency than at the beginning.

But now...hell. He respected her too much. He admired her. Damn it, he actually *liked* her. She was the first human being he had genuinely admired in a very long time.

He'd taken advantage of women before. He'd played with them like pleasure toys and then discarded them when he was done. But he couldn't do that with Emma.

There were so many reasons for her to stay away from him. But what it boiled down to was that he was no good for her—or for anyone for that matter—and he was too damned cowardly to show her the truth.

His steps slowed, and he paused, staring at one of the gaslights that glowed onto the street in a circular pool of gold, a color that would always remind him of Emma's eyes.

Perhaps that was the answer. He wouldn't have to tell her everything, but just somehow find the strength to tell her one thing. One thing that would certainly scare her away.

* * *

He didn't return. Not until an early morning hour when Emma was so deep asleep that when she woke, she couldn't recall whether the feel of him drawing her into his arms was a dream. But he slept beside her, smelling of whisky.

It had been whisky the previous night, too. She shouldn't be surprised it would be his drink of choice now that they were in Scotland.

She slipped from under the covers, trying not to wake him. She sat on the edge of the bed, her legs dangling over the side, her back to him.

"Good morning, Emma." His voice was deliciously rough with sleep.

She looked back over her shoulder at him. "Good morning."

His arm slipped out from under the covers and his hand closed over hers. She stared down at it.

"Are you angry with me?"

Yes. No.

"I don't know," she admitted. His kiss yesterday had left her weak-kneed and light-headed. But then he'd left her alone in that state, and in the hours that passed after he'd walked out the door, she'd come to her senses.

This was Luke. Sensual, seductive, but changeable and confusing. Watching him walk away from her last night had broken something inside her.

She was trying to steel herself, to build impenetrable

shields around herself so that he wouldn't be able to hurt her. Because God knew, she'd been hurt enough by Henry to last a lifetime. The problem was, Luke could melt down those steely walls quicker than she could build them.

Behind her, Luke blew out a breath. She felt movement, then he was sitting beside her, his presence strong and masculine, and there it was. That melting. That feeling—no, the certain knowledge—that whatever he asked, she would want nothing more than to give it to him.

His hand was still on hers, engulfing her much-smaller fingers in his own.

"Emma—" He broke off, shaking his head. His fingertips played with the lace at the edge of the long sleeve of her nightgown.

She glanced at him. He was wearing his shirt as always—in fact, she had never seen him shirtless—and drawers. The bed linens were partially draped over his lap. With his dark blond hair curling to his shoulders, his blue eyes, his shirt open at the collar, showing a hint of pale flesh, he looked like he could be etched in marble. He was beautiful—a blond Adonis.

God, how she wanted him.

She looked away.

"I shouldn't have done that last night," he said.

She lifted her chin, gave him a defiant look. "Shouldn't have done what? Kiss me or leave me afterward?"

"Kiss you."

"You did notice that I didn't complain?"

"Yes, I did notice that. But you should have."

She shook her head stubbornly. "I refuse to listen to

more of that nonsense about the incompatibility of angels and devils. I told you—I am no angel. You've seen that I am no angel. This is a silly excuse. There must be something more."

"You have never begged," he said softly. "I promised I wouldn't touch you unless you begged for it." His fingers tightened around hers.

"Another excuse," she said. "If I were to beg, it wouldn't matter. You'd still be afraid. You'd still run away and drown your fear in drink."

He stiffened. "You don't know what you're talking about."

"Don't I?"

Silence for a long moment, then he turned to her, his fiery blue eyes capturing her gaze. "I meant it when I said I could offer you the heights of pleasure. I meant it when I told you I'd take you to that pinnacle if you begged for it. But now, and I swear I am not using this as an excuse, I know without a doubt that you're too good for the likes of me. I didn't understand that at the beginning, but I do now."

"You're going to drive me mad," was all she could say. Because no one in the English-speaking world would say that Emma was too good for Lord Lukas Hawkins. The truth was, her social status was far below his. He was the son of one of the noblest families in England, both his feet firmly entrenched on the highest rung of society's ladder.

By contrast, her family's money—even when they'd had money—was new money earned from trade and looked down upon by society. Everything her family had—from the admission to the elite boarding school in Hampshire to the two Seasons she'd had in London—

they'd had to fight for, to claw through upturned noses and haughty set-downs.

She pulled away from him and stood, moving toward her clothes. They needed to go. Today was an important day.

But he stopped her. He came up behind her and set his hands on her shoulders, turning her around. "Listen to me, Em. I'm trying to explain myself. Be patient with me. It isn't easy."

She stilled, staring up into his face, at his unshaven jaw, his straight, aristocratic nose, his burning blue eyes gazing down with an intensity that simmered through her bones.

She didn't say anything. She waited, gazing at him. Probably, to him, she appeared completely still and calm, but her insides were roiling.

"You deserve gentleness," he finally said.

She made a scoffing noise. *Gentleness?*

"You deserve tenderness and care."

"Good God, Luke—"

He pressed a finger to her lips, cutting her short.

She'd been going to say that in the past week, he'd showed more tenderness and care toward her than anyone had in her life.

"I can't give you any of that," he said.

"Yes, you—"

Now his hand covered her mouth entirely, and his free arm wrapped around her waist, pinning her in place so she couldn't have backed away even if she wanted to.

"Let. Me. Speak."

She ground her teeth. But she allowed him to speak, even though it took several seconds before he began again.

"You are a beautiful lady, and you deserve someone who will offer all those things, and more. You're intelligent and assertive, and you could get anything out of this life if you set your mind to it. You're a woman who deserves permanence and consistency." He shrugged. "But you're also very naïve."

She made a noise of disagreement, but his palm pressed harder over her mouth.

"You don't understand what kind of a man I am."

She narrowed her eyes at him. She knew more than he thought.

"I am not the sort of man who would ever offer permanence to a woman. I can't give you any of those things you need. And"——he took a deep breath, his broad chest rising and falling behind the shirt——"my tastes in the bedchamber do not coincide with yours."

How on *earth* would he know what her tastes in the bedchamber were? She hardly knew them herself.

Slowly, cautiously, he removed the hand covering her mouth. As soon as she could, she snapped out the question, "And what, exactly, are your tastes in the bedchamber, my lord?"

His eyes narrowed. The arm wrapped like a steel band behind her back didn't budge.

"Would you like details?"

"Yes." She narrowed her own eyes back at him.

He tilted his head, his gaze seeking hers, as if trying to pry under her skin and see what hid there.

Then he looked down. "God, Em. Are you really going to make me talk about this?"

"I need to know." She pressed her hand against his chest, her palm flat and firm. "I need to know this big, jagged secret that you hold so close it cuts you inside."

He gave a humorless chuckle. "A big, jagged secret? And you think I have just one?"

"Start with one," she whispered.

He was quiet for a moment, then he nodded, not quite meeting her eyes. She'd never seen him so shifty-eyed before, and it made something twist inside her.

"I have done things to women that would horrify you."

She stood firm. "What kinds of things?"

His eyelids sank down. His chin tucked into his chest. And yet his arm remained clasped in a solid curve around her waist.

"I've taken them two at a time. I've shared with other men. I've participated in orgies."

She released a measured breath. This came as no great surprise. She knew as much, from their encounter with that awful Smallshaw man.

But Luke wasn't finished.

"I have...I have been cruel to women." His voice twisted with anguish. "I don't want to be cruel to you."

"You have never been cruel to me, Luke."

"But"—he shook his head bleakly—"it is how I am."

"Are you talking about the ruination of that girl you told me about before?"

"That is just one example. Her name was Mary."

She gazed at him, waiting for him to continue.

"She was a servant at Ironwood Park. Eighteen years old. I was twenty and had just given up on Cambridge. I came home, argued with my brother, as usual, and was generally restless and ill-tempered. I was planning to return to London, when I discovered Mary." He looked directly at Emma and said in a low voice, "She was all angelic sweetness and innocence. Rather like you, Em."

She frowned at him, feeling her brows pulling tightly together.

"I seduced her most thoroughly. I made it a game to have her in every room of Ironwood Park. That's all it was to me. A droll game. Very soon, we were caught in flagrante delicto. If you'd asked me beforehand, I would have predicted it, and I wouldn't have cared. I had no concern for the repercussions to her should we be caught. Of course Trent, being Trent, said I should do the gentlemanly thing and offer marriage. I refused."

Emma took a measured breath, but her gaze didn't leave his face.

"I turned my back on her and left Ironwood Park, leaving her to her fate."

"What happened to her?"

"She was sent away. After that...I don't know."

Emma stared at him, wondering why none of this shocked her as much as it should. Jealousy and anger swirled through her. A part of her hated him on behalf of Mary. But she still wanted him just as much as ever.

What was *wrong* with her?

After a long silence, he said, "So do you see why you should run from the likes of me? I've done it before and I'm more than likely to do it again. There is an evil that resides inside me, Emma. You mustn't take that risk."

Slowly, Emma shook her head. "You have taken responsibility. You feel remorse for what you did to that girl. I hear it in your voice."

He blew out a breath. "People who care about me always end up regretting it. Invariably, I will hurt them. And I am the worst to women." He closed his eyes. "I seduce them. I take wicked pleasure from their bodies. Then I escape."

Just like he did from her, every single night. It seemed Luke made a habit of escaping.

"Is that what you want, Luke? To seduce me? To take wicked pleasure from my body?"

He hesitated, then his expression darkened. "Yes."

"Tell me how."

He started to turn away, but in a move quicker than she'd ever have thought possible, especially with her emotions in this roiling state, she whipped her arms out, wrapped them around his waist, and clasped her wrists behind him, trapping him in the circle of her arms.

He looked down at her with stormy eyes. She pressed her body against him, feeling all his hard, masculine ridges pressed to her. Fire kindled under her skin, aching, needing...

So many emotions crossed over his face she couldn't keep track of all of them: pain, shame, desire, others she couldn't define. But then he stilled, his gaze clearing and his eyes growing so intensely blue they glittered like sapphires.

"You'd be bound," he said, his voice rasping. "On your knees. Or on your stomach, your legs spread, so I could see all of you."

Emma's breath caught and refused to leave her body.

"I'd blindfold you so you'd be unable to see what I'm doing to you." His tongue swiped over his top lip. "So you'd feel sensations you've never felt in places you've never felt them. I would teach you how to pleasure yourself and then I'd watch you do it."

He paused. Emma didn't move. Her breath was still

caught somewhere between her lungs and the back of her throat.

Ever so quietly, he continued. "Most of all, I want to hear you lose that control you hold on to so tightly. I want you to scream for me. I want you to beg for release. Sob for it."

Through the roar in her mind, Emma vaguely heard the sounds of the outside world. A carriage rattling over cobbles. A baby crying somewhere in the hotel. A slam of a door.

"I am bad, Emma," he said softly. "Bad, wicked, and depraved."

Something released in her, and she finally let out the long breath she'd been holding. She gazed evenly into his eyes. "You are not evil, Luke. Everyone has those kinds of desires. They are *human*."

The vehemence of her voice surprised her. And Luke recoiled as if she'd punched him. The glitter in his eyes faded as he tore his gaze from hers. "If you don't believe my depraved fantasies to be evil, then what about what I will invariably do to you afterward?"

He'd escape afterward. Leave her debauched and alone. Or at least he thought he would be compelled to do so, because of this evil he believed resided within him.

But what if he was wrong?

Oh, Lord, it was an enormous risk. But she wanted him badly enough, she was willing to take it. "What if I told you I didn't want to think about afterward? That I don't care if you were to walk away? That I am a grown woman who can make her own choices, and I choose *you*?" She pressed closer to him. "I want to exist in the present, Luke. I want to stop worrying about the future."

His eyes widened, then narrowed. He stepped infinitesimally closer to her. "You say you believe everyone has dark desires? Then tell me about yours."

She stiffened. "That's unfair. I haven't had the same opportunities as you. I'm inexperienced. I don't know—"

"But you still crave something. What is it you crave? Did your husband give it to you?"

Her chest felt so tight. "No," she breathed.

Luke reached up and swiped the back of one of his knuckles down her cheek. "What? When you were lying there on your back and performing your marital duty, what did you crave?"

She was breathing hard now. Panic swarmed in her chest. There were certain things a person never revealed, to anyone.

"Tell me, Emma. Tell me what you wanted."

"It was only three months," she whispered. "I was so new to...to experiences of the flesh. I didn't know, exactly."

"But you had an idea."

"Yes."

"Tell me."

"Luke," she breathed. "I've never told anyone this. Ever. I'm not sure I can..."

She'd hardly admitted them to herself. And when she had, she'd pushed them, deep and hard, into the farthest recesses of her soul.

"Tell me." His voice was firm and commanding. Her knees felt watery. She took a shaking breath.

"I wanted..." She stopped. Licked her lips and tried again. "I wanted him to try something else."

"Something other than lying on top of you?"

"Y-yes." She couldn't look at him. She was mortified, but there was so much more than mortification swirling through her. Something delicious was unfurling in her belly, and she was flushed and hot—not only on her face, but also all over, inside and out.

This was the utterly forbidden. These were thoughts she'd never, ever dared allow herself to dwell upon.

"Like what?"

"Once...I saw horses in a meadow once...and... and...I wondered what it would be like to be on my hands and knees while—"

Luke inhaled sharply. Somehow, the sound of the air rushing through his teeth strengthened her.

"I wanted to be on top," she admitted, the words coming easier now. "I wanted to be standing against a wall or leaning over the edge of the bed while you—while *he*," she corrected quickly as flames leapt to her cheeks, "took me. I...I wanted him to have his wicked way with me. To tie me up and tell me what to do and how to do it. I wanted to please him." A note of desperation rang in her voice with the final sentence.

"Bloody hell," Luke muttered. And then he drew her into his arms and was kissing her, and his lips were strong and soft against hers, his tongue nudging into her mouth. With a little gasp, she wrapped her arms around him and gave in to it, opening and allowing him access, feeling him sweep through her as if her mouth belonged to him.

Her knees finally gave way, but his arm, that steely band, was around her back again, holding her firm against him.

His arousal touched her stomach. Flutters trembled

through her, starting at the spot where that hard ridge pressed against her.

He sucked at her bottom lip, trailed his tongue over her top one. His kisses slowed, the urgency softening into exploration. She moved her hands up his back, feeling the hard ridges of muscles below her palms.

His hand cupped her jaw, moving her face this way and that, covering her skin with languid, soft kisses as though he needed to taste every inch of her. His lips moved up the side of her face, then pressed down on her closed eyelid.

"Emma," he whispered on a groan. "God, Emma."

He stopped kissing her, his hand dropping from her jaw to join the other hand behind her back. He held her close, and she pressed her face to his chest, feeling the rapid beat of his heart against her cheek, the rise and fall of his torso with each quick inhalation.

Then there was a knock at the door. Slowly, hesitantly, he pulled away until he stood facing her, arms at his sides.

"Yes?" he called.

"Excuse me, sir," a woman's voice said softly. "I've the washing water and breakfast you ordered."

He raised a brow, and Emma nodded, signifying that last night, she had indeed requested these things to be delivered at eight o'clock this morning.

"Come in, please," Luke said.

Three servants dressed in black dresses with white aprons entered, carrying trays of food and a basin of steaming water.

As the servants bustled about, Emma gazed at Luke. He hadn't moved from where he stood facing her. He looked shaken.

She swallowed back the huge lump that had formed at the top of her throat. She glanced at the servants who had finished their tasks and were waiting with downcast eyes for further instruction. "Thank you, that will be all," she told them. They curtsied and left.

She turned back to Luke, resolve straightening her spine. "We should eat and dress. Then...we need to go find C. Macmillan."

Chapter Seven

❧

$\mathcal{I}$t was a half-hour drive out to Duddingston Parish.
As Luke drove them through the village of Wester Duddingston, he slowed the horses. When Emma glanced
over at him, she saw that he was gazing at a middle-aged
woman who was emerging from behind the church, staggering under the weight of what appeared to be two very
heavy baskets slung over her forearms.

"Here we go." Luke halted the horses and handed
Emma the ribbons. "Stay here. I'll be right back."

Bemused, she held the horses and watched him saunter
up to the woman. Emma was too far away to hear anything more than snippets of their conversation, but she
could tell by the woman's quick speech and fretful motions that she was overcome by Luke's handsome bearing. And perhaps also by the fact that he was English and
very clearly of the aristocracy.

"Do ye mean Colin Macmillan? Oh, aye," the woman

said, and went on chattering in a lower voice, her tone conspiring. She was probably telling Luke everything she knew about the man.

Emma had to admit that watching Luke flustered her, too. Even now, after spending almost every moment with him over the past several days. She mused over this as she watched him. At first, perhaps, it had been simple lust. A product of her innate and unwise attraction to rogues and scoundrels that she'd been trying to suppress. But now, even though the lust had grown into something so powerful it threatened her control, there was more to it than that. Much more.

"Och, aye, sir," she heard the woman say. "'T'isn't far. Over that hill, yonder, and through the grove of yews."

Luke reached down and retrieved the two baskets the woman had been carrying but had lowered to the ground in order to speak to him. "May I help you with these? Where were you going?"

Emma shook her head, smiling wryly. And the man claimed he wasn't a gentleman.

The woman protested, saying it was too far, that he "shouldna fash" himself over her. But Luke gently pressed her until she gestured to the other end of the street, where Luke and Emma had entered the village.

Luke walked by the curricle carrying the heavy baskets, winking at her as he passed. She grinned at him, then smiled at the woman, who gave her a respectful curtsy before hurrying after Luke.

Moments later, Luke returned alone. "Well, she told me a little about C. Macmillan," he said as he climbed up and took the reins from her.

"Do tell."

"He seems to dabble in industry, dipping his fingers in many different pots. He owns a great deal of land along the shore and manufactures salts there. He's a partial owner of the Duddingston Coal Works and employs most of the workers here in Wester Duddingston. And he owns a soap manufactory nearby."

"Goodness. A busy man," Emma murmured.

"Yes." Luke frowned. "I am curious as to why such a man would associate with someone like Roger Morton."

"Well, I can think of one way we might find the answer to that."

"By asking him," Luke said.

"Exactly."

Ten minutes later, they rode through the iron gates of a mansion that reminded her of her father's house in Bristol. But this one was older, its modern design belied by round fairy-tale towers, topped by battlements and arrow slits at each end of the façade.

Luke pulled the horses short and gazed at the house. "It's a little early for a social visit."

"Our visit isn't particularly social," she mused.

A stable boy ran toward them and took the reins from Luke. Luke jumped down with practiced ease, then came around to help Emma.

"Ready?" he murmured.

She nodded and blew out a measured breath. "I am."

He smiled at her and led her to the massive entryway. As they approached, a man opened the door. A butler, certainly. He was older, and very thin, and stood straight as he gazed at them impassively.

"Sir. Madam."

Luke looked at him with an utterly bored expression.

"Lord Lukas Hawkins and Mrs. Henry Anderson. Here to see Mr. Macmillan."

She released a breath. She'd asked him to use her maiden name, afraid that Macmillan would become suspicious if he heard Henry Curtis's wife had come to see him.

"Have you a card, sir?" The butler sniffed, and Emma noted that he didn't have any trace of a Scottish accent.

Luke rolled his eyes. "No. No card."

"Very well, sir. I shall see if Mr. Macmillan is at home. Please excuse me."

The butler retreated, and the door closed with a low, resonating boom.

She glanced at Luke. "What if he refuses to see us?"

Luke shrugged and spoke without inflection. "My name gets me into most of these kinds of homes." He grimaced. "Not because it belongs to me, of course, but because it is linked to the Duke of Trent."

"Oh," she murmured.

"Everyone knows Trent. Of him, anyhow. And everyone wants to wheedle their way into his good graces."

"Do you often use your name for the benefit it can give you?" She asked the question without rancor; she was truly curious, because she hadn't seen him do this before.

"No." His voice was flat. "I despise doing it. I did it for your sake today. And for the sake of my mother."

She reached out to touch his arm but dropped her hand quickly, because the door was already opening again.

"Mr. Macmillan was on his way to the manufactory, but he will see you now," the butler announced with a sniff. "Follow me, if you please."

They followed the man into a cavernous marble entry

hall. Everything inside was white marble except the glints of gold in the chandelier and the few pieces of gilded furniture placed against the wall.

Their footsteps echoed ominously as they traversed the wide space. Beside her, Luke shuddered and said under his breath, "Just like Ironwood Park."

That surprised her. She'd imagined his childhood home to be grand and imposing but not cold and barren. There wasn't time to ask him about that now, though.

They followed the butler through an arched doorway and up a winding oak staircase. At the landing, he opened a monstrous carved door and announced them. "Mrs. Anderson and Lord Lukas Hawkins, sir."

He stepped aside, allowing them to gain entry into the room.

It was an elegant drawing room designed with dark furniture and enhanced by marble tabletops and gilded sconces, not unlike the drawing room where her father had received visitors—back in the day when visitors had come to their house in Bristol.

A man stood in the center of the room. He was thin, like his butler, but old and grizzled, with a shock of thick gray hair. He grinned and held out his hands in welcome as if they were old friends he'd been expecting for days.

"Well, good morning," he said warmly to Emma. His voice contained a soft Scottish burr, but his accent was very slight, as if he had spent many years in England. "Ye must be Mrs. Anderson."

"It is a pleasure to meet you," she murmured, somewhat mystified. She'd expected a very unpleasant man, but his vocal tone was nothing like the tone of his letter to Morton.

"And Lord Lukas, how fine it is to finally make your acquaintance. I had the honor of meeting your brother the duke at a dinner in London last spring."

Luke slid her a glance, and beyond the mocking expression on his face, she didn't miss the glint of pain in his eyes. At that moment she realized how much he truly hated how people treated him as an extension of the Duke of Trent rather than as his own person.

"A pleasure to meet you," Luke said politely. But a muscle worked in his jaw, and she could practically hear him grinding his teeth.

"I was pleased to hear of his recent nuptials as well. I sent a letter of congratulations a few weeks ago. Do ye know if he received it?"

"Sorry," Luke clipped. "No idea."

Macmillan didn't glean Luke's mood from his tone. "I wrote also about the measure in parliament providing some relief to those of us merchants who lost our salt at sea in last winter's storms."

"Mmm." Luke's expression darkened.

"I hope ye will convey to your brother that it is a start, but no' enough, if Britain—Scotland, in particular—is to see future growth in its salt trade."

"Mr. Macmillan," Luke growled, "I am not a message boy for my brother. Tell him your damned self."

Oh, dear. Emma stepped forward as Macmillan's eyes widened. "Mr. Macmillan, thank you so much for seeing us today, and for your generous welcome into your home."

Macmillan turned his now-wary gaze to her.

"We were hoping you could be of assistance to us in a very important matter."

Macmillan studied her for a moment, and in his assessing gaze, she found a hint of the man who'd written that letter to Roger Morton. But then he smiled and made a grand gesture toward a cluster of sofas and chairs on one side of the room. "Please, sit down, and we'll talk. May I offer you some refreshment?"

"Thank you," Emma murmured. Luke was still glowering, so she touched his arm and mouthed, *Sit*, as Macmillan spoke to the servant who'd been standing at attention by the door.

Luke puffed a breath out of the side of his mouth and gave her a slight nod.

She lowered herself on a sofa upholstered in rich shades of burgundy and gold. Luke sat beside her, a little closer than would generally be considered proper for acquaintances, but they were so much more than that now. And she didn't care a whit what Macmillan thought.

Still, she saw his assessing gaze take in her and Luke's proximity as he returned from speaking to the servant.

He sat in a matching chair across from them, laying his forearms over its tasseled arms. He gave them a polite tilt of his head. "Now, then, how may I be of assistance?"

She flicked a glance at Luke. His clenched jaw told her that he was still annoyed, so she steeled herself. It looked like she would be the one to explain.

"We are looking for someone who might have information pertaining to the disappearance of the Dowager Duchess of Trent."

Macmillan's brow furrowed. He, like everyone else in the country, must know by now that the dowager had been missing since spring.

Luke shifted uncomfortably beside her. She wanted to

touch him. But she was in a strange man's house, and he was watching them carefully. Her desire to soothe Luke would have to wait.

Macmillan's gaze moved to Luke. "I had heard about the dowager. Unfortunate business, that."

"Yes," Luke ground out. "Unfortunate."

"We have evidence that the duchess's disappearance might be connected to a man named Roger Morton," Emma said softly. "We have reason to believe you might know this man. That you might know where we could find him."

At the mention of Roger Morton, Macmillan went very still. His gaze strayed from Luke to Emma and back to Luke again. His fingers tightened over the arms of his chair.

"Aye, I do know the man. What's led you to believe he was involved in the duchess's disappearance?"

She glanced at Luke again. When he didn't seem like he was going to respond, she said, "There were many eyewitnesses who saw them together. In particular, the family located one of the duchess's servants, who claimed that the duchess left her home with Mr. Morton and went with him to Wales, where he procured a house for her and where they lived for several weeks over the summer."

Macmillan stared at her, then he shook his head and muttered, "Just like Morton, to involve himself in such business."

Emma hesitated, then decided not to ask him about Roger's association with Henry just yet. The link to the duchess seemed to be enough for now.

"Would you mind telling us in what capacity you know Mr. Morton, sir?"

"Aye, of course. He worked for me several years ago at one of my offices in London. He was an ambitious man, and very intelligent. He made a few excellent investments, and five years ago, he told me he was leaving my service to engage in certain potentially profitable prospects of his own."

"But you have communicated with him since then?"

"Indeed. I kept my eye on him, as it were. I was interested in his progress, as I am in all men of ambition who prove their talents to me."

Luke stared at Macmillan with narrow-eyed interest. "Did you find him to be an honest, honorable sort of man?"

Macmillan gave a humorless chuckle. "Honest and honorable perhaps have different meanings in my world than yours, my lord."

Luke glanced around him. "Hmm. Last I noticed, Mr. Macmillan, we were residing in the same world."

"True, true." Macmillan's tone was gracious. "However, what I mean to say is that in order to find success and riches, one must not only be willing to work for it day and night, but one must also fight for it. Sometimes that requires a kind of fighting that might not be considered strictly admirable."

"I see," Luke said. Emma wasn't sure if he truly understood. She certainly did. There was something very intrinsic—deeper than money—that separated people like Luke from people like her and Macmillan.

Two servants came in bearing trays—one covered in sweet-looking little cakes and the other with a teapot and cups.

When the tea was poured, and Emma held her cup in her hands and was sipping at it, Macmillan said, "In spite o' that, I never was given any reason to believe that Morton was involved in anything untoward, or illegal."

"When did you last hear from him?" Luke asked.

"About a year ago. During the spring a year prior to that, he'd told me of a new scheme he'd been considering investing in—a brewery near Bristol. He asked for a loan to assist him and his partner with the cost of investing."

Two years ago—that was the Season she'd spent in London. When she'd met Henry.

"And you gave him the funds he requested?"

"I *lent* him the funds. As I said, he was a man of competence. I analyzed the information he sent me regarding the business he was considering and deemed it a fine investment. However, his partner was a fool—"

"His partner—what was his name?" Emma breathed.

"Curtis. Something Curtis." Macmillan frowned. "Harry?"

"Henry," she corrected softly.

Henry had been in league with Roger Morton from the beginning. Emma gazed down at the half-full teacup in her lap, blinking rapidly.

Luke's hand closed over hers, stopping the frantic drumming cadence her fingers had been tapping out on her thigh. She stilled. When she looked up at Macmillan, he was studying their joined hands with interest.

"Tell us the rest," Luke said harshly. "What happened with the loan and with Morton and Curtis's brewery?"

She remembered the brewery—Henry had "borrowed" several thousand pounds from Papa to invest in it. Money Papa had never seen again.

She'd been nothing but a pawn in a grand, horrible scheme to steal her father's fortune.

Macmillan shook his head. "Betimes when men of little means become men of fortune, they lose their wits and turn to debauchery and vice. When I sent Morton a letter requesting the promised payments, the lad told me Curtis had turned to drink and gambling, that the potential of their investment was slipping through his fingers because the man was a fool. He requested more time."

Macmillan's face went stern, his eyes dark, and Emma suddenly knew why this man had done so well for himself. He did not suffer fools gladly.

"I sent him another letter—a threatening one, for he had broken the terms of our agreement—and quite legal and proper terms, they were, too. I told him to rid himself of Curtis and continue on his own. I warned him that if he did not remit the funds to me in the allotted time, I would involve the authorities."

"I assume he remitted the payment on time?" Luke asked.

"He did. He paid in full, a week before the due date."

"What happened to Curtis?" Luke asked. "Did he tell you?"

"Nay. The name wasn't mentioned. I assumed he'd taken my advice and got rid of the fool."

It seemed Morton had "got rid" of Henry just in time. By drowning him that night in the Avon.

"Do you know where Mr. Morton is now?" Emma asked over her scraping throat.

"He kept a flat in Bristol."

"He's long gone from there," Luke said gruffly. "Where do you think he would have gone? Back to London?"

"Undoubtedly."

"But where in London?" Emma asked, her heart sinking. The city was so enormous and so crowded that finding a single man within it seemed as difficult as locating a needle in a haystack.

"He resided near the docks last I knew." Macmillan shrugged. "But his fortunes have certainly changed since those days."

She leaned forward. "Is there anything, any information or clue that you could give us to help us find his whereabouts, Mr. Macmillan? What about his family? Do you know where any of his relatives live?"

"Aye, there's that." Macmillan tapped his chin. "His family. He'd a married sister, if I recall. We were introduced once, quite by chance."

"Do you know where she lived?" Luke asked.

"What did she look like?" Emma asked.

"Sorry, my lord. I truly cannot recall. But the one time I met her was outside a church in Soho. They had just emerged from services—Morton and his sister, and her husband as well, who was a redheaded and red-cheeked Irishman who appeared as though he'd just arrived in London from that country. As to what *she* looked like..." Macmillan scrunched up his face. "She was dark-haired like her brother. Of average height and build like him, too. They were very much alike—I remember commenting on that. I thought they were twins, and said so, but they said no, they were more than a year apart in age—the sister being the elder of the two."

"Do you remember the husband's name?" asked Luke.

"O'Binn? O'Brien? I'm not sure—sorry. It was O-somethin' or other, however."

"That's helpful," Emma breathed. "Thank you so very much."

Luke glanced at her. "Looks like we'll be heading south."

"Yes," she murmured. "To London."

Macmillan tilted his head again, but this time there was a curious gleam in his eye. "If you don't mind me asking, Mrs. Anderson, what is your relation to the Dowager Duchess of Trent? You seem quite invested in Morton's whereabouts."

She opened her mouth to respond, but then she stopped, something black and ugly twisting in her gut. She didn't want to admit she'd married Henry Curtis. She didn't want to be associated with that bastard in any way anymore. She wondered vaguely if it was even possible for her to change her name back to Anderson.

"She's a close family friend," Luke said, coming to her rescue. "Very close. My mother had a way with children, and over time, she became practically a mother to Mrs. Anderson as well. Of *course* she is invested. Our mother is important to all of us."

Luke sounded pompous and aristocratic, and there was a warning edge to his voice that had Macmillan retreating immediately.

"Of course," he said sympathetically. "Well, then. I do wish you the very best. I hope you find Morton and that he is able to help you locate your dear mother."

"So do I, Mr. Macmillan," Emma said softly. "So do I."

* * *

That night, their last night in Edinburgh, Luke and Emma ate dinner in their sumptuous lodgings at Cameron's Hotel.

The food was splendid, and they had been given a small staff to serve it. After a first course of cold soup and cucumbers, they enjoyed a salad, then Scottish fare consisting of bannocks, haggis, duckling, and sage stuffing soaked in savory gravy. The dessert consisted of a variety of fruits with sweet cream topping it, and cheese and dried sweetmeats.

Feeling pleasantly full and content, Luke glanced at his wineglass—no, it was still nearly full, so that wasn't the reason for his contentment. It was the woman sitting across from him.

They'd barely spoken throughout the meal, but that suited Luke. He liked that they could be comfortable with each other in silence without feeling the awkward need to converse about mundane topics.

Emma took a bite of the cream-covered pear and sighed. "Heavenly," she murmured. After she swallowed, she grinned at him. "Far preferable to the haggis."

"You didn't like it?"

"Not particularly. But now I can say I've tried it."

He chuckled. "That you can."

They ate in silence for a few more moments. Then, "Luke?"

"Mmm?"

She gazed at him steadily, stirring at her ice with a spoon. "Why do you dislike being associated with your brother?"

His stomach clenched. All the peace that he'd seemed to have found snapped away.

It had been an illusion, anyhow.

He rubbed the bridge of his nose, suddenly tired. "Do you really want to talk about this now?"

She gazed at him for a long moment. Then she looked away. "No. Not if it upsets you."

"Ah, Emma." He shook his head as a feeling of hopelessness settled through him. It seemed every other topic of conversation upset him these days.

He laid his spoon on the table and sat back in his chair, the silky upholstery caressing him. "It's not that I dislike being associated with him," he said quietly. "It's that I dislike being compared to him and found lacking. It's that I dislike the fact that I am found lacking even before any comparison is made. It's that I dislike that I always have been, and always will be, his inferior."

She stared at him, her lips parted. Her brows lowered in a frown. "That's not true."

"Try living your life with a brother who is a paragon. Try competing with him and losing, in every way possible."

"Luke," she said in a low voice. As if she was about to chastise him for his words.

His lids were so heavy, they sank under the weight. He was suddenly bone weary. "I don't want to talk about this. I don't want to talk about Trent. Because every time his name is mentioned, I'm dragged back under his shadow." He forced his eyes open. "I am trying to step out of his shadow, Em. I want to do things on my own, live on my own terms, be my own man. But every time he's mentioned, every time someone reminds me of how perfect he is, I am reminded that the probability of doing so is negligible."

With a nod, Emma pushed away her food. "Are you finished with your dinner?"

He blinked at her, shaken by the sudden change of topic. "Yes."

She rose and called a servant to clear the dishes. The staff of Cameron's Hotel seemed to pride itself on the expediency of its service, and within two minutes, the table was completely clear of food—the soiled dishes replaced by a vase filled with blooming heather.

The two women curtsied and left, closing the door softly behind them.

Luke remained in his chair, watching as Emma latched the door. His lips quirked. "Locking me in?"

She turned to face him, folding her hands demurely in front of her. "I've told you before, I don't like it when you go downstairs and drink. Like you did last night."

"Last night," he repeated softly, staring at her lips, remembering that kiss that had twisted him into so many knots he had hardly been able to stop himself from ravishing her. He'd hardly been able to walk out of the room. God, he loved her lips. He loved their color—such a deep red. He loved their shape—plump and smooth. He loved how they tasted . . .

He loved—

"And the night before that," she said.

He dragged his gaze up to her eyes.

"And before that."

"You needn't remind me," he said dryly. "I haven't been *that* sotted. I do recall each of those nights."

She leaned back against the door and crossed her arms over her chest before raising her gaze to his again. "I want you to know something, Lord Lukas Hawkins."

He quirked a brow at her, bemused by her use of his name. "What's that?"

"You won't like it. I find it necessary to mention the person you dislike speaking of."

He ground his teeth. Bloody hell. Trent. Again. Of course she would bring the topic of conversation back to his damned sainted brother.

"I don't know him," she said, "but I have heard only good things about him."

"Of course." He tried to keep his voice mild, but the words came out as a growl. "You admire him. If you met him, you'd adore him. Everyone does."

"But I know *you*, Luke." Her voice softened. "And it's you I admire. It's you I adore. I don't care to compare you with anyone else, because you're you. Just the way I like you."

"Good." He sure as hell didn't want Emma, of all people, comparing him to Trent. Because, like everyone else, she'd find him lacking.

He hoped she never met his brother.

"It's getting late," she said softly. "We need to have an early start tomorrow if you want to arrive in London in five days."

She took her nightgown from a drawer and slipped behind the standing privacy screen off to the side of the bed.

Fabric rustled as she changed into her nightgown, and he closed his eyes, remembering last night. Remembering this morning. What she had told him about her desires.

He wanted to give them to her, and more. He wanted to soak her in pleasure. Bring her to a height of ecstasy Curtis had never come close to reaching with her.

He stood beside the bed when she emerged from behind the screen, wearing that innocent white nightgown that had driven him to the brink of madness again and again over the past several nights.

She had told him she wanted to exist in the present. That was how he lived most of the time. Only since he'd known her had he grown cautious.

He didn't want to hurt her. But the need to give her pleasure, to take his own pleasure from her, drowned all reason.

She'd braided her hair into a thick plait down her back. That would have to be remedied.

She'd stopped next to the screen, and he held out his hand. "Come here," he said gruffly.

She approached, taking his hand. He pulled her close. "Turn around," he murmured.

She complied, and he undid the thin ribbon at the bottom of her braid and laid it on the table. He slowly untwined her hair, reveling in the smooth, thick waves he so seldom had the opportunity to see in full, coppery glory.

He pressed a kiss to the top of her head. "I'm not going downstairs tonight."

She released a relieved breath.

"Because I want to stay with you. Is that what you want?"

"Yes." It was a whispered word, but it was solid. There was no hesitancy behind it.

He closed his eyes. Already, his cock was hard, his body hot and demanding and impatient. "Tell me if I do something that you don't want. That you don't like. That you find demeaning or unacceptable or too wicked or debauched—"

She spun around, facing him. "Stop, Luke."

"No. You need to know. If I become too..." God, how to say it? Feral? Animalistic? Wild? "Just tell me to stop. Promise me you'll do that, Emma."

He couldn't countenance taking this woman beyond her limits.

She gazed up at him, golden sparks lighting her eyes. "I've wanted this...wanted you...since that very first night. You do know that, don't you?"

He hadn't known her that first night. All he'd seen was her beauty, how much pleasure her body could bring him.

He found her more beautiful now. The way she looked at him—with trust, with desire, with need—made him want her in a way that was so much deeper than that first night. But he was afraid of that look changing into one of distrust, disgust, dislike. If that happened, he didn't know if he could bear it.

"You didn't know me then," he said.

"I know you now, and I want you even more."

He kissed her, dragging her to him with one arm snagged around her waist. The other he wrapped in her glorious, soft mass of hair, holding her locked in place against him as he took her mouth.

He nipped her upper and lower lips. His tongue thrust into her sweet mouth, mimicking the action his cock would take within her soon. He pressed himself against her, trying to give his cock some relief. But there was only one way for it to find relief.

He moved his lips to the edge of her mouth. "You taste so good, Em." He groaned, then licked the shell of her ear. "So good," he whispered.

He felt her shudder under the palm that he'd pressed to the small of her back. He moved that hand now, lower, until it cupped the taut, round flesh of her buttocks.

Untwisting his hand from her hair, he dropped that arm, too, until he was cupping the globes of her arse in both hands. Kissing her jaw, her cheek, the side of her nose, he ground against her.

She gasped. God, he loved that heavenly sound. "You're an angel," he murmured.

Taking handfuls of her nightgown, he pulled it upward until he felt the bare skin of her buttocks, and squeezed it.

She nuzzled her arse into his hands, then grabbed him around the neck and pulled him in, kissing him deliciously, her tongue making little darting explorations between his lips.

"Em," he murmured between kisses. "God, Emma."

He'd squeezed her bottom hard, so now he tried to soothe the area with gentle strokes of his fingers. Then he dropped her nightgown and moved his hands to her chest, untying the ribbons that closed her neckline.

"Take this off." His voice shook. His fingers shook. His grip on his control was too weak, too tenuous.

God. He was such a damned disaster. A wild, feral animal, struggling against these base urges. Trying—and failing—to be a good man. A solid man. Like his brother. He'd never be like his brother.

He would hurt her. He'd hurt Emma like he had everyone else.

He dropped his hands from her nightgown. *No.* This was wrong. Like every other decision he'd ever made in this damned cursed life, it was wrong.

Chapter Eight

Emma saw the rising turbulence in his blue eyes. She saw the fear and the shame.

She still didn't completely understand this beautiful, tortured man, but after this morning, she comprehended so much more.

How could she convince him to stop fighting with himself? How could she force him to believe that his desires were not evil? That she wanted to explore all these things with him, the consequences be damned?

She kissed him hard, remembering the cloak he'd given her. Remembering those little things he did for her all the time. "Lock the door, Emma," he'd told her on the second night. Earlier that same day, he'd wanted her to stay inside the inn so she wouldn't be seen with him. He'd punched Smallshaw because the man had maligned her honor.

And today he'd helped a woman carry her heavy baskets across town. He'd held Emma's hand when Macmillan had exposed her husband's true nature.

He. Is. Not. Evil.

She wanted him desperately. She wanted to lie with him, then sleep naked in his arms. She wanted him to tie her to the bed and blindfold her, and do whatever else he wished to do to her. She wanted to throw off her night-gown, bare herself to him, and let him have his wicked way with her. In whatever way he wanted.

She *craved* it. Every inch of her body craved it. Her heart and her soul craved it. Why wouldn't he believe?

He took a step back, pushing her arms away from him and pressing them to her sides.

"No," she said on a groan. "Don't stop. Please."

He gazed at her, that turmoil running rampant in his expression.

"You're too good——" he began.

She cut him off by dropping to her knees in front of him. "Please, Luke. Please take me to bed. I am begging you. I need you tonight. Part of me will die if I can't have you. *Please.*"

Slowly, terrified, her heart beating so rapidly she thought it might jump out of her chest, she raised her head. He was gazing down at her, his fists clenched at his sides.

Something in his expression had changed. Softened.

"Please," she whispered. She looked up at him, pouring all her hope and desire and need into her gaze.

Please, Luke. Don't turn away from me. Don't go downstairs. Don't get yourself so drunk you stop fearing what you might do to me...

"I want to be yours tonight," she whispered. "Completely yours. I've never wanted anything more. *Never.*"

He sank to his knees in front of her. His turbulent gaze

had calmed into something sharp as a blade. He was determined, intent.

Hot.

"You'll regret this."

"No."

"You'll hate me eventually."

"Never," she said. She meant it with all her heart.

His hands were on her, dragging her to her feet. Her nightgown gaped open at her chest, and he lifted the hem, then pulled it up. She raised her hands, and he removed it with jerking motions, then tossed it aside. Then he said, "Stand still," the tone of command in his voice unmistakable, and he stepped back to look at her.

His gaze raked over her. Hot and hungry, it traveled up and down, leaving burning trails of heat and desire in its wake.

"God," he rasped. "You are so beautiful. So. Damn. Beautiful."

The way he looked at her made her *feel* beautiful. And desired, and so feminine.

"Get on the bed," he ordered.

Instantly, she backed up until her bottom touched the bedclothes. Then she scooted onto it, sitting on its high edge.

"Lie down," he directed her, his blade-sharp gaze never leaving her body.

She watched him as she obeyed, feeling the heat of his hunger as his gaze swept over her body once more.

He came to the edge of the bed and stood there for a long moment, looking down at her in silence. She shuddered. She hadn't expected this, lying here completely naked while he stood over her, staring. She felt so exposed.

Then his hand rose to cup her cheek, forcing her to look at him. His gaze softened, and suddenly he wasn't that predator she'd met on the first night, but the multifaceted Luke she'd grown to care so much for.

"Do you know how lovely you are, Emma? That was my first thought when I saw you. That you were the loveliest thing I'd seen in a very, *very* long time."

His voice was raw. There was an honesty in it that she'd never heard from anyone else. His tone elicited some deep, almost painful emotion she'd never felt before.

He reached toward her. "Come here. Move closer to the edge so I can touch you."

Staying on her back, she scooted toward the edge of the bed as he tucked his arms under her and helped her move toward him. His gaze traversed her body yet again, his expression possessive, his hand cupping the top of her knee protectively.

She had done this to herself. She had opened herself to him, given herself over to his hot gaze ... and whatever else he chose to give her. The most shocking part was that she wanted him to partake of her body. He gazed at her like she was a tempting morsel of food, and she wanted to provide him with the most delicious meal he'd ever tasted.

His fingertips skimmed over her hip bone, and she shivered. No one had ever touched her there. Even though she'd been married, there were so many places she hadn't been touched.

"I want to feel every part of you," he murmured. "Kiss every inch of you."

"Please," was all she could manage over the enormous lump in her throat.

She was begging. Over and over. Just like he'd promised her she would.

He trailed his fingertips down over her hip and the front of her thigh, over her knee and shin and to her feet. He lifted her feet one by one, then kissed the tops of the one closest to the edge of the bed, running the flats of his hands up her calf and shin until he bent her leg at the knee. Then his lips ran over the side of her calf, soft, tickling. The dampness of his tongue swiped over her flesh. Finally, he raised his head and looked at her with hooded eyes.

"Do you know how much I want you?"

She gazed at him, wondering if he knew how much *she* wanted *him*. She shook her head.

He chuckled. He kissed the side of her leg, up and over her thigh. His mouth was like velvet. The sensation so foreign but so exquisite she couldn't contain the little moans that escaped from her throat with every press of his lips.

He kissed her hip bone, then moved closer toward the triangle of hair at the apex of her thighs. She tensed in anticipation, and he looked up at her, his gaze hungry, his breath hot on her sensitized flesh.

"Do you want it, Emma? Do you want me to kiss you there?"

She shuddered all over. She'd learned long ago that it felt good to touch herself there. Sometimes, she'd rub her fingers through that slick flesh and imagine a man's mouth touching her there, kissing her.

She never, ever had believed that it might someday actually happen.

"Emma?"

Hardly able to breathe, she nodded.

His lips curved into that wicked, sensual, self-possessed grin he'd given her that first night and so many times since. That smile that made her insides melt and heat radiate through her body.

In one smooth, graceful motion, he was up on the bed beside her, moving over her. Distractedly, she realized he was still fully dressed. But she didn't have time to give a second thought to that, because he moved down her body, pushing her legs apart with his hands and settling himself between them, looking down at her body with a wicked glint in his eyes.

She was...overcome. A part of her felt shy. She'd been indoctrinated to avoid showing her *ankles* to men, and now he not only had access to a view of both her ankles, but also her calves, her knees, her thighs. Her *sex*.

But another part of her felt victorious. That part gloried in the heat of his gaze and the hungry look in his eyes. Everything he did, every movement he made, was for her. He'd called her beautiful, and for the first time in her life, she believed it.

He kissed her skin, starting with a spot on the inside of her thigh she'd never known was so sensitive. He moved up her leg, nipping the flesh, then soothing the burn with soft kisses.

She lay back on the pillow, her eyes sinking shut. Sensation traveled from her thigh to her core, heating, coalescing into a tight, toe-curling ball of fire somewhere below her navel.

He licked the inner part of the very top of her leg, and she let out a low moan. "Please, Luke."

"Please? What are you begging me for, Em?" His voice was slightly muffled against her skin.

"I...don't know." She had no idea. She was on the verge of some kind of precipice, and she wanted to grip his hand and jump with him.

"Kiss you?" He kissed the inside of her upper thigh. So very close to her sex, which was now pulsing with need.

"Yes," she gasped.

"Lick you?" The flat of his tongue moved over her skin. So hot and warm, stoking the fire inside her.

"Yes!"

"Where, Em? Where do you want to be licked?"

"I...don't know...," she choked out in frustration.

His hand closed over the top of her leg, hot and dry, and her skin was so sensitive her body gave a little jerk.

"I think you do know," he said wickedly. He looked over her body at her, and he raised a brow. "How will I know how to please you if you don't tell me?"

He was playing with her. And she hadn't been lying, really—she truly didn't know *exactly* where she wanted his mouth. But she certainly knew the general location— that place that was wet and aching and pulsing, waiting for...for...*something*.

For him, that place of power within her whispered. *It's waiting for him. Tell him.*

"Here," she whispered. She moved her hand to cup the place between her legs, slipping her fingers slightly into the folds and trying not to squirm at the sensation of her own touch. She was wetter than she'd ever been before, and if she thought her inner knees and the skin of her thighs was sensitive, this place was burning with sensation.

Of course she was sensitive. Of course she was wet. Lukas Hawkins, the most intriguing, most beautiful man she'd ever known, was making love to her.

Luke sucked in a breath. His eyes were on her fingers, watching them intently. She pressed harder, sliding her fingers through the wetness. "Here, Luke," her voice was huskier than usual, rasping with need.

His tongue moved over his lower lip, leaving a glistening sheen, and then he lowered his head to press a chaste kiss to the top of her hand. Then he took her hand and moved it to her side, holding it firmly in one of his own. With his other hand, he pushed her thigh open wider. For a long moment, he gazed at her.

"You have such a pretty pussy, Emma."

Oh, God. He was staring at her, not touching her. She'd never felt so raw and open. Like she was one single, exposed, shuddering nerve.

"Have you ever looked at it?"

She tried to wiggle her hips, close her legs, but his hands were firm on her, pinning her to the bed.

"Have you? Have you ever used a mirror to look at your pussy?"

If a combination of mortification and lust had ever killed anyone, she'd drop dead at this moment.

"Tell me." His voice was firm, brooking no argument.

Was this what he meant when he'd talked about his tastes? To her knowledge, carnal relations had been simply about the physical congress between a man and a woman. She wasn't aware that people actually spoke to one another in the throes of lust. Luke was turning this into an erotic conversation, and she had no idea how she felt about that.

Vulnerable.

The word popped into her mind. She'd never enjoyed that feeling of vulnerability that tended to creep up on a woman in this world. She'd always fought against it, tried to be strong, tried to take care of everything after her mother died.

This kind of vulnerability...it was deeper and more intimate than anything she'd ever experienced. She was helpless, defenseless against him, against his touch, against his mouth, against his penetrating blue gaze.

And she wanted *more.*

She was tired of being in control. Of caring for her father, worrying about her sister. Running a household, paying debts. Thinking of how to save her family, how to locate Roger Morton and find a way to return her father's money to him.

Right here, right now, she had no responsibility, none of that crushing weight that had strangled her for the past year. Right here, right now, Lukas Hawkins was commanding her. She had surrendered control. Of the situation, of her body, even of her mind.

And she loved it.

"Emma?" His voice was ripe with warning. "Answer me. Have you ever looked at yourself here?"

"No," she whispered.

He let out a breath. Of relief? She couldn't tell. "It's pink, such a deep pink, it's almost red. Take a white rose petal and a red one. Combine them, and that is your color."

Slowly he released her hand, then touched her, moving his fingers through her slickness just as she had moments ago.

She quivered under his touch, feeling the edge of his fingernail scrape gently over her. "You're so wet," he said gruffly. "So swollen. God, Emma, you're so responsive."

His words, his touch. Her mind was swirling. The world was quickly fading away around her. There was only Luke and the way he was touching her, only the sensations tightening her body and shuddering through her.

His fingers moved to circle an area so excruciatingly sensitive, her hips bucked. But using his free hand, he pinned her against the mattress. He circled the tiny area again, and she gasped. "Do you know what this is?"

"N-no." She gulped in great breaths. What he was doing was beginning to feel like some kind of teasing torture. Would it ever end?

"This is your clitoris, Em. The center of your pleasure."

"Oh," she said. Then she squirmed, willing him to do it again.

He did. He touched her there, circled her there, brushed over her clitoris until the sensations were so strong and so powerful, she was overwhelmed by them. Her vision began to go black around the edges. No one... no one could withstand this kind of assault. It hurt and felt so good and so frustrating. She was still on that edge, and it seemed like she'd been standing there forever, the urge to jump only growing inside of her with his every touch, every swipe and stroke.

And then he moved his fingers lower, circling her entrance before, ever so slowly, pushing a finger inside.

Emma let out another strangled moan. She felt him everywhere. Inside her, around her. The thrust of his fingers pleasured her clitoris, too—and as he moved his finger in and out, sliding decadently over her inner walls, it stopped its tortured scream and began to hum. That hum resonated through her whole body, once again flaming that ball of desire deep within her core.

He withdrew one finger, and when he pushed in again, there were two fingers. She could feel them moving, scissoring inside her. Her senses were so heightened, she could feel everything.

"Now," she heard him say, as if from very far away. She registered the tone of male satisfaction in his voice. "Now you're ready."

Ready for what? she wondered.

But as he continued to thrust his fingers inside her, his mouth went above them, covering her clitoris, his tongue swiping over that tiny area.

The effect was electric. Emma jolted and cried out. Her hands scrabbled for something to hold on to, and then she found his head. Her fingers sank into his silky blond hair, holding him to her.

She felt disembodied. Her body was making movements she could not control, thrusting against his mouth, against his fingers. God—he was so deep inside her. She felt so full.

He licked her. Kissed her. Suckled her on that most intensely sensitive place.

She heard herself begging, panting. She had no control. Her fingers tightened in his hair, but she couldn't control those either. The fireball inside her was growing, burning. Her toes were curled over the edge of the precipice.

He breathed against her, his breath so hot. He panted and growled against her. He was saying things she couldn't completely understand—she could only hear single words: "damn," "burn," "yes." She didn't know if he was telling her to do something, but even if he was, there was no way she could comply. Every muscle in her body had gone stiff, every limb straight.

His thrusts grew more powerful. Emma's back arched. Her body welcomed him, wanting more, deeper, harder. He seemed to understand its demands, and his rigid fingers drove fiercely into her. His breath whispered over her clitoris. And then his lips circled it again, and he sucked. Hard.

She didn't step off the precipice—she leapt off it. Her body bucked violently on the bed, but she was hardly aware of it. There was only the sweet pulse of light inside her as the ball that had been coalescing inside her unraveled. She didn't fall—she was soaring through the air, every part of her body undulating with the pleasure.

Slowly, the pulses receded, turning into languid glides under her skin. His fingers had stilled as her body clenched rhythmically over them. His mouth had stilled, too, and now pressed gently against her.

The release loosened every muscle in her body, until she lay limp and boneless on the bed, her vision hazy.

Ever so slowly, he pulled out of her, and her sex clenched at the raw sensation of the movement over her flesh.

She struggled to focus on him. He was gazing at her, his lips wet—with her juices. Her heart, which was still pounding furiously, clenched a little at that observation.

The way he was gazing at her—his eyes were filled with *wonder*.

"Damn, Emma," he whispered huskily.

Still staring at her, he crawled up her body. When he was face-to-face with her, he lay down beside her, turning her, pulling her naked body against his clothed one.

"What?" she asked, concern and self-consciousness flooding through her. "Did I do it wrong?"

He blinked. "Wrong? Hell, no." He pressed a gentle kiss to her lips. "It's just... I don't think I've ever made a woman come so hard."

"Oh." Her cheeks heated. Her eyelids fluttered closed as he kissed her again, his lips pressing hers open.

"See how good you taste, Em?" he husked out.

She couldn't answer that. She wrapped her arms around him, kissing him harder, feeling the need to somehow thank him for the experience she'd just had.

She pressed her body against him, feeling the tautness of his erection behind his trousers. She rubbed her pelvis against it.

If that was what he wanted, she'd give it to him. She'd give him anything right now.

"Tell me what you want," she whispered against his mouth.

"It's no longer a matter of want. I need you. I need you so much it's about to kill me."

"Then take me, Luke."

Still kissing her, one hand behind her head to keep her lips pinned against his, he shuffled a bit and then she felt his hand reach down and begin fumbling with the falls of his trousers. Still kissing him—she'd never get enough of this man's lips—she helped him by pulling his shirt up, running her fingers up his chest beneath the linen.

But he stopped her, moving his hand from behind her

head and pressing her hands to his falls. "Help me," he said roughly. "Unbutton them. Take them off."

Her fingers more nimble than she'd expected, she opened the front placket of his trousers. His erection bulged behind his drawers, and she untied the string that held them in place. Then, as he lifted his hips, she pulled them down, swallowing hard as his erection sprang free.

He was larger than her husband had been. Thicker.

Her eyes flickered up to his. He was gazing at her, a soft smirk on his face. It made her smile as she continued removing his clothes.

After she'd pushed them over the curve of his buttocks and he had kicked them away, he rolled her to her back and lay atop her, his organ pressing into her belly. He moved his hips, sliding himself over her gently.

"Do you feel that? That's going to be inside you soon."

"Yes. I feel it." She met his gaze. His expression was so hot, so delicious, she wanted him inside her this instant.

But he bent his head, sliding down her, his length passing over the top of her still ever-so-sensitive sex and down to press against her thigh. He kissed her between her breasts and licked his way up the slope of one of them. Then he swirled his tongue around her nipple, and it tightened and puckered for him as if begging for more of his attention.

He gave it. Moving from one side to the other, cupping the globes of flesh in his hands, he kissed and suckled her.

Moans escaped from her throat again, like when he'd kissed her thigh—but this was stronger. Arrows of pleasure seemed to shoot from each of her breasts to the target deep in her womb, where the heat built quickly into a simmering, burning ache.

"Please, Luke," she gasped. Her fingers threaded through his hair, and she didn't know whether to push him away or drag him closer.

"You have the loveliest breasts I've ever seen," he said, pulling up briefly before he bent down again to take a nipple into his mouth. He licked her, his tongue swirling over the puckered flesh, and she drew him against her, her body arching against his.

He still wore his shirt. She would take it off now, but— Oh, Lord. He moved to the other side, drawing that nipple into his mouth while his hand came to the one he'd just left, his fingers deftly moving over the damp flesh and then pinching her hard.

Emma cried out, her body bucking uncontrollably. That arrow had met its target, stabbing her in a place so deep and pleasurable inside her, she couldn't define it.

His mouth gentled over her nipple as his hand drifted down her waist. He pulled her leg open wide and slipped his fingers between her legs.

"God," he murmured. "You're so wet. Is all that for me?"

"Yes," she said. "All of it."

"Good."

He released her breasts, moving up her body once more. He braced his arms on either side of her, and his blue, blue eyes gazed down at her. "Are you ready?" he whispered.

"Yes."

He shifted a little, one of his hands moving down to align his shaft with her entrance. He swiped the broad head of himself over her a few times, touching her clitoris, making her quiver beneath him.

She wrapped her arms around him, and he stilled. Looking into her eyes, he notched himself at her entrance. Slowly, ever so slowly, he pushed himself in.

"Oh, Luke," she whispered. "Oh, Luke." She was nearly sobbing, though she couldn't comprehend why. Her pelvis tilted upward, trying to take more of him, to take him faster, deeper.

But he held his pace—his slow pace that was going to drive her insane. And then he stopped altogether, gazing down at her. "Do you want more?" he ground out.

"Yes. Yes, please."

His smile was feral. But she only saw it for an instant, and then he surged into her. Emma's body bowed up off the bed. She nearly screamed. The sensations were so strong. He was so large. He made her feel so tiny and feminine, so deliciously helpless.

"Like that?" he growled. Even though he kept most of his weight on his forearms on either side of her head, his chest was heavy and hot on hers behind the fabric of his shirt. She liked it there, pressing her down into the bed. Holding her. Keeping her safely trapped beneath him.

His mouth moved against the shell of her ear. "Like that, Emma?" he repeated.

"Yes. Just like that."

"Not too hard?" And for the first time in a while, she detected that hint of insecurity in his voice.

"Harder," she told him.

He was still for a moment, but she felt his response in the tremor under his skin.

And then he jerked out of her. She arched up, trying to

hold him in her body, trying not to lose him. But when the blunt head of him was at her entrance, he surged inside her again, filling her completely.

"Oh, God," she whispered. She was shaking. He was so hard. So big. So strong. So intensely masculine.

He did it again. And again. Over and over, he pounded into her, his thrusts so powerful she thought she might splinter. Splinter in the most delicious, most pleasurable way possible.

She wrapped her arms around him. She wrapped her legs around the backs of his. She grabbed bunches of his linen shirt in her fists. And she could only hold on as he turned her body into one massive, sensitive nerve— a nerve that was getting stroked again and again by his powerful thrusts, by his hot, hard, heavy sex.

Sweat broke out across Emma's chest. Her body burned, inside and out. She whimpered, making sounds she was hardly aware of. Luke's breaths were harsh and rasping, his body tense, his muscles engaged and steely. He surrounded her. His scent—salt and smoke and soap—sank into her skin, became part of her.

He didn't slow. He kept up his punishing pace until both of them were slicked with sweat and every thrust pushed Emma's breath from her body in a harsh pant.

The burn was scorching. So hot. She fisted his shirt in her hands. Her back arched, and her pelvis met him thrust for thrust.

And then Luke moved his weight onto one arm, slowing his pace and shifting so he could pull her leg farther up. She matched it with her other leg, pulling it up over his buttocks and wrapping it around his lower back. "That's right, Em. Good."

He took a few experimental strokes inside her. The change in position, she realized, had changed his angle inside her. And this...oh, Lord. Pleasure swept through her, so powerfully she closed her eyes on a whimper.

Luke's rhythm slowly changed, increased in force and depth until each thrust matched the intensity of those that had come before.

And, for the second time, Emma unraveled. She fell apart. The single nerve that she had become shattered like glass, piercing and sharp, cutting through her with no pain, but with the most excruciating pleasure she'd ever experienced. She cried out as her body spasmed uncontrollably.

"Bloody. Hell," Luke whispered harshly. Then she felt his fingers in her hair, wrapping into the strands, pulling nearly to the point of pain. Her body was still moving, her sex clenching over his. But with a low groan, he jerked out of her. He sank his head into her hair as he pulsed over her, and she felt the warm flood of seed as he spent himself on her lower belly.

He lay there for a long moment, his heavy, hot body slick with sweat, then he rolled off her. She chanced a glance at him to see him staring at the ceiling as if stunned. Then, as if he felt her gaze on him, his eyes slid toward her, watching her with a certain wariness.

Slowly, her lips curved into a smile that stretched her mouth. She felt deliciously and utterly happy. This was what she had always secretly desired when she'd engaged in carnal congress before. She'd wanted it to be rough and raw and sweaty. Wild and feral. With Luke, it had been all of those things...and more.

His gaze focused on her smile, and he seemed to relax minutely, the blue of his eyes lightening.

"I was going to ask you if you were all right," he said softly. "But if I judge by your expression, I'd say you are."

Her smile widened—if that were even possible. "I am," she confirmed.

She turned her body toward him, and he put his arm around her and tucked her up against him.

His seed was still on her stomach, a damp reminder of the wicked things they'd done. She was damp between her legs, too, and a little sore.

It would probably be good manners to clean herself up, put her nightgown back on. But she didn't want to do either. She wanted to press her naked, languid body against Luke and fall asleep like this with his sweat and his smell and his semen on her, and the feel of his touch still on her skin.

She gazed up at his stubbly jaw. "Can you sleep?"

He gave a low chuckle. "Probably."

"Mmm."

They were silent for long moments, and a languid, heavy drowsiness spread through Emma.

"Luke?"

"Hmm?"

"It was...perfect."

And she drifted into oblivion.

Chapter Nine

Luke awoke with a start in the middle of the night. But it wasn't a nightmare that woke him this time. He kept his eyes closed, remembering Emma's lips closing over his cock in his dream.

He was as hard as a rock.

Emma stirred beside him. She was turned away, and her delectable backside brushed against his aching flesh.

The force of need came on him with brutal ferocity. He wanted her. He needed to be inside her.

He slid his hand over her buttocks. She wiggled against him. God, she was so damned receptive to him. Even in sleep.

It was completely shocking. Almost bewildering.

He reached between her cheeks gently, smoothing his hand at first softly, then exerting more pressure. He stroked her in long, slow glides. She was still wet from their last joining, but as he stroked, she grew wetter. Her breathing changed, and she hummed a little on her exhales, making little *Mmm* sounds as her body moved against his hand.

Everything about this woman was so beautiful.

He lifted her leg with one hand and with the other guided his cock into her.

She gave a soft moan as he slid home.

He pressed his lips to the back of her head. "Am I hurting you?"

"Luke," she moaned. He'd stilled within her, and she wiggled her hips in frenetic movements, mimicking the thrusting action. "More."

"Shhh, Em. Be still. I'll give you what you want."

She quieted instantly, and he thrust in and out of her in long, deep, slow drags. She was burning hot. A wet glove that closed around him in a tight fist that made him clench his teeth so his breath hissed out from between them.

He wrapped his arm around her waist, clutching her tight against him. Her body molded perfectly to his in this position. His lower stomach touched her round arse each time he pushed deeply into her.

He buried his nose in her hair, smelling that delicious lavender-tinged feminine scent of hers. His eyes sank shut, and he pressed his lips to the back of her head.

There was nothing like being inside Emma. Being close to her this way. It was a feeling as close to perfection as he'd ever come.

She was making little whimpering noises now. God, he loved the sounds that she made. He loved that she was vocal. He loved that she showed him her reaction to him by the noises she made as well as by the movements of her body.

So—*thrust*—damn—*thrust*—responsive.

She was tightening around him. So tight. She was going to squeeze him to oblivion. To heaven.

"Emma," he murmured into her hair, releasing a husky word with every thrust, "my sweet. My angel."

Her groans were drawing out, becoming longer, more pronounced. He crossed his arm over her chest, reveling in the heavy, soft feel of her breast against his forearm.

He was going to come soon. Spirals of pleasure wrapped around the base of his spine, tugging from his cock all the way through him, tightening. *Hell.* The pleasure. It would destroy him. He closed his eyes and pressed his lips and nose into the thick fall of her hair again, finding the back of her neck with his tongue and pressing little licking kisses there.

She was moving now, her body undulating, her muscles tautening under his arm and against his chest and stomach.

Holy hell. Was she going to come? Again? He'd done so little to prepare her...

And she did. With a harsh gasp, she clamped over him, her body rigid, and then squeezing him in rhythmic pulses that drove him mad. He wanted to come, too. He needed to. He wanted to pour himself deep, deep inside her. But he wouldn't—*couldn't*—risk her that way.

He clenched his teeth and willed himself to see her through it this time. His arm remained wrapped around her tightly. He nipped her neck, whispering encouraging words to her. "Yes, Em, that's it. Come for me. Hell, that feels so good. Yes. Yessss..."

Ever so slowly, her muscles relaxed, going limp against him. The contractions of her sex slowed, then abated. But he kept up his rhythm throughout, and now he sped up, thrusting into her hard and fast. She was open to him, accepting, taking everything he had to give.

Her hand closed over the forearm clasped around her, a simple but meaningful gesture. It was a gesture of oneness, of acceptance. To him, it meant everything. He thrust furiously. The pleasure built and tightened, and then he yanked himself out of her just in time, dragging her hard against him.

When it was over, he stayed there. He liked how her arse cheeks cradled his cock. She was so soft and feminine, yet strong and courageous at the same time.

As he drifted back to sleep, he thought that perhaps it wasn't so impossible for him to love after all.

* * *

They were able to get an early start the next day, but ominous clouds had rolled in and gathered over the Pentland Hills. Luke pushed the horses because he had a bad feeling about the weather, and indeed, it began to rain at about noon. It started as a slow drizzle, but two hours later, it had turned into a downpour. The road had grown muddy, and Luke had had to slow the horses significantly, negotiating them around puddles and areas of deep mud.

As Luke had climbed into the curricle this morning, he'd hesitated, his gaze scanning over it. The poor vehicle had seen better days. It had already been well used and a touch shabby when Luke had purchased it in Bristol. Now it was mud-caked and scratched, its cushion torn in at least three places. Still, those defects were cosmetic. Every day he checked its shaft, axle, undercarriage, and wheels thoroughly before driving, and all of those parts appeared intact and strong. Despite its currently less-than-elegant appearance, it had proved to be a sturdy vehicle.

He glanced at Emma. She'd been right—although they'd raised the hood at the first hint of rain, they were both soaked through. He hoped the boot hadn't sprung a leak, otherwise all their luggage would be soaked, too.

Clumps of wet copper-brown hair hung down from her bonnet strings, and she wiped a stream of water from her cheek with the back of her hand. Feeling his eyes on her, she turned to him.

He'd half expected her to be angry and sullen at this uncomfortable turn of events, but she grinned at him.

"Wet," she said, her voice raised above the patter of rain on the hood.

"Extremely," he agreed. He sighed. "We're going to have to stop for the day, I think. The road is too muddy." The last thing he wanted was to drive the curricle into a mud bank.

"Yes. That would probably be a good idea. Those poor horses."

He glanced at the beasts—they had been in fine form this morning but were now bedraggled and miserable-looking.

This had not been the plan—they had just crossed over the border into England. He'd intended to cover another thirty miles or so. "Do you know of an inn?"

She shook her head. "And I daren't take out *Paterson's Itinerary* now. I'll ruin it and then we'll never find our way to London."

He chuckled. Of course that wasn't true. Almost all

roads led to London, and even if they chanced upon one that didn't, there were always villages, towns, houses, farms. People to ask.

He'd learned, on their travels so far, that Emma disliked asking people for help in that way. She'd much prefer to manage their course on her own.

"All right," he said mildly, and he continued to drive. Soon they entered the bustling little town of Berwick-upon-Tweed. Luke drew the horses to a stop at the first person he saw, a man huddled in an oil-slicked coat, and asked where he might find the nearest lodgings. The man directed him to the King's Arms two minutes away.

When he started the horses again, he slid a glance toward Emma. "See, now that wasn't so difficult, was it?"

She made a little growly noise, and he laughed. "Are you pouting, Mrs. Curtis?"

She gave him a very dry look. "I do not pout, Lord Lukas. Surely we could have found the inn on our own. Look"—she gestured at the stone building where they'd stopped—"we are already here."

And so they were. They performed the tasks they'd become accustomed to over the days—Emma directing the luggage while Luke dealt with stabling the horses.

They planned to stay in Berwick-upon-Tweed for one night. What they didn't know then was that the rain wouldn't let up for five days.

Five cold, wet, long days.

Five glorious days, in a small inn in a small town, with nothing for Luke to do except keep Emma occupied...in bed.

On the third morning, she woke, slipped her nightgown over her naked body, and padded to the window, crossing her arms over her chest and shivering a little.

Luke gazed at her, focused on the curve of her bottom through the thin fabric.

She cracked open the curtain and stared outside, sighing heartily. "It's pouring, and the sky is a most uniform, most dreary color."

"Gray?" he supplied helpfully.

She sighed again. "Yes. Gray." She turned to him. "What are we going to do?"

He gave her a wicked smile. "I've some ideas."

"You don't think we should push forward?"

He sobered. "No. Too dangerous." For the horses, the carriage, and for her health. As much as he wanted— needed—to find Morton and his mother, he didn't want to repeat her getting soaked through again. He wouldn't risk her getting ill.

When had Emma Curtis's well-being become his primary concern? He wondered this vaguely as she approached the bed and sat on its edge.

He laid his hand on her thigh. After so long forcing himself not to touch her, now he couldn't seem to get enough of touching her.

"Come back to bed," he murmured.

Her teeth closed over her lower lip. "I feel like...like I should be doing something. Something that will help us find Morton."

"There's nothing to do. Not here. Not now."

Her brow furrowed. "How long do you think it will be before the rain stops?"

He shrugged, tugged her onto the bed. She allowed him to arrange her limbs into a comfortable position, then he said, "I've waited six months to find my mother. You've waited a year to find Morton. As much as I want to find her, I know by now that a few rainy days won't make a difference in the grand scheme."

She sighed and turned to face him. "You're right."

He traced the edge of her face with his fingertips, pushing away the hair that had fallen over her cheek. "Are you still so eager to kill him?"

"Morton?" Her lips firmed, and he saw the shadows pass behind her eyes. "Yes. Perhaps even more so now."

"Do you mean that literally?" he asked softly. "Would you hold a pistol to his head and pull on the trigger?"

"Y—"

He pressed a finger to her lips. "Murder, Emma. Are you truly capable of it, or is it your anger speaking?"

Her breath whispered over his finger as she exhaled, and her eyes sank shut. He could tell she was picturing in her mind what it would actually be like to murder a man, because she shuddered. "He destroyed my family."

"Yes."

"I want him to suffer for what he's done. I want him to pay. But..." She opened her eyes and looked at him, her golden gaze flat in the dim gray light. "I don't know if I could really kill him."

He slid his arm over her stomach. "I don't want you risking yourself."

"What do you mean?"

"He's dangerous. He's a murderer and a thief. I won't have you recklessly putting yourself into danger for that man."

"I—"

He tightened his hand around her waist, holding her

protectively. "I won't risk you, Em." In that moment, Luke knew that if Morton threatened Emma's safety in any way, he wouldn't hesitate to kill the man himself.

She sighed, and they lay in silence for a long moment. He let his hand trail up and down the curve of her waist.

"Can you sleep?" she eventually murmured.

Coming out of the haze of desire that touching her had evoked, he blinked at her, then chuckled. "Sleep? Did you really think I had sleep on my mind?"

Her expression relaxed. "Well...I wasn't sure..."

"Be sure," he said softly. "If there have been more than a few hours since the last time I had you, having you again will always be what's foremost on my mind."

"That's nonsense," she murmured. "It is new for us both now. But it won't always be like this."

"Why not?" he asked her. He couldn't even conceive of growing tired of this woman.

"It never is."

"How can you know that?"

She gave him a half-smile. "I suppose I don't. But I thought that was the way of it. Especially for men like you."

"Men like me?"

"Rakes. Scoundrels. Rogues." The words emerged in that low, whisky-smooth voice of hers that stroked along his nerves. That was one thing he'd never get enough of, for certain: her voice.

"Is that what you think I am? A rogue?"

"I know that's what you are. I've known that from the moment you looked at me over that glass of ale."

"But you know me better now. Your opinion hasn't changed?"

"My opinion of you has changed in many respects, but in that one, no. In fact, I do believe you are more of a rogue than I originally thought."

"If I'm not mistaken, you seem pleased by that."

She laughed softly. As always, his body responded to that sound.

"I suppose I am pleased by it." Her eyes flashed at him in a wicked glint. "My lord."

"Why?" he asked her.

The slightest tinge of pink infused her cheeks. "You know why."

"Perhaps. But I want to hear it."

She licked her lips, the action so erotic his breath caught. "Very well," she said in that soft, rasping voice. She was silent for a moment, then said, "I thought rogues were men who took what they wanted from the world with no regard for the people they hurt."

"They do," he said softly. He knew that firsthand.

She pressed a finger to his lips.

"But I've learned there are different kinds of rogues. There are those who behave like that. There are those who pretend to be rogues but are really gentlemen at heart—"

He raised his brows in disbelief. "You believe I am one of them?"

"Not at all." Her lips curled seductively. "You are the third kind."

"Oh? And what's that?"

"The true rogue. The man who lives by his own rules and refuses to be cowed."

She said it with such pride, like that was the kind of man she admired above all.

"The kind of man who follows his heart, who takes risks." She reached up and touched his cheek.

He captured her wrist in his hand, pulling it down but keeping it firmly clasped in his own. "And that's me?"

"Mmm. Yes."

"Stay here," he ordered. He slipped out of bed and found his cravat lying over the back of the chair, tucked underneath his trousers. He pulled it free and returned to the bed.

She gazed at him, all innocent freshness, but her words belied her expression. "What are you going to do with *that*, my lord?"

He grinned. "Hmm. I think you're growing too cocky. And do you know what happens when my woman grows too cocky?"

"Nooo..." She stretched out the word, her eyes riveted to the cravat dangling from his hand.

He went onto the bed and on his knees beside her. Bending down close to her ear, he whispered, "I teach her her place."

"My place? Where's my place, my lord?"

"Under me," he growled. He captured her wrists and wrapped the cravat around them in one full loop but not tying it.

"Do you like to be bound, Mrs. Curtis?" he asked, mimicking the question he'd asked her on that first night in Bristol.

Her eyes flicked from her wrists, where he held the cravat, to his face. "I...I don't know," she whispered. "I've never been bound."

"But you need to be, don't you?"

"I..." She swallowed. He studied her, trying to read her

expression. Uncertainty or anticipation? He wasn't sure. He needed to be certain. "...don't know," she finished.

He bent down and kissed her, running his cravat loosely over her wrists so she'd feel the rasp of the material against her skin.

"You'll tell me if you're scared. You'll tell me if it hurts. You'll tell me to stop, if you need me to."

"I will?" she breathed.

"Yes."

"But I want you to go far," she said shyly, blinking up at him.

After the last three days with her, he believed her. That tinge of fear still frayed the edges of his consciousness— that worry that he'd do something to ruin everything. But each time they made love, her enthusiasm and responsiveness shrank that fear.

He leaned down and licked the shell of her ear. "I'm going to take you hard, Em. Are you ready to scream?"

He felt the tremor run through her body at his promise. And he gloried in it.

She didn't answer. But then, he hadn't expected her to. He ran his lips over her ear, down her jaw and the silky slope of her neck. She tasted so damn good. She could make him forget everything.

Rising back up onto his knees, he secured her wrists in front of her. He knotted the cravat tightly, knowing it would make indentations in the lovely, soft flesh of her wrists. He wanted to see those later. To have her bear his marks on her flesh.

"There." He glanced up at her face. Her eyes were closed. "Keep your hands right there, Em. Don't move unless I tell you to."

She took a shaky breath. But she complied.

"Good," he murmured in approval. She was compliant, hot, responsive.

His cock was pulsing with burning, demanding need.

Yanking up her nightgown, he pushed his hand between her legs without preamble. She was wet already. He groaned.

He grabbed her wrists with his free hand and pulled them over her head, tugging her nightgown up her body until her breasts were exposed. They beckoned him, so full and soft, with puckered pink nipples begging for his mouth.

With one hand stroking between her legs and the other pinning her wrists above her head, Luke bent down and suckled her sweet, taut nipples, one at a time. Licking, nibbling, tasting. So soft, so good. He could lose himself in her breasts.

Vaguely, he heard her panting. "Luke," she whispered. "Please, Luke."

He continued making love to her soft flesh, pushing his thumb inside her tight channel. She gasped with pleasure, thrusting her body against him.

"Shhh," he told her. "Be still. Just feel, Em. That's all I want you to do. Feel."

With a small whimper, she relaxed. He licked up the side of her breast, rubbed his lips over the tight nub of her nipple. He thrust his thumb in and out of her, reveling in the slick, hot clasp of her body.

But his body was making demands of its own, and they were growing more urgent by the second. He pulled his hand away from her sex, giving it a light squeeze.

"Turn over," he told her, his voice gruff.

She did as he told her, flipping onto her stomach without a word. Her immediate compliance in bed always surprised him. When they weren't naked, she was different—confident and in charge. But then, when they weren't naked, he was different, too. And he liked her transformation. It suited his desires perfectly.

He looked down at her and swallowed. She lay before him like an offering, her hands stretched overhead, bound by white linen. Her hair fanned in loose silken waves across the pillow. Her head was turned to the side, and she faced him, gazing up at him with complete trust in her gold-tinged eyes.

What the *devil* had he ever done to deserve such a look?

The way she offered herself was a precious gift, and unworthy as he was, he couldn't understand why she chose to give it. But what he did know was that he wanted to give her a gift in return: the most pleasure he could possibly bestow.

Her back was smooth, her complexion a soft, uniform olive shade. There were two small dimples above the cleft of her arse, and he bent down to press a kiss to each of them, one at a time.

He lifted his head again, admiring the slope of her behind. Her curves were so generous. Her breasts were large and firm, her hips narrow, her arse round and plump, her legs long and well formed.

"You are so perfect," he murmured.

"Luke," she said on a sigh. He glanced at her face as she continued in a voice so soft he had to strain to hear. "So are you."

He closed his eyes. When such words came from her lips, he could almost believe. *Almost.*

He trailed his hand down her spine, watching the shiver that chased it, and then he palmed her cheek.

"Up on your knees," he told her. "Keep your forearms on the bed."

He helped her into the position, then studied her again. His hand wandered down to his cock, and he gave it a few tugs, trying to give himself some relief as he studied how her arse tilted in the air. Waiting. Ready for him. He glanced at her to find her watching him ardently. Her gaze snagged his, and she licked her lips.

No more teasing. For her or for him. He needed her now.

He moved into position behind her, guided himself to her entrance. There was no preamble this time. He thrust home in one hard push. She bucked, her spine curving.

Oh. *Yes.* She was on her knees, her bound arms in front of her, her head bowed. He bloody *loved* to see her like this.

He gripped her hips. Her skin was soft and warm under his. The curve of her supple waist made perfect notches for his hands to hold her.

He thrust into her, her body caressing him in a silken glide.

"So good," he told her. "You're so tight and sweet around me." At her low moan, he added, "Yes, that's right. Let me hear your pleasure."

Soon, she began to buck and arch, her body slamming into his each time he pushed home. That telltale clamping of her body around him told him she was going to come.

"Yes," he encouraged. "You're getting tighter." He ground his teeth at the intensity, trying to keep himself from exploding inside her. "You're going to drive me mad, Em." He squeezed his fingers over her hips, directing her body's movements against him.

Her breaths emerged in harsh "Ah! Ah! Ah!" sounds. Her back curved, then straightened. Her forehead pressed into the bed. Her pelvis tilted back, allowing him the deepest penetration possible.

And then her back arched and she threw her head back, and she came. Glorious pulses of pleasure milking his cock.

Damn it. Damn it, he thought to himself. *Wait. Wait, damn it.* He wanted to be inside her for the duration of her climax, but oh, *God* how he needed to come.

As soon as her tremors began to subside, he thrust hard into her, his fingers digging into the soft flesh of her hips, his cock digging into the tight grip of her sex.

Once, twice, three times. And then he pulled out of her, wrapped one of his arms around her while he braced his weight on the other, and shuddered out his release in the cleft of her arse.

As his own tremors subsided, he collapsed to his side, clutching her against him.

With fumbling fingers, he untied her bonds. He blindly tossed aside the cravat, then rubbed soothing fingers over the indentations it had left in her wrists.

"Mmm," she said.

"Does that mean you do like being bound, Mrs. Curtis? Because I've asked you several times now, and you've yet to respond."

"Mmm," she repeated. And then, a few moments later, she added in her low, sultry voice, "Yes, Luke. I like being bound. I like it very, very much."

Chapter Ten

O ver the next few days, Luke made very good use of his cravat. And her stockings. And the two yards of soft cotton rope he'd purchased at one of the stalls on the town's market day.

Emma really did like to be bound, he discovered. And he very much enjoyed tying her up. He bound her wrists. Her ankles. He tied her to a chair and had his wicked way with her. He secured her to the bedposts, spread for his pleasure—and hers. He wished there was more furniture to experiment with, but alas, this was a simple country inn.

And she cried out his name. She screamed in ecstasy. She came more times than he could count. And not once did she ask him to stop. He was fairly certain she never even came close, even when her legs and arms were bound in intricate knots, precluding her from moving at all.

Emma bound was a compelling erotic picture. It awed him. He'd bound women before. Some women hated it—

more than one had called him a bastard afterward. Some did seem to enjoy it, but none to the extent Emma did. She seemed to revel in it; her skin grew so sensitive that the merest touch sent her to shuddering and the softest stroke made her come.

He'd never been more sexually sated. He'd never felt calmer. Those sharp edges within him, the ones that seemed to scrape incessantly at him, had dulled to a low throb.

And yet, on their final night in Berwick-upon-Tweed, the plague of nightmares returned.

He'd fallen asleep after another bout of vigorous bed sport and had slept soundly for several hours. Then it began.

Luke ran as fast as he could. Twigs and gravel crunched under his feet. He was near the stream at Ironwood Park, trying to reach the forest, where he could find a place to hide under the cover of the trees.

But it was no use. Fingers encircled his arm in thick, powerful bands, pulling him back. And he looked into the angry, twisted face of his father. He smelled the sherry on his father's breath and winced. He hated the smell of sherry.

"How dare you run from me?" Papa growled.

Luke didn't answer. He was too afraid to answer.

The duke moved even closer, his sharp green eyes seeming to dive into Luke's soul. "Look at you. You'll never hide your true ugliness, Lukas, your inherent malevolent nature. So stop bothering to try. You'll never be anything like your brother. You will never inherit, because you aren't worthy. Do you hear me? You will never be worthy. *Never*."

Why? Luke always wanted to ask. *Why do you hate me so much? What have I done?*

But he knew what he'd done. He existed. His very existence disgusted his father.

The duke sighed, and Luke winced. He knew what was coming. "Turn around. If you refuse to banish the evil yourself, then I'll need to beat it out of you."

"No, Papa," Luke whimpered, but his voice was so small compared to the booming, overpowering voice of his father.

The duke shoved him to the ground, jerked his shirt up, raised the riding crop. Luke curled up in a ball on the ground, but the crop was whistling through the air, coming down to slice at his skin...

Luke's body surged up to a seated position. He bent forward, gasping. His back stung from the blow. Was he bleeding? He twisted his body, trying to see.

Gradually, he realized he was in bed. He wore his shirt, and it was damp from sweat, not from blood. And Emma stirred beside him.

"What is it?" she murmured. "What's wrong, Luke? Are you all right?"

Blast. He was shaking, he realized. Trembling from a childish fear of a man who'd been dead for twenty years.

He can't get to you now.

But his self-reassurance fell on deaf ears, as it always did.

"Luke?"

"Ah," he said shakily. He couldn't...stop...shaking. What was his problem? "Yes."

She was more awake now. She rose to a sitting position beside him, laid her hand on his shoulder. He tried not to flinch away. His skin felt raw. Like his flesh had just been beaten to ribbons, even though he knew it was just a dream. He wasn't hurt. He *wasn't*.

"You're shaking."

"I'm all right," he growled. Lying, of course.

"No. You're not all right." Her voice was calm. Soothing. But something about it... *Pity*. He couldn't do this right now. He'd shared so much with Emma—so much more than he had with any other person. But there were places he couldn't go, and this was one of them.

He stumbled out of bed, trying to remember where he'd put his trousers and his coat, fumbling around until he found them in the darkness.

"What are you doing?" Now she was beginning to sound alarmed.

"I need to go for a walk."

"Luke, it's the middle of the night. It's all right..."

He struggled with the legs of his trousers, which he'd found on the floor. "No," he pushed out through his closing throat. "I need to walk. I'll be back. Later."

"Luke, don't run away. Stay with me."

His trousers weren't buttoned properly, but he could hardly drag air into his lungs. He had to get out of here. He grabbed his coat from the peg where it had been hanging, took the key from the lock, then opened the door and went out into the corridor. He struggled to get the key into the lock—his hands shook violently—but finally he locked the door. He knew Emma hated being locked in, but if he couldn't do anything else, he'd take some steps—however weak and meaningless—to keep her safe.

Then he slumped against the door, closing his eyes,

clenching his fist around the key. He could breathe a little better out here in the darkened corridor.

He ran a rough hand through his hair, his fingers still shaking.

This was all an illusion, he realized. What he was doing with Emma. It was a teasing taste of heaven, but it wasn't real. Sooner or later he would need to run from his demons again, only to be grabbed, reminded of his failings, and beaten into the dust.

And he had brought Emma into this mad world of his. He was destined to disappoint her, ultimately hurt her. It was inevitable. He always hurt the people he cared about. Like his mother. Like Trent.

He straightened on unsteady legs and made his way downstairs. He wished the tavern was open, but it was too late—or too early, he supposed. There would be no drink to help him soften those cutting edges tonight.

He walked down the corridor of the silent inn and burst outside into the misty street. A thin layer of snow whitened the street. Winter was definitely on its way.

At least it had stopped raining.

* * *

Emma couldn't sleep after Luke left. She lay there for what felt like hours, staring at the ceiling. Wondering what he'd dreamed about. He wouldn't tell her. Should she try to pry it out of him, or should she let it go?

Let it go, she decided. Luke had divulged certain secrets to her, but only when he had been ready to do so. If he ever wanted to tell her about his nightmares, it would have to be on his terms.

But she wanted so badly to know. To help him. She hated feeling so helpless. She closed her eyes and tried to sleep, but it was impossible. As dawn turned the world to a dull gray around her, she stared at the ceiling, at the crack running across it that grew clearer, deeper, longer as the sun shed its light on the world.

By the time Luke returned, Emma had bathed and dressed and was gazing out the window. When she heard the door open, she turned to watch him enter.

He hesitated on the threshold. "Did you get any more sleep?"

"No."

He winced. "I'm sorry."

"It's not your fault."

A humorless laugh rasped out of him. "Oh, yes, it is."

She gave him a small smile. "It's all right. I'll sleep tonight."

She was always assuring him that it was all right. But was it? She wasn't so certain right now.

He came up to her, put his arms around her, drew her close. She slipped her arms around him, too, and pressed her lips to his neck just above his collar. His skin was cool. He'd been outside. She inhaled deeply, loving his salty scent.

"Em," he said softly. That was all.

They stood there for a minute, holding each other. Then, gently, he pulled away. "It snowed last night."

"I saw," she said. "At least it's not raining."

"The roads will be bad, but we should try to get some miles behind us today."

"Yes." Their days here had been nothing short of ex-quisite—Luke had showed her erotic pleasure she'd secretly fantasized about, but he'd given her much more than she'd ever dreamed possible. He was rough in bed, but tender at the same time. Loving and attentive. A rogue who took her to the edge, then thrust her over again and again.

She'd loved every moment they'd spent here, but those stolen moments had been necessary due to the weather. Finding Roger Morton was still the priority. They needed to hurry to London, locate the man, and hopefully find the answers to all their questions about Henry and the dowager duchess.

Then what would happen?

She was trying not to think of that. She still had the gun in the bottom of her satchel. The rain hadn't ruined it, thankfully—the boot had ended up keeping their luggage dry, after all.

Luke still hadn't discovered her gun. That was for the best. After their conversation last night, she knew that if he found out about it, he would take it away.

An hour later they'd eaten breakfast and were once again on the road—the now-muddy, pitted road, with melting patches of snow on its edges—bound for London.

Luke was quieter than usual this morning. Emma knew the reason why—his nightmare—but she was loath to broach the subject after mulling it over in her head all morning.

They traveled slowly, much slower than their usual speed. Emma understood the roads were bad, but after hours of plodding along at a snail's pace, she thought she just might crawl out of her skin.

"Can't we go a little faster?" she begged.

Luke didn't remove his focus from the road. "No."

She sighed as he negotiated around a muddy puddle, remembering how reckless she'd thought he'd been for purchasing this curricle in the beginning. In truth, he'd been a conscientious and careful driver from the start.

"At this rate, we'll arrive in London sometime in January."

He shrugged. "Better alive in London in January than dead in Northumberland in October."

Well, she couldn't argue with that. So she sat back and studied the scenery as they began to climb a steady incline. The forest was thick here, encroaching on the road on both sides. Red-and-gold-leafed sycamores, green pines. Fallen leaves in stunning autumn browns, reds, oranges, and golds blanketed the ground, and the snow, though melting, showed through in patches of white on the leaves, tucked in shady corners of tree trunks and on the ridged edges of the road.

They topped the rise. The road here began to descend in a sharp grade, curving sharply under the canopy of an exceptionally large and heavily leafed sycamore whose golden and red leaves had clung tenaciously to its branches. Just off to the right, Emma saw water—a pond, perhaps, its surface placid and edged with snow and weeds.

The sycamore shadowed the road here, and a thin layer of snow blanketed the next several feet. The strip of dirt stretching out before them appeared even, but the rocky movement told Emma that was an illusion caused by the uniformity of the snowfall.

Suddenly, they dipped into a large patch of slush, and the carriage jerked wildly. The earth seemed to grab at the wheel on Emma's side. The horses kept straining forward but clinging fingers of mud and water and snow held the curricle back.

Crack! The carriage buckled, the motion catapulting her from the carriage and sending her flying through the air. She scrambled desperately to hold on to something, but the seat had been ripped out from under her. She reached out for Luke, but he was gone, too. Wood cracked and splintered all around her. And then, a sudden, sharp pain shot through her ankle and up her leg. She tumbled headfirst through ice-cold water. Her hand sank into mud. Something struck her cheek.

For a brief second, everything was perfectly still. Perfectly quiet.

And then the excruciating pressure came off her ankle and arms closed around her and hauled her out of the water.

"Emma!" The voice was loud. Anguished. Close.

She was laid on a soft bed of leaves.

"Emma, are you all right? Speak to me, please." Hands closed over her shoulders, shook her slightly, and she smiled.

Slowly, she opened her eyes. Luke was bent over her, his expression wild. As he saw her eyes open, he bent down and gathered her close against his chest. "My God," he breathed. "Thank God. I thought...thought...I'd lost you."

She shook her head, confused. And then sensation returned to her body in a rush. Wetness seeped through her cloak and all the layers of garments beneath it. Her ankle burned with pain. And it felt like there was a cold, wet weight on her face.

She reached up in curiosity and found a mud-laden leaf

stuck to her cheek. She pushed it away. Luke still held her, muttering apologies as he kissed her hair.

"What...what happened?" she managed when she found her voice.

"We hit a patch of snow—or that's what it looked like. It was clearly some kind of ditch filled with water, though. The mud trapped the wheel on your side, and the axle failed. Look."

Pulling away slightly, Luke helped her to a seated position, then turned toward the road. She followed his gaze. The horses seemed fine—they stood on the road placidly, nuzzling at weeds along its edge. But the carriage—their curricle—was in pieces, its major parts on the road and one wheel near their feet. "Oh, no," she breathed.

"You were propelled out of the carriage and into the water..." Luke paused, swallowed. His voice shook when he went on. "You landed headfirst. And then you were so still, I thought you'd hit your head...I thought you'd..."

"I'm all right," she reassured him. Her wits were returning, and trying to think beyond the frigid cold, she assessed herself. Her head felt fine. Her body, too. Well, except for her foot.

"Are you...were you hurt?" she asked him, running a hand over his cheek.

"No. I leapt after you. Landed on my feet. There's not a damn scratch on me." His lips twisted bitterly. "Of course."

She made a *tsk*ing noise. "Stop that. Are you wishing you'd been hurt?"

"If it meant you weren't, then yes," he said without hesitation.

"I'm not hurt."

He released a slow, audible breath. "Are you really all right?"

"Yes." She hesitated, then added, "But I think something happened to my foot."

He moved to her feet. "Which one?"

"The right."

Slowly, he removed her sodden shoe. Every touch near her ankle was excruciating. His fingers ran gently over the surface of where it hurt the most. "Here?"

"Yes."

"That damn wheel fell on you. I had to get it off before I could pull you from the water. It must have crushed your foot."

His gaze moved from her ankle to her face, his expression hard. "You're chilled to the bone. You need dry clothes. Then we need to find you a doctor."

"Out here? I think our first dilemma is what to do about the carriage."

Luke ground his teeth. Then he reached down and scooped her into his arms as if she were a child. "Luke! I'm too heavy. I can walk."

"No." He tugged her tighter against him and rose to his feet with surprisingly little effort. She wrapped her arms around his neck, and he climbed the embankment and stepped onto the road. He turned slowly, keeping her snug against him. "There's nowhere for you to sit. Can you stand on one foot for a few moments?"

"Of course," she told him.

Ever so gently, he set her down, and even though her heart was still beating with fear and shock, and even though pain wound through the bottom of her leg, she felt a quickening in her womb.

He felt it, too. When her feet touched the ground, he looked down at her with a heated gaze. "I want you so damn much right now."

Then take me, she wanted to say. *Right here in the middle of the road.* But she shivered instead. Even though it was a shiver of need, he took it as a chill, and after ensuring she was steady, he stepped away.

She looked down at the rocky, wet ground, acknowledging that it would have probably been highly uncomfortable to make love to Luke right here. Sometimes, practicality ruled.

She watched Luke rummage around in the boot, drawing dry clothes out. He returned with her extra chemise and a petticoat. "We'll start with these. Stand still."

She stood as he removed her dripping, heavy silk cloak. She nearly cried when he drew it off and she saw that it was caked with mud and leaves. "Do you think it's ruined?"

"No," he said softly. He went behind her, not allowing her to move, and worked on the buttons of her dress—she'd been wearing the white muslin. It, too, was dirty, wet, and mud-splashed.

The dress came off, followed by her petticoat. And, half naked in the middle of a thoroughfare in Northumberland, she began to shiver uncontrollably. She'd never been so cold.

Luke saw—she couldn't have hid it from him—and his jaw tightened. "I'm sorry," she whispered. "It's just... chilly."

"It all needs to come off," he said darkly. "You're soaked. If anyone drives by in the next five minutes—" He glanced up and down the road as if willing all nearby vehicles to halt where they were until Emma was decent again.

And then he went to work. Balancing on her one good foot, she helped him unlace her stays, then lift the chemise over her body.

His eyes flickered over her when she was naked, but then he saw her shivering, her hands wrapped around her chest. A muscle jerked in his jaw again, and he tugged the dry chemise on over her.

"No stays," he snapped. "They're too wet." She didn't have an extra set of stays anyhow.

"All right."

He helped her into her petticoat in silence, his movements efficient but gentle. Then he buttoned her into her black-and-white half-mourning dress.

No vehicles passed by. Which was rare, since the road had been relatively crowded earlier—all the farmers and travelers making their way north or south after the days of rainy weather.

Now that she was fully dressed, she'd expected to warm up. But the cold had settled into her bones, and she couldn't stop shaking.

He removed his coat and laid it over her shoulders, murmuring, "It's only damp on the outside."

He was right. The inside was warm and smelled of him. She wrapped it tight about her as he went to the carriage—what was left of it—and fetched the blanket they'd had since Bristol.

He laid that on her shoulders over his coat and then pulled her close. He rubbed her back briskly, trying to infuse warmth, but his gaze went to the curricle.

"Someone should be by soon. We'll have him take us to the closest doctor."

"Really," she told him, "I don't think it's so bad. Just a bruise."

He scowled at her. "A bruise you cannot stand on? I don't think so."

They went to the carriage, Luke supporting most of her weight as she hobbled over the muddy ground. Emma leaned against the one still-standing wheel while Luke unhitched the horses.

Before he finished, they heard the clomping of hooves coming from ahead. Emma watched as a coach and four with a driver on the front seat and another man seated at the rear came into view. They'd been moving at a very fast pace—compared, at least, to the speed Luke and Emma had been traveling at earlier—but the driver slowed the horses as soon as he saw the wreckage scattered across the road.

Luke stopped his work on the horses and went to meet the vehicle as it came to a halt just ahead of the ditch where the curricle had lost its wheel.

Men poured out of the coach to view the wreck, their curious gazes roaming over the curricle, then over the intimate wet and muddy clothing spread over the lopsided seat. Then their attention moved to Emma. Luke, who was speaking to the coachman, broke off, his gaze going to the men, then to her.

He was beside her in a few long strides. He scooped her up, as he had before. Ignoring the five men who'd emerged from the carriage, he approached one of the coachmen, who was dismounting.

"I'm sorry—I used my real name," he murmured to her. Then to the coachman, "My companion was injured in the accident."

"I hope it isn't serious," the driver said in a compassionate tone, but Emma could see the glint in his dark eyes as his gaze perused her. He thought she was Luke's mistress.

Which, she supposed, she was.

"Really, it's not so bad—just a bruised ankle." And to Luke, "Please put me down, my lord."

Luke ignored her and said to the coachman, "You will drive us to the nearest physician."

The man raised a brow. "Sorry, my lord. I'm from London—not even sure physicians exist this far from civilization."

The second driver had descended from his perch and stood beside the first. "We're an hour from Belford. There is a coaching inn there. They're likely to know where to locate a doctor."

Emma nearly groaned. They'd passed through Belford a while ago. They'd be going backward.

"Good. We'll join you, then," Luke said.

The men helped to move the wreckage of their curricle to the side of the road. They secured the horses behind the mail coach and fetched Emma's and Luke's luggage. Luke assured her he'd also gathered her wet clothing and had returned it to her valise. Then, three of the men sat on the top of the mail coach, leaving plenty of room for Luke and Emma inside. Luke carried her in, setting her gently beside the window, then sitting beside her.

The hour was long. Luke glared whenever either of the two men glanced at her. So Emma sat quietly, her skin numb with cold, but the outside of her foot throbbed with pain.

Belford was only fifteen miles south of Berwick-upon-

Tweed. After all they'd been through today, they would have only fifteen miles of progress to show. And no carriage. Emma wanted to discuss what they were going to do from here with Luke, but she didn't want to talk in front of strangers.

So it was with deep relief that she alighted from the mail coach in Belford. Practically before she could blink, the driver had grabbed a bundle of mail from the open window at the inn, and the coach was on its way again, kicking up mud onto the luggage that had been deposited at Emma's and Luke's feet as they stood there, Emma balancing on one leg with Luke's supporting arm around her, the reins of the two horses gripped in his free hand.

Luke stared after the mail coach, supreme annoyance in his expression, then he looked at his feet. His shoulders rose and fell with a deep, deep breath.

He looked up again. "Sorry about that."

She raised a brow. "About what?"

"The way they were looking at you."

Ah. That.

"God help me, I wanted to wipe those smirks off their faces. It was all I could do not to."

She laughed softly. "I admire your self-control, but truly they were not that bad."

"I don't approve of anyone looking at you like that." His eyes narrowed. "Except me, of course."

Two servants wandered out from the inn and took their luggage. Another took the horses and promised to give them a good rubdown and a clean stall for the night.

"I require a pint of red paint, I believe," Luke muttered.

Emma turned to him, wide-eyed. "What on earth for?"

"So I can write 'Property of Lord Lukas Hawkins.

Anyone caught staring will be immediately throttled' on your forehead."

She laughed. "I doubt all that would fit on my forehead." At the same time, a part of her secretly thrilled at the idea of being his "property." Which was unsettling, because ever since her disaster of a marriage, she didn't like to think of herself as anyone's property but her own.

And she wasn't Luke's property. She hadn't promised anything to him, nor had he promised anything to her. Even if they had made promises, she didn't know if she could ever again accept the concept of belonging to any man. She'd spent her life first as her father's property, then Henry's. Now she was her own woman, making her own decisions. And she liked it that way.

But she couldn't dwell too much on such thoughts right now. They had more pressing matters to deal with.

"What are we going to do?" she murmured, gazing at the bend in the road where the mail coach had disappeared.

"First, let's get you inside. You're still cold. Then a doctor for that foot. After that I'll find us a new carriage." He gave her a cocky grin that warmed her from the inside out. "If all goes well, we'll be on our way again tomorrow."

Chapter Eleven

The doctor prodded Emma's foot. She gritted her teeth but didn't complain. Finally, he pronounced a badly sprained ankle—the wheel landing on her lower leg had only produced tenderness and bruising, but the true injury must have been upon her impact with the ground, when she twisted the ankle. Truly, she couldn't quite remember exactly how it had happened. It had all been such a blur.

The doctor reassured Luke that it was a relatively minor sprain and should heal in a few weeks, as long as she kept off it as much as possible. He wrapped it tightly in a linen cloth, directed her to keep her leg on level with her body, ordered hot towels to be brought at regular intervals, and gave her a cane.

When the man left the room they'd procured at the Blue Bell Inn, Luke stood still, glaring down at where she was seated on the bed with her back propped against the wall. His hands curled into fists at his sides.

He was furious. At himself. For allowing her to get hurt.

Yet another reminder of his inadequacy.

Not to mention the fact that he'd lied to her from the beginning...

He took a measured breath. He needed to see about a carriage. He tried to smile at her but was certain it emerged as more of a grimace. "A post chaise."

"What?"

"We'll hire a post chaise to take us to London."

She seemed to consider this, then gave him a wry smile. "I would have loved that idea back in Bristol."

He frowned. "But not now?"

"I grew fond of our little curricle, I suppose. I was sorry to see it in pieces like that."

He went to the edge of the bed and sat, gathering her delicate, feminine hand in his own larger one.

"I shouldn't have bought it. I should have known better."

"I saw all of England, from the south to the north. I breathed fresh, clean air every day. The experience was incomparable. I'd no idea back in Bristol how much I'd end up appreciating all that."

"But you were hurt," he said gruffly.

"Not badly."

"It could have been worse." So much worse. He remembered her body lurching through the air like a rag doll, then slamming into the water. The wheel spinning through the air after her—God, the most sickening images had run through his mind all afternoon. His stomach was still a twisted mess.

"But it wasn't worse," she told him. "I'm all right, thanks to your careful driving."

He brought her knuckles up to his mouth and kissed the top of her hand gently. "Rest. I need to go down and find us a new carriage."

She sighed. "All right. I'll write to Jane while you're gone."

He brought her her writing supplies and arranged them so that she wouldn't have to get out of bed in order to write the letter. Then he took his coat and left her.

Half an hour later, he'd arranged for a post chaise to depart from the Blue Bell promptly at nine o'clock the following morning.

As he was heading back up to Emma, his eye caught on the pub across the street from the inn, which was growing busy for the dinner hour.

He'd have a drink before heading up for the evening. Just one, and then he'd join Emma for dinner, perhaps carry her down so they could eat together.

* * *

The sun went down, and a servant came in to light the lamps. Emma didn't ask for dinner to be brought up, because Luke had mentioned something about eating downstairs.

Another hour passed. And another. Another servant brought her a batch of hot towels for her ankle. She took them with thanks and sent the servant away.

By now, Emma knew where he'd gone. She set the towels aside, hobbled to the window, and pressed her forehead against it.

The man brought out such conflicting feelings in her. From unadulterated happiness to deep despair and just about everything in between. She'd never even known she was capable of feeling so much.

Right now, the prevalent feeling was despair. She hated that compulsion he had to leave her. He would have done it every night, she knew. The only reason she'd had a reprieve in Berwick-upon-Tweed was that she'd kept him so completely occupied in bed.

Tonight she would have been happy to keep him occupied in bed as well. That surge of desire at the scene of the carriage accident hadn't dissipated as the day had slipped by. It still resided somewhere deep and dark and delicious inside her.

But those desires surely wouldn't be satisfied tonight. Luke wasn't here. He was gone. In the pub across the street she'd seen him glancing at as they'd gone into the inn earlier.

As she stood there gazing out into the black of night, the despair transformed to anger. She briefly contemplated limping down there to fetch him. No. She wouldn't make a scene, and she was too furious with him not to. She felt like railing at him. She felt like punching him.

The pane of glass pressed against her forehead, cold as a block of ice. Their room was at the back of the inn, and the lane, as well as the mews and stables beyond, were dark. It was cold, and everyone had gone home for the evening. Everyone except Luke, evidently.

She pressed her palm against the windowpane, realizing she was feeling possessive about Lord Lukas Hawkins. She was feeling entitled to have a say in what he chose to do in the evenings. But, in truth, that wasn't at all the case. Technically, he owed her nothing. He'd made her no promises. He could do whatever he pleased. Even find a woman downstairs, if that was what he chose.

Still, her heart told her otherwise. Her heart told her that they had shared too much intimacy to be indifferent toward each other.

Which was a dangerous thing. She was becoming too involved. She knew Luke well enough now to understand that he was unlike anyone she'd ever met—charming and dark, teasing and sensual, demanding and generous, content yet aching for something mysterious she wished she could give him. He was a maddening, intriguing combination of lightness and darkness, but he kept so much of himself hidden from her, even now.

How could a woman tell her heart what to feel?

She waited for hours. A maid came in with her laundered damp clothing and hung it. Hopefully it would dry overnight, because it would need to be packed early in the morning if Luke did indeed intend to leave tomorrow, and she didn't want it to sour.

And then she sat on the bed, keeping her foot level with her body as the doctor had ordered.

She waited. And waited. Growing more angry. More sorry for herself. Tears gathered behind her eyes, but she didn't let them fall.

Why, Luke? Why do you do this to yourself? To us?

She donned her nightgown and attempted to sleep. That was a fruitless endeavor. She was too agitated. Too angry and hurt and confused. Her mind was too consumed by Luke. For the first time since she'd known him, she wondered how she was possibly going to survive this man.

Finally, in the early morning hours, he returned.

Emma hadn't slept at all. She turned away from the door at the first fumble of the key in the lock, then feigned sleep as he stumbled in, cursing under his breath. She heard him lock the door, strip down to his shirt. Then he climbed into bed beside her. She could smell the liquor on him, and again, she felt that heavy pressure of tears behind her eyes.

"Emma?" His voice was thick, and he pronounced her name as if it were a foreign word he'd yet to master.

She closed her eyes and didn't answer.

His lips pressed into her hair. "Beautiful angel," he slurred. "Sleep, my love."

It was only then that a single tear escaped from her clenched eyes. It slid slowly down her cheek in a hot, painful trail.

* * *

The next morning, Emma awoke to the smells of eggs, ham, toast, and steaming coffee.

She stirred, stretched. Remembering last night, something inside her clenched as she saw Luke rise from the chair across the room bearing a tray. She schooled her face to passivity as he approached her.

He sat on the edge of the bed, the tray in his lap, and gazed down at her, an expression of infinite tenderness on his face. "How is your ankle?"

She moved it experimentally, and pain flashed through her foot. "The same."

"I have your breakfast."

"Thank you." She sat up and scooted back, leaning against the wall but keeping her bad leg straight, trying not to wince at the pain of the weight of the blankets on her foot as it slid up the bed.

Her eyes widened at the tray Luke held. It contained two cups of coffee—hers heavily creamed the way she liked it—and a single plate piled high with ham, eggs, toast, sweet bread, and butter.

"For your strength," he said, and there was a hint of hopeful boy in his expression.

She reached for the plate, but he caught her hand and placed it firmly at her side. "Let me feed you."

"I am not an invalid. I can feed myself."

"I know. But...I would very much like to feed you your breakfast this morning."

She knew exactly what he was doing: trying to make up for leaving her last night.

Sighing, she said, "I'll never be able to eat that much food."

"I hope you'll share."

With a small, false smile on her face, she nodded.

He buttered the toast, tore off a piece for her and one for himself. Using the same fork, they shared bites of egg and meat until Emma's stomach was pleasantly full.

Luke moved the tray to the table and then sat on the bed again. Cradling her coffee cup in her hands, she gazed at him, all kinds of questions barreling through her mind. Accusations, too, for the memory of how he'd made her feel last night was a dark, festering pit inside her.

She'd felt *abandoned*.

That was exactly what he'd told her he'd end up doing to her. Why was she surprised? Still, she asked in a small voice, "Why didn't you come back last night?"

He gazed at her, his expression unreadable. Then he said, "I'm sorry."

Could such a simple, flat apology soothe all the dark feelings inside her? She didn't think so.

"I sat in that tavern last night," he said, "and all I could think about was what a liar I've been. How I've been lying to you."

She gazed at him, her heart suddenly feeling like it was kicking against her ribs.

"I can't lie to you anymore, Em."

"What is it?" she asked unsteadily. What now? What on earth was he talking about? Was he married? Did this have something to do with his secretive outing in Worcester?

His throat moved as he swallowed, and he suddenly looked so unsure. "I discovered something last summer. Something that has altered my life but also explained a great deal about my past."

He swallowed again, looked down at the bedclothes, then back up at her. "My mother went missing in April, as you know. In the course of searching for her, my brother became involved with Baron Stanley. Have you heard of him?"

"No."

"Stanley's lands are adjacent to Ironwood Park. Stanley wanted his daughter, Georgina, to marry Trent, and he attempted to extort marriage from my brother."

"How?" she breathed.

"He had information—potentially devastating information. About my two brothers Mark and Theo. And about me."

She shook her head, confused. "What kind of information?"

He jerked his gaze away from her, looking toward the window she'd leaned against for so long last night.

"I am not the Duke of Trent's full brother," he said dully. "I am his half brother, on my mother's side. I am the illegitimate son of the Dowager Duchess of Trent and Lord Stanley."

She gazed at him uncomprehendingly.

"When Trent was a baby, my mother became embroiled in a short-lived affair with Lord Stanley. The old duke knew about it and was furious, of course, but he agreed to raise me as his own if the truth about my mother and Stanley's liaison was never revealed."

"Good Lord," she murmured. "And...and you never knew?"

He shook his head slowly. "No. For almost twenty-eight years, I thought the Duke of Trent was my father."

"Oh, Luke. I'm so sorry."

"None of us knew. Not Trent, not me, not my other brothers or my sister. We were kept in the dark until Stanley revealed the truth last summer in his attempt to force Trent to marry his daughter."

"But the duke didn't marry her," Emma mused. "He married the housemaid."

"Sarah...yes." Luke's lips quirked at one edge. "Trent managed to avoid that potential disaster. Georgina Stanley is quite the brat. She and my brother never would have suited."

"Miss Stanley...she is your half sister, then?"

"Yes." Slowly, his head turned until he was looking at her. The depth of sadness in his gaze undid her. Unraveled her completely.

Oh, Luke.

To spend one's life thinking you were the son of a duke, only to discover at twenty-seven that not only are you not, but that you're illegitimate as well. Your father is a stranger. You have siblings who are strangers. The siblings you thought you had are only half the relations you believed they were. The name you believed was yours for your whole life no longer applies.

She couldn't imagine what that felt like.

"Are... are you sure?" she stammered.

He closed his eyes in a long blink. His jaw firmed. "Yes. The proof is incontrovertible."

"And your brothers, Mark and Theo? Are they Lord Stanley's as well?"

"No." His voice sounded thick, as if he were speaking through syrup. "They are the illegitimate sons of the old duke and one of his mistresses. Stanley possessed proof of that as well. So... my two younger brothers? We have no blood in common. They're not really my brothers at all. Trent and Sam, my two older brothers, are both half brothers on my mother's side, and my sister—no one knows for certain what her origins are. Stanley raised some questions regarding her legitimacy as well."

"All this in an attempt to force the Duke of Trent to marry his daughter."

"Yes," Luke said simply. "The man is a conniving bastard."

And this was the man he'd just learned was his true father. Emma leaned her head back against the wall and closed her eyes.

He inhaled shakily. "So you see, I've been lying to you about who I truly am. My entire existence is a lie. My identity as the son and legitimate brother of the Duke of

Trent—as his heir—is false. I'm nothing but a bastard pretending to be someone he is not."

Emma squeezed her eyes more tightly shut. For a long moment, they sat in silence. Not moving, not speaking.

Luke was still Luke. He was still the man Emma admired and desired, who drove her to distraction in so many ways. Nothing had changed about any of that. All that had changed was her understanding of him. Now she had further insight into the depths of him.

Emma dragged her eyes open. "You said this could change what we have between us. But I don't understand how."

Luke's lips pressed together in a flat line. He gazed at her. "I don't belong in the position I was raised to believe I occupied. I'm a charlatan. And I'm inherently evil. Spawned in sin."

She blinked at him. "What are you talking about?"

"I deserve nothing of what I have. I receive an allowance from the ducal estate, but do I even deserve that? No, I don't. I'm a bastard's bastard. I should have nothing, but I have lived such a life of leisure I can't survive without taking the money of a dead man I have no legitimate ties to."

"Your brother wouldn't agree!"

He gave a humorless laugh. "You seem to know so much about Trent."

"From you. You've told me about the duke. I know you and he don't often agree, but I can tell you care for him. It is obvious he cares for you, too. I doubt he gives a damn about this stupid discovery."

"Oh, he gives a damn," Luke said softly. Turning away from her, he pushed a rough hand through his hair.

Emma ground her teeth. Luke had taken this discovery of his paternity as some kind of proof that he was a lesser man, an undeserving man.

"You *foolish* man."

Luke blinked at her. She struggled to move toward him, trying not to move her foot too much. She took his neck and pulled him to her. She kissed his lips, then pressed her cheek to his stubble-roughened one. He hadn't yet shaved this morning.

"Don't let this destroy you, Luke. It doesn't change who you are."

"Doesn't it?" His voice was rough with emotion.

"No." She kissed his lips again, hard. "No." Her lips pushed against his. "This changes nothing of how I feel for you. Nothing of what I think about you. It changes nothing of what's inside you. Here." She pressed her palm against his heart.

He gripped her shoulders. His blue eyes shone at her, two bright sapphires. "Every time someone calls me 'my lord,' it is a lie. I'm not who you thought I was."

"Yes. You are. You're exactly who I thought you are. You're the man I want. The man I need. Right now."

She fumbled with the hem of her nightgown, pulling it up, feeling the twinge in her ankle but not giving a damn.

"I need you," she whispered, peppering kisses over his face. She pulled away for a second to jerk her nightgown over her head. Then it was off and she was naked, and Luke's hands were fumbling over her, touching her waist, her stomach, her breasts.

She lay back, pulling him over her. She reached down to his falls. His arousal grew as she touched him there, and a whimper of anticipation escaped her throat.

"Emma," he groaned. "God, Emma." And then he took command, strong and powerful, like he always did. A deep shudder began at her core and traveled outward through her limbs. She wiggled against him, yearning, wanting. She'd wanted him last night—she'd pined for him—but now her need had grown. Her need eclipsed rational thought. She yanked his trousers over his hips, and he kicked them away. She wrapped her arms around him, over his shirt.

"Need you," she whispered. "I need you. Please. Please."

With one heavy push, he was deep, deep inside her. She gasped as her body took him in. And she looked up at him. His wild blue eyes gazed down at her.

"More, Luke. Give me more of you."

With a low groan, he began to move in powerful, heavy thrusts. He bent down and took her mouth, sweeping his tongue in with each plunge of his body into hers. One hand went to her breast, squeezing.

And that quickly, her body tightened. His kiss, his touch, his presence inside her, all of it combined to make the pleasure nearly unbearable. Her body tautened from head to toe. She felt like a violin string, with Luke the virtuoso playing her until she vibrated with pleasure.

He tasted like salt and man, with a hint of coffee from their breakfast. He was hard and warm. Each thrust that entered her body seemed to go impossibly deep, and he pushed so far inside her, she was certain he touched her very soul.

She came so hard black spots crowded her vision. Her body pulsed and shuddered. Her eyes rolled back in her head. She grabbed his shirt for dear life.

But Luke was over her, protecting her. As pleasure rolled in thundering waves through her, she knew he'd keep her safe.

Slowly, she emerged back into the world, panting, her heart galloping. He was breathing hard, too, each exhalation a harsh rasp that blew strands of hair from her face. His thumb moved over her too-sensitive nipple, and she squirmed. The wetness from her orgasm made her slick and hot between her legs, and he glided into her now, still so deep and so hard she felt him to her core.

He didn't stop. He was relentless, his body moving through hers like this was where he belonged and he had no intention of ever leaving. In minutes, Emma's body began that sweet rise to her peak once again. The orgasm came sharp and hard, and as she came down from it, she whimpered, boneless and replete beneath his onslaught. Seconds later, he pulled out. Reaching down, he circled his fingers around himself, and she felt the warm splash of his seed as he released onto her stomach with a low groan.

He dropped onto her, heavy but not too heavy, because he kept much of his weight on his arms and knees, and she wrapped her arms tight around him, reveling in the feel of his masculine, powerful body on top of hers. Her face was in line with the curve of his shoulder to his neck, and she kissed him tenderly there as he panted into her hair.

Minutes later, when both their breathing had calmed somewhat, he raised his head slowly, as if it weighed a ton.

"Did you mean it?" he asked, and the expression on his face was so young and so vulnerable, a lump rose in her throat. "Am I the man you thought I was? The man you want?"

"Yes," she said, her voice husky and firm. "I swear to God and on the lives of everyone I hold dear, I meant it. I meant every word."

His eyes closed and he lowered his head again. But his lips pressed to her hair and his arm tucked itself between the bed and her body, hugging her to him.

"You're an angel," he said softly.

"No, Luke, I'm not. I'm just a woman who cares for you."

And… who just might be falling in love with you, too.

Chapter Twelve

They drove at a brutal pace for four days, changing horses often, hiring a new pair of postilions to drive the horses every day. The weather wasn't ideal, but Emma and Luke were in a closed carriage now, and rain didn't have as great of an effect on their travel.

From Belford to Darlington that first day, then Doncaster the second. On the third day, they became more intimately acquainted with the interior of their post chaise. Emma was leaning on Luke's shoulder, half asleep, and his hand was on her thigh. Slowly, it began creeping upward. With every inch, Emma's awareness rose. She reciprocated by touching his thigh, too. When they reached each other's upper thigh, Emma looked up, and their lips met in a long, languorous kiss.

Luke lifted her from the carriage seat, then settled her to a position on her knees in front of him.

"Loosen my falls," he commanded, his voice husky and laced with erotic promise.

She glanced toward one of the windows. The curtains on both sides of the carriage were open, letting the sunlight cast golden rays inside.

He quirked a brow. "Do you want me to close the curtains?"

She almost said yes, but then she caught herself. There was something wickedly intoxicating about the idea that someone might see whatever it was they were about to do. A farmer at the side of the road might chance to look up at the passing post chaise and see Emma and Luke in the throes of passion.

Her heart quickened at the thought. For the life of her, she couldn't understand why the idea was so arousing, but it was.

On her knees in front of Luke, the movement of the carriage rumbling under her shins, she looked up at him and slowly shook her head no.

His lips curved. "Good," he said. "Now loosen my falls."

She did as she was told, her body trembling in anticipation.

He was hard already, and she wondered if it was the kiss or the open windows that had aroused him. Perhaps both.

With deliberate slowness, she unbuttoned his falls, allowing her fingertips to skim over his length whenever they came near it. Then she opened his trousers.

The largeness of his arousal never failed to astound her.

She stroked a finger down his length. He shuddered, and she looked up at him. She wanted—needed—his instruction.

"Tell me what to do."

"Grip me in your hands," he murmured. "Gently at first, then tighter."

She touched him in a loose grip, lightly circling her fingers around him. His skin was so soft here, over the steely hardness of his length.

"Good," he murmured. "Tighter now, and slide your fingers over it like this."

He moved his hands over hers, showing her how to stroke him in an up-and-down movement. His eyes fluttered closed. "Oh, yes. That's so good. Just like that."

She wanted to kiss him. So she did, running her lips over his blunt head and stroking back and forth. His salty taste was more pronounced here.

They'd done so many wicked things together, but this was so deliciously naughty, her breaths quickened and her pulse galloped.

He released a low growl as her lips pushed over the fleshy tip of him, and the sound encouraged her. She licked him, following the path of her hands with her tongue as she moved up and down over his long, thick length.

His fingers dove into her hair. Vaguely, she heard her pins clattering to the floor of the carriage, and she smiled. Luke loved her hair, loved digging his hands into it.

The coil of her braid came loose, and he anchored his fingers tight against her scalp. "That's so good, Em. Now wrap that pretty little mouth around me."

She opened and took him inside her mouth, going down as far as she could before pulling up, licking his shaft as she moved over it, using her lips for pressure. Now, her lips followed the path of her fisted fingers over him, up and down, her tongue swirling around him, paying special attention to the blunt head of him, because whenever she licked him there, his fingers tightened in her hair.

Arousal flushed through her. She pressed her thighs together to combat the building need at their apex. Her body wanted this, wanted him to press this steely, hot organ deep inside her. Hard and fast, like he always did. It wanted that deep, intense friction only Luke could provide.

She began to whimper over him, feeling like she was going to squirm out of her very skin.

"Yes. That's so damn good. Keep making those noises. They feel so good."

He had begun to move into her mouth, thrusting deep, using the fingers wrapped in her hair to push her over him. She wanted to take him all, swallow him down. He was so hard and hot and delicious. Whenever she took him in especially deep, he groaned in appreciation.

"Yes. God, yes," he murmured, thrusting into her mouth. As she worked her mouth and hand over him, he grew impossibly harder, impossibly longer. She could almost feel the pulse of blood and heat through his shaft. Her body was on fire—hot, needy, and wanting, so open and ready for his invasion.

His fingers grew so tight in her hair it almost hurt. His hips moved, and all she needed to do was give over to his direction. She relaxed, letting him thrust into her mouth, letting him direct her with his hands cupping her head and tangled in her hair.

She loved this—being locked against him like this, him controlling her every movement.

She glanced up at him from beneath her lashes. The look of ecstasy on his face made her own body clench.

"Em...going to come..."

She released a long, shuddering whimper. He thrust into her mouth. And then he stilled, locking her there against him, his shaft pulsing under her lips and tongue and fingers. And the salty fluid of his release spilled onto the back of her tongue. She swallowed, took more, and swallowed again.

Every muscle in his body seemed to go limp, and so did she. She slowly pulled her mouth off him, then spread small, wet kisses over his relaxing shaft.

She lay against him until she felt his hands on her, pulling her back up to the carriage seat. Sitting beside him once more, she wrapped her hands around his neck and pulled him to her in a wet, erotic kiss. She knew he tasted himself on her, and she squirmed—teased and pleasured by that fact.

* * *

That third night of travel in the post chaise, after she'd given him pleasure and straddled him on the carriage seat and found her own release, they stopped in Stilton. As the sun began its descent behind a heavy layer of clouds on the fourth day, they reached the tollgate at Hyde Park Corner.

London. They had finally arrived.

It was a cool evening, the dull gray skies heavy with the promise of more rain as the post chaise stopped at the front of Luke's town house in Cavendish Square. Emma knew this area to some extent—before last year, her father had owned a house near Bedford Square, less than a mile away.

She gazed up at the narrow façade of Luke's house, a three-story structure of whitewashed brick. They hadn't discussed her staying here. It was the only obvious choice, she supposed, since they both knew there was nowhere else for her to go. Yet it seemed a huge step, to sleep with Luke in his home.

His hand closed over hers, warm and large. "What do you think?" he murmured.

"It's lovely."

It was. Stately but not overly opulent. It suited a single gentleman of Luke's pedigree—or, she supposed, of his false pedigree.

They alighted from the carriage, and Luke gave instructions to the postilions while Emma leaned on her cane and studied her surroundings. The gardens lay on one side of the street, a large, round splash of green in the midst of the city. Tight rows of buildings—mostly houses—lined the square. Luke's house was in the center of one row, with nothing significant about it to set it apart from the others.

The front door of Luke's house opened, and a man appeared at the threshold. He wore black pantaloons and a coat with a black stock at his neck. He wasn't tall or short, old or young. His hair wasn't quite black but not brown either. Receding at the top, it hung straight over his ears, and he had no trace of the sideburns that had recently come into fashion.

His gaze flicked impassively over Emma, then landed on Luke. He stood silently, keeping his gaze on Luke, until Luke was finished speaking to the postilions. The two uncommonly small-statured men went to the rear of the carriage to unload the luggage while Luke joined Emma.

He took her hand. Such a public display of affection, in such a public place. He probably knew half the people who resided in the square. She was certain more than half of them knew him. Luke wasn't only the Duke of Trent's brother, but he also had a reputation about Town, and this—his home—was certainly where that reputation was rooted.

So him holding her hand...it was surprising. But she was glad for it. It reassured her to be touching him right now.

He tugged her toward the door, and they mounted the few steps that led to it, Emma limping slightly although her ankle was improving daily. The man standing there bowed. "My lord," he said without inflection.

"Baldwin," Luke said in return. He turned to Emma. "Em, this is Baldwin, my one and only servant. Baldwin, this is Mrs. Curtis. You shall treat her as you would me, as your employer and your superior in all things."

Emma blinked at Luke. *Goodness!* But Baldwin's face remained completely expressionless. "Yes, my lord. Good afternoon, Mrs. Curtis."

She nodded and smiled at him. He stepped aside as Luke led her inside. They entered a small receiving room tiled in black and white marble with a flight of stairs directly in front of them. Luke pulled her through the entryway and to the right of the stairs, speaking over his shoulder to the servant. "Hire a cook tomorrow, will you? I'll be taking most of my meals here indefinitely, and I wouldn't want you overcome by the work."

"Yes, sir," came Baldwin's dry voice from behind them.

"And a maid, too. One who will assist you with maintaining the house but who is also familiar with waiting upon ladies."

"Yes, sir."

"I'd prefer to be the one to help you dress," he murmured to Emma with a wicked glint in his eyes, "but a maid might be able to assist you in other things."

Emma had had her own maid ever since she'd entered adolescence, but over the past year, she'd become quite accustomed to doing things on her own. "That's not necessary," she told him.

"Of course it is." And the subject was closed.

Luke gestured through an open door as he pulled her along. "Dining room. I think I've been in there once, when I bought the place. This is my study. I spend more time in there." He grinned. "Sometimes."

He waved to an arched doorway at the far end of the corridor. Beyond the arch, Emma could see a small table and a square-paned window beyond. "That's the breakfast room, and the kitchen is down there." He gestured to a set of stairs at the end of a short corridor to the right.

He swiveled around and they returned to the stairway. On the first floor he showed her the drawing room, which looked out over Cavendish Square. Then he took her into his bedroom. "We'll be sleeping here. But now, what do you think about harassing Baldwin for something to eat?"

She smiled. "That sounds excellent. But what's up there?" She pointed to another set of stairs.

"There are three additional bedrooms on the second floor—rooms I haven't ever used—and servants' quarters in the attic."

They went downstairs and sat in the breakfast room while Baldwin served them an extremely simple dinner of beef stew with apples and a bottle of wine.

For some reason, it was the most excellent dinner Emma had eaten in ages. Perhaps because it was the first time in weeks she wasn't eating inn food.

As they ate, they discussed their plan for locating Roger Morton.

Tomorrow, they would head to Soho to see if they could find anyone who knew his whereabouts. If that didn't work, they'd go to church on Sunday and look for the sister and her Irish husband—today was Tuesday, so they'd have to wait a few days for that.

"What if we don't find him?" she whispered. "London is so enormous, it's quite possible we won't—"

"We'll find him, Emma." Luke said it like a promise. She hoped he was right.

* * *

The next day they went to Soho. They questioned just about everyone they saw—all the people who seemed to be fixtures in Soho, from the boy selling the *Times* on the corner of Oxford and Dean Streets to the orange lady on Frith Street to the bookseller in Soho Square.

It was true that their account of Roger Morton wasn't very helpful—the man had brown hair, brown eyes, and was of average height with no marks or scars or other distinguishing characteristics. That description could have described anyone from Henry Curtis to one of Luke's younger brothers.

They asked about the sister and her husband, too, but with no more than the fact that the husband was a red-headed Irishman with an O' name, they only received blank stares and reminders that every tenth person who resided in Soho was red-haired and Irish.

With the vague information they had, Emma worried they'd never find the man.

Luke, however, was optimistic. "There's still Sunday," he told her. "We'll find the sister and her husband at church."

Emma wasn't so sure, but she gritted her teeth and nodded. There was nothing to do but wait until Sunday.

They spent the better part of Thursday in bed. In the afternoon, they met the new cook and went to Bond Street for a little shopping Luke insisted on, because Emma's dresses had grown wretchedly shabby during the journey to Edinburgh. Both of them were a dull shade of gray rather than white now, and both had ugly dark stains near their hems. The velvet ribbons on the half-mourning dress had begun to fray, and the muslin had already looked well used when she'd packed it. Now it was hardly wearable.

Of course, Emma didn't possess the funds to purchase new dresses. A part of her didn't want to accept Luke's charity. Another, more practical, part of her knew she couldn't saunter about London in nothing but her chemise, so she gritted her teeth and allowed Luke to buy her two ready-to-wear dresses, both of finer quality than she would have chosen for herself.

On Friday, the Duke and Duchess of Trent came for a visit. Emma and Luke were still in bed when Baldwin knocked on the door. As usual, his voice was completely flat and devoid of emotion. "Sir? The duke and duchess are here. Are you at home?"

Luke pulled back from Emma. He'd been lying over her, making a sensual perusal of her body with his lips. She stared at him with wide eyes. Oh, God. The Duke of Trent was in Luke's house and she hadn't a stitch of clothing on her body.

Luke rolled his eyes. "Very well, Baldwin," he said, sounding exasperated. "Put them in the drawing room. Offer them refreshment and all that nonsense."

"Yes, sir," Baldwin said, and they heard his retreating footsteps.

To Emma, Luke growled, "How like my brother to show up at such an ungodly hour."

"It is ten o'clock," Emma pointed out.

"Too early for visiting." With a grumpy sigh, he rolled off her and went into the dressing room. Emma rose more slowly, acutely aware that the drawing room was on the other side of the wall. Here she was, naked, and the Duke and Duchess of Trent were hardly more than ten feet away from her.

With the new maid's help, Emma dressed as quickly as she could in one of her new plain white muslins. Luke left the room to greet his brother while Delaney went to work on Emma's tangled hair, taming it into submission and then twisting it into a tight chignon just above her neck.

She took a deep breath, looking into the mirror. Her cheeks were flushed—whether it was from the attentions Luke had been bestowing upon her moments ago or from nerves about meeting the Duke of Trent, she didn't know.

She was about to meet the Duke of Trent, in the flesh. Jane—and the rest of Britain's female population—would be so jealous.

She rose, smoothed her skirts, straightened her shoulders, and left the bedroom, leaning on her cane as she hobbled next door.

"Here she is," Luke said warmly as she opened the drawing room door. He went to her side, grasped her hand, and slid his other arm around her, supporting much of her weight. Again, she was surprised at his flagrant show of affection. What kind of message did this send to the duke and duchess?

The duke had risen as she'd entered. His hair was a few shades darker than Luke's, but they were of a similar height and build. His eyes were green, though, while Luke's were blue.

His wife stood beside him, a demure woman an inch or two shorter than Emma, with a slender build, black hair, and pale skin. Her stomach showed the first signs of increasing with pregnancy. Her gray-blue eyes immediately struck Emma as kind, and even before she said a word, Emma knew she'd like the duchess.

"Emma, this is my brother, Trent, and his wife, Sarah." He held up her hand. "This...is Emma."

Well, that wasn't a particularly standard introduction. And to a duke, no less. Emma swallowed hard.

But both of them smiled at her. "Lovely to meet you," the duchess said. "But do you mind if I call you Emma?" She flashed a gently quelling look at Luke. "Lord Luke does enjoy being informal, but would you prefer a different name?"

"Oh, no," Emma said. "Emma is fine. Wonderful, in

fact. So few people call me Emma, but I'd be honored if you would, Your Grace."

The duchess made a noise low in her throat. "Then you must call me Sarah."

"Thank you," Emma said, pleased. She glanced at the duke. Amusement danced in his green eyes.

Amusement was far, far better than disapproval. Which she might have expected, given the way Luke still firmly held her hand and the way the duke kept glancing down at their entwined fingers. This was...completely improper.

According to some people, anyhow. Evidently the Hawkins family was rather relaxed when it came to matters of propriety.

"We heard you were back in Town," Sarah told Luke, "so we came right away."

Luke smiled at Sarah, then gave his brother a wary look. "Any luck in finding our mother's whereabouts?"

The duke shook his head. "No. What about you? I heard you had traveled north."

Luke raised one brow. "Now where did you hear that?"

The duke just shrugged. "I have my sources."

"Are you having me followed?" A slight edge of fury resonated in Luke's otherwise mild voice, and every muscle in Emma's body went tight.

The duke shrugged. "Not anymore. I called him off when you were in Bristol."

Emma could virtually feel the righteous anger rise in Luke. The temperature of the room seemed to rise by ten degrees in that instant. She squeezed his hand, hard.

"Why?" Luke pushed out.

Sarah stepped forward. "We wanted to be sure you were all right, my lord."

"Sarah, how many times have I asked you to stop calling me that?"

She frowned. "I don't know. Once? Forgive me, I forgot."

Luke took a deep breath. "You're my sister now. Did you forget that?"

"Sometimes..." She flushed a little. "Well, sometimes, yes, I do."

"Luke," he growled. "Just call me Luke."

"I'll try to remember." Sarah directed a soft, defusing smile at Luke, and Emma liked her even more.

The duke cleared his throat. "In any case, after he was in Bristol, I brought my investigator back to London. Where he found nothing. I'd hoped you were more successful."

"That scarred man. That was him, wasn't it?" Luke ground his teeth.

The duke just gave him a noncommittal shrug in response.

Luke slid Emma a frustrated glance. She gave him a nod of encouragement, and he blew out a slow breath, seeming to release all his tension. He gestured to the brown-and-white striped chairs arranged around a low table near the hearth.

"Sit down, Trent. This will require a few minutes."

The four of them sat on the scattered chairs, Luke helping Emma into hers like a true gentleman, then laying her cane aside. When they were all settled and Baldwin had entered with refreshments, Luke glanced at Emma. He raised a brow. "The story begins with you, Em, so perhaps you should tell it."

Emma bit her lip, then nodded.

And she told them everything. From her ill-fated court-ing by Henry Curtis, to her short-lived marriage and Henry's subsequent death. Her father's missing fortune, and her discovery of the connection between Colin Macmillan, Roger Morton, and her late husband.

She told them about how she'd heard Lord Lukas Hawkins had come to Bristol asking after a man named Roger Morton. Finally, she told them how she'd accosted Luke in a hotel in Bristol and had proposed to join him in his search for Morton in exchange for information that might lead to his whereabouts.

Luke took over the story from there. "We found Macmillan in Edinburgh."

Both the duke and duchess were poised on the edges of their seats, the tea that Baldwin had brought them for-gotten on the table. "And?" the duke asked. "What did he tell you?"

"His arrangement with Morton appeared to be one of an entirely legal nature. He'd loaned Morton money to go into a brewery venture with Emma's husband, but when Morton failed to pay the loan, Macmillan grew impatient. He threatened to seek legal reparations, at which point Morton—" Luke broke off and looked at Emma.

"Killed my husband," she finished softly. "He stole my father's fortune and used part of it to pay off Macmillan."

"We don't yet know what he did with the rest of the money," Luke added.

"But where is he now?" the duchess asked.

"Mr. Macmillan believes he's in London," Emma told her.

"His sister and her husband live in or near Soho," Luke told them. "So we thought Morton might live there as well. We went yesterday but didn't get very far. The problem is that he seems to possess no distinguishing characteristics."

"We're planning to attend holy services on Sunday. We're hoping his sister will attend," Emma added.

Sarah clasped her hands in her lap. "It sounds to me like you have made great strides toward finding the duchess." She gave an optimistic smile. "I think we'll know everything soon."

"I hope so," the duke said.

"So do I," Luke said. The two men's gazes locked for the briefest of seconds, then they both looked away. For the first time, Emma wondered how brothers showed affection. She and Jane were quite affectionate, but men were so different. From the subtle messages they gave with their expressions and words, it was clear to her that these two men cared for each other, but they were also uncomfortable with each other.

"Do you require my help on Sunday?" the duke asked.

"No!" Luke nearly roared it. Then he added in a softer voice, "No, Trent. Allow me to do this, will you?"

"Of course," the duke conceded. "But if you need any help—"

"I don't," Luke bit out.

The duke's lips firmed, and Emma saw a hint of Luke in that expression. They might only be half brothers, but they certainly *were* brothers.

The duke glanced at Sarah. "I'm required at parliament in an hour. I'll take you home to Esme—I know the two of you have plans for this afternoon." He turned his attention back to Luke. "Contact me if you learn anything."

Luke ground his teeth. "Yes, sir."

The duke rolled his eyes heavenward. "Stop being ridiculous. Come, love." He held out a hand to his wife and helped her rise from her chair.

She smiled sweetly at Emma, and Emma was struck by the oddness of it. Strangers in a carriage in the middle of Northumberland had gazed upon her as if she were the Whore of Babylon. This woman was a duchess, and she surely realized Emma was sleeping with her brother-in-law, but she offered her a genuine, heartfelt smile.

"I do hope we will have the occasion to see each other again soon," she said to Emma.

"So do I," Emma said softly. She meant it.

The duke was more reserved. "Luke," he said. Then he inclined his head toward Emma. "Mrs. Curtis."

He'd evidently gleaned her family name from her story. She wasn't surprised; he'd listened in rapt attention.

She curtsied. "Your Grace."

He wrapped his arm around his duchess, and, side by side, they left.

As soon as the door shut behind them, Emma released a breath she hadn't realized she'd been holding.

So that was the Duke of Trent and his duchess. She didn't know exactly what to think.

She'd liked them, she supposed. Mostly because they hadn't seemed to pass immediate judgment on her.

She glanced at Luke to find him studying her intently. "Well?" he asked.

She wasn't sure what he wanted from her, so she simply shrugged. "They seemed...nice."

His brows jumped toward his hairline. "Nice? Really? Is that all you have to say about them?"

She nodded, and he laughed. He took her hand, then

pulled her off the sofa and gathered her into a tight hug. "*Nice?* Now why do you think you using that word to describe my brother makes me so happy?"

She burrowed her body against him, reveling in his warmth. "Mmm...I don't know, Luke. Why does it make you happy?"

He nuzzled his nose into her tightly bound hair. "Half the women who meet Trent are besotted at first sight. I was worried you might be one of them."

"What? First of all, he's married—"

Luke pressed his hand over her mouth. "But there are certain things about you that I understand now, Emma. And one of them is this: *nice* is never a word you'd use to describe a man you're besotted with."

She mock-pushed him away. "What words *would* I use, then?"

"Hmm..." His blue eyes danced with mirth, then he bent down and licked the shell of her ear. "Demanding bastard, perhaps?"

A shudder ran through her—because that was just what she wanted. From Luke. This very instant. She gazed at him. "Back to bed?" she whispered.

"Oh, no." Luke's voice was so silky it made her nerve endings tingle under her skin. "We're going to finish what we started. And we're going to do it right here."

And after he'd stripped her, Luke made sweet, rough love to Emma on his drawing room floor.

Chapter Thirteen

❦

That night, Emma was dragged out of sleep by Luke coming out of a nightmare. She'd been so deep asleep, she lay there, half conscious, only partially aware of him leaving the bed.

Time passed. She might have fallen asleep again. Then she jerked awake, suddenly aware that he had not returned.

Her eyes opened, and she saw him on the other side of the room. Moonlight filtered in through the curtains, bathing his body in a silvery light.

She lay very still, but her eyes widened. He was shirtless, wearing only his drawers, which rested low on his hips. It was the first time she'd seen his torso. He always wore a shirt to bed, and when he'd changed his clothes on their travels, he'd always done so behind a screen or when she wasn't in the room.

His torso was a magnificent thing to behold. Pale and hairless save for the thin trail leading from his navel down into his drawers. Rippling with lean muscle. She'd asked him how he was so strong, given that he lived such a leisurely life, and he'd laughed and told her it was because he rode every day, oftentimes for several hours. Then he'd kissed her and said their bed sport didn't hurt matters, either.

He was washing himself. Water trickled as he squeezed a towel in the basin, then lifted it to wash his shoulder and underarm. He turned a little, and moonlight bathed his back.

Emma's breath caught in her throat.

His back was covered in sores. Some circular, some more oblong, like teardrops. There were more than ten, all about the size of Emma's thumbnail. A straight line of them marred the top of his back, starting below his left shoulder blade and continuing almost all the way across. There was another line of them down his spine.

No. Not sores. *Scars*, she realized as he turned more fully into the light. They were flat, darker in color than the pale tone of his skin, with a darker red rim around their circumferences.

What on earth had happened to him?

Now she knew why he never removed his shirt. His torso was beautiful, but the scars were blemishes that spoke of violence and pain.

After he finished bathing himself, Luke put his shirt back on and sat in one of the upholstered armchairs. He sat for a long time, perfectly still, his elbow on one of the arms of the chair and his forehead resting in his hand.

After a while, she couldn't bear it anymore. She slipped out of bed and pulled her light robe over her shoulders and limped over to him.

He looked up at her, his face darkening. "I woke you."

She put her hand on his shoulder. "Come back to bed?" she asked in a husky voice.

"Not sure I can sleep."

"Try?"

He looked unsure.

"I'm cold," she murmured. It wasn't a lie. She was starting to shiver. "Come warm me?"

It was manipulative, because she knew he wouldn't deny her this. But she wanted so badly to lie with him, to wrap him up in her embrace.

"Just for a little while?" she begged.

"Of course," he said softly.

They went back to the bed, and she twined her arms around Luke and peppered kisses to his chest over his shirt. He pressed his lips to her hair. "Sleep, Em," he said gruffly.

But she wouldn't sleep until he did. It took a long time, but finally, when she heard his breaths grow even and deep, she allowed herself to slip away into her own dreamless slumber.

* * *

On Friday, after they'd eaten a late supper, Luke told Emma he was going to his club. He hadn't been there in months and wanted to make an appearance. At least, that was what he told Emma. The truth was, he couldn't face sleeping with her, waking from one of the nightmares, then seeing the look of pity on her face.

He knew she didn't approve from the way her lips pursed and her gaze faltered before she smiled and said, "I'll see you later, then."

He was treating her despicably. He knew this. He hated himself for it.

But the next night—Saturday—he did it again. At Boodles he played vingt-et-un with a group of exceedingly dull men while he drank copious amounts of brandy.

He ended up losing ten guineas. It seemed a pittance compared to the risk of another nightmare.

He arrived home staggering drunk and fumbled his way into his bedchamber. She was asleep, her beautiful, thick hair fanned over her pillow. He lay beside her as carefully as he could since the world kept tilting under him. And then he gazed down at her.

Emma. He fingered one of her soft curls. She'd accepted him in a way that no one in his life ever had. In bed and out. She was so strong, but also sweetly submissive.

He dropped his heavy body on his own pillow, still gazing at her smooth skin, at the thick russet brows that swept in arcs over her eyes.

Something in his chest squeezed hard. He wanted to gather her close and hold her against him and never let her go.

* * *

On Sunday, Luke and Emma rose early to attend church services at St. Anne's church in Soho. They'd learned there was more than one church in Soho, and Emma had fretted over whether they should go to St. Patrick's, the Catholic church—after all, Macmillan had said the husband of Morton's sister was Irish.

But Luke thought that surely Macmillan would have mentioned that Morton was Catholic if it were the case. So it was to St. Anne's they went for early divine services at eight o'clock in the morning—an ungodly hour, as far as Luke was concerned.

St. Anne's was a plain rectangular brick building with tall, narrow windows. Its only distinguishing feature was the bell tower—a square structure that rose above the church and whose bell pealed as Emma and Luke entered the church.

They sat quietly in the back so they could have a better prospect of the congregation, which numbered about two hundred persons packed into the pews. The sermon was on the seventh commandment, and while the preacher droned on, Luke took careful stock of the parishioners.

There were two possibilities—two red-haired men accompanied by dark-haired women. One of the men sat in the third row, and it appeared as though the entire row was made up of his family—him, his dark-haired wife, and at least eight children. The other couple looked like just a man and his wife, sitting in the middle of the congregation across the aisle from Luke and Emma. The man was very large in stature and girth, and the woman was thin and of an average height.

"The body was not created for fornication; rather, it was made for the Lord," the preacher said. "Further, according to the words of St. Paul, 'To avoid fornication, every man should have his own wife and every woman her own husband, for it is better to marry than to burn.'"

Luke fidgeted. Obviously the reverend had decided to take this sermon a step further than the seventh commandment and the sin of adultery. Luke slid a glance at

Emma. She was sitting with her hands folded in her lap over her prayer book, looking utterly serene.

Just looking at her calmed him.

The reverend preached about casting away filthiness of the soul, and Luke cast his own eyes heavenward. Before he met Emma, he might have agreed with all this talk about filthiness and impurity and uncleanness, and how it was related to all the sins he'd committed.

But somehow, sitting beside her, in spite of all the debauched, lustful things they'd done, Luke felt purer than he ever had. He wondered what the reverend would think of how tying a woman to the bed and having his wicked way with her over and over again had somehow helped to cleanse Luke's soul.

With a last admonition to all the men in the congregation to find themselves a prudent wife who would prevent them from looking at other women with lust in their gazes—which was, evidently, just as sinful as the act of fornication itself—the preacher finally ended the sermon.

Luke let out a relieved breath. He glanced at Emma. She still sat there placidly, except now the corner of her lips wobbled as she fought a smile.

She looked down at her prayer book, turning it to a marked page. Then she glanced at him and gave in to the smile, and all was well in Luke's world.

When the service ended, Luke subtly indicated the couple he'd pinpointed earlier.

"Mmm, yes," Emma murmured. "I saw them, too."

They made their way to the front of the church—being in the last row they were among the first out—and waited for a few minutes. Finally, the redheaded man exited, his wife at his side.

Emma blew out a breath. "Ready?"

"Always." Luke narrowed his eyes on the couple. He wondered if they knew anything about their brother's nefarious deeds.

Soon enough, they'd find out.

They fell into step behind the man and woman as they wove through traffic to traverse Dean Street. Emma leaned on her cane, and he wanted badly to put his arm around her and support her weight, but if anyone who knew him saw them—well, it wouldn't end well, because he wouldn't tolerate talk about Emma around Town. So he kept a respectful distance from her and ground his teeth. God, he hoped she didn't reinjure her ankle.

When they were close to the couple, Emma called to them. "Excuse me."

They stopped and turned, curious expressions on their faces. Emma limped up to them, Luke on her heels. He was content to let her do most of the talking. She managed very well in these kinds of situations, he'd learned.

"I'm so sorry to bother you." Emma gave the woman a dazzling smile. "But are you Roger Morton's sister?"

The woman glanced at her husband, who shrugged. She turned back to Emma and said in a low, soft voice, "Yes, I am Veronica O'Bailey. This is my husband, Colm."

Emma clasped her prayer book to her chest, looking delighted. "Oh, that's wonderful. I saw you in church and had hoped to make your acquaintance, but I wasn't sure I'd catch up"—she gestured toward her foot—"due to this blasted twisted ankle."

The woman's brow furrowed. "Are you...acquainted with Roger?"

"Oh, yes. You see, he was a business associate of my husband's. I'm Emma Curtis. It is lovely to finally make your acquaintance."

Both the woman and the man gazed at Emma with utterly blank expressions upon their faces.

"Oh, I'm so sorry." She turned to Luke, motioned him forward. "This is Lord Lukas Hawkins."

Mrs. O'Bailey gave him an owlish blink, then curtsied. "It is an honor to meet you, my lord."

O'Bailey bowed over his excessive girth and echoed his wife. "Milord." His voice was deep, with a pronounced Irish flavor.

"Lord Lukas is also acquainted with Mr. Morton—through his mother, the Duchess of Trent."

Mrs. O'Bailey looked aghast. "Is that so?" she asked, her voice so breathy he could hardly understand her words. "You are a relation of the Duke of Trent, then, my lord?"

Luke fought not to roll his eyes. "Yes, madam," he said, proud of his patience. "He is my brother."

Her eyes widened, and she looked from Luke to Emma in awe. "Oh, my goodness," she murmured. "I'd no idea Roger possessed such esteemed acquaintances."

"We had heard he might be in London," Emma said. "We'd so like to see him. Would it be possible for you to direct us to his place of residence?"

Again, Mrs. O'Bailey glanced at her husband. Again, he shrugged. "He keeps an office and rooms in Wapping," Mrs. O'Bailey said. "We haven't seen him in a few months, though."

"Can you tell us where? We'd love to surprise him!"

"Of course." And she rattled off a location in Wapping High Street.

"Thank you so much," Emma gushed.

Luke bowed to Mrs. O'Bailey and her husband. "A pleasure to meet you."

"And you, my lord," Mrs. O'Bailey said, her brown eyes still a little wide with awe. "Such a pleasure." Her more reticent husband just bobbed his head.

Emma and Luke stood on the curb and watched them turn and walk a ways down Dean Street.

"They know nothing of their brother's illicit activities," Emma whispered.

"You're right. They're innocents, I believe. Nonetheless, I should follow them. Remain here and rest your ankle. I'll return as soon as I see where they've gone."

She nodded. Luke kept himself a good distance behind the couple, watched them turn down another street, then another. They finally disappeared into a very small brown-brick residence tucked between two far larger ones.

"All right," Luke murmured when he'd returned to Emma's side. "That should be easy to find again, should we need to."

As they walked back to where they could find a hackney, Emma asked, "Why would he keep rooms in Wapping? That's near the docks, isn't it?"

"Perhaps they're the same lodgings Macmillan told us about, and even though his fortunes have changed, he has chosen to continue residing there."

"But he can certainly afford much finer lodgings now."

Luke shrugged. "Perhaps he's hiding the money. Perhaps he prefers the thievery to the spending of his illgotten gains. Come, let's go."

The hackney they hired took them directly to Wapping

High Street. There, above one of the open warehouses, they found Roger Morton's office.

They only knew they were at the right location because the number 6 was painted in heavy black above the door just as Mrs. O'Bailey had described. They stood in a dim first-floor gallery, gazing at the door. Windows flanked the door, but they had been painted black as well.

Emma shuddered. "I wonder what kind of business he conducts in there."

Luke was sorely tempted to break in. After his knock was met with silence, he tried the door and the windows, but all of them were locked. Since it was Sunday morning, the warehouse was essentially abandoned. It would be so simple to punch a hole in one of the windowpanes and climb in.

Emma clearly read his thoughts in his expression, because she narrowed her eyes at him. "No. We'll wait."

"What if he doesn't return?"

She took a deep breath. "Well, he'll need to, eventually. We'll come back tomorrow, and if he hasn't arrived by then, we can ask the landlord about his habits."

Finished with their investigations for the day, Emma and Luke returned home in another hackney, then spent a leisurely afternoon together in the drawing room, Luke reading while Emma worked on her sewing. It was so *domestic*. Unnervingly so.

Something compelled him to put an end to that.

Luke set aside his newspaper. He went to Emma and took the needle and thread out of her hands, setting it aside. Then he stripped her bare and made love to her, laying her out over the drawing room's velvet sofa and taking her from behind, stroking his hands up and down her beautiful, flawless back as he pumped deeply and deliciously inside her.

* * *

Emma lay bent over the arm of the sofa, her breasts pressed against the velvet cushions. Luke's hands roamed over her back as he moved inside her, caressing the deepest, most intimate parts of her.

She had learned that her body loved this position—him entering her from behind like this. There was something utterly and decadently submissive about it. It was wicked and wonderful, and the angle of his penetration stroked her in a way that made her squirm and clench.

She moved her face to the side, pressing her cheek into the soft sofa cushion. Her fingers curled around the edge of the sofa as her body went taut. She came in a warm rush of pleasure, letting the sensation take over her until she sagged limply over the sofa. He bent down over her, whispering, "I love to watch you come. I love watching your body move helplessly beneath me. So beautiful."

His thrusts had decreased in speed, and now he slid languidly in and out of her hot, slick, and oh-so-sensitive channel. He set a slow, leisurely pace, rare for Luke, whose lovemaking was usually so powerful and intense.

He remained bent low over her, his shirt and chest pressed against her back, his lips grazing the back of her neck. Emma closed her eyes and sank into the sensation. Sweet, smooth heat. So deep.

She was building to that pinnacle again, but this time it was a slow, meandering journey, a gentle road toward that ultimate peak.

She lay on velvet with Luke over her, stroking her, teasing, coaxing her ever so expertly. She could feel all of him—his length and breadth inside her, his texture, his strength.

The orgasm came, starting with a low, rumbling pleasure deep in her womb and rolling through her entire body until she was overcome with pleasure.

Moments later, he came, too, releasing his seed on her lower back. Eventually, he lifted off her. She didn't have the wherewithal to move, so she just lay there draped over the side of the couch, completely spent. Moments later, she felt a cloth move gently over her back. When he finished cleaning her, he gathered her in his arms and took her to the sofa, where he helped her don her chemise. Then he tucked her against his body as they sat on the sofa.

They sat there for a long while, murmuring to each other about meaningless things. She cuddled up against his chest and wondered whether it would rain tomorrow when they went to Wapping. And Luke talked about buying Emma another cloak, since the silk had been torn on her old one. They spent several minutes guessing what the new cook would make for dinner.

The dinner, served in the dining room as it had been ever since the cook arrived, happened to be a white vermicelli soup followed by pork cutlets with red cabbage and stewed watercress, and a baked pear pudding for dessert.

It was simple but delicious. Baldwin had done an excellent job in hiring the cook. The maid he'd hired, Delaney, had worked out very well, too. She'd had experience as both a housemaid and a lady's maid—just what Luke had requested. The best part about both Delaney and the cook was that they both appeared to be exceptionally discreet, treating Emma with the utmost deference and politeness. She wondered what Baldwin had told them about her.

When Emma rose from the table, her belly pleasantly full, Luke rose with her. She headed upstairs to the drawing room, planning to continue her work on the new chemise she was sewing. Luke might have insisted on buying her new dresses, but she could certainly make her own chemise.

Tension settled over her as they walked up the stairs. Luke had left her for the past two nights only to return sotted in the early morning hours. Would he do it again? What would she do if he did?

At the door to the drawing room, he turned her gently to face him. "Emma, I'm going out."

She'd expected it. Still, it felt like he'd knocked all the wind out of her.

Of course he was "going out." That was the pattern, wasn't it?

She tried to force a smile. She struggled to find at least something decent to say. But she could do neither, so she just gave a jerky little nod.

"I'll be back. Later." He kissed her on the forehead, turned, and retreated back down the stairs they'd just mounted.

Damn it!

She stood there for long moments, hands clenched at her sides, unsure whether to fall to her knees and sob or to walk out the front door and never come back.

But she couldn't leave him. Not completely. The logical part of her told her that she had nowhere to go, that she still needed his help to find Morton. But to her soul she knew it was more than that. Luke had become too important, too much a part of her. She couldn't walk away.

She couldn't accept this, either. And that was exactly what she'd been doing so far: She'd never liked his drinking and his late nights, but she'd accepted them. She'd allowed Luke to run away because . . . Well, she didn't exactly know. Because he had nightmares. Because he had scars on his back. Because he'd been through something terrible and had convinced himself he couldn't face it without drowning himself in ale or whisky or brandy every night.

Because, at first, she'd felt like it was none of her business, none of her concern.

Now it was both her business and her concern. Perhaps it shouldn't be, but it was. She and Luke had shared too much for it not to be.

Emma spun around and went into the drawing room. She rang for Delaney. The two of them spent the remainder of the evening cleaning and preparing the front-facing bedchamber on the second floor.

* * *

Sometime in the early morning hours, Emma was awakened by a pounding on the door. "Emma? Em? Are you in there?"

As she came out of sleep, the first thing she recognized was that his words were slurred. It came as no surprise.

"Go to bed, Luke," she called groggily.

"Can't. Door's locked."

"Go to your own room. I assure you, *that* door is not locked."

A long moment passed. Silence. Then, "Em?"

"Hmm?"

"What are you doing?"

She sighed. "I'm sleeping here tonight. And every night henceforth that you choose drunkenness over staying at home."

"No." His voice was rough.

"Yes," she told him.

"Why?" he demanded.

"I can't do this anymore."

"Can't do what?"

She slipped her legs over the side of the bed, both her hands gripping the edge at her thighs. She took a deep breath, then looked bleakly at the locked door. She was fully awake now.

"I can't lie awake in a cold bed, wondering when you'll come home. I can't keep wondering why you run away from me every night. Wondering why I can't give you what you need. Wondering how drunk you'll be when you finally return."

"You do give me what I need."

No, she didn't. At least she hadn't so far.

"Let me in." His voice was soft, cajoling.

She closed her eyes. Didn't say a word.

"Please."

She gripped the edge of the bed tighter. It was difficult for her to deny this man anything. But if she was going to survive, she needed to deny him this. This was too important. She needed to be strong. If she didn't do whatever was in her power to stop this, Luke would continue down this path of self-destruction. She couldn't bear to see him destroy himself.

"Emma, let me in."

"No," she said, her voice firm.

"Why?"

"I already told you why."

"I need you."

"As much as you need to drink?"

"More. A thousand times more." His voice sounded broken, and she closed her eyes. "Open the door."

"No," she pushed out.

"I need to lie beside you."

"You survived without me for twenty-eight years, Luke. I'm sure your sleep will be perfectly adequate alone in your bed tonight."

"Survived without you? If that's what you call survival," he said gruffly. Then, in a whisper, he repeated, "I need you."

She closed her eyes, fisting her hands in the blankets. "You're drunk."

"Just a little," he admitted.

"You have to know I won't sit by and watch you destroy yourself."

"It might be too late."

I know. She blinked hard and looked down at her lap.

He was silent for a long moment. Then he said, "So you'll deprive me of my only comfort?"

"Oh, I am clearly not your only comfort, Luke." Her tone was far more bitter than she'd intended it to be.

"But you are...you have become...something...

my..." He seemed to be struggling with the words. Not surprising, given how drunk he was.

"You're more important to me. Than anything," he finished clumsily.

If he'd said that to her sober, she might believe it. Now she knew he just wanted in the room and was trying every tactic he could think of to wheedle her into unlocking the door. Still, she slipped out of bed and walked to the door and leaned against it.

"If that's true, then you need to stop this," she said through the wood that stood between them. "You need to stop running away."

"I will," he said, too quickly. Then, "May I come in?"

"No." Her voice was soft.

"I'm not leaving until you let me in."

"Then you might wish to get comfortable." Because she knew, now more than ever, that she *couldn't* let him in. Just telling him he needed to stop wasn't enough. Him promising to stop wasn't enough. He needed to show that he could—that he would try.

She heard a pained sigh, then fumbling as he sat on the floor on the other side of the door. "Very well," he said. "I will remain here all night. A guard posted at his lady's door."

She sank down, too, leaning her back against the door and crossing her legs on the carpet.

"Why do you do it?" she whispered. When he was silent, she wasn't sure if he'd heard her.

Finally, he spoke, his voice gruff. "Drink?"

"Yes."

"Ah." There was a soft *thunk*, as if the back of his head had banged against the door. "It makes me stronger."

She bristled at this, but she ground her teeth, refusing to show her frustration at that nonsense. Instead, she asked, "How?"

After a moment of silence that seemed to ring in Emma's ears, he said, "Keeps the nightmares away."

"How does that make you stronger? You can't help having nightmares. Nightmares don't make you weak."

"Mine do. Sometimes I think...I think they're... they're doing something to me...driving me mad."

"How?"

"Em," he groaned. She imagined the pained frustration on his face. She'd seen it before.

A part of her wanted to soothe him, to reassure him and say he didn't have to tell her this. But he did have to tell her. She needed to know. How could she help him if she didn't know? How could he help himself?

"How, Luke?" she pressed.

"When I wake up, the...the *panic*. It doesn't go away like it ought. Sometimes hours pass before I convince myself that he's not after me..." His voice was choked. Every word that he said twisted her heart. "That he's not going to kill me."

"Who?" she asked.

"My father. No," he corrected quickly, voice strained, "not my father. The old Duke of Trent. The man I thought was my father. And even though I know he's dead, my mind convinces me that he isn't. That he's coming after me and that this time he's going to kill me."

"And you can't wake?"

"I am awake, though. But I can't...I can't...make him go."

Good God. Every part of her wanted to open the door

to him. To hold him. Tell him it would be all right, that she was there, that she would be there whenever he woke. That she'd help him.

She couldn't do that, though. He needed to understand, no matter what, that he couldn't continue down this path.

"Why do you have nightmares about him?" she asked softly.

Silence.

"He was cruel to you, wasn't he?"

"He gave me what I deserved."

"I doubt that."

"That's what he said." Luke sounded so alone. So vulnerable and small. He never sounded like this. "He said I needed to be punished. He said it was the only hope to cure me."

"Cure you of what?"

"My inherently evil nature."

"And you believed him?"

"I was a boy."

"But you still believe him, don't you?"

Luke gave a humorless laugh. "I haven't exactly been a model of goodness."

"Yes, you have."

"You don't know me very well."

"You're wrong about that." She knew very well the goodness that lay beneath the irreverent mask of the rogue he showed to the world.

"Maybe," he said softly.

"The old duke turned his anger at your mother and Lord Stanley upon you."

Silence for a long moment. Then, "I never thought of it like that."

"How did you think of it, then?"

"He knew I was a bastard and therefore evil. He also knew that I was second in line to the dukedom. He truly intended to cure me, in the unwelcome event I held his title one day."

But Emma was stuck on the first part of what he'd said. "You were a bastard and therefore evil? What are you talking about?"

"For God's sake. You know."

"No, I don't. Please explain."

"Haven't you gone to church? Haven't you read the doctrines? It is common knowledge that bastards are evil because they inherit the evil nature of their sinful parents."

"That's rubbish," she snapped. "All children are born innocent."

"No. I was born of evil and I became evil. Just like the old duke predicted."

"Rubbish!" she repeated, her voice shaking with certainty.

He was silent for a minute. Then he said, "You are a very opinionated woman."

"Only when I know I'm right."

"Are you right, Em?"

"Yes." She was so angry red tinged the edges of her vision. She would find her gun and shoot the old Duke of Trent if he weren't already dead. How dare that man try to beat the evil out of an innocent child? And she had no doubt that he was also the one who'd made those marks on Luke's back.

Luke had spent his whole life believing he could never be good, could never be saved. How was a person supposed to survive that? How could a person who believed such a thing ever be happy?

"He should never, ever have done that, Luke. You were a *child*."

"I was never a very good child. I never followed orders. I couldn't sit still like my brothers could. I picked fights. It only grew worse as I went into adolescence. I stole kisses from girls behind barns. I gambled away my allowance. I was hateful to my brothers and sister."

"Some of that was certainly a result of your father's cruelty. I know you well enough to know that they are not inherent traits within you."

"Are you sure?" He sounded so hesitant. Uncertain. *Hopeful*.

"I've never been more certain of anything," she said in a near whisper.

He was quiet for a while, perhaps mulling it over. Then, "Emma, can I come in?"

She closed her eyes tight so the tears wouldn't leak out. Because it was physically painful to say it this time. "No."

Chapter Fourteen

The next morning, Emma woke early. She hadn't had enough sleep—it had been almost dawn by the time Luke had convinced her to go to bed.

The first thing she did was slip out of bed and hurry to the door. Her ankle felt better this morning. Almost as good as new.

She unlocked and opened the door to find Luke curled on the floor fully dressed. She dropped to her knees beside him. "Luke?"

He blinked groggily at her, disoriented. She touched her fingers to his cheek. "Come to bed for a while?"

He gazed at her for a long moment, his expression unreadable. Then he said, in a scratchy voice, "Yes."

He rose to his feet on unsteady legs, reminding her of a newborn colt.

She took his arm and led him to the bed. She helped

him undress down to his shirt and tucked him into bed. Then she leaned down and kissed him on the forehead as if she were kissing a child.

"Sleep," she murmured.

He grasped her wrist. "You're not coming back to bed?"

"No."

He frowned, but she gazed steadily at him, and he released her wrist. She grabbed her robe and, wrapping it over her shoulders, left the room, closing the door quietly behind her.

She went downstairs to the drawing room and sat in one of the chairs with her legs drawn up under her chin. She sat there for a very long time, thinking about Luke, about what they'd discussed last night. About her new understanding of him.

Had she been too harsh? He'd opened up and told her everything—well, everything except the details about the scars on his back—and she'd brutally refused him.

Yet, a part of her knew that if she coddled him, he'd have no reason to stop his current behaviors. She hoped that part was right. At one point last night, when he'd continued to beg her to let him in and she'd refused, she'd wondered if she was hurting him irrevocably. If she was being as bad as the man he'd thought was his father.

No...never that bad, she thought bitterly. After last night, she knew she'd never hated anyone—not even Roger Morton—like she hated the late Duke of Trent.

She sat there for a good hour, mulling over things, and then with a sigh, she went into Luke's bedchamber and dressed. She called on Delaney to help her with her hair. Luke still wasn't awake after that, so she fetched her sewing basket and went back into the drawing room to work on her chemise.

It was almost noon when Luke appeared, fully dressed, in the door of the drawing room. Emma had been sitting in silence for hours, lost in her thoughts as she stitched away, and the sound of him at the door made her gasp.

"Did I startle you?"

"Yes. It has been so quiet."

He gazed at her for a long moment. Then he came over to the sofa where she sat. He tilted her chin up, then bent down to kiss her on the lips. "Are you ready to return to Wapping?"

So that was how it was to be. They weren't going to discuss last night. A part of her was relieved. Another part was confused. She studied him carefully, wondering if he even remembered all that had been said. If so, he showed no sign of it.

"Have you eaten?" she asked.

A shadow crossed over his expression. Then it cleared and he said, "I'm not hungry." His voice was quiet and emotionless.

She released a slow breath as she set her sewing aside. Perhaps he did remember, after all.

"I'm ready. I'll just fetch my cloak."

* * *

Morton's office and residence in Wapping was about five miles away from Luke's house in Cavendish Square. As Luke sat beside Emma in the carriage—a hired hackney—he considered investing in a carriage. He'd never owned a carriage of his own. He'd never needed to. He always kept a horse or two, and he'd simply ridden everywhere.

But now Emma was with him. She shouldn't be traipsing about in London in dirty hired conveyances. She should have her own coach with a driver.

He glanced at her from the corner of his eye.

Caught.

She saw him glance at her and turned to him fully, giving him a soft smile.

Something clenched in his stomach. Was that sympathy in her eyes? He didn't want her sympathy.

Why had he said so much last night? He'd been so desperate to hold her, to have her open that damned door. He'd tried everything save fury—how could he be furious with Emma? She had every right to lock him out. He'd behaved like a weakling and an idiot.

But he'd told her some of his deepest secrets—all those things that showed him in the worst possible light. He didn't want her thinking of him as some weak, browbeaten simpleton.

He much preferred the looks of innocent awe that she gave him when he made love to her. Or the look on her face when she cried out in pleasure. Or that sleepy, sated, trusting look she gave him after they'd both reached orgasm.

He adjusted himself in his seat. Probably not a wise idea to think of how she looked at him after she came. He'd want to take her right here on the carriage seat, and given that Wapping was only a mile or so away, that probably wasn't the wisest idea.

Instead, he'd think of last night. That was about as effective as a bucket of cold water thrown directly over his cock.

He was a bloody fool.

Emma put her hand over his and squeezed. He took a breath, then squeezed back.

A few minutes later, they arrived at the warehouse in Wapping. The area was far busier during the noon hour on Monday. The streets were crowded with Londoners going about their business. Sailors, merchants, traders, men of business, messengers, servants—they all mingled on the street, intent on going wherever it was they needed to be.

Luke helped Emma out of the carriage. She didn't have her cane, but she was hardly limping today. "How is your ankle?" he asked her as they headed toward the warehouse.

"Very nearly healed, I think," she told him. "I hardly feel it anymore."

Men glanced at Emma as she walked by. He knew why, of course. She was beautiful. Her lovely curves would make any man think carnal thoughts. And her face—that heart shape with those big golden-brown eyes and a mouth shaped for sin...

He wanted to lock her away from all those admiring eyes. All those lascivious thoughts.

But what was he doing having proprietary feelings for Emma Curtis? What the devil was he thinking?

Where was this going?

It had already gone so far. Too damn far. And yet he couldn't stop it. He didn't want to. He wanted to see whatever this was played out to its ultimate conclusion. And he hoped to hell it wouldn't be to see her return to Bristol to be with her father and sister.

They entered the warehouse, passing all the workers carrying crates and heading to the utilitarian stairs on one side. They ascended the two flights and exited on the second-floor gallery.

Halfway down the gallery, they hesitated at Morton's door. It was as dark and still as it had been yesterday. Luke knocked. No answer. He ground his teeth.

Hell…if Morton was planning another scheme like he had with Emma, it was possible he wouldn't return to London for months.

Emma released a frustrated breath. "Let's talk to the landlord."

He nodded tightly. They descended the stairs and were told the man in question's name was Merrow and he could be found on the ground floor in one of the larger offices.

This was one occasion in which Luke knew it would be better for him to do the talking. Emma seemed to realize that, because she hung back as he approached the man, a plump, balding fellow who looked to be in his late forties.

. Merrow was taciturn until Luke told him his name, and then the floodgates opened.

"Oh, yes, Roger Morton lets number six upstairs," he told them.

"Does he live there all the time?"

"No, he isn't always in residence; however, he does appear to spend two or three nights a week in residence. And he oft conducts business from his office."

"Has he been here recently?" Luke asked him.

"He was here last week sometime—I'm sure I saw him about."

"Will you let us see his rooms?"

At that, Merrow grew squeamish. "Sorry, sir. I can't let you in. Not unless you are in possession of a warrant to search the premises."

Luke blew out a breath. "Very well. We should like to hire a boy to notify us when Morton returns to the building."

"That sounds reasonable," Merrow said.

They arranged for Merrow to take care of hiring the boy, as he informed them that he had several boys he used as messengers and one of them would surely suit.

"Good," Luke said. "We will await your message."

As they left Merrow's office, Luke saw a man lounging against the wall in the corridor. He stopped dead, studying the man, who'd turned away from him, but not before he caught a glimpse of the scar that ran down his cheek.

And he knew exactly who this man was. He thought he'd seen him in Bristol from afar, the morning of the day he'd met Emma. He'd definitely seen him at Ironwood Park, entering his brother's study last summer.

"Trent," Luke growled, fury rising so fast he could hardly breathe through it.

Emma glanced at him in surprise. "Stay here," he snapped at her, then he stalked over to the man. He grabbed his collar and pushed him, hard, against the wall. Emma gasped behind him.

The man's face broke into a scowl, and he tried to shove Luke off him.

"My brother sent you," Luke said. It wasn't a question.

"Unhand me, if you please, my lord."

Of course, the bastard knew exactly who Luke was. He let go of his collar but kept his face close to the man's. "What's your name?"

"Grindlow," the man said, red-faced. His hands went to his collar, straightening his stock.

"Why are you following me?" Luke asked, even though he knew the answer.

"On the orders of the duke, sir."

Luke cursed under his breath. He'd asked Trent not to become involved, and still he'd sent his man to watch Luke's every move. His brother didn't trust him to do anything correctly.

For a moment, Luke was too furious to speak. Then he clenched his teeth and said, "Stay away from me, Grindlow. Tell my brother I know what he's about. Tell him I caught you red-handed. Tell him to stay out of my life."

Grindlow frowned. "Er, very well, sir. I will tell him."

Luke gave him a tight nod and backed up a step. Then he turned and went back to Emma. "Let's get out of here," he said under his breath, taking her hand in his.

Holding her hand was immediately comforting. The tight knot of rage in his chest loosened. And though he directed the hackney driver to take him to Trent House so he could storm in and rail at his brother, halfway there, he changed his mind, deciding that it would be much more fulfilling to go home and take Emma to bed instead.

* * *

That night, Luke felt that pull trying to take him out of the house. It was so damn powerful. Like a steel cord yanking at his chest and toward his club. Or any damned place that would serve him a drink.

After dinner, he looked up at Emma.

Seeing the expression on his face, she murmured, "Stay with me, Luke."

How could he? He knew what would happen.

"Em," he said softly, "the drunken version of me is so much better than the nightmare version."

"The best part of you is the real you. Not the you that has been dulled and subdued by drink."

He closed his eyes, resigning himself to whatever might happen. Then he looked back up at her. "I'll try."

She gave him that warm, wide smile he adored, and he felt a little better.

Later that night, he awoke with a jolt. He heard the hiss of burning skin. The stench of charring flesh was thick in his nose. It was a smell he'd never forget. A smell he hated. He twisted, trying to escape, moaning with fear and pain.

"Luke. Luke!"

No, no, not again. Not two in one night. The first one still burned like a hot poker was jabbing into his back.

Something brushed against his back. His body jerked away violently, his arm reaching up in pure instinctual self-defense, smacking into flesh.

He heard a feminine gasp and realized someone else was in the room with them. Someone was seeing what was happening to him. Shame coursed through him. He curled up in a ball, wanting to hide, not wanting anyone to see him like this.

"Luke, shhh. It's all right."

He vaguely recognized the voice. He knew it. But he didn't want to listen, because, no, it wasn't all right. Nothing was all right. "Go away," he muttered, sounding petulant.

"I'm not going anywhere," she said firmly.

And it hit him. *Emma.*

What was she doing here?

And then he realized he was in his own room at his house in Cavendish Square. He was a grown man, and Emma was lying beside him.

But he still smelled the charred flesh. He still heard the sizzling noise. He still *felt* it, and damn it, it hurt.

"Luke! Wake up!"

He blinked, and Emma came into focus as she leaned over to turn up the lamp. Her beautiful hair framed her face in loose, tousled curls. He'd taken her braid out last night when he'd made love to her.

But why was she here?

And...oh, God. Her cheek was turning pink in stripes—the shapes of fingers. His fingers. He'd hit her, thinking she was his father and that she was after him with the cigar. God, no. His airway constricted. His chest felt like a horse stood upon it. His heart was beating too fast. He had to go.

Choking, shaking, he tumbled out of bed. He found his trousers and jerked them on. She was talking, saying something, but he couldn't hear over the roar in his ears. He'd hurt her. He'd struck Emma. His angel.

He'd known he wouldn't be able to do this. What had he been thinking? *God. God. God.* It was half prayer, half curse.

Her arms went around him, holding him tight. And finally, he could hear her. "No! I'm not letting you go."

He froze, because he was afraid he'd hurt her. He stood like a statue, except for the deep-rooted shaking he couldn't seem to contain.

She was behind him, her arms wrapped around his torso. She pressed her cheek against his back, and he shuddered, because his burns hurt when she did that.

No. No, damn it, they didn't hurt. That had happened long ago. They didn't hurt anymore. His mind was trying to fool him, taking a memory of something that had happened long ago and turning it into something real.

He took a deep, shaky breath. The pain receded a little. He closed his eyes and breathed, again and again, telling himself it wasn't real.

Emma stroked his chest, whispered against his back, but he was too focused on trying to twist his mind back into the present to hear her words.

They stood there for several minutes. Slowly, Luke's breathing and pulse returned to normal, and he returned to himself. When he felt like he had control over his mind and body once more, he dropped his hands, which had been frozen on the buttons of his falls.

It took another several minutes before he gently pried Emma's hands off him. Then he turned to look at her.

She gazed up at him, relief burning bright in her eyes. "Are you...are you all right?"

The red outlines of his fingers showed on her cheek. Something in his chest clenched hard, and he closed his eyes in a long blink.

Slowly, he reached up, skimming his fingers over her face. "I...hurt you."

"It's nothing."

"I hit you."

"You were dreaming, Luke. You were dreaming of something awful, and you thought I was going to hurt you. I shouldn't have touched you."

"*I* shouldn't have touched *you*."

She looked up at him, cupping his face in her palms. "Listen to me. It is nothing. I can't even feel it." Her expression softened. "But are you all right? You're cold."

Belatedly, he realized he'd begun to shiver.

"Come back to bed," she coaxed.

He stepped out of her hands and wrenched his gaze to the bed.

"You're staring at it like it's going to bite," she murmured. "It's just a bed, Luke. It'll be all right. Come, let me warm you. Let me hold you."

She was right. The damn bed was not going to bite him. Still, his steps were hesitant as he forced his legs to move him to the bed. She undid the one button he'd buttoned on his falls, then sat him down on the bed's edge and pulled off his trousers the rest of the way. "Lie down," she commanded.

He blew out a breath and looked at her askance. But she just stared at him. So he laid his body onto the bed. She tucked the covers up around him, then went to the other side of the bed and slid in beside him. He turned to hold her as she nestled against his body.

He pressed his face in her mussed hair and took a deep breath in. She smelled so good.

"I don't want to hurt you," he said gruffly. "I can tolerate most of the stupid, boorish things I do...but I draw the line at hurting you...or any woman."

"I know," she said simply. "But you cannot—you mustn't—blame yourself for what happened. You weren't yourself."

He sighed, feeling marginally better. He knew he

wouldn't have done it on purpose. But the fact he'd done it at all was another burn on his soul.

"You were afraid of something," she continued in a whisper. "Was it *him*?"

He closed his eyes. "Yes."

"I hate him," she said with soft vehemence. "I hate him so much."

"He's dead, Em."

"Yes, but not in your heart."

He didn't answer her.

"Have you had these nightmares all your life?" she asked a moment later.

"No. When I was a child, after he died. Then not until recently."

"When did they start again?"

He knew the exact date. How could he not? "Last summer. It was the day I learned he wasn't my real father." Somehow, the revelation had opened all the gates of his mind, releasing those past painful memories, allowing them to flood back.

Emma pressed herself more tightly against him. "Can you sleep?"

"I don't know," he said honestly. Usually he didn't bother to try after a nightmare woke him. But last week he'd fallen asleep holding her after she'd come to him in his armchair. Maybe he could do it again.

"Try," she murmured.

"I'm sorry," he said.

"It's not your fault."

He tried his damnedest to believe her. Yet a part of him rebelled, told him it was all his fault, that everything was his fault. That he should leave her before it was too late to save her, because the duke was right—he was inherently evil.

Eventually, he thrust that voice aside. She'd told him it wasn't his fault, and to his knowledge, Emma had never lied to him.

With that truth soothing him, he fell back to sleep.

* * *

Morton didn't return to his rooms in Wapping until a week later, when a messenger came to Luke's house saying he'd seen Morton arrive just before noon. He was in his office, the boy said, working.

Luke and Emma locked eyes. Today was the day. Luke would learn what had happened to his mother. Emma would learn what had happened to her father's money.

This might get complicated, Luke knew. He might have contemplated going to Trent or his brother Sam, but after that scene with Grindlow, Luke was determined to manage this on his own. While Emma was upstairs fetching her cloak, Luke went into his study and readied his pistol.

He didn't intend to use it, of course. To kill Morton would be to bury whatever secrets the man kept. But it might prove to be a useful tool of intimidation.

The hackney ride was tense, both Luke and Emma hardly speaking. It was a forty-minute drive in good traffic conditions, but at this hour on a Tuesday, it took over an hour.

By the time they arrived, Luke saw that a tiny bead of sweat had appeared on Emma's forehead, though it was frosty outside. Gently, he brushed it off, then gave her a reassuring smile.

He needed to succeed today. For Emma. If he was able to reestablish her father's fortune, perhaps it would make up for some of the hell he'd put her through. Perhaps it would prove to her—and to himself—that he was worthy of her.

He almost laughed at himself for having that thought. He couldn't comprehend ever thinking of himself as worthy of Emma.

They went upstairs, Luke helping to bear some of Emma's weight even though she said her ankle was almost completely healed. And then they hesitated at the closed door. He took a breath, looked at her.

"Ready?"

"As I'll ever be," she murmured.

He rapped on the door. Silence. He knocked again, this time harder, and heard a muffled, "Just a moment."

Standing beside Emma, he waited. Finally, the door opened.

Emma gasped, the sound drawing the gaze of the man who was standing there. Roger Morton was dark-haired and dark-eyed and of average height, just as he'd been described by various people to Luke. He was wearing a white shirt and a simple black waistcoat with black cloth buttons.

He saw Emma. His eyes widened. The blood drained from his face.

"Emma?" Morton choked out. He blinked rapidly. His eyes flickered to and fro, as if he was looking for an escape route.

How did Morton know Emma? Luke glanced at her, but she seemed frozen, as still and cold as an ice statue.

"Bloody hell," Morton muttered. Then he thrust forward, out the door, pushing between Luke and Emma and then sprinting down the corridor.

Luke turned to race after him, Emma on his heels, bellowing, "Stop! Come back!"

Then he heard her cry out in pain. He glanced over his shoulder and saw that she had fallen. Saw that tears streamed down her face. He rushed back to her.

"No, no!" she cried. "Go after him, Luke. Stop him!"

Luke hesitated for a moment. But she kept shouting at him to go, so he did. He spun around and ran down the stairs where Morton had disappeared seconds ago.

On the ground floor, he saw Morton exiting the warehouse, the white of his sleeves stark among all the pedestrians in their dark coats. Luke raced after him, bursting out into the chill of the street seconds later.

There, he came to a grinding halt. The street was crowded with both pedestrians and vehicles. Luke turned slowly, looking first up the street, then across the street and down it.

He saw no men wearing just a waistcoat. It was too crowded. Morton had melted into the crowd.

Luke clenched his fists. "Damn it," he cursed, causing a passing older woman to look at him askance.

His steps heavy, he returned upstairs. He hadn't expected Morton to run like that. Hell, the man was guiltier than he'd thought.

Why had he recognized Emma? Emma didn't know him. Perhaps Curtis had pointed her out to Morton without Emma knowing.

He hurried toward her. She was standing upright but balancing precariously on one foot, and he knew she'd reinjured her ankle. Damn it again. This had really not gone how he'd intended.

"You...didn't...catch...him?" It seemed like each of her words was emitted with a gasp of pain.

"No."

She blanched, gazed off in the direction where Morton had run.

"It's all right. Morton will need to return here eventually. Next time we'll be more prepared. How's your ankle?" he asked as he approached her.

She stared at him, seemingly not understanding what he'd said.

"Are you in pain?" he asked, suddenly very concerned.

"L-Luke..."

"Lean on me," he murmured, sliding his arm around her. She was stiff as a board.

"Y-you don't understand," she whispered.

All his senses went on high alert. Her tone was...odd. "What is it?"

"Luke," she breathed. "That wasn't Roger Morton. That was Henry Curtis. My...husband."

Chapter Fifteen

Emma allowed Luke to carry her. She sat in the hackney on the ride home unspeaking, unfeeling, stiff as an automaton.

She was completely numb.

When they reached Luke's house, he lifted her out of the carriage and held her against him. Baldwin opened the door, impassive as ever.

"Mrs. Curtis has reinjured her ankle," Luke snapped at him. "Summon a doctor right away."

That was completely unnecessary, but she couldn't even bring herself to tell him that.

Henry...Henry was alive. Despite believing he'd had a hand in the loss of her father's fortune, she'd mourned him for a year. But he'd never been dead. She'd despised Roger Morton for murdering her husband, but Henry had been alive all along.

Unless there had never been a Henry at all. Or there

had never been a Roger Morton. Could they be one and the same?

In any case, she wasn't a widow. Her husband hadn't died. She remembered the sermon at St. Anne's two Sundays ago on the seventh commandment. She'd been living in sin with Luke, but now that sin was much more poignant.

Adulterer.

Luke carried her upstairs and laid her on the bed. He took off his coat—the pockets of which she knew contained papers taken from Morton's—*Henry's*—office. The door had still been open, and Luke had done a quick search of the place before they'd left, finding a small satchel that contained soiled men's clothing and the sheaf of papers.

After depositing his coat over the back of one of the armchairs, Luke returned to her. He untied the string of her cape, gently slid it from under her, and set it aside.

He didn't speak, and for that she was glad. She couldn't talk—not to him or to anyone right now.

He went to work on her boot, gently removing it and then rolling down her stocking and taking it off. She watched him numbly.

Setting her stocking aside, he looked up at her. "Is it very painful?"

She shook her head.

"Good." He went to sit on the edge of the bed closer to her. "That was your husband?" he asked softly.

She opened her mouth to speak. No words would emerge. She nodded.

Luke's chest rose and fell. He was silent, perhaps having similar thoughts to hers. Finally he said, "They never found Curtis's body, then?"

She shook her head. They had dragged the Avon downriver of where Henry had last been seen, to no avail. That was common, the authorities had told her. By then, the body could have traveled all the way to the Bristol Channel.

"God, Em." His voice was low. Heavy with the enormity of this revelation. "He counterfeited his own death so he could steal your father's money."

And never have to see her again. Never again be forced to play at the false marriage she had so naïvely thrown herself into.

Suddenly, she felt so heavy. Heavy enough to sink deep into this bed, so deep she'd never have the fortitude to climb out.

"He truly must have despised me," she said, her voice raspy. "And...and he's my husband. *Till death us do part*...It was all a lie. He lied to me from the beginning. Even his death was a lie. I mourned him. What...what kind of man does that to a person?" She blinked hard, staving off the tears that pressed behind her eyes.

Luke shook his head as if he, too, couldn't fathom it. "A very sick bastard," he said softly.

She dissolved. It came suddenly, her tight muscles melting, her chest loosening and setting her pent-up emotions free. And she bent her head. Tears crested her bottom lids and rolled down her face, and she began to sob in great heaving gulps.

She cried for her lost innocence. Because she'd been a stupid, naïve fool. Because, thanks to her, Jane had not been able to have her second Season in London. Because her father and Jane had collected the last scrapings of their money to buy her a half-mourning dress that now held no meaning whatsoever. She cried for all the loss she'd put her family through since she'd met Henry Curtis.

And she cried for Luke. For the loss of his mother, the only person who'd tried to understand him. She cried for the demons he struggled with every day. She cried for his lack of belief in himself.

She loved him so much. So much more than she'd ever loved the man who was her husband.

He gathered her against him and rocked her, murmuring soothing, comforting things into her hair.

Had Henry ever been so loving? So kind? *No. Never.*

That horrid truth just made her cry harder.

She didn't know how long it lasted, but eventually the well of tears ran dry. She had nothing left. So she just lay, still and limp, while Luke held her and dried her eyes and wiped her nose.

"It's getting late," he murmured.

She blinked, glanced around the room, realizing for the first time that dusk had fallen and the room was growing dark. She'd cried for hours, and he hadn't left her side for one second.

And suddenly she was embarrassed. Heat suffused her cheeks, and she scrambled to a seated position, wincing at the pain that shot through her ankle. "I'm sorry," she murmured.

"Shhh," he said. He pushed a lock of hair that had fallen from its pin behind her ear. "There's nothing to be sorry about. Are you hungry?"

She wanted to say no—how could she manage food? Her stomach felt like a brick had taken up residence inside it. But she was sure Luke must be hungry, so she gave him a faint nod.

"All right. And the doctor is here—"

"Oh no!" she gasped, then cringed. God knew how long he'd been waiting for her to finish falling apart. "When did he arrive?"

Luke shrugged. "Doesn't matter."

She was appalled. "Why didn't you tell me?"

"We were otherwise occupied, Em," he said softly. "Come. We'll see him now."

He carried her to the drawing room where the doctor awaited them. Pronouncing her ankle resprained, he wrapped it and commanded her to keep it level with her body at all times for the next three days. No walking at all for three days, and when she did walk after that, she must use her cane at all times for at least a month. And no traipsing up and down stairs during that entire time.

"Can one of your men carry her?" the doctor had asked Luke. "Because if not, I suggest you make arrangements for her to remain downstairs for the month."

"I'll carry her," Luke said mildly.

When the doctor left, dinner was served in the dining room. It was a quiet affair, and Emma moved around the food on her plate, managing only a few tiny bites. Luke noticed—she saw him glance at her plate multiple times—but he didn't comment. She was thankful for that.

After dinner, they went to the drawing room. He made no mention of leaving her to go out. But as the hour drew nearer to go to bed, her anxiety increased.

Finally, she looked up at him. He was reading a book on horticulture. When he'd first started reading it yesterday, she'd found it so endearing that she'd teased him about it. He'd given her an arch look. "I happen to be quite fond of horticulture," he'd said, and she'd laughed.

Now she swallowed hard. "Luke?"

He glanced up from the book. "Hmm?"

"You know...I can't...sleep in your bed tonight, don't you?"

He stared at her. Then he closed the book and very slowly set it aside. "Do you plan to return to your husband? Do you plan to resume marital relations with him?"

The thought made her stomach lurch. "No."

"Then you can sleep with me tonight."

"No. I can't. I really can't." She'd made a vow to Henry Curtis. Even having some idea of what he was, she couldn't bring herself to willfully break it. She looked down at her lap where her hands were twisting together. "I'm sorry."

"Is this it, then?" he whispered.

"What do you mean?"

"Are we finished, Emma?"

She opened her mouth to say yes, but the word wouldn't come out. She looked back down at her lap. "Don't make me answer that."

He released a harsh breath.

"Please...give me time. I just found out that I'm still a married woman. That I've been..." Her voice trailed off.

"I don't want to give you time," Luke said darkly. "I want to take you to bed and make love to you for so long and so hard that you forget all this and realize that you're mine. That you've been mine ever since that first night in Bristol."

She closed her eyes. Because a very, very large part of her wanted that, too. But...she couldn't. She shook her head.

"Stubborn woman," he murmured. "Very well. I'll give

you time, because I know you're confused right now. But I'm not a patient man. And if I see that you're suffering, it's going to be very difficult for me to stay away."

She gave him a wavery smile.

She loved this man *so much*. Why had she only realized it now?

Now... when she couldn't even tell him.

He sighed. "I've something to tell you. I'd hoped we'd have things resolved by tomorrow, but evidently not. And now I have to leave London for a few days."

She gazed at him, bewildered. "Leave London?"

"I need to be in Worcester by Friday."

She tensed. "Why?"

"For the same reason I needed to be in Worcester last month when we were there."

So here it was again. His mysterious task in Worcester.

"And this is necessary? Now? When we know Roger— Henry—is nearby?"

He flinched but he recovered quickly. "I made a promise, Em. You wouldn't understand."

"Oh," she said bitterly, "I understand promises. Far too well."

"True enough. I meant you might not be able to understand this particular situation until you see it firsthand."

"You're not going to tell me why? You're going to continue to tease me with this mystery?"

He was silent for a moment. "Sorry, I don't mean to tease you. I was hoping you'd come with me," he said softly.

"Do you mean come with you to Worcester and stay at the inn and worry and have all kinds of wild thoughts about what you might be doing?"

He blinked. "Is that what happened last time?"

She nodded.

"Well. No. I was thinking this time I'd take you with me so you can see for yourself."

* * *

Three mornings later, they rode up to a tall, sweeping, wrought-iron gate. The journey out here had taken two long days. Emma still couldn't walk, so Luke carried her everywhere.

Both of them were out of sorts. Not being able to touch him was driving her mad. And she hadn't touched him—well, except when she'd fallen asleep in the carriage and woken with her head in his lap and his arm wrapped possessively around her. She'd insisted upon them taking different rooms in their lodgings, and this time he'd ground his teeth but had granted her request.

He still hadn't told her what this visit to Worcester was all about. He'd been surprisingly tight-lipped, maintaining that she needed to see for herself—that he couldn't adequately explain it to her until they arrived.

They'd spent much of the two-day journey mulling over the papers Luke had taken from Henry's office. Now that Emma had calmed down from the initial shock of seeing Henry alive, she was more focused than ever on finding him and seeing him brought to justice.

The papers from the office consisted of letters and various agreements. There were documents regarding a transaction of property, the purchase of a new carriage, a bill of sale and delivery instructions for a race horse, drawing room furniture, a fine Persian rug.

There was no mention of a Henry Curtis; the few papers that were signed all bore the name Roger Morton. Which led Emma to believe that Henry Curtis might have been a false identity from the beginning. Roger Morton *was* Henry Curtis.

Oh, how he had fooled her.

"But where is he keeping all these things he has purchased with my father's money?" Emma had mused after reading yet another receipt.

"We need to find his true place of residence," Luke said, "because clearly he's not keeping any of it in Wapping." After a moment of silence, he asked her, "Where did he live when he was courting you?"

"He lived near my father's house...his lodgings were..." She thought hard, trying to remember. "I believe they were in Percy Street?" She shrugged. "But he's long gone from there. When we married, he gave up his rooms to move to Bristol."

"Yes, but we should question the landlord, and perhaps the neighbors. They might have insight."

The letters were mostly related to gambling debts and business settlements, all containing names of people Morton knew and who might have information about his whereabouts.

By the evening they arrived in Worcester, they'd developed a plan. They already had someone watching Morton's offices. If he returned, they'd be better prepared next time. Luke would call on his brother Sam—he was still too furious with the duke—for help. Sam, Luke said, had been a soldier and was used to dealing with men like Roger Morton.

And, Luke had told her darkly, next time he wouldn't

risk her safety by bringing her to Wapping. Next time she was to stay home.

Emma knew it was useless to argue. Further, she was beset by feelings of incompetence. She'd brought her pistol with her to Wapping last time, and after she'd fallen, she'd fumbled in her cloak for it, but by the time she'd grasped it in her hand, both her husband and Luke were long gone.

While Luke and Sam waited for Morton to return to Wapping, they'd systematically go through the names in his correspondence, finding the people mentioned and then questioning them.

Luke and Emma slept at the inn in Worcester they'd stayed in last month. Emma was in the room adjacent to Luke's, and as she prepared for bed, she heard the creak of his door opening.

She gripped the table. No...maybe he wasn't going down to the tavern. Maybe he was coming to see her to wish her a good night...or...Well, she couldn't think of another reason for him to leave his room.

But he didn't come to see her.

He'd gone downstairs. She lay in bed for a long while, unable to sleep, fighting with herself about whether she should try to stop him. But how could she? She had no power over him anymore, no right to tell him what he shouldn't be doing. She couldn't hold him as he shuddered from his nightmares. They couldn't even touch. She belonged to someone else.

She'd never felt more alone. More hopelessly miserable.

The following morning, they drove back in the direction of London. After they'd been on the road for about half an hour, the carriage slowed in front of this tall wrought-iron fence.

They stopped outside the gate. There were already a half-dozen carriages standing out here, as well as several tethered horses.

"Welcome to Bordesley Green," Luke murmured.

She gazed through the gates as Luke spoke to the postilions. Beyond the gates was a vast green lawn dotted with small clusters of strolling people. The lawn wrapped around an enormous, dark house with Gothic beams and cornices. If the day wasn't so bright and the lawn so green, she might have called it forbidding.

Luke came around to lift her out of the carriage. "Put all of your weight on me," he told her sternly. "I do not want you to hurt that ankle again."

She complied, gripping her cane in one hand and slipping her arm around him. He moved his own arm around her waist to support her.

She gazed at the house in the distance. "What is this place?"

"It is an asylum for idiots," he said tersely. "Come."

He nodded to the man at the gate, and he opened it. They went through, slowly traveling down the graveled path that meandered to the house.

"Is it visiting day?" she murmured to Luke.

"Yes. Second Friday of every month."

"And you come every month?"

"Yes, but only since August."

They passed groups of people walking on the lawn, and she could now tell the residents of the asylum apart from the people who visited them. Family members and loved ones, she thought. The residents didn't wear nightgowns to set them apart, but it was obvious who they were anyhow. They spoke differently, gestured differently, walked differently from the people who'd come to see them. Their expressions were less guarded, easier to read. There was the man of at least forty years, bouncing on his toes and grinning like a lad on Christmas morning. There was the young woman with her arms flailing wildly about, a man and woman with her speaking in soft voices, trying to calm her.

She took a breath. "Who are we visiting, Luke?"

He didn't answer. They approached the door, which was opened by a stern-looking woman. "Friend Luke," she said in a businesslike tone, "it is a pleasure to see you again."

"It's a pleasure to see you, too, Friend Hannah," Luke said.

Emma tried to hide her surprise. This woman was clearly a Quaker, and Luke seemed totally at ease with their way of communicating.

The Quaker woman's gaze went to her, curious but not unfriendly.

"This is my friend, Mrs. Curtis."

The woman nodded politely, then turned back to Luke. "He's quite excited to see you. He hasn't stopped talking about visiting day for the last week."

Luke smiled. "Where is he?"

"He is in the art room. I'll take you to him. This way."

Hannah led them down a long, dark corridor. As they were walking, she glanced back at them. "Do not be surprised by the state of the art room. We like to give the idiots some freedom of expression...and they do take advantage of the opportunity."

Trepidation rose in Emma as they walked. Who was this person? An idiot? What did that mean, exactly? It was disconcerting to be walking toward something she knew nothing about.

Hannah stopped at a door, and choosing a key from the thick ring she wore about her neck, she unlocked the door. "Wait here," she said, and slipped inside. A moment later, she opened the door wide and smiled at them. "Come in." Turning to look back over her shoulder, she called, "Friend Bertram, someone is here to see you."

Emma stepped into a room the likes of which she'd never seen. It was a very large room—perhaps meant to be a hall or drawing room in the original vision of the house—but it was splattered with paint. The wood floor was patchy—black and red and green and blues. Swirls and dabs. Big blocks of one color, then dull brown mixes of colors, then cheerful, bright stripes, strips, and swirls.

There were a few paint-spattered easels strewn across the room. As they walked in, a thickly built, blond-haired man turned toward them, a broad smile splitting his round face.

"Luke!" he called. "Luke, Luke, Luke, Luke, Luke." And he dropped his paintbrush, spattering yellow paint over his bare feet and onto the floor, and ambled toward Luke.

"Bertram!" Luke said cheerfully.

Emma watched him carefully to see if this cheer was manufactured. But it wasn't; she was sure of it. Luke was truly pleased to see this man.

Bertram threw his arms around Luke, sending Luke stumbling backward. Laughing, the man held Luke in a big bear hug and squeezed him tight. With a grin, Luke looked back at Emma. "Bert, this is my friend Emma. Emma, meet Bertram, my brother."

His...*brother*? She glanced at Hannah, who gave the two men a benevolent look.

"Emma!" Bertram hugged Luke even tighter.

"Let me go, man," Luke said good-naturedly. "You'll squeeze the life out of me."

Bertram let him go immediately and began to pat his chest. "No squeezing, no squeezing." His words emerged fast and slightly slurred. Emma could hardly understand them.

Luke put a hand on his shoulder. "You may squeeze, brother, but not too much, all right?"

Bertram's head bobbed up and down, and he smiled. His teeth were very small—it looked like he'd never lost his infant teeth.

Emma studied him. He looked...odd, like his facial features had been somewhat flattened. He was shorter than Luke by several inches—about her height, actually—and he was far softer than Luke. His skin had a pale, doughy complexion. His face was round, his nose small and flat, his eyes tilted a bit upward at their corners. He looked quite young, but his features were so smooth and soft, she couldn't be certain of his age.

But there was something of Luke in those eyes—in the crystal-clear blue of them. His hair, too, was a dark blond, nearly exactly the same shade as Luke's.

He wore a white shirt and black wool trousers—the ensemble completely paint spattered. She glanced at Luke to see that he'd been smeared with paint, too, but he didn't seem to mind.

"I know we usually walk and play on the grounds,

Bert, but Emma has an injured ankle. Would you mind if we stayed inside for a while?"

Bertram blinked at Emma, his blue eyes clear and guileless. In that way, they were definitely not like Luke's. His gaze landed on her cane. "Injured ankle?"

"I twisted it," she explained, smiling at him. "I'm not supposed to walk at all."

"There is no one else here in the painting room, so you may stay if you like," Hannah said. "Perhaps you could show your friends your paintings, Friend Bertram."

Bertram looked down and shuffled his feet bashfully, his ears turning red. "Aw."

Something in her heart softened at his sudden shyness. "I'd very much like to see them," Emma told him.

Luke flashed her a relieved smile. "As would I, Bert."

Bertram looked up, but his expression was still tentative.

"Good," Hannah said firmly. "Now I must go see to our other visitors. If you require anything, please do not hesitate to call upon us. Friend Bertram, do be good to your guests."

"Thank you, Friend Hannah," Luke said.

Hannah slipped out of the room, closing the door with a *snick* behind her.

"What a room this is, Bert," Luke said, looking around as if impressed. "I didn't know you were a painter."

"I like painting." Bertram made a flourish with his hand as if he were holding a paintbrush and making a grand sweep of color with it.

"Will you show us something you painted?" Emma asked him.

He turned, and they followed him, Luke supporting

her as Bertram walked toward the easel where he'd been standing as they entered. He walked around it and stopped, frowning.

They came to stand beside him.

"Well," Luke said.

"That's lovely," Emma said.

"Flowers," Bertram said bashfully.

It was, in fact, a bunch of yellow daffodils growing in a green field with a blue sky overhead. It was a colorful, cheerful, happy painting, and quite good. Not something Emma would have expected an "idiot" capable of.

"Pretty yellow flowers. And orange. Using red with yellow, like this." And then Bertram launched into a description of all the colors he'd used in the painting, speaking so quickly he slurred a bit and showing them his pots of paint in various colors. Emma couldn't keep up with all he said.

"Well," Luke said finally, and there was admiration in his voice as he clapped his hand over Bertram's shoulder, "you, brother, are a very talented artist indeed. Have you any other paintings you can show us?"

Bertram looked up at him brightly. Then he turned from the easel and scurried over to a far wall, where canvases lay piled on the floor. He got down on his knees on the painted-over floor and began to spread them out.

"All mine, my paintings," he told them, looking up and grinning.

Luke raised his brows at the pile on the floor, then murmured to Emma, "There aren't any chairs in here for you. Can you sit on the floor?"

"I think so."

He helped her down so she could have a closer look,

then he moved beside her. Bertram handed them canvases, and Luke held them up one at a time.

There were many garden scenes. Brightly colored flowers. Trees. Sunshine. All painted in bold, bright, heavy strokes. There were structures, too. A barn, and a picture of a simplified Bordesley Green that made it look cheerful and open rather than dark and sinister. Just looking at all these happy paintings infused an odd kind of well-being in Emma.

And then Luke held up another house. This one was obviously a fine home—regal with its redbrick façade and front colonnade. Luke's jaw worked as he studied it. Finally, he looked up at her. "The Stanleys' country home."

And now she knew how Bertram was related to him. Bertram wasn't a Hawkins—he was another disregarded son of Lord Stanley's.

Which was why, too, Luke hadn't visited Bertram until this past August—August was when he'd learned that Stanley was his true father. It must have been when he'd found out about Bertram, too.

"Mama's home," Bertram corrected Luke now. "And baby Georgie is right there." He pointed to one of the tiny windows.

"Georgina," Luke explained softly. "Our sister."

Emma nodded rather than spoke—her throat was too constricted for her to say anything.

Bertram rifled through the paintings and pulled out a smallish one. It was of a beautiful blond, blue-eyed baby lying upon a blanket, holding up a chubby fist. Bertram gave the picture directly to Emma. "Georgie," he told her, pointing at the infant.

"She is lovely," Emma mused.

Luke smirked but quickly relaxed his expression and moved on to the next one. "What's this?"

She watched them mull over the remaining paintings, marveling at their easy camaraderie. She couldn't help but notice how much easier Luke was with Bertram than he'd been with the Duke of Trent.

The duke was his half brother on his mother's side, Bertram his half brother on his father's. Luke and Trent had gone through childhood together, but Luke and Bertram had only known each other since August.

It was so interesting to Emma how some bonds seemed completely natural, while others had to be forged by blood and sweat. And even then with no guarantees that they would hold.

They remained with Bertram for several hours. They talked and laughed. They shared the luncheon Luke and Emma had brought with them. Bertram wanted badly to show her the gardens behind the house, so Luke helped her downstairs and sat her on a bench while Bertram festooned her hair with little pink flowers.

And then visiting day was over. They said their goodbyes. Luke hugged Bertram—it was an odd sight to see an aristocratic man like Luke behaving in such an affectionate fashion, but then again, Emma knew firsthand that he was naturally an affectionate person.

Luke carried her to the carriage and set her gently inside. She settled in, waiting for him as he instructed the postilions.

Moments later he climbed in and sat beside her, and the carriage began to move. It was afternoon, but the days were growing so short now, it felt like dusk was upon them.

He gazed at her, his expression inscrutable. "Well?"

She smiled at him. She touched her hair, and her thumb and forefinger came away trapping a tiny flower. "He's lovely, Luke. I can see why you couldn't bear to break your promise to visit him. But," she added slowly, turning the flower between her fingers, "what I don't understand is why you didn't tell me sooner. Heavens, why didn't you tell me last month when we were here?"

He leaned his head back against the soft velvet squab. "Hmm, and what would I have told you? That I have an idiot half brother who lives in an asylum? That would not have given you the correct impression. Bert is…" He shook his head. "I didn't understand either, back in August when I first saw him. I thought he would be a drooling imbecile. But then I met him and…" His voice trailed off.

"And…?" she prompted.

He gazed at her seriously. "I've never met anyone so simply pure," he told her. "He's so full of innocence and…and *joy*. I find him, I don't know, soothing somehow."

"I think he is comforted by your presence as well."

"And it turns out he's a talented artist," Luke mused. "I didn't expect that at all. I've thought about pulling him from that place and bringing him to live with me. To be with family instead of those strangers." Luke studied her as if to gauge her reaction to this.

She nodded.

"On the other hand, I am not sure. He seems content there most of the time. But sometimes I see hints of loneliness in him. Though if I brought him home and then went about my business as usual, would he be lonely there, too?"

"I don't know," Emma said softly. "But I am certain he'd love to be close to you."

"Also, he'd be in London. In a crowded city. His paintings show how much he loves nature, gardens, and open skies. Would I stifle him by bringing him into the city?"

Emma gazed at him. Luke—the man who called himself "evil"—was consumed with worry about the happiness of a brother he'd only known for one day a month for four months. A brother whose parents had obviously decided to tuck him away and ignore him. Their lack of attendance at today's visiting day didn't escape Emma.

She couldn't help it—she took Luke's hand in her own and brought it to her lips, kissing his knuckles and breathing in the leather of his glove.

"You don't need to make such decisions now," she told him softly. "The people at Bordesley Green seem very compassionate and focused on the well-being of the people who reside there. I'm sure Hannah will help. Maybe you could start with bringing him home with you for a few days at a time to see if he will be happy in London."

"Do you think so?"

At that moment, Luke seemed so eager, so young. So intent upon doing the right thing for his brother. She wanted to wrap her arms around him and hold him tight.

She was a married woman, though. Swallowing down the bile that threatened to rise, she released his hand and turned away. "I do think so."

And she knew, above anything else, that Bertram Stanley was lucky to have Lukas Hawkins as his brother.

Chapter Sixteen

✦

They spent the night at Ironwood Park, Luke's childhood home. It was the right distance from Bordesley Green, so they arrived just at dusk.

When he first told her where they were going, Emma had raised her brows, remembering how flatly he'd refused to visit Ironwood Park the last time they were in the area. But Luke just laughed. "Last month, my brothers and sister were in residence. Now they've all gone. We'll have the entire mausoleum to ourselves."

That didn't sound promising. Indeed, when they went through the gates of Ironwood Park and down the long, meandering driveway, the massive gray edifice looked dark and forbidding under the gathering purple clouds of dusk.

But as soon as they dismounted from the carriage, Luke swept her into his arms and carried her up the steps. An older woman with thick white hair piled atop her head opened the massive front door. As soon as she saw them, she beamed.

"Why, if it isn't Lord Lukas. I thought I might see you tonight, my lord."

Luke's brows rose. "Did you?"

"I did indeed. The duke told me you'd be venturing in this direction monthly and that you might be gracing us with your presence."

Luke glanced down at Emma, still surprised. "It's as if he's omniscient sometimes," he grumbled. At the top of the stairs, he set Emma gently on her feet. "Mrs. Hope, this is Mrs. Curtis. She is providing assistance with the search for my mother. Mrs. Curtis, this is Mrs. Hope, the housekeeper."

Mrs. Hope seemed to accept this incomplete introduction of Emma at face value. She curtsied. "A pleasure, Mrs. Curtis."

"Good evening," Emma said.

"She sprained her ankle," Luke said. "Badly."

Mrs. Hope made a *tsk*ing noise. "Now I see why you brought her here, my lord. Because I'll surely have a poultice just for that."

She led them inside the house, clucking and talking. Emma blinked at the vastness of the marble entry hall and the lavish paintings along the corridor. Mrs. Hope ushered them into the opulent drawing room and told Emma she'd be back with the poultice in a trice.

She bustled out, leaving Emma blinking after her as Luke helped her to one of the two ornate sofas.

"Goodness," Emma murmured. "I never thought a single person could make such a colossally cold place so inviting." Then she winced. "I hope you do not take offense—"

"Not at all." Luke laughed. "I was the one to call it a

mausoleum, was I not? And, yes, Mrs. Hope does have a way about her. She's been here ever since I was a boy. Sometimes she feels like the only beam of light in the gloom of this place."

Moments later, servants brought in refreshment. Then Mrs. Hope entered with a soothing salve that she gently rubbed into Emma's ankle. Dinner followed in the impossibly enormous dining room. Emma drank a glass of sherry in the drawing room afterward, while Luke joined her with a glass of port—Emma had noticed that sherry was the one drink he refused to touch.

Finally, Mrs. Hope led them up to their rooms. She had brought a footman to carry Emma upstairs, but Luke scowled at the man. "No. I'll do it."

With a pleasant nod, Mrs. Hope dismissed the footman and led the way to the guest bedchamber that had been assigned to Emma. Luke settled her onto a soft armchair as one maid brought in her luggage, another a basin of water, another a pitcher, and yet another maid held nothing—her sole purpose was to turn down the bed.

When they'd finished their tasks, the maids trickled out, leaving just Luke and Mrs. Hope.

"Might I fetch you aught else, Mrs. Curtis?" Mrs. Hope asked.

"Oh no, thank you. Thank you so much for all you have done, and without any advance notice that we were coming today," Emma said with feeling.

"Of course, dear." With that, Mrs. Hope took her leave, shutting the door behind her, not seeming to notice she was leaving Luke alone in the room with Emma.

Emma gazed after her. "She doesn't condemn me for coming here with you."

Luke shrugged. "If she were that sort of a woman, she wouldn't have held her position here for very long."

"Goodness," she mused as she took in her surroundings. The guest room—one of many, she was told—was simple but elegant, decorated in ivory and trimmed in gilt.

His voice gentled. "Will you be all right?"

Looking up, she met his gaze. "Yes." Her voice was lower and huskier than she'd intended it to be.

"I miss you, Em," he said softly. Slowly, he stroked a knuckle down her cheek. The simple action brought warmth to her face that spread all the way through her body.

"I miss you, too," she murmured.

He leaned down and whispered in her ear, "Do you know how much I want to take you to my room and tie you to my bed and make you scream?"

Her breath caught. The warmth inside her deepened.

"*I miss you*," he said again, placing quiet emphasis on each word. "Have you made your decision?"

"My decision?"

"About leaving your husband. About coming back to me. To my bed."

"I'm not with him right now," she reminded him.

"But you're not with me, either."

She blinked up at him.

"Being with you yet being unable to touch you... It's driving me mad."

It was driving her mad, too. But she couldn't tell him that.

"Let's find Henry first," she said. "It will be soon. I know it will."

She didn't know if she could ever betray her vow to

Henry. But seeing him, talking to him, somehow having a deeper understanding of what he'd done and why—she needed all of that before she could move forward.

Luke gazed down at the floor, then back to her. "For you, Em. Only for you." He turned and walked to the door, glancing over his shoulder. "I'll send someone in to help you prepare for bed."

He slipped out, closing the door firmly behind him.

And she prayed that the chaos in her mind wasn't causing him to slip through her fingers.

She was a married woman. She belonged to another man. If Henry discovered what she and Luke had done, he could bring legal action against Luke. He could publicly destroy Luke. And Luke had been destroyed enough as it was.

She gazed at the door. Something deep inside her, intrinsic to her well-being, had become inexorably entwined with Lord Lukas Hawkins.

She didn't want to lose him.

* * *

Two days later, they arrived back in London. Luke helped Emma up the front steps—her ankle was improving again, and she'd insisted he stop carrying her everywhere—and looked up when Baldwin opened the door.

"Good afternoon, Baldwin," Luke said.

Baldwin's face bore a fierce expression. It was the strongest emotion Emma had ever seen from him. Luke, too, because his steps ground to a halt as he took in the look on his servant's face.

"What's wrong?" he asked darkly.

"There are men here, sir," Baldwin said. "Bow Street officers. They've a warrant to search the premises. I told them you were returning this afternoon and to wait, and they agreed."

"Search the premises?" Emma asked.

"For what?" Luke asked.

"It seems they're searching for evidence of some sort," Baldwin growled. "I haven't any idea what, though. They would not say."

"Where are they?" Luke added.

"In the drawing room upstairs, sir."

"Stay here," Luke said to Emma, and he strode into the house. Emma watched him disappear up the stairs.

She glanced warily at Baldwin. "What's happening?"

"I really do not know, Mrs. Curtis," he told her. But his Adam's apple shifted as he swallowed. "Please come inside and wait for his lordship."

She was still standing outside the door. It was a cold afternoon; the wind whipped across the square, and leaves had gathered in every available nook and cranny. She glanced across the street to find only a few tenacious leaves clinging to the tree branches. Winter had descended upon them.

She limped inside, gripping her cane. The postilions entered behind her, bringing her and Luke's luggage. They slipped away quickly to tend to the horses and carriage, leaving her alone with Baldwin in the small entrance hall.

She twisted her hands over the smooth polished wood of her cane, gazing up the stairs, hearing the muffled sounds of masculine voices from above. She wanted so badly to go up and see what was going on, but Luke had told her to stay. She stared at her cane, balanced on one foot, and waited, standing in the center of the small entry hall for an indeterminate length of time. Baldwin stayed by her side, silent but solid.

Minutes later, Luke came downstairs, followed by two men. He was angry—that much was evident in the harsh ice blue of his eyes and the tight, flat line of his lips. His expression softened minutely when he saw Emma waiting for him.

"Come," he murmured, wrapping his arm around her and drawing her close. "We'll go up to the drawing room. You need to get off that ankle. Baldwin, please bring us some refreshment. It has been a long day of travel." He didn't deign to glance at the two men as they brushed by and turned toward the kitchen.

"What is this about?" she whispered as they began to ascend the stairs.

He bent his head so his lips were close to her ear. "They're searching for evidence. They've a warrant. There's nothing we can do but wait."

She frowned at him. "Evidence of what?"

He helped her settle onto the chair that had become her favorite—a soft, velvety brown armchair that seemed to swallow her up in comfort every time she sat in it.

His expression was bleak. "I don't know. They wouldn't say."

"Oh...Luke," she breathed. "Did you...do anything?" Perhaps one night, in a state of drunkenness, he'd done something awful...

He shook his head. "I don't know." Turning away, he pushed a hand through his hair and went to fetch the footstool for her.

She raised her leg, and he slipped it under, grasping her calf and adjusting her foot gently on the footstool's cushioned surface.

"Do you think it was...recent?"

He shook his head. "It can't be. I haven't done anything untoward since I met you in Bristol. Hell, I haven't even made any wagers recently."

"What about when you have been...sotted?"

"No."

"So it must have been before that. Can you remember anything?"

Still on one knee in front of her, he gazed at her steadily. "I'd rather not remember anything before you, Em."

She reached out to him, and he covered her hand with his. "Believe me," he said softly, "I cannot think of anything I've done—ever—that would result in two Bow Street officers searching my house with a warrant."

"I believe you," she told him, her eyes locked onto his. She added softly, "I will always believe you."

The corners of his lips curled upward, and he kissed her hand before rising.

Delaney came in with a tray of refreshments. They both stared at the tray, covered with cakes and other freshly baked sweet delicacies from the cook, along with a steaming pot of tea and two cups.

Neither of them touched the food or the drink. Acutely aware of the two men searching the house, Emma was sure her stomach would rebel if she ate anything right now, and it seemed Luke felt the same way.

They didn't wait for long. It was less than five minutes later when the door burst open.

"My lord, we are arresting you for the theft of six hundred pounds from Lord Winchell. You will come with us."

Emma's mouth dropped open. "What?"

Luke shook his head. "You've the wrong man. I am not acquainted with Lord Winchell."

"Nevertheless, you are in possession of a false bill of sale for a blood-horse. Lord Winchell became aware of the fact you duped him after your agent took his banknote and then did not return with the beast as promised," the man, a dark-haired giant, said. "You will come with us, sir. You will come willingly or we will take you by force. The choice is yours."

"This is absurd," Luke spat. "I know nothing of this."

"We found the bill of sale in your valise."

And it all came together. The bill of sale regarding the horses sold by Roger Morton in Newmarket had been among the papers she and Luke had found in Morton's office... Emma vaguely recalled that one of the men she and Luke had intended to seek out had signed his name as simply, "Winchell."

Morton was responsible for this.

Emma rose to her feet. Luke rose at the same time. The men came forward, grabbing his arms simultaneously.

Her eyes locked with his.

"I didn't steal anything," he growled.

"I know," she told him.

"That is for the jury to decide, I'd wager," one of the officers said grimly.

She was strong. So was Luke. This was simply another of Morton's nefarious schemes. But the ruse was over. Finished. She wouldn't let him get away with it this time.

The two men began to lead Luke away. He appeared to be too stunned to do anything other than comply. But at the doorway, he turned to face her. "Stay here."

"What? I can't—"

"Trust me," he told her, his voice strong and even. "I will acquit myself of this ridiculous charge and be home with you soon."

And then he was gone, pushed out by the two men, the door closing with a thud behind them, leaving Emma alone in the shrieking silence of the drawing room.

* * *

The Bow Street officers had taken all of the evidence—all of the papers Luke had removed from Morton's office in Wapping. Emma was furious at herself for not making copies of those documents, but then again, she'd hardly been given the chance.

She sat in the drawing room as twilight began to cast shadows through the room, wondering where they'd taken Luke. To Newgate? Was he spending the night in some dank prison cell in the company of violent criminals?

Would he have nightmares tonight? She hated the thought of him waking from a nightmare among strangers.

Baldwin came in to light lanterns and stoke the fire. He asked if she'd like dinner brought up, and when she demurred, he said quietly, "I will bring you a light meal, Mrs. Curtis. You will require nourishment."

A little while later, he brought up a tray of food, along with a letter that had arrived while Luke and Emma had been in Worcester.

"For you, ma'am," he told her. "It arrived just this morning."

"Thank you, Baldwin," she murmured.

She opened the letter distractedly...God, she wanted nothing more than to run to Newgate and demand they release Luke immediately. But that wouldn't work. What would? What could she do?

Start with this Lord Winchell...and the horse market in Newmarket. It was all she had, for now. Tomorrow, she'd go there.

My Dearest Sister,

I hope this letter finds you well. Further, I hope that you have made great strides in recovering that which you seek.

I do not wish to cause you worry, but our father's doctor has refused to see him until he is given additional compensation, since we have not paid him. There are no funds with which to pay...I did sell the desk in the study last week, but I needed to use that to pay for the workmen and materials for that leak in the roof I wrote about in my last letter.

Perhaps we must give up our tea next. I will certainly do that before selling Mama's jewelry, but I have been taking tea with Papa every day like you used to, and it seems it is the only time a little life flows through him. Otherwise, he is much the same, if not a little more listless and dull than usual. And the swelling in his body increases, now that the doctor will no longer provide him with his medicine.

I know you are busy, dear sister, but we need you here. I fear for Papa. I fear our creditors. Another man came yesterday and said Papa owed him a great deal of money and warned that he could take the house from us. The house is all we have left, Em. Where will we go if we lose it?

I am sorry. I fear I reveal too much of my melancholy. I want so badly for you to succeed in your endeavor, but I feel helpless and impatient staying in this lonely house and waiting for word of your success.

I will continue to pray for you... and for all of us.

> *Your Loving Sister,*
> *Jane*

Emma stared at the letter, despair welling in her. She knew the man Jane referred to—Mr. Childress. Using his silver tongue, Henry had convinced Childress and her father to invest in a coal mine. Less than a month later, he had taken Childress's money along with Emma's father's. There had never been a coal mine.

It struck her that her father had been just as taken with Henry as she had. He'd *trusted* him. Even before their marriage, Henry had come to her father with schemes and investments, and her father—in some ways as naïve as her, evidently—had given him whatever he'd asked for.

But how to answer this letter? Emma wasn't sure she could.

Dear Jane, Henry is alive! Imagine that! He counterfeited his own death and absconded with our father's fortune...

Or...

Dear Jane, Well, not only is Henry alive, but he's also somehow managed to have the Duke of Trent's brother arrested for an act of thievery he no doubt committed himself.

The Duke of Trent. Surely he could help.

She closed her eyes. *No.* Luke didn't like involving the duke in his affairs. But Luke had three other brothers on the Hawkins side. There was Sam, the eldest—he had been in the army, and Luke had told her he worked in some secretive business in service of the Crown. There were the two younger brothers, Lord Theodore and Lord Markus. Luke hadn't spoken much about them, but she recalled that they both resided in Cambridge.

Sam would be the one to ask. If she could find him. She didn't know much, beyond the fact that he lived in London. Maybe Baldwin would know the location of his home.

She called for the manservant. Moments later, he entered the drawing room. "Yes, ma'am?"

She gazed at him for a long moment, then said softly, "I need help, Baldwin."

He gave an impassive nod. "Of course. How may I assist you?"

"I must inform the Hawkins family as to what has happened," she told him. "But your master... Well, I hesitate to involve the duke. Do you know where Lord Lukas's older brother, Mr. Samson Hawkins, lives?"

"No, ma'am."

She released a noise of frustration. "How can you not know?"

"I am acquainted with Mr. Hawkins, ma'am. He is a

secretive, private man. I doubt many know the location of his residence."

"What about Lord Markus and Lord Theodore? Do you know where they reside?"

"Yes, ma'am. They are in Cambridge."

"Do you know where?"

"I believe so. I've a general idea. But unlike Mr. Hawkins, the two young lords have no reason to keep their location secret. They'd be easy to find."

"But...Cambridge?" She rubbed her temples with her fingertips. "How long would it take to travel there?"

"The better part of a day."

The thought of Luke in prison for that long...it hurt her chest.

She knew where the duke lived. In St. James's Square. *So close.*

Luke had said he could take care of himself, and she didn't doubt it. But the thought of him being locked up for one minute longer, and all because she'd brought him into Morton's sights, broke her heart. His brother was a duke, an extremely powerful and influential man. He would help Luke. She knew he would.

And yet...it infuriated Luke whenever Trent became involved in his affairs.

It would have to be Cambridge, then.

Of course, she didn't have the money to hire a post chaise to take her there. She'd have to take the mail coach, and she'd have to beg for the money from Baldwin for that. At least the mail coach would transport her to Cambridge quickly.

And then the solution struck Emma like an anvil to the chest—Luke's sister, Lady Esme! She was in residence at the duke's house in St. James's Square. She would know where Sam resided.

Finally, Emma had a palatable plan.

* * *

The following morning, after a night of tossing and turning and worrying about how Luke was faring, Emma waited as long as she could tolerate. Still, it was only a little past ten when she arrived on the Duke of Trent's doorstep.

This could be a huge mistake, she admitted to herself as she raised her hand to knock. Within moments, a man—presumably the butler—answered the door. He raised an impassive brow at her. "Yes?"

"Good morning. I'm Mrs. Curtis, a…a…*friend* of Lord Lukas. I'm here to see Lady Esme."

Oh, that had sounded quite bad. What would Lady Esme say to her brother's mistress coming calling so early in the morning?

"Please wait here. I will see if she is at home."

Emma waited. And…waited. She paced across the landing, wringing her hands, knowing that her patience had already frayed. Several minutes later, the butler opened the door again.

"Lady Esme will see you. Please, follow me."

Breathing a long sigh of relief, she followed him into a drawing room decorated in shades of blue, with light blue wallpaper and royal blue furniture. "Please wait here, ma'am. The lady will be in shortly."

Another several minutes passed. Emma moved restlessly. She hovered over a rich wooden card table containing a chessboard. It looked like the chess game had been half played—and white was winning.

She had gone to the window and gazed out onto the bustling St. James's Square when the door opened behind her. She spun around as a young, dark-haired woman entered the room, followed by Sarah, the duchess.

Emma forced herself to smile as Sarah made introductions.

"It is lovely to meet you, Lady Esme," Emma said. She was rather surprised at the lady's appearance. Lady Esme's coloring and features were quite different from both the duke's and Luke's. Her skin was olive-toned, her eyes deep brown, and her hair so dark as to be nearly black.

"Likewise," said the lady, although judging by the befuddled expression on her face, she'd no idea who Emma was.

Emma thought of Luke in a dank, disease-ridden cell. She thought of the violent men undoubtedly surrounding him. She couldn't wait. She'd half expected the duchess to be here, and she'd thought of ways she could ask Esme to speak alone.

But Luke was in danger. Nothing else mattered but his safety.

She licked her lips and tried not to focus on the duchess. "Lady Esme, I am a friend of your brother, Lord Lukas."

Lady Esme's eyes widened. She flicked a glance at Sarah, then back at Emma.

"Come, let us all be seated," the duchess said with a sweep of her arm toward the blue-upholstered chairs and sofa. "Would you care for any refreshment, Mrs. Curtis?"

"Thank you, no." Emma strode to one of the armchairs and bent herself into it, although her body protested. Her body wanted to be in action—running to wherever they were keeping Luke and dragging him out of there.

"I've come to ask for your help, my lady, in an urgent matter regarding your brother."

Again, Esme, who was seated on the sofa across from Emma, glanced at Sarah.

"The best person to help Lord Lukas would be the duke," Sarah said.

Emma swallowed hard. With strength she didn't know she possessed, she gazed evenly at the duchess. "Forgive me, Sarah, but His Grace and Lord Lukas's relationship is...strained. I'm not sure he'd approve of me appealing to the duke in this matter."

Emma knew she'd fall on her knees and beg the duke for his help, but only if it were her last resort.

Sarah nodded and said quietly, "I have known Lord Lukas most of my life, Mrs. Curtis. Believe me when I say I understand."

Emma breathed a sigh of relief.

"But," the duchess added, her gaze hardening, and for the first time, Emma saw a steely will behind the duchess's gentle demeanor, "if he is in any kind of danger, the duke must know about it. Their dealings are not always on the best of terms, but my husband cares deeply for his brother."

Emma tried to smile. "I know he does. And his brother cares for him, too."

The duchess quirked a brow, and Emma knew what she was thinking: *Well, he doesn't show it very well, does he?*

They gazed at each other in silence for a moment, both holding their ground. Lady Esme looked back and forth between the two women, her own gaze serious.

Esme was the one to finally break the silence. "May I speak with her, Sarah?"

After an additional moment gazing at Emma, Sarah gave a curt nod. She excused herself and left the room, closing the door softly behind her.

Emma released a long breath as she watched the duchess go, then she turned to Lady Esme, who was gazing expectantly at her, her dark brows drawn closely together.

Emma had the feeling this young woman wasn't one for politesse. And she was grateful for it. She got straight to the point. "My lady, I fear Luke is in grave danger."

Esme raised her brow at Emma's familiar use of Luke's name. But clearly, the duke and duchess knew of her intimate relationship with Luke. If Esme didn't know by now, she would soon. In any case, Emma was beyond pretending.

She continued. "I must find your brother, Samson. I feel he might be the only one who will be able to help."

Now it was Esme's turn to give her an assessing gaze. "Help with what?"

Emma clutched her hands together in her lap and said softly, "Getting Luke out of prison."

Chapter Seventeen

*H*alf an hour later, Esme and Emma arrived at a small town house in a middle-class neighborhood. They were showed in to Samson Hawkins's office by a male servant. As they entered the small, shabby space, Mr. Hawkins rose from behind a large, well-used desk.

He was dark, tall, and broad. Taller than both his brothers—who were tall themselves—by a few inches. His skin was several shades darker than his brothers', too, and his eyes were a deep, rich brown—very similar to Esme's.

He walked around the desk, focused on Esme. He gathered her hands in his own. He didn't waste time with formal greetings. "Esme, why are you here? What's wrong?"

"Sam, this is Mrs. Curtis, a friend of Luke's. Mrs. Curtis, this is Mr. Hawkins, my brother."

The brown gaze of Samson Hawkins settled on her, and Emma felt vulnerable and exposed. It was clear this man wasn't going to beat about the bush.

His voice was brusque. "Mrs. Curtis. How may I help you?"

She took a slow, steady breath, bracing herself limb by limb. "Thank you so much for seeing me, Mr. Hawkins. I've come to beg for your help. You see, Luke has been arrested."

Mr. Hawkins's face showed no emotion. "On what charge?"

"The theft of six hundred pounds from Lord Winchell."

"I see."

"They took him away last night," Emma continued. "I don't know where he is, or what's going to happen, but we need to—"

"Did he do it?"

Her mouth dropped open in surprise. Then she snapped, "No! Of course not."

"Are you sure?"

Anger boiled up within her faster than she could contain it. She had always strongly believed that a family should support their own unconditionally and without reservation. Luke was a self-confessed rogue and a scoundrel, but that didn't exclude him from this rule.

Did Luke's own family not implicitly trust him? If that was the case, then it explained so much. It was no wonder he had never truly healed.

She crossed her arms over her chest and glared at the big man. "I'm sure."

His expression still didn't change, but he lifted one brow slightly. "You'll forgive me, Mrs. Curtis, but as you probably know by now, my brother is prone to excesses of drink and other debauched pursuits. A drunkard's actions can be quite different from his actions when he is sober."

Tears choked her throat and stung her eyes, but she didn't let them free. "Luke is not a drunkard," she bit out, her voice harsh with certainty. Luke did drink to escape from the hard realities of his life, but he was no more a drunkard than she was.

That dark eyebrow crept higher on his forehead. "Is that so?" he asked dryly.

"It is."

Mr. Hawkins stared at her for a long moment—the members of the Duke of Trent's family stared at her too much. All of them were evidently attempting to delve under her skin in an effort to understand her motives. She didn't like it, and Mr. Hawkins's calm perusal of her now did nothing to allay her anger. It remained, bubbling close to the surface.

His gaze dropped to the fists clenched at her sides, then he gestured to a chair behind the desk. "Please sit. You must tell me everything you know of what has transpired."

Woodenly, she walked to the chair and lowered herself into it, aware only vaguely of Mr. Hawkins going to the door and ordering someone to bring in another chair for Esme.

She was so angry. She *hated* the fact that she'd had to defend Luke to his own brother. That one, small question—"Did he do it?"—riled every possessive and protective instinct within her.

Nonetheless, one tiny remaining rational part of her told her that she was overreacting, that she was already overwrought, and it had only taken Mr. Hawkins's innocent question to push her over the edge.

A servant placed a chair beside hers, and Esme lowered herself into it. Mr. Hawkins strode around to the other side of the desk and sat in the seat across from them.

"Now," he said, still wearing that unnerving, unreadable, flat expression on his face, "tell me what happened."

She told him about the Bow Street officers who'd been waiting at Luke's house when they'd arrived home from Bordesley Green, about the papers they'd found in Morton's office and how the officers had believed the bill of sale was sufficient evidence to arrest Luke.

"Are you certain they were referring to the receipt you found in Morton's belongings?" Mr. Hawkins asked eventually.

"What other paper could they possibly be referring to?" she asked in exasperation. "In any case, the papers were gone when I looked for them later. It was the obvious conclusion."

"Did the officers show you the evidence? Did you see it firsthand?"

"No, but—"

"They could have confiscated Morton's papers as possible evidence, but the true evidence could have come from anywhere," Mr. Hawkins said.

"No," Emma said mulishly. "You cannot believe that. There is no other true evidence. The only other possible evidence would be the false word of my villainous husband."

That infernal dark brow rose again. "Why do you believe that so strongly? You haven't known my brother long, Mrs. Curtis. What makes you so certain he is innocent?"

"He is a good man," she ground out.

"Hmm. I suspect Luke himself would be the first to disagree with you on that count."

Her chest was so tight with emotion it hurt. She felt slicing daggers shooting from her eyes toward Samson Hawkins. "Because he has been told so many times that he isn't good that he has come to believe it," she said coldly. "That lie was brutally beaten into him as a child, and he still believes it."

Esme made a small noise, but she ignored it, knowing full well that she had spoken too plainly, but she was too angry, too scared for Luke, to censor her words. Her voice was bitter with accusation as she continued. "He is trying, ever so hard, to prove himself to his family as a man capable and dependable, but at every turn the lot of you decide that he is unworthy. Every day he has come close to giving up altogether, but the goodness of his nature doesn't allow him to. And still you all make him believe he has failed."

"That's not true!" Esme breathed.

Emma rose on shaking legs. "Perhaps I shouldn't ask for your help at all. I was unaware of the extent of your disloyalty to him."

"Mrs. Curtis," Mr. Hawkins snapped. "Sit down."

Her hand curved around the back of the chair. The instinct to obey this man's hard, commanding words was strong, but she held her ground. "No. Either you promise to help your brother in whatever way possible, or you let me go so I can help him on my own. But I will not tolerate you questioning his innocence."

She glared at him, noticing for the first time that he'd lost color and that his eyes were wide with surprise rather than narrowed with anger as she'd expected.

She turned to Esme. The young woman was staring at her lap, blinking furiously as if to hold back tears.

Feeling Emma's gaze on her, she glanced up. "B-beaten?" she asked, and a tear slid down her cheek.

Esme was much younger than Luke—she'd probably been an infant when the old duke had died. Could she really not know, though?

Emma looked at Mr. Hawkins, who wasn't looking at his sister at all. He was staring at Emma, his brows flat, his expression stark and pale.

"You didn't know?" she asked them.

Slowly, Mr. Hawkins shook his head. "No," he said gruffly.

Her jaw dropped in amazement. Surely brothers knew such things about one another.

"Who...who did that to him?" Esme breathed.

He'd told no one. The knowledge that Luke had borne his abuse throughout his whole life without anyone knowing slammed into Emma, leaving her breathless.

She closed her eyes, imagining him as a blond-haired, blue-eyed little boy, frightened and alone, unable to go to anyone, his attempts to hide what his father was doing to him only resulting in more scoldings from the people around him. Enduring a cycle of pain and fear no child should ever have to endure.

Then she pictured him as she had all night and all morning, as a man alone in a cold, dark cell in Newgate. At this moment, she wanted nothing more in the world than to drag him out of that place and hold him in her arms.

And never let him go.

And then, of course, she remembered who her husband was. The man responsible for this situation.

She opened her eyes and looked directly at Lady Esme. This was a young, sheltered woman she was speaking to, but Emma didn't intend to mince words. "It was the old Duke of Trent—your father. Evidently, he made a ritual of punishing Luke. But it was more than punishment—it was abuse. It was *torture*. Haven't you seen his scars? His back is riddled with them."

Esme's gloved hand went to her mouth to stifle a gasp of horror. Mr. Hawkins's dark eyes narrowed. "Christ," he spat out.

Emma continued. "The duke thought to beat the badness out of him. He convinced Luke he was evil. Luke has believed this ever since and feels that his every action is further proof of his evil. Horrible nightmares torment him. He suffers every day because of what that man did to him when he was a child." Emma turned to Mr. Hawkins. "You, of all people, should know about this. The old duke evidently despised his 'sons' who weren't his true progeny. Did he not deliver the same treatment to you?"

It was a ridiculously forward question. Impossibly forward—she had met this man minutes ago. But Emma was beyond caring.

"No," Mr. Hawkins pushed out. "He did not."

So Luke truly had been the sole recipient of all the old duke's cruelty and vengeance. Emma's lips tightened, and she turned to go.

"I can't stay here," she said. "I'm wasting time. I need to help him."

"Wait, Mrs. Curtis," Mr. Hawkins said, his voice raspy. "You need to know I'll do whatever I can to help my brother. Please stay."

Emma glanced at Mr. Hawkins over her shoulder. He

was standing, and true concern was etched into the lines of his face. Esme had risen, too. She twisted her hands in front of her and wore a pleading expression.

Forcing her feet to move, Emma returned to her chair.

* * *

"Come with me, yer lordship."

Luke warily rose from his haunches from the stinking floor.

He'd pressed himself into the corner of the wall all night and for most of the day. It was damned cold in this place, and for the few hours when the sun had provided a little square of light through the tiny barred window, he'd moved under it, hoping to absorb a little warmth.

He hated small, enclosed spaces. The duke had, more often than not, locked him in a closet for several hours after a beating, not allowing Luke out until he was certain Luke was recovered enough not to blurt out the truth. More than once, the governess had punished him for "running off" without telling her. But her sharp raps on his knuckles were nothing compared to the discipline his father had wielded.

Luke had dozed fitfully last night, waking from nightmare after nightmare, shaking, sweating, even though the temperature in the cell had dropped to near freezing levels.

After one such dream, his heart had pounded so hard, he was certain it would kill him. He'd felt the walls pressing in on him, squeezing the life out of him. He kept telling himself that was impossible, that he wasn't dying, but his body wouldn't believe him.

Finally the feeling had ebbed somewhat, and he'd drifted off into another fitful sleep, only to be awakened an hour later in the throes of another nightmare.

It was now late afternoon. He'd been here, locked in this nine-by-six-foot cell, for twenty-four hours. He couldn't bear it much longer, that much was for certain. It wouldn't take this place very long at all to drive him to real madness.

But, really, it didn't matter. If he was found innocent, he'd be set free. If he was found guilty, he'd hang. Either way, he wouldn't have to bear it for much longer.

The barred wooden door creaked as the guard opened it.

He looked into the man's lined, unfriendly face. "Am I to be arraigned?" He'd been looking forward to that moment all day, to informing the court of his innocence and his intent to prove it.

"Nay," the man mumbled. "You're to be released."

Luke narrowed his eyes in suspicion, but the man turned with a brusque, "Come," and began to lead him down a long corridor. He shuddered as they passed cell after depressing cell, some with hands reaching through the bars that topped each door, others with moans and cries emanating from behind the thick slabs of wood.

The man opened the door onto a cloud-dimmed day and gestured at Luke to exit through it. "Good day, then, milord."

Luke paused. So this was it? He was free? He quirked a brow. Since he'd entered this place, the turnkeys had demanded money from him at every turn. He'd paid for a private cell in the state area. He'd paid for water, a plate of food, release from the shackles they'd placed on him when he'd first arrived, the soiled and torn sheets that he'd failed to sleep on last night. And now this man was letting him go. Free and clear, with no expectation of additional payment.

A sick feeling began to twist in Luke's gut. This was too fast. Too easy. It reeked of Trent's involvement.

Grinding his teeth, Luke stepped out of Newgate Prison and into a brown dirt courtyard. The thick wooden door closed with a hollow *thud* behind him.

His brother's carriage stood ten yards away. He recognized the gold crest on its side.

Of course. He really wasn't surprised. Still, his chest felt tight, the skin taut over his body.

As he stepped forward, Trent alighted from the carriage.

Luke pushed forward, striding resolutely toward his brother. His heart felt like a dead rock in his chest.

This had to be Emma's doing. But why? He'd asked one simple thing of her—for her trust. Yet she hadn't trusted him. Instead, she'd gone to Trent.

Because Trent was more capable. Trent was *better*.

His brother met him a few steps away from the carriage. For a moment, they just gazed at each other. Luke knew he should be furious. Should be railing over the duke's involvement.

But it was Emma who had betrayed him. And that made him feel like an integral piece of himself was being forcibly ripped away from his body, leaving him without the energy to argue with his brother.

Trent gestured toward the carriage. "I'll take you home."

Luke nodded. He went around the back of the carriage, climbed in, and slid onto the seat. Trent rapped his knuckles on the ceiling, and they lurched into motion.

Luke sat perfectly still, staring straight ahead. What would he say to Emma when he arrived home? Would she even be there?

Feeling his brother's eyes on him, he glanced over at Trent.

"I'm sorry," Trent said.

Luke blinked at him. What was he talking about?

"For what my father did to you."

Every single muscle in Luke's body went completely rigid. He couldn't move. Couldn't react. Couldn't breathe. His lungs were frozen.

"I didn't know, Luke." Trent sounded as though he were on the verge of tears, but that was stupid. Trent didn't shed tears over him. He seemed at a loss for what else to say, so he repeated, "I'm sorry."

Luke wrenched his face toward his window. He couldn't speak. His throat was incapable of producing sound. At this moment, he wanted nothing more than to jump out of this carriage and to run away. From all of it. But that was folly. He was an adult. He would stay and endure his brother's judgment... or sympathy. Whatever Trent chose to give him.

But Trent didn't speak further. He gazed out his window. His hands drummed restlessly over his thighs. The action reminded Luke of Emma's nervous finger tapping.

Emma.

He closed his eyes. She'd told Trent the deepest, most personal secret he'd shared with her. He'd never felt so betrayed.

They didn't speak again. Luke didn't want to talk to Trent. He didn't need to find out how Trent had set him free. He had probably gone to the source, to Lord Winchell, and handed over the six hundred pounds.

The point was, Luke hadn't been able to do it himself. As always, Trent had cut in first, solving all his problems, proving once again that Luke was incapable of doing so himself.

And in the interim, Emma had told Trent his darkest secret. That one shameful bit of himself he'd never revealed to anyone but her.

He closed his eyes. He really didn't want to face her—his anger was far too close to the surface. But he knew he must.

"How much do I owe you?" he asked Trent finally.

Trent waved his hand. "Don't worry about it."

Luke huffed out a breath.

They were close to Cavendish Square now. It had been less than a three-mile drive from Newgate to his home.

"I like her," Trent said.

Luke's fingers curled into fists. "Who?" But he knew the answer.

"Mrs. Curtis."

"She's married," he pushed out, as if that explained everything. It didn't, of course.

"Perhaps not," Trent mused. "If the man's name is truly Roger Morton, then he married her fraudulently by taking on another man's identity, and the marriage isn't legal. It could be annulled, and you could step in."

"What are you saying? That I should marry her?"

"Yes," Trent said. "I think you should."

Luke blinked at his brother. Trent had never approved

of Luke's paramours as topics of conversation, much less suggested marriage.

Trent gazed at him, his green eyes solemn as the carriage rolled to a stop in front of Luke's house. "She loves you, man. You'd be a fool to let her go."

Emma was waiting for him. She burst out of the door when Trent's carriage stopped at the front of Luke's house, and she hobbled out to greet him as fast as her injured ankle would allow.

Luke stepped down from the carriage, his heart heavy. Hell, his whole body felt like it had quadrupled in weight in the last half hour.

In public situations, Emma was usually quite cognizant of appearances. She refrained from touching him except when necessary due to her injury, and she was always aware of people witnessing them speaking intimately. But she didn't seem to care about any of that now. She rushed toward him and threw herself into his arms.

"Oh, Luke," she breathed, burying her face in his chest. "I was so worried."

He stiffened, his arms straight at his sides, and she felt it, for she took a step back, wariness seeping into her expression as she looked up at him. "Come," she murmured. "Let's go inside."

He gave her a tight nod, then looked over at his brother, who was watching them, his brows drawn together in an unspoken question.

Trent had already poked his nose too deeply into Luke's relationship with Emma. He gave a shake of his head as if to say, *Not now.*

Trent nodded. "Call upon me if you require anything

tonight. I'll come over tomorrow, and we'll discuss further action."

Right. Luke didn't think so. But he didn't say that. He turned away from his brother and followed Emma inside, for the first time in days not making any attempt to support some of her weight off her ankle.

He should have offered to support her. But he couldn't bring himself to, because he was too damned angry with her right now. He supposed that just served as more proof of what an ass he was.

She led him inside and upstairs to his bedchamber. The servants were notably absent. A steaming bath was prepared, and clothes had been laid out for him.

Except, despite the fact that he'd been steeped in filth for the last twenty-four hours, he was in no mood for a bath.

He followed her into his room, closed the door behind them. She turned to him. "Are you all right? They didn't hurt you, did they?"

"No," he said flatly. A sufficient answer to both questions, he decided.

She looked down. "I'm sorry, Luke. I know you didn't want to involve anyone...especially Trent."

At least she knew why he was angry. At least she wasn't pretending she hadn't betrayed him.

"Then why did you?" His voice was sharp, cracking like a whip, and she cringed.

"I tried not to. I went to Mr. Hawkins—Samson—instead. I told him of your wish to handle this alone, but he insisted. He said Trent knew Lord Winchell personally and could resolve the situation quickly. I just wanted you out of there. I could hardly think straight knowing you were in danger."

Luke's fists clenched at his sides. He stared at her. "Really? You went to Sam? You went to Sam and honestly thought he wouldn't involve Trent?" Obviously she didn't understand in the least how his family worked. Everyone went to Trent. For everything.

For the first time, challenge blazed bronze in her eyes. "Nothing mattered but getting you out of that place."

"So you went against my plainly expressed wishes."

"I tried to think of other options—"

"I asked you to trust me to handle this, Emma. Me. Ultimately, you did not. That is all there is to it."

Distress washed over her features. "I'm sorry."

"You know how I feel about this. I have been very clear with you about how Trent interfering with my life affects me. I could have handled this on my own, but even you wouldn't give me the chance."

"I was just so...so very scared for you." Her voice was small.

"Is that why you told him about..." Luke swallowed thickly, then forced the words out. "About what his father did to me?"

She recoiled. "I didn't tell him that."

He narrowed his eyes at her.

"Oh, Luke," she whispered. "It slipped out when I was talking to Mr. Hawkins and Lady Esme. And then they must have told Trent. I am so very sorry."

Holy hell. Now his whole family would know. Esme had probably already written to Theo and Mark and told them everything.

"I thought they knew," she whispered. "I had no idea they didn't know about any of it. I...I wasn't thinking very rationally at the time."

He gazed at Emma with new eyes. Her betrayal burned acid holes in him.

"I can't do this," he said. His voice was flat. Cold.

"Luke," she begged, "please. I am so very sorr—"

"I'm going out," he said, cutting her words short. "Don't wait up."

He turned his back on her.

"Don't run from me, Luke. Not this time."

Ignoring her pleas, he strode out of the room. Without bothering to change out of his stinking clothes, he went downstairs. And after stopping in his study to fetch his pistol, he went out the back door and into the mews. He went straight into the stable, where he saddled his horse. Then he rode into the encroaching darkness.

He didn't go to his gentleman's club. He didn't go to a pub or a gaming hell or a whorehouse. He went to none of those places that were usually his first choices to help dull those blades that cut at him. And those blades were sharp now, slicing deep.

Yet tonight, he avoided his usual haunts. Instead, he went to find Roger Morton.

* * *

Emma stood still in Luke's bedchamber for a long time. She gazed at the door, stunned. By his anger, by his abrupt departure. By her inability to stop him from leaving.

Her heart throbbed and ached.

He was furious with her. And could she blame him? She'd gone against his wishes. She'd told Sam everything, and Sam would not be dissuaded from going to the duke. Worse, in her worry and anger, she'd revealed Luke's secret—hadn't known how deep of a secret it had been until after she'd blurted it to his brother and sister.

The hours passed excruciatingly slowly. He'd said not to wait, but she waited anyhow. What else could she do? She didn't know where he'd gone. Her best guess was to his club, and as much as she wanted to go looking for him, she knew that if she went there and demanded to speak to him, she would be turned away.

She went to her room on the second floor and prepared for bed with Delaney's help. Then she lay on the bed. Shivering, she stared up at the white ceiling. This bed-chamber would always feel cold and lonely to her; it was plainly decorated, sparse and painted white, with plain oak floors. There were no colors, no carpets, no excess decoration, because Luke never came up here, and he rarely, if ever, hosted guests.

But it was more than that, she acknowledged. Luke had never lain beside her in this room. He'd never made love to her here, nor warmed her in the circle of his arms. That was why it was a lonely, sterile place.

She felt his absence keenly—she'd felt it like an open wound within her ever since the Bow Street officers had taken him away yesterday.

Lying here in the cold, lonelier than she'd ever been, Emma realized a truth that she'd been avoiding for days.

She wanted to be with Luke in every way. It didn't matter that she was married to someone else. She needed him…and a deep, intrinsic part of her told her that he needed her as well. She truly wanted to be beside him through thick and thin. She wanted to help him heal, and she wanted him to help her heal. He had already gone so far in doing so. Since she had been with him, she'd never felt so confident. So cherished or so protected.

Luke made her whole.

By being with Luke, she would consciously be committing the most grievous of sins—one that had always disgusted her. Yet, Henry had been dead to her for a year. And somehow, seeing him in the flesh for those brief seconds had solidified his death in her mind. There was no doubt about it—Henry was dead to her in every way that mattered. In the eyes of the law, he might be her spouse, but he would never be her true husband again.

She remembered the preacher in Soho, the sermon about adultery. A twisting sickness welled in her gut. She closed her eyes and prayed for understanding.

She lay awake for hours, her ears straining for the sounds of movement in the house below. Once the servants had gone to bed, there were none. Luke wasn't coming home.

Chapter Eighteen

❧

Emma woke to a scratching sound at her door. She bolted upright, instantly awake. Luke had returned and wanted to see her. *Thank God.*

She hastened out of bed and hurried to the door. She unlocked it and flung it open as her heart fluttered in anticipation. She would fall to her knees and beg his forgiveness if that was what it took.

"Luke, I . . ." The words died on her tongue.

Luke wasn't at her threshold. It was Henry—*Morton.* He stood there, wearing a fierce expression and holding a pistol pointed at her chest.

"Emma," he said softly, "don't make a noise, or I'll shoot. I swear it."

She froze, her lips parted, staring at him. "What are . . . what are you doing here?" she stammered.

He gave her a tight, false smile. "We need to talk."

"T-talk?" Her gaze went to the weapon. His forefinger

rested on the trigger. One little movement of that finger and her chest would be blown open.

"Right. Talk. But not here. You'll need to come with me."

"Now?" she breathed.

He huffed out a breath. "Yes, now. Do you think this is a social visit? It's two o'clock in the morning, for God's sake."

Her mind worked frantically. "I need to . . . dress."

His jaw firmed. That jaw she'd once pressed her hand to—that jaw she'd once thought she loved . . .

No, she couldn't think of any of that right now. This man was a stranger to her. He always had been.

He was silent for a long moment. Then he nodded. "Very well. Dress. Quickly. I'll give you five minutes. And don't make any noise, Emma, because I don't want to be forced to use this"—he waved the gun—"but I will, if it comes to that."

"I understand," Emma murmured. She believed him. His hair was tousled, his cravat askew. He bore the expression of a desperate man.

"Go, then." He gestured the gun in the direction of the armoire but made no move to close the door or give her any privacy.

She gathered her courage. "Will you . . . will you wait outside?"

His glance darted to the window. "I don't think so."

"Do you honestly think I'd jump out the window? We are two stories up. I'd kill myself."

He ground his teeth audibly. "You've four minutes now. Don't attempt to lock the door. If you do, you'll regret it."

He stepped back and pulled the door so that it was almost, but not quite, shut. She knew he was hovering just behind it, his fingers on the handle, his foot at the threshold to prevent the door from closing. He was fully prepared to rush in should she attempt to do anything untoward.

Hurriedly, she donned her chemise and one of her muslins. Then she fetched the old wool and ermine cloak that looked so bedraggled now. It had deep, concealed pockets sewn into it, and like the day they'd ventured to the docklands, she removed her own pistol from the bottom of the drawer where she'd stowed it and slid it into one of the pockets.

She was pulling the edges of the cloak together and stepping toward the door when Henry—*Morton*—opened it again. His eyes raked up and down her body. Evidently satisfied, he gave a brusque nod and stepped aside to let her out of the room.

"You will go downstairs and out the back door. I've a carriage waiting in the mews. Don't make any loud noises."

"Where are you taking me?"

"Somewhere safe."

She didn't like the way he said "safe." As though it would be safe for him but not necessarily for her.

And suddenly it all made sense. He wouldn't kill her here—it would be too conspicuous. Instead, he'd take her somewhere "safe" and do away with her there. In a place where he wouldn't be immediately implicated for her murder.

How could he do that? Murder a woman he'd once pretended to love?

"Are you a murderer, too, Henry?" she asked him, the words coming out before she could censor them.

"No," he said. But he didn't meet her eyes. "Go on, then." He gestured toward the stairs. She went down, and he followed close behind her. As strong as a touch, she felt the barrel of the gun aimed at her back. They left the house through the open back door.

It was cold outside, the air crisp and clear. The moon shone bright, and what seemed like a million stars glittered overhead.

He nudged her toward the waiting carriage.

The comforting weight of her own pistol knocked against her leg as she walked. With a growing sickness inside her, she realized that she truly didn't have any idea how to handle a gun. She'd never shot a weapon in her life.

All she could do was wait until he least expected it, then bring out the pistol. Hopefully he'd be in a position where he'd have no choice but to let her go. Hopefully she wouldn't have to attempt to shoot him.

The sickness in her gut twisted and tightened. She was glad she hadn't eaten anything for dinner, because she wouldn't have been able to keep it down.

Morton opened the door for her, and she stepped inside. As she turned around to settle onto the seat, she saw the broken remnants of the open dining room window. Morton had shattered the panes and climbed through it. She hadn't heard the sound of breaking glass, and clearly the servants hadn't either, but there must be ways to quiet it. And the floor in the dining room was carpeted, so that would muffle the noise of glass falling onto it.

Morton pushed in next to her and closed the door, and

the carriage jerked into motion. She scooted across the squab and pressed herself into the opposite door, as far away from him as she could manage.

He still held the gun. He held it balanced on his leg, ominously pointed at her.

"I could kill you now," he murmured quietly. "It would be so easy. And it would fix everything. Do you realize how eliminating you will rid me of all my problems?" He sighed, as if he thought her cruel for putting him in this untenable position.

"It won't rid you of your problems," she said confidently. "Luke will come after you."

"Lord Lukas Hawkins?" he scoffed. "Last I heard, he was in prison for theft. The evidence against him is very strong indeed. I have no doubt he'll hang."

So he hadn't heard that Luke had already been released. He quirked a brow at her. "Hanging is a well-deserved fate for that man, wouldn't you agree? Taking my wife into his home as if she were a common whore..." He made a low noise of disgust.

Emma's stomach cramped and twisted.

"But then again, I wouldn't have expected that of you, either, Emma."

"I was a widow," she ground out. Then she pressed her lips together, refusing to speak any more on the subject. Above all, she didn't need to defend her actions to this man. Instead, she asked quietly, "So that is your goal? Have Lord Lukas hanged for a crime he didn't commit, then kill me so neither of us will implicate you? But you're not a murderer. You said so."

"Yet I can't allow you to implicate me, either. Don't you see? It's you or me."

"What if I didn't implicate you?" she asked quietly. She hated this man so much right now. She despised the way he spoke of taking her life as if it were a business transaction. "All I want is my father to have his money back."

He barked out a humorless laugh.

"And Luke—Lord Lukas—needs information regarding the whereabouts of his mother. Just give us our money and give his lordship the information, and we will leave you alone."

"But you're *my* wife, Emma. Or have you forgotten?" His voice was soft.

"You're dead, Henry. Or have *you* forgotten?"

He blinked at her. She'd changed since she'd last known him. Circumstances had forced her to become a much stronger person. She was a woman of action now, a woman who'd fought for her family's survival for the past year.

Hopefully Henry would soon know the extent of that strength. When she escaped from him. When she forced him to unearth her father's money and the Dowager Duchess of Trent. When she saw him called to task for all that he had done to everyone he had wronged.

"How'd you end up with Hawkins?" he asked her. "Did you think you could win a duke's brother to save your father's fortune?"

"It has nothing to do with that." She clutched the door handle to steady herself as the carriage rattled over a deep rut. "He came to Bristol looking for Roger Morton. I was also looking for Morton, so—"

"*You* were looking for Morton?"

"You didn't escape as thoroughly as you believed,

Henry. You left plenty of evidence of Morton behind. For over a year, I thought he'd murdered you."

He raised his brows.

"Lord Lukas and I followed you all the way to London."

"Where you somehow located my offices."

"You are Roger Morton, then," she murmured. "Who is the alias? Are you Henry, or are you Roger? Or are both of those identities false?"

He grimaced, then shrugged, as if thinking that revealing the truth would not affect matters between them. Strengthening her theory that he indeed intended to kill her. "My real name is Roger Morton."

She released a slow breath. She'd known it—all the evidence pointed toward it. But it cut deep to know that even his name had been a part of his fake courtship. He'd played her false from the moment she'd made his acquaintance.

"You're still my wife," he muttered now.

"Please don't be a hypocrite."

He narrowed his dark eyes at her. "You've taken him into your bed, haven't you?"

"That is none of your concern."

"The courts wouldn't agree."

"Is that so? Would you begin criminal proceedings against Luke, then? After faking your name and subsequent death and leaving me and my family penniless for a year?" She made a low, scoffing noise in her throat. "Would the courts even acknowledge our marriage?"

"Henry Curtis existed in truth, Emma. I could become him again. Easily."

"Is that what you want?" she asked, well aware of the

bitterness lacing her voice. "To return with me to Bristol and resume our life there?"

His expression soured. "Of course not. That monotonous existence wasn't for me."

Clearly.

"Where is our money, Henry? Or, forgive me, *Mr. Morton?*"

His expression went blank. "Your money? I don't know what you're talking about."

"The money you stole from my father."

"I stole nothing."

"So you'll admit that you counterfeited your identity and your death, yet you will insist you didn't take my father's money from him? If you didn't do it for the money, then for what? Certainly it had naught to do with me. You're a liar as well as a thief."

He studied her with slitted eyes. He reminded her of a snake assessing whether it would be beneficial to strike out at a creature who'd disturbed its lair.

She glanced down at the weapon still pointed at her and took a slow, steady breath. She was no less convinced that he wished to kill her—he was just waiting for the right time and place so that he could make himself appear as innocent as possible. He was a wily, conniving liar, and while it might be easy to associate him with the man she'd once thought she'd loved, she mustn't forget his villainy. Not for a second. It could mean her life.

"I would suggest you cease your accusations, Emma. I don't believe you're in the position of power here." He looked meaningfully at the pistol.

She released a slow, controlled breath. She didn't think he'd murder her in cold blood in a carriage in the middle of London. Even in the dead of the night, there would be witnesses, and he didn't want that. Still, he'd made rash decisions before without being entirely careful. He'd staged his own death while leaving evidence of the existence of Roger Morton, for example. He was a villain, but he wasn't the most thorough of villains.

If she made him angry enough, she didn't doubt he'd to something rash. To his own detriment...and hers.

She bit her lip. "Will you tell me one thing?" she asked softly. "What was that business with the Duchess of Trent?"

Morton's lip curled, and he relaxed into his seat, but that blasted gun remained trained unerringly on her breast. "That woman is a virago. Did you know that?"

She shook her head.

"What is it, then? Is word going round that I kidnapped her and did away with her?"

"No one is exactly sure," she murmured.

"It was nothing like that." He gave a short, mocking laugh. "I endured that month for an old man I owed a debt to. He forgave the debt in exchange for my services."

"Ah...a wager, I take it? Like the one you made stating I'd be with child in three months?"

He raised a brow. "Similar, yes, I suspect. So did VanHorne demand his payment?"

She stayed still, clenching her fists in her lap to prevent herself from lashing out at him. "He did."

He frowned. "How much was that for? A hundred guineas?"

"Five hundred," she choked out.

"Ah." Morton made a dismissive motion with his hand. "Well, this wager was of a similar nature. When he offered to forgive the debt if I fetched the duchess for him, it seemed like the easiest of payments. Plus, at the time I thought it might be an entertaining endeavor. I needed a diversion."

"Who was this man?"

"An old gypsy." Morton shook his head. "He had the manner of an English gentleman but the disposition of one of the most vile of his race."

"So you kidnapped the duchess?"

He made a *tsk*ing noise. "*Kidnapped* is a rather strong word, Emma," he drawled. "By all means, I did not kidnap the woman. She came willingly enough, once she ceased throwing things at me."

She frowned. "But...why?"

"Wasn't much of my business. But from what I could gather, the two were lovers. And he wanted her back."

"What?"

"Is that so surprising?"

She looked down at her lap, thinking of all that Luke had told her about the Dowager Duchess of Trent. She'd kept many lovers, had had at least two children out of wedlock. It wasn't such a stretch to think that one of those lovers might have been a gypsy.

"Why didn't he go to her himself?"

"Ah. You sound like the duchess. 'Why isn't he here, then?' she squawked at me. 'Tell him I won't go, not unless he comes to me first,' she harped. But he was unable to come—which was why he'd given over the task to me. I ultimately convinced her to go with me."

"You took her to Wales?"

"Yes, to Cardiff." His dark eyes met hers. "So close to my Emma. I checked up on you, you know."

Fury rose hot in her cheeks. If he'd checked up on her, he'd undoubtedly seen how she'd struggled. He'd done nothing to help, nothing to ease what he had done to them. "You had no right," she bit out.

"That is a matter of debate," he said calmly.

"You cannot imagine to claim any sort of responsibility or ownership over me when you were—and are—legally deceased."

He merely shrugged. It seemed the argument was pointless to him. Clearly he had decided that though he believed them to still be technically married, they certainly wouldn't be once he'd killed her.

She changed the subject. This topic would certainly gain her nothing. But for Luke's sake, she needed to find out what had happened to his mother.

"So you took her to Cardiff. What happened then?"

"We waited for the gypsy to show up. And he took his time about it, let me tell you. I think he intended to torture me with that woman's whims for as long as possible. He only rescued me when I was on the verge of throttling her."

"What is this man's name?"

He gazed at her for a moment, then shrugged, seeming to deem telling her to be inconsequential. "His English name is Steven Lowell. I don't know what they call him in that heathen language of theirs."

She committed the name to memory. "And he came, eventually, to fetch the duchess. How did she react to him?"

"I do not know," he said dryly. "I was not present for their reunion. Lowell came to me and said he had no further need of me. I left Cardiff immediately. I'd had enough of the place."

"Do you know where he intended to take her?"

"Of course not. I imagine he intends to take her all over the place, though. Isn't that what gypsies do? Live nomadic lives by illegally squatting upon properties that rightfully belong to others?"

"You said that he had the demeanor of a gentleman. I thought that meant he might have a home somewhere."

Morton snorted. "I doubt that." He waved his free hand. "It is of no consequence. I have washed my hands of that virago the duchess, and I have washed my hands of Lowell as well. It is merely one less debt to repay."

What of the debt he owed Emma? And her father? The caustic words were on the tip of her tongue, but she didn't set them free. There was no point. Morton had admitted to everything except his most villainous crime, and he didn't seem likely to confess that.

In truth, out of all his crimes, it was the theft that was the most likely to get Roger Morton hanged. Maybe that was why he didn't intend to confess it, even to a woman he intended to murder.

She nodded, shifting in her seat to feel the comforting weight of her pistol. When should she use it? Surely it would be unwise to draw it now, when he still had his own pistol resting on his leg and aimed at her.

She gritted her teeth, her fear and anxiety making her fidget. Thoughts of Luke kept creeping into her head. If he returned home drunk in the early morning hours, would he look for her? She'd left the door to her room open, so if he came upstairs, he'd notice right away that she was gone. What would he think when he saw her empty but tousled bed?

If he was still angry with her, would he go upstairs to

check on her at all tonight? And even if he noted her absence, what could he do? She didn't know where Morton was going, and Luke wouldn't know either.

She closed her eyes. She felt her separation from Luke as a deep pain in her chest that grew as the distance stretched farther between them. She couldn't count on him coming after her.

A part of her knew without a doubt that if he saw that she was missing, he *would* come. Despite everything that Luke had done, despite all the challenges they had faced, he cared for her. She was sure of it.

He might be angry with her, but he would come if he could. He would save her if he could. Those simple thoughts calmed her, soothed her, even as she knew he probably wouldn't come at all.

Chapter Nineteen

$\mathcal{L}$uke had not found Morton in London. He had gone to the man's offices, broken in through the blackened window, and rifled through every bit of evidence he could find. He found more addresses and more names—one of particular note. It contained more details on the property Morton had purchased—including its location in the parish of Chiswick, a few miles outside of London.

When he left the warehouse, Luke rode straight to Morton's sister's house in Soho. Though by this time it was growing late in the evening, she received him in a shabby parlor and served him what was probably the last bitter dregs of her tea supply.

"I'm so sorry to bother you at this late hour," he told Mrs. O'Bailey, "but I must ask you some urgent questions pertaining to your brother."

"Of course, my lord. What would you like to know?"

He gazed at her, mildly disconcerted. Her acquiescence had been too easy, but he also knew why she was so accommodating—because he was the Duke of Trent's brother.

He didn't have the energy to be annoyed by that tonight.

He asked her if she knew anything about Morton's dealings in Bristol. "No, sir," she told him. "I never knew he'd gone to Bristol."

"Have you ever heard of Henry Curtis? He was an associate of your brother's there."

"No, sir."

"Do you believe your brother's investments have been successful ones?"

She seemed to ponder this one for a moment. "Well," she finally said, "I believe so, but it isn't something we've spoken of often."

"Does your brother keep his only residence in London?"

"Yes, my lord. Except when he travels outside of London for business."

"What, exactly, is the business that compels him to leave Town?" he asked her.

"I'm not certain, but I believe it's to do with prospecting."

The woman was such a simple, honest sort, he couldn't bear to tell her the truth. He didn't want to be the person to destroy her assumption that her brother was a decent, hardworking man. He didn't want to tell her that the bastard was a criminal whom he intended to have hanged.

He thanked her and left. He glanced in the direction of Cavendish Square—and Emma—but he didn't go home.

Not yet. He wouldn't go home until he had something to bring home to her, something solid they could use against Morton.

They.

She had betrayed him. She hadn't trusted him, and she'd revealed his deepest secret. He should be furious with her.

But she had apologized, and her apology had been heartfelt—he knew Emma well enough to understand this. And despite himself, despite all the bitterness and anger he'd always held inside, he had already forgiven her. It seemed she'd somehow leached that bitterness and anger out of him.

He loved her. How long could he stay angry with the woman he loved?

She had betrayed him, yes, and as much as he continued to feel the burn of that inside him, another part of him was convinced that she had done what she'd done only out of worry and care.

Instead of going home to Cavendish Square and to Emma, he turned toward his brother Sam's house. He had no desire to face Trent right now, but he and Sam needed to talk.

He secured his horse and knocked on Sam's door. It was answered by his brother's manservant, who led him into Sam's back study. As always, Sam was working—scribbling away, probably a report on the mission he'd just completed for the Crown. He looked up, brows raised, as Luke entered, but he didn't rise.

Luke didn't bother with platitudes or decorum, either. He went straight to the chair across the desk from Sam's and sank into it with a tired sigh.

There was no reason to beat about the bush. "She told you."

Sam knew exactly what he was talking about, of course.

"She did." His voice was mild.

"And you told Trent."

Sam nodded. He placed his pen in its tray and steepled his fingers at his chin.

"Why?" Luke asked him.

"I thought he should know."

"I disagree."

A corner of Sam's lips quirked upward. "That much was obvious, considering you haven't deigned to tell him—or any of us—for the last twenty years."

Luke's fingers tightened over his knees. "It was my problem to manage on my own."

Sam scoffed. "You were a child."

"So were you," he shot back.

"But older," Sam said. "I could have protected you."

Luke rolled his eyes heavenward.

Sam's lips tightened. "It is a family's responsibility as a whole to keep a child safe. We failed you in that regard."

Luke fidgeted, feeling more uncomfortable by the second. He gazed down at his lap as his throat tightened with some emotion he couldn't name. He sucked in a breath. "I c-came..." His voice cracked loudly. He cleared his throat and tried again. "I came here to let you know that I won't tolerate anyone speaking of it. It happened in the past. It is over."

"Not to you, evidently. Mrs. Curtis said you have nightmares."

Luke closed his eyes against yet another unwelcome jolt of betrayal. "Let it go, Sam."

"Very well," Sam said, too easily. When Luke opened his eyes, he saw a glint in Sam's. "Word of advice, Luke: You need to stop interpreting all that Trent does for you in the worst possible light."

"What do you mean?" Luke demanded.

"Everything he does for you comes from a place of deep caring. You don't seem to see that, though. Even when he arranges to have you exonerated from a hanging offense, you have no doubt found a way to blame him. The truth is, however, that there's only one reason he left parliament early today and nearly killed himself to ensure you were cleared of the charges brought against you. And that reason is that you are his brother. He loves you."

The word *love* plowed into Luke like a deadly arrow finding its mark. It was not a word that had ever been bandied about freely in the Hawkins household.

He stared at his brother, who was gazing at him, his expression inscrutable.

"Forgive Trent," Sam said quietly. "He doesn't always express his love in the most forgivable of ways, and he has a tendency to push you to extremes. Hell—you have a tendency to push him to extremes, too. But he means well. The news of your abuse at his father's hands has devastated him."

"I...don't want it to devastate him..." Luke pushed out.

"What do you want, then?"

"I didn't want him to know at all."

"It's too late for that," Sam said, a rare gentle tone in his voice. "He does know. So does Esme, and no doubt

Theo and Mark will know soon as well. You'll need to live with that."

Luke thrust a frustrated hand through his hair.

"Why does it vex you that we know, Luke? Is it because you feel it makes you look weak? Because we will see you as less of a man?"

It felt like a giant fist tightened around Luke's chest. He stared at his brother for a long moment. "Maybe."

"That's stupid," Sam said flatly. "You were just a boy."

"Exactly. It all happened long ago. So I should not be dwelling upon it now, and neither should the lot of you."

"You were brutalized at your father's hands."

"Not my father," Luke said quickly.

"The man you thought was your father, then. Those kinds of scars do not fade quickly." Emotion bled into Sam's flat brown gaze. He knew what it was like to be beaten. Perhaps not in the exact same way, but he'd fought in wars and had been injured in battle. He'd endured the deaths of two wives and an infant son.

"How do you live with it, Sam?" Luke murmured.

"I live a day at a time," Sam replied, equally quiet. "I can't think too far ahead. If I think only of today, then I can endure it."

It was odd, but for the first time, Luke felt he had gained a deeper understanding of his stoical brother. Sam had endured worse than Luke had. Sam had suffered, but those close to him had suffered even worse. Luke couldn't even begin to think of how he would feel if Emma died. All he knew was that he'd succumb to madness once and for all.

"Sometimes," Luke said in a low voice, "it feels like I'm going mad. Like *he's* driving me straight to insanity."

"I know," Sam said. "And I'm sure he is attempting to do it, in your mind. Attempting to drive you straight into the welcoming arms of Bedlam. But you've battled against him for this long, and I've no doubt that you'll continue to fight. Harder, even, now that you have Mrs. Curtis."

Luke jolted at her name. "What about Mrs. Curtis?"

Sam's expression subtly softened. "Come, now, brother—"

"What about her?" Luke demanded.

"She is a tigress."

Luke narrowed his eyes. "What does that mean?"

"She was prepared to bare her claws and tear into the flesh of anyone who would slander you, much less throw you into prison on false charges. She fought hard for you, and with great passion." Sam sounded impressed.

"She did?"

"Yes. And I thought she would kill me when I told her I needed to take the problem to Trent. She begged me not to go to him, but in the interests of expediency, there was no other choice. I had to entreat the duchess and Esme to calm her. Still, she paced my corridor like a prowling cat all afternoon. And when Esme and I drove her back to your house in Cavendish Square, she snarled if anyone so much as mentioned your name."

Luke was surprised to feel a smile curling the edges of his lips. "Did she, now?" he asked softly. Love for Emma bloomed in him, swirling sweetly. He wanted to go home to her. Tell her how much he loved her. Ask her for forgiveness for speaking to her in anger earlier.

Nevertheless, the problem of her marriage vows and her unwillingness to consciously break them hung like a dark cloud over his head. As much as he wanted to take her straight to bed and make love to her until dawn, the fact remained that she wouldn't allow him to touch her.

And there was still the matter of Roger Morton. Whoever the hell the man was, Luke needed to find him and resolve this once and for all.

"Trent said if Morton married her under a false name, then the marriage would be annulled. Is that true?" he asked Sam.

"Yes. But given everything that has happened, don't you think Morton will be hanged once he is caught?" Sam asked. "Either way, the man is irrelevant. She'll ultimately be free."

Not so irrelevant, Luke thought. If Morton was hanged as her husband, she would have to endure the stigma of being the widow of a criminal, not to mention the additional stigma of having been Luke's lover while she was still married. Furthermore, if he knew Emma, she'd feel she would have to endure yet another year of mourning before she could truly be free to be his.

If the marriage was annulled, however, she would be free and clear. She wouldn't feel like an adulteress. She'd be able to start anew.

Luke studied his brother. "You too?" he mused. "You think I ought to marry her?"

"Of course. You'd be a damned fool not to. And while I know you've made many, many stupid decisions in your life, brother, I don't think you're stupid enough to allow this one to slip through your fingers. This is a brave woman. One who will stand by your side and fight for you. Best of all, she loves you."

That word again.

Hell.

Luke was beginning to feel rather overwhelmed. He needed to leave. He had much to accomplish this night, and the hour had grown late. He rose.

"I hope you're heading home to propose marriage," Sam said, the barest hint of a smile curling his lips.

"Not yet," Luke replied. "I'm heading out to Chiswick to follow up with a lead about Morton's whereabouts. I need to confront the man."

"I suppose you'll insist you require no assistance from Trent and me."

Luke's hands tightened over the back of the chair. For a long moment, his throat was too crowded with emotion for him to speak. Then he said, "Let me do this on my own, Sam. Let me . . . try."

"I hope you will absorb into your thick skull that we come to your assistance not because we believe you are incapable, but because we care and want to lend our help in whatever way possible. I know it is an alien concept to you, but it is natural for people to wish to help those they hold in high regard. Promise me you'll remember that."

Luke couldn't move, much less make a promise like that.

Sam sighed. "We'll stay away from Chiswick tonight. But if you're not back by noon tomorrow, there's no army that could stop Trent and me from finding our brother and ensuring his safety. Do you understand?"

"I'll find Morton, I promise you," Luke choked out. "Then I'll find our mother."

Sam sighed. "I hope you're right, Luke. I really, really hope you're right."

* * *

It took almost an hour before Luke reached the location in Chiswick that had been written on the bill of sale. He rode down a long, overgrown driveway, glad for clear skies and a good amount of moonlight to guide him, and stopped his horse in front of a large house that might have once been grand but was now in disrepair, with peeling paint and an overgrown lawn. The place was quiet and dark, but it was after midnight now, and if anyone lived here, it was possible they were all abed.

He dismounted, secured his horse in a small clearing surrounded by trees, and walked around the place, keeping his steps quiet and his body hidden in shadows so he wouldn't make himself known if there was anyone about. From what he could gather by rubbing at the dirt-encrusted windows and peering into the darkened interior, the house was abandoned.

He tried the doors—which were locked—then the windows one by one. He finally found one he could push open a few inches. He reached inside and forcibly pushed it the remaining way up by grasping its frame from the inside. Then he swung his leg over the ledge and vaulted inside.

He landed in a crouch on the floor of a large kitchen. There was a rectangular table and a few overturned chairs, all covered with a fine layer of grime. When he stepped forward, kicking up a cloud of dust, a small animal he didn't care to name scuttled across the wooden floor.

The fact that the kitchen wasn't in use confirmed that the place was abandoned. It was a large house, and it could certainly be made to be elegant given a great deal of work. That was probably what Morton had intended—to use some of the money he'd stolen from Emma's father to remodel this pile into a stately home.

Luke systematically searched the house. He went through every room, from the downstairs galleries, with their stripped wallpaper and scuffed floors, to the upstairs rooms with once-grand but now blackened fireplaces, peeling paint, and crumbling walls.

There were three notable rooms. The first was a vast hall—perhaps a ballroom—that was piled high with furniture and other items that had been covered by large white linen cloths. When Luke moved the cloths aside, he saw that everything beneath was new and of the highest quality. There were gilded mirrors, ancient-looking statues, Greek urns, Persian carpets.

This must be where Morton had stored some of the items he'd purchased with his ill-gotten gains.

The second room of note might have once been a library. Its furniture, including a grand assortment of bookshelves, had been piled in the center of the room. Oddly, one wall had been completely stripped of its wallpaper and repainted. The same white paint had been used on one wall of what had clearly been the drawing room, with its dusty pianoforte with several missing keys and a nest that rats had created out of shredded newspapers in one corner.

Luke went upstairs to the servants' quarters and into the attic. The house was still and quiet. Eerie, really, in these early morning hours. Luke felt his way about in the darkness, relieved whenever he encountered a west-facing room, where the moon could offer some additional light.

He returned downstairs, his mind working furiously over the various ways to catch Morton the next time he appeared here, when he heard a noise that made him stop dead in the middle of the corridor. He listened. There it was again—a rattle coming from outside.

The noise came from the back of the house and sounded very much like a carriage traveling over a rutted road. Luke made his way to the kitchen, to the broken window where he'd entered the house, and, keeping his body out of sight, he peered out.

The dark, shadowy form of a small carriage came into view as it rounded a bend in the driveway. It stopped in front of a smaller rectangular building Luke had earlier assumed was the stable—he'd intended to search it after completing his inventory of the house.

The coachman remained in his seat, sitting stiffly. A man alighted, holding his hand aloft, and Luke stiffened. The man held a gun, clearly silhouetted by the moonlight. He waved it at another occupant of the carriage, gesturing at that person to quit the vehicle as well.

Luke's hand went to his own pistol, still tucked into his pocket.

Skirts fell from the doorway. Slippered toes reached for the step, and then she emerged, setting every single one of Luke's senses screaming.

Damn it. The bastard had Emma.

He watched, his body so tight he couldn't have moved even if he wanted to. They spoke, but Luke couldn't hear the words from here. The man gestured in the direction of the stable, then turned to the coachman, snapping out instructions. The coachman nodded, then turned the carriage around and left in the direction they had come.

Luke's fingers tightened on the sill. He couldn't see her face. He needed to see her face, needed to know if she was all right.

But she turned away from him and headed toward the stables. Morton—or whoever the hell he was—followed her, keeping the gun pointed steadily on her back.

Hell, no.

Luke was not going to let that bastard hurt the woman he loved.

* * *

"Open the latch," Morton told Emma when they reached the stable door. She did as she was told, still acutely aware of the gun aimed at her.

She hadn't been able to see much from the window as they'd approached this place. They'd driven down a long, winding, narrow road to get here. She'd seen the large, dark house through Morton's window and this stable through her own. She'd no idea where they were.

She breathed steadily, keeping her fear in constant check. Time was running short for her. Could she whip out her pistol and shoot him before he could shoot her?

No, she thought, panic twisting her innards tighter and tighter. She didn't think so. If only he'd point that infernal weapon at something else for a moment...

But he didn't. His dark eyes were watchful, too, not straying from her for longer than the blink of an eye.

"What are you going to do with me?" she breathed.

"Just walk inside, Emma."

She did, feeling old bits of hay under her slippers.

"Go into that stall on the end."

Oh, Lord. She didn't like the sound of his voice. It had become low and rough. On shaking legs, she forced herself to go to the end stall. Inside, it was dark, but as her eyes adjusted, she saw the shadowy shape of a bale of hay.

"Sit on that," Morton said, gesturing at the hay bale, "and face me."

Again, she did as she was told. She gazed up at him. His face was drawn into tight lines. The hand that held his weapon trembled.

"You...give me...no choice, Emma," he bit out. "Lie down. Stomach onto the hay."

He intended to...to *execute* her.

Oh Lord.

"Please," she whispered. It was too late for her pistol, but her shaking hand moved toward her cloak pocket anyhow. It was her only hope.

"You have forced me to these ends," he said in that rough, odd voice. "This is not my fault. I am no murderer, but you have made me into one, do you hear me? *You*."

"No," she murmured. "You're not a murderer...Henry. I know you." She was lying but she didn't know what else to do, how else to convince him...

"Lie down," he said sharply. His weapon drew inexorably closer.

She did it. She lay on her stomach. Stray pieces of hay poked at her through her bodice and prodded the bare skin of her chest.

"I won't tell anyone," she whispered.

"It's too late for that, isn't it, Emma? The damned Duke of Trent knows about me now. The only way out of this for me is to eliminate you. Once you're gone, I'll find a way to turn his suspicion to you."

Luke would never believe that. If she had to die, she'd die believing he'd know she was innocent.

She couldn't let Morton murder her. Luke needed her. She needed *him*.

She turned to face Morton. He stepped closer. The barrel of that horrid gun headed toward her temple. Now it was pressed against it, the metal cold against her skin.

Her body trembled violently, and her hand fumbled, searching for the opening of her pocket. She couldn't find it. Her weight was on a fold of her cloak, blocking it.

Morton cocked the pistol, and she sucked in a breath at the sharp cracking noise. Lord, she thought in despair. She knew so little about firearms. The gun hadn't been cocked this entire time. She should have taken the chance and tried to shoot him. She probably would have succeeded.

But now it was too late.

She gazed at him, saw his eyes dilate even as they narrowed.

Luke, she thought, *I love you. Please know that I love you...*

They heard the sound at the same time. A scuffling, followed by a low slam—like the wooden stable door had crashed against its inside wall.

Morton reared backward, trying to see who was coming without taking his eyes off her, which was impossible. He finally gave up and swung his gaze toward the stall door.

Emma sprang into motion. She scrambled up, digging into the folds of her cloak for her weapon. Just as her fingers touched metal, a large, dark figure surged into the tiny space. The silver of his pistol glinted in the dimness.

"Luke!" Her voice broke on a wrenching combination of relief and fear.

Morton barreled into him. She heard the thud as one of their pistols fell to the floor. Their arms flailed, punctuated by the dull sounds of gasping breaths and fists connecting to flesh. Both men tumbled to the hay-strewn floor, locked in a brutal battle.

"Stop!" she cried, raising her own gun in her shaking hands. She couldn't shoot—Luke's and Morton's limbs thrashed violently in the dimness of the tiny space, and she couldn't tell whose belonged to whom.

Morton surged to his knees, his dark eyes widening at the sight of the pistol in her hand. Before she could blink, he raised his gun. Again, toward her. And she was facing the barrel of a gun pointed directly at her chest once more.

Everything ground to slow motion. Like someone had poured syrup into the stall and they had to push through it with every movement. Her vision became precise, hawklike. She saw everything. Saw Morton's eyes narrow. Saw the tiny movement of his finger tightening on the trigger.

Her own quaking finger awkwardly cocked her pistol.

"No!" Luke roared, and Emma jerked back, because his voice cracked like a gunshot. In a blur of motion, he jumped in front of her, knocking the pistol from her hand and the wind from her lungs as they tumbled to the floor. A much louder *crack* pierced the air. Luke's body jerked over her.

Oh, God. He'd been hit.

Morton had shot Luke.

Something thudded to the floor. Morton's gun? Luke's

body was heavy atop hers. She lay sprawled across the hay. She couldn't see Morton beyond Luke's large form. Luke groaned, and suddenly, all her senses went on high alert.

"Luke!" she cried, searching his body desperately with her hands. With a grunt of pain, he slid off her, leaving her right hand wet with blood.

Luke tried to rise to his knees but faltered, weakened by his injury. Morton, his face twisted with fury, lunged toward him, hands out, poised to kill.

Just as Morton reached him, Luke surged up. A weapon—Emma's pistol—glinted in his hand. The gun fired with a deafening roar, and Morton staggered backward two steps. His backside hit the door, and he sagged into a heap on the floor, instantly unconscious.

Luke dropped Emma's gun, then he, too, slid bonelessly to the floor. Emma scrambled over to him.

"Luke...Luke, where are you hit?"

His eyelids fluttered. "Emma," he said in a rasping voice. He reached weakly toward her. "Are you all right?"

"I'm fine, but you're shot..." Tears streamed down her face in hot stripes. "Wh-where were you shot?"

"Don't know...My stomach...it burns..."

"Just lie still." She glanced at Morton. It was so dark, she couldn't tell where he'd been hit either. But he didn't move or speak, so she assumed he was either unconscious or dead.

She hoped he was dead.

She turned back to Luke. "Stay here. I'm going for help. I'll be back soon."

He caught her wrist with his hand. "Em...stay with me. I need you, Em."

What he needed was help—a doctor. She gently pulled out of his grip.

"Need you with me..."

"I love you," she said in a vehement whisper. "I'll be back soon. You wait."

His eyes began to sink shut.

"Wait for me, Luke!" she commanded.

He was losing consciousness. She swallowed down the sob that welled in her throat, rose, and hurried to the door. It devastated her to leave his side now. If he died while she was gone, she'd never recover.

Marshaling all the strength she possessed, she ran for help.

Chapter Twenty

※

$\mathcal{L}$uke woke to early morning sunlight streaming into the room. His side ached, but the pain was now only a dull throb. Three weeks had passed since Morton had shot him. The bullet had pierced the side of his stomach, missing vital organs by less than a fraction of an inch, the doctors had told him.

His recovery had been long and painful, but Morton had fared far worse. Luke hadn't dealt him a killing wound—he'd shot him in the shoulder. But once the doctor who'd helped Luke had seen to Morton's injury, he'd been charged with a multitude of crimes, from forgery to theft to kidnapping, then transferred to Newgate Prison.

The wound had festered in the filth of the prison, poisoning Morton's blood, and seven days ago, he had died.

But not before his marriage to Emma had been annulled on the grounds of the husband having forged his identity on the marriage license. Luke had Trent to thank for that. While Luke and Emma had been overcome by the immediacy and seriousness of Luke's wound, Trent had taken it upon himself to see that Morton and Emma's marriage was declared null and void.

When Trent had come to tell them the news, Emma's eyes had cleared of the pain that had resided there since the moment she'd seen her "husband" was alive. And perhaps for the first time in his life, Luke had taken no offense to Trent poking his nose into business that didn't concern him.

Maybe it was the start of a new, better relationship between them. Luke hoped that would be the case.

Anticipation welling sweetly within him, he turned his head to the woman lying beside him. She was awake, too, lying still and gazing at him with those lovely amber eyes.

"I didn't know you were awake," he murmured.

"I heard you stir."

His lips quirked into a smile. She'd gone to get help on the night he'd been shot, but she hadn't left his side since.

God, how he loved her. She'd saved his life. In more ways than he could possibly express.

"Doctor says I am free to finally leave this bed today," he reminded her.

Her smile was as bright as the morning sunshine. "I know. Are you ready?"

"More than ready. You know that. I want to do it right now."

She raised her brows. "I thought we'd wait for your brothers and Esme."

His siblings came to see him every day. Even Theo and Mark had come up from Cambridge. Sam's words about brotherly love still resonated in Luke's head. For the first time in his life, Luke was able to appreciate the different ways his siblings showed they cared.

Trent made things—like the annulment—happen. Sarah showered him with motherly attention. Sam was a stoic, stable presence. Esme fretted and wrung her hands, and then she scribbled furiously in the notebook she always carried about with her. Theo and Mark chattered about nonsensical things, told jokes that made him laugh until the stitches pulled in his side, and asked him over and over to regale them with the story of how he had "saved Emma and defeated the dastardly Roger Morton."

Through it all, Emma was there. Beside him. Loving him in her quiet, steady way.

"I don't want to wait," he told her now. "I want to do it with you. I want to walk to the drawing room and receive my family there instead of here."

She grinned at him. "I think that's a wonderful idea. They'll all be so happy to see you up and about."

He was certainly ready. He'd been restless and anxious to get out of bed for the past week, but the doctor had said no—the wound needed more healing. As she had since that first night, Emma insisted he follow the doctor's orders to the letter.

She slipped out of bed, then came around to his side. Slowly, he lifted himself up to a seated position, feeling the pull—but no pain—in his injury. She held his arms as if to steady him, but he well knew he was too heavy for her. It didn't matter—he was quite capable of lifting his own body weight.

Equally slowly, he slid his legs over the edge of the bed. He was wearing his drawers and the shirt he wore to bed every night.

"Well done," she said, beaming.

He grinned up at her.

"Does it hurt?"

"Not at all."

"Good," she breathed. "Baldwin laid out your clothes last night. Can I help you into them?"

The last three weeks had been difficult and painful. Emma had probably seen enough blood and raw, oozing, pustulant flesh to last her a lifetime. But somehow, even though she'd never left him, he'd managed to continue to hide his back from her. There were times he'd asked her to turn away as Baldwin helped him out of his shirt and bathed him, and she had done so willingly but not without revealing the slightest tinge of hurt in her expression.

But today...today was the first day of his new life— at least he hoped it would be. And today was the day he needed to expose that last bit of himself he'd kept from her.

"Yes," he said gruffly. "Please help me to dress."

She sucked in a breath, surprised. Then her expression relaxed. "I'll call for a basin and cloth to wash you." Her gaze met his evenly. "Let me do this for you, Luke. You'll feel so much better."

There was a deeper meaning infused in her words. He understood it. She hadn't really ever commented on it or complained about it, but she knew as well as he did that he kept his shirt on in her presence for a reason.

"All right," he told her. His heart suddenly felt like it was galloping. The only person who'd seen the scars on his back was Baldwin, and he'd always discreetly refrained from mentioning them.

She was gone for a moment, ringing for Delaney and

then speaking to the maid. A few minutes later, the girl and Baldwin brought up a basin, soap, and several towels.

"Oh, sir," Delaney exclaimed when she saw Luke sitting on his own, "'tis so good to see you up!"

"Thank you, Delaney," he said. He glanced at Baldwin and thought he saw a hint of a smile on the man's imperturbable face.

"Shall I bathe and dress you, my lord?" Baldwin asked.

"No. Miss Anderson will do it." They all addressed Emma by her maiden name now that her marriage had been annulled.

"Very well, sir," Baldwin said flatly. He and Delaney took their leave, closing the door softly behind them.

Emma smiled at him as he sat there, frozen. Trying to fight back the fear and shame that had begun to well in his gut. Her smile thawed him, somewhat. Gave him the courage to go forward.

She gestured to his shirt. "Let me help you with that."

Taking her time, her hands gentle, she untied his neckline, then grasped his hem in both hands and began to lift.

Luke sat rigid. God. *God.* He didn't think he could do it.

"Lift your arms," she murmured. Her voice was so gentle.

With an extreme force of will, he did so. She lifted the shirt over his head and laid it over a nearby chair. When she returned, she checked his bandages. "Good. No bleeding."

She turned away to dip a cloth in the steaming water, then scrubbed the soap over the wet fabric.

She stepped back to him, her arm poised to wash him. He raised his arm, grasping her wrist in his hand, stopping her.

"Em—" His voice sounded reedy and thin.

Her sweet bosom rose and fell with a heavy breath. She gazed into his eyes, her expression somber. "I know, Luke."

He tilted his head at her, uncomprehending.

"I know why you have never removed your shirt in my presence."

"Wh-what?" he stammered through his closed throat.

"I saw you once. Soon after we arrived in London. You'd woken from a nightmare and had removed your shirt. You were washing yourself." She paused, and then said in a throbbing voice, "I saw the scars."

He stared at her, unmoving, unspeaking. His mind roared. She knew. She'd known all this time.

She reached forward, cupping his jaw in her hand, her thumb rasping over his unshaven cheek. "I didn't mention it because I wanted to give you time. I knew you would tell me about them when you were ready." Again, a pause. Then, softly, "Are you ready now?"

"I—" His voice broke, and he cleared it. "I don't know," he said roughly. He lowered her wrist and released her. She returned the cloth to the basin and came to sit beside him on the bed on his uninjured side. She snuggled up against him. "It was the old duke, wasn't it? He made those scars on your back?"

"Yes."

"You told me he beat you. But this…this was different."

"Yes." His voice was so dry it felt as insubstantial as an

autumn leaf, so easily crushed under any passerby's boot heel.

"What did he do?"

He pushed out a painful breath. Then he closed his eyes. "He burned me." And a long-subdued part of him, that frightened boy who'd endured those burns, resonated in his voice.

"How?"

"Cigars," he muttered. Fear and shame swirled heavily within him. He didn't want to tell anyone about this. Hell, he never had, although sometimes he thought his mother had guessed. But even she had never broached the topic.

Emma made a pained noise and pressed herself more tightly against him.

"He said the reasons were twofold. The first was that he might burn the badness out of me. The second because he wanted me to be forever aware that I belonged to the House of Trent. To no one else."

"Oh, Luke."

"That's why the scars are in the shape of a T. He intended to brand me." The words came easier now. "But he didn't completely succeed—he died before he could finish it. So now..." A bitter noise choked out from his throat. "Now...I have an incomplete *T* branded upon my back."

"It doesn't matter—" Emma began.

"He didn't succeed in burning the wickedness out of me, but he did succeed in one way: I will never forget that I bear the mark of the House of Trent upon my back."

She shuddered against him. "And that bleeds over, somehow, to the new duke. Even though he never knew what the old duke had done to you."

"Yes," Luke admitted. "Every time I see him, a part of me remembers what his father did to me. A part of me remembers that he owns me, that a part of me will essentially remain a slave to him for the rest of my life." He swallowed hard. "I try not to link the two. I know Trent had no part in it. But I can't help it. I see him and..." He shook his head.

"It must be so hard to look at the duke and see his father in him."

"Yes." That was exactly it.

"How old were you when he...when he burned you?"

Groaning softly, he bent his head and ran his free hand through his hair. "Over years, starting when I was five or six. He'd add a new burn after a few months, after the last one healed." Luke clenched his jaw, remembering the pain, the pulsating fear that had seized him each time he was summoned into his father's study. "He said...he said it was because he wanted me to always feel it, always feel the pain of the sores as my shirt rubbed against them. That way, it was more likely to work."

"He was mad," Emma said flatly. "A mad bastard."

He nuzzled his nose into her hair. "I never thought so," he muttered. "I believed him."

"You were an impressionable child. He was your father, a duke, revered by all."

"You are the first person I've ever known who has made me believe that maybe he *was* mad—"

"He was!"

"For the first time, I have begun to think that his punishments were a product of his own insane reaction to my mother's affair with Stanley. That maybe, just maybe, they had nothing to do with me."

"How could they have had anything to do with you? You. Were. Innocent." She said the last words with a solemn forcefulness, as if she were trying to physically drill those words into his soul.

He pressed a kiss to the top of her head, breathing her in. She smelled so good. Fresh and sweet, and so familiar to him now.

Somehow, he did believe her. If drilling those words into his soul had been her intent, she had succeeded.

They sat there for a long while, and when she finally pulled back, he turned away from her, for the first time baring his ugly, scarred back to her view.

"Will you bathe me?" he asked softly.

"Always." She retrieved the cloth and with soft, smooth strokes, she washed his torso, starting with his back, pressing her lips to various spots after she'd finished rinsing them.

He closed his eyes. They hadn't made love in weeks—not that his body had stopped responding to hers, but there had been too much pain that first fortnight, and the third week, she'd been adamant about his need to heal.

Now he wanted her. His pulse throbbed between his legs, and his cock hardened, pressing against the front of his drawers. Her kisses pressed harder as time went on, and when she nudged him to turn so she could clean his front, the color was high on her cheeks and her thick, dark lashes were downcast. She was so beautiful his breath caught in his throat.

She rinsed him and dried him, then her hands went to the waist of his undergarments as she looked up at him through her lashes. "Let me bring you pleasure."

They held each other's gazes for a long moment. He

nodded. "Yes. Make me come. My body needs you, needs to come in you."

Her color deepened at his words. She opened his drawers and lowered her mouth to him. His cock jerked at the first touch of her lips, the soft, hot feel of her pressing against him sending pleasure rolling through his body. Leaning back on one hand, he threaded the fingers of the other through her hair, locking her against him. "Yes, Em. That's it. Lick me. It feels so damn good."

She stroked her tongue over him in long, hot drags. He was so full, so thick, and every touch of her mouth made him harder. Made him want to bury himself inside her.

Made him mad for her. For every bit of her.

His fingers tightened in her hair when she opened, and his cock slid deep into her mouth. "God," he growled out. "That's right, angel. Take me in your mouth. Deeper. That's it. Yes."

She grasped the root of him between tight fingers, circling him, gliding up and down concurrently with her lips tightened into a round O of pleasure as they moved over him. Up and down. Tight and hot and wet.

He groaned as hot waves of sensation undulated from his cock and through his body. She set the rhythm with her long slides up and down him, but he needed control. He locked his hand in her hair, stopping her, then he thrust into her mouth and hand.

She took him. Deep, soft, wet. So sweet and hot and carnal. She relaxed over him, allowing him to set the pace, keeping herself open and accepting of whatever he demanded of her.

He loved that so damn much about her. He loved her

strength and her loyalty. Her passion and her intelligence... and her acceptance.

This was the woman he wanted to be with. Forever.

"I love you," he murmured, pumping into her mouth. "I love you, Emma."

She couldn't respond, couldn't reciprocate, couldn't repeat the words back to him. His bollocks drew up tight against his body, and sensation coalesced at the base of his spine. He was going to come.

With a harsh gasp, he pulled her off him. Seed dribbled from the tip of his cock. When she bent down, he allowed her to lick it off, closing his eyes at the near painful pleasure of it.

"I... need to... be inside you," he ground out.

He lay back on the bed, dragging her along with him. She scrambled up onto the bed. She was still wearing her nightgown, but he knew from experience she was naked underneath.

"Ride me," he commanded huskily.

She settled over him, her knees on either side of his hips, her hot, slick center sliding over him. She was ready for him. Taking him into her mouth had aroused her.

"I don't want to hurt you," she gasped.

"You won't," he promised. "Take me inside you. Now."

She reached down to guide him. They both groaned as the steely length of him penetrated her lush body. "God, Em. You're so wet. So tight," he murmured, closing his eyes to the onslaught of sensation.

Her body swallowed him in a hot sheath, and when she leaned forward, the hard points of her breasts brushed against him through the fabric of her nightgown. When they moved over his own sensitive nipples, he gave a low growl of approval. He clutched her buttocks in his palms, lifting her up and slamming her down over him. Even though he was on the bottom, she surrendered control.

She cupped his face in both her hands, sinking her fingers into his hair, and gave in to his movements. She tightened over him, and he ground up into her, stroking her most sensitive places with his body.

She grew tighter and tighter, releasing tiny whimpers whenever he buried himself the deepest. God, how he loved the sweet little noises she made.

And then her body clamped over him, and she came in a hot, tight rush, her channel undulating over his cock. Damn. The pleasure—it was too much. He pumped furiously inside her, then exploded into her, giving a hoarse shout as he did. "Emma!"

His body released its seed in hot ropes. It went on and on. Luke had no control of his wild, frantic thrusts as he poured himself into her, as pleasure overwhelmed him in crashing waves.

She slumped over him—even that slight movement making him shudder. Her weight was distributed over his body, slung across him, but he felt no pain in his gunshot wound. Further proof that he was almost healed.

They lay still, both trembling occasionally in the aftermath.

Finally, she murmured, "You came inside me."

He turned his face, his lips brushing over her ear. He kissed her there. "Yes. Is that all right?"

She pulled back slightly so she could look at him. He gazed into her beautiful eyes.

"Yes, Luke. It is more than all right. I . . ." Blushing, she averted her gaze.

"You what?"

Her breath whispered against his neck. "I hope you will come inside me every time. It's…"

"Erotic?" he asked.

"Yes. So erotic. And…so much more."

He understood. They had been together so many times, but never like this. Coming inside her was a statement almost stronger than any vow. It was a silent promise he made her. A commitment. A guarantee that she belonged to him, and he would take care of her, no matter what. He hoped she understood all that. He believed she did.

There was a knock at the door.

Blowing out a breath, Luke called, "What?"

"Your family is here, sir," Baldwin said.

"All of them?"

"Yes," Baldwin confirmed dryly. "All."

"Very well. Show them into the drawing room. We'll join them there in a few minutes."

It took a while longer than he'd expected. Emma dressed him carefully, paying special attention to his cravat, chewing her lip in concentration as she attempted to get every fold just right. A smile tugged at his lips as he sat docilely, allowing her to fret over him.

Then she called in Delaney to help her dress, even after he'd insisted he could serve her in return. He only relented when she promised him she'd give him that privilege when his bandages were off for good.

Finally, bathed, dressed, and combed, they entwined arms, and Luke rose from the chair he'd been seated in for the past half hour. Again, his wound pulled but it didn't hurt. Still, he tugged Emma tight against his body. He liked her close. He wanted her close forever.

His family awaited him in the drawing room: Trent and Sarah, Esme, Sam, and Theo and Mark. They all stood when he and Emma entered, and Mark began to clap. They all joined in the applause, and Luke found himself blushing and embarrassed.

"Good God, I'm not a child," he grumbled. "I've been walking for over a quarter of a century, after all."

"Oh, Luke," Sarah said, her smile reaching her blue eyes as she clasped her hands together over her expanding belly, "it is so good to see you up and about."

Trent came and clapped him on the back. Sam helped him onto the sofa. Theo, the youngest of his brothers, dark-haired and still retaining that air of boyish innocence, asked, "Does it still hurt?"

"Not at all," Luke assured him.

They all settled in with tea and sweet cakes the cook had prepared, chatting comfortably among themselves. Luke gazed at them, from Esme, the youngest of them all, to his brothers and Sarah and finally to Emma. She gazed at him with what could only be described as adoration in her eyes.

It was fitting. Because he damned well adored her, too.

For the first time, they were all gathered together. He'd wanted this. He'd planned it.

He and his siblings spoke of their mother with far less tension than they had in the past months. Emma had told them everything Morton had told her, and they no longer had that black cloud of her possible death hanging miserably over them.

"She's all right," Esme said. "I truly believe that."

Everyone agreed. There was still the matter of finding her and Steven Lowell, but to Luke it felt like a huge weight had been lifted from his shoulders. His mother was alive. He just hoped that wherever she was, she was happy.

"I would make it a personal mission of mine to find her," Sam said. "If only..." He sighed, glancing toward the window that looked out over Cavendish Square.

They all knew what he meant. Tomorrow he was leaving on yet another mission for the Crown, he'd told them, and he'd no idea when he'd be returning to London. To abandon that mission to find their mother would be considered nothing short of an act of treason.

"We'll keep looking," Trent assured him.

"Always," Mark agreed, and Theo nodded.

"But she's alive," Luke said. "That's what matters. And I hope this gypsy man is what she wants."

Mark shrugged. "Our mother is so whimsical. Perhaps it's what she wants for now. But I wouldn't be surprised if she came wandering back to Ironwood Park one of these days, full of apologies for making us worry."

Esme made a low growl in her throat, and all eyes turned to her. "If she does, I do believe I shall throttle her."

"You and me both!" Theo agreed.

Luke laughed as the odd image of his two gentlest siblings—Esme and Theo—throttling their mother invaded his mind. They all joined him in laughter. Even Trent.

When the laughter began to die down, Luke took a steadying breath and rose, shocking everyone silent. Emma gave a small gasp as his body separated from hers.

He raised his hand, asking for quiet, even though everyone was already staring at him. "There's something I need to say. I want all of you to listen and to hear me."

Suddenly his heart was beating so fast his vision went blurry. He blinked hard and calmed himself. He'd do this. For Emma and for himself. And for hell's sake, he refused to faint.

It was his only chance at happiness, and he needed to grab on to it with both hands and hold it tight.

* * *

Emma gazed up at Luke, confused. He stood over her, looking tall and handsome in a tailcoat that hugged his broad shoulders and an embroidered waistcoat and snowy cravat that she had worked so hard to tie just right. A part of her had wanted to show his family how very perfect Luke could be. And he was perfect, standing over her. He looked so hale and strong, too—the paleness of his skin over the past three weeks replaced with a flush of color.

She smiled up at him, waiting. She didn't know what he wanted to tell all of them, but pride bloomed in her chest at the sight of him. He was confident, healthy...and virile. Right now, there was no hint of that sullen, angry man whose face his family had seen too often.

This was a man who made her proud. And she knew he'd made his family proud, too. None of them could stop talking about how he'd gone after Roger Morton. About how he'd leapt in front of her. How he'd taken a bullet for her. How he'd saved her life.

In their eyes, he was a hero. In her eyes, he was *everything*.

He looked down at her, and their gazes locked. He reached down with one hand, gesturing for hers. She raised it, and he clasped it in the hard strength of his fingers.

"Emma," he said, his voice a low rasp. "I need to do this here and now, with my entire family to bear witness to it."

A frown drew her brows together. "What...?"

He squeezed her fingers. "Two months ago, I was a lost, wandering soul. I didn't know who I was or where I belonged. And then I met you."

Her breath caught.

"You were kind but firm. Gentle but resolute. And so very beautiful. At times I wondered how you could be real."

"Luke," she began, her voice a reedy whisper, but he raised his hand to stop her.

"You really are my angel, Emma. You've helped me to find my way. You've taught me how to be a man. How to love."

As Emma stared up at him, the room seemed to shrink. His surrounding family members faded into the background, leaving only Luke. Only his firm grip on her hand, the expression of devotion on his face, the clear look of unadulterated love in his blue eyes.

"I love you, Emma," he murmured. "When we are together, I am"—he drew in a shaky breath—"a man who is whole again. Who is complete."

Very slowly, carefully due to his injury, he lowered himself to one knee. He brought his other hand up so he was clasping her one hand in two of his own. "I know I am difficult. I am changeable and moody and temperamental. I am not an easy man to live with. You know this—you've seen all of my darkness. But you have pushed me toward the light. You make me want to be a better man. Moreover, you make me believe I can be that man.

"I will never stop loving you, Em. Since the first moment I saw you, you have been the only woman for me. That will never change. You bring me peace. You bring me light."

He bowed his head, brought her hand close, and pressed soft lips against her knuckles. Then he looked back up at her, his crystalline blue eyes shining.

"Be mine, Emma. I want you." His voice rasped as he spoke. "For the rest of my life, and yours. Be my wife."

For a few seconds, silence filled the room. That last word, *wife*, resonated over and over inside Emma's head.

Be his wife.

She slid forward, off the sofa and onto her knees before him, her skirts belling around her.

"Yes," she whispered. There was no hesitation, no second thought, no concern or insecurity. Unlike in her first marriage, this time she knew her heart. Luke had become as essential to her as her next breath.

She looked up into his handsome face, into those compelling eyes. "I love you so much, Luke. I want nothing more in this world than to be your wife."

"Em..." he choked out. He released her hand and wrapped his arms around her, pulling her against him. She held him tight, her breaths short and rapid, her heart pounding in a staccato rhythm against her breast.

Luke's wife. Luke, in her heart and in her life... and in her bed, for the rest of her life. She raised her face toward him. He captured her lips with his own in a tender, possessive kiss.

"Mine," his kiss said. "Mine. Forever."

And she was. His. Forever. He was right—it wouldn't be easy. They hadn't solved all their problems completely, not his nightmares or his tendency to run or drink. But he'd showed her that he was willing to work, willing to make adjustments ... and try. She had a feeling that that was what people in love did. Make compromises, change, grow.

Hearing movement from somewhere beyond, Emma jolted back to the present. She jerked backward, heat slamming into her cheeks. She'd completely forgotten about Luke's family.

Luke kept her pressed tightly against him as he glanced over his shoulder. Mortified, she peeked up, but all she saw were smiling faces.

She blinked at them as they gathered round: the Duke of Trent and his wife, Sam, Mark, Theo, and Esme. Sarah and Esme helped Emma stand as the brothers crowded around Luke, helping him to his feet as well.

Congratulations and laughter, hugs and backslapping reigned for several minutes. Through it all, Emma and Luke were acutely aware of each other, of the powerful new bond they'd forged between them—a bond that neither would ever break.

Epilogue

*L*uke's intuition had led him back to the rambling mansion Morton had bought in Chiswick. He brought workers with him who tore down the walls in those two rooms with new paint.

As soon as the first hunk of plaster crumbled away, money began to pour out of the walls. All in all, they found eight thousand pounds hidden within that old house's plaster.

It only accounted for about a third of the money Morton had stolen from Emma's father. But Mark had taken it upon himself to look into Morton's affairs, and he'd assured them that they would probably double that amount once they'd sold off Morton's "assets"—many of which they found in the house's ballroom.

They'd never have all the money the man had stolen—no doubt he'd spent much on personal extravagances—but it was enough. Enough for Emma's father to rebuild his family's life in Bristol.

Two days after they found the money, Emma and Luke married by special license in London. It was the most beautiful day of Emma's life. Watching Luke express his love to her in a church, before God and his family, was intensely emotional for Emma. Tears leaked from the corners of her eyes as they spoke their vows.

They were married. They were one.

The very next day, they headed for Bristol in a private carriage. A second carriage containing the most renowned heart doctor in London, as well as three servants, followed. They arrived at the house on a snowy winter's day.

The days since Luke's proposal had been the happiest of Emma's life, but the dismal sight of her father's house through the falling snow sobered both her and Luke.

Emma left the carriage, huddled against Luke under the umbrella the coachman held for them. They ascended the steps and went to the tall, black door and knocked.

Emma glanced at Luke. "It's so odd to be knocking on the door of the house I considered home for so long."

"You should walk right in, then."

"No," she said softly. "My home is with you now."

It was Jane who answered the door. Emma's sister looked tired and thin, with dark circles of worry smudged beneath her eyes and her lips turned down in a frown. But when she saw who was at the door, she threw herself into Emma's arms with a low exclamation of joy.

"Oh, Emma! You're home! I missed you so very much!"

Emma held her sister fiercely. "I missed you, too."

It took several seconds before Jane gathered herself

and pulled away, then she flushed as she glanced at Luke and the servants who had gathered behind them.

"I'm so sorry," she murmured. "You mustn't stand here in the rain. Please, come inside."

They all gathered in the entry hall, where Emma made the introductions. She hadn't sent a letter home since Luke was recovering from the gunshot wound. At that time, Luke had insisted she send a hundred pounds to cover any immediate expenses and debts. But that had been before the proposal. Before the marriage. Before they'd found the money Roger Morton had stolen.

"Jane," she said now, "I'd like to present Lord Lukas Hawkins. My husband."

Jane's mouth fell open. Her gaze darted between Luke and Emma. Smiling, Luke slipped his hand over Emma's and threaded his fingers with hers. She grinned at her sister.

"Close your mouth or you will trap a fly," she teased. Their mother used to tell them that.

Jane's mouth snapped shut. "It's winter," she said, using the retort that had once earned Emma a swat on her bottom. "There are no flies in winter."

Emma just smiled, and Jane's expression softened. "I...suppose I should say congratulations," she murmured. "I am surprised...but"—she glanced at Emma—"your letters. I could tell you possessed strong feelings..."

"As I do for her," Luke said softly, squeezing Emma's hand.

"I am so glad to hear that," Jane told him.

"Is Papa in his bedchamber?" Emma asked. "We want to tell him the news."

Jane smiled and nodded. "He'll be so happy to see you."

They went upstairs to Emma's father's room. Her heart constricted as she entered the room, Luke staying near the door while she went forward to greet her father. He was as she'd left him, small and fragile, his hair now completely white, his features swollen from the dropsy.

He looked at her, his eyes not seeming to recognize her for a long moment. Then his expression softened. "Emma," he said in a cracking voice that had once boomed across the Bristol docks, "you've come home to me."

She bent down and hugged him the best she could. "I've brought something for you."

"Will I like it?" he huffed out.

"I think so."

She introduced Luke first. Her father was wary but accepting, and Luke—oh Lord. Her heart surged at the way he behaved toward her father—with such polite deference she'd never thought possible from him. But she knew why—because the man in the bed was her father, and Luke had told her he'd wanted so much for her father to like him.

Second, she introduced the doctor, a man who was known for his excellent work with ailments of the heart.

Third, she had the servants carry in the large satchel into which her father's money had been carefully packed.

"Twelve thousand pounds, Papa. I know it's not everything, but we're promised more."

"I'd heard...you'd found Morton," her father said, breathless and wide-eyed, "but the money...I didn't know...God Almighty, Emma." He looked at her as if seeing her for the first time, his brown eyes showing a rare clarity. "You have become a magnificent woman."

By the way Luke smiled, she knew he agreed.

* * *

Later, they ate a meal with Jane prepared by the cook they'd brought with them from London. It was clearly the first excellent meal Jane had partaken of in some time, for she ate with rare enthusiasm. Afterward, they went into the drawing room, where the doctor joined them.

He told them their father suffered not only from dropsy but from melancholy. The dropsy he could treat with a very exact prescription of digitalis along with certain other remedies, and he was confident that that aspect of their father's illness would improve.

The melancholy had begun after the death of their mother, and it had grown worse with the theft of their money along with the encroaching illness and the feelings of helplessness resulting from both. After hours speaking to Emma's father, the doctor developed a plan for a cure. It consisted of prescribed interaction with people outside the house, daily walks, social events, adding furniture back to the house to infuse some sense that the living actually inhabited it.

After listening to what the doctor had to say, Luke, Emma, and Jane all agreed to join to work on curing this aspect of their father's illness together.

They began that very evening, helping him down into the drawing room. He lay on the sofa covered in blankets, and for the first time in a very long while, he played a game of chess with his eldest daughter.

* * *

Emma and Luke remained in Bristol until the spring, when the snow melted away, the sun shone brighter and warmer, and the daffodils began to reveal their cheery yellow faces.

Emma, with Luke and Jane's help, had restored the house to its former glory. Emma's father was on the long path to recovery, though he'd never be the powerful man with the booming voice she remembered from her childhood.

Bertram had come for a visit every month. They'd begun with an overnight visit, which in the subsequent months had stretched to a week. And now he was going with them to London, along with Jane, who was to have her second Season this year, and their father.

They'd received word a few days ago that Sarah, the Duchess of Trent, had given birth to a healthy baby boy, who was to be named Lukas Samson Hawkins after the duke's two eldest brothers. Trent and Sarah had asked them to be the child's godparents, so Emma and Luke's first order of business in London would be to attend the christening.

After the christening, Luke planned to talk to Trent about locating their mother once and for all. In his letter, Trent had alluded to some kind of clue relating to the whereabouts of Steven Lowell. It seemed like the brothers were finally close to a long-overdue reunion with the dowager.

Emma's family all seemed excited about traveling to London, especially her new brother-in-law, Bertram, who'd taken to painting Jane wearing different-colored dresses and suggesting what colors she should ultimately wear in Town.

"Janie," he'd say, "sky blue it is. Blue is so so pretty." But the next day he'd change his mind to lavender. Then buttercup. Then lilac. Then primrose. Bertram loved colors.

Luke and Emma had lived and loved hard over the past months, their bond growing ever stronger, their relationship ever closer, as the days flew by. There had been nightmares. There had been arguments. But Luke and Emma's fierce love and loyalty for each other never wavered.

Now they stood outside the house on a fine spring day, hand in hand. Servants bustled about, preparing for their departure by loading their luggage into the carriages. Emma raised her face to the sun and inhaled a deep breath of warm air. Then she glanced at Luke, who smiled at her.

"London," she murmured.

"London," he agreed.

"Home," she said, and she heard the lilt of surprise in her voice. His hand squeezed hers tighter.

"Is London home to you?"

"It is. I've missed being there with you."

He bent down and kissed her softly on the lips. "Me too. I've been thinking of my bed. All the things I did to you there. All the things I wish to do to you in the future."

She shuddered and said in a voice lower than a whisper, "Will you tie me to the bedposts again?"

"Most definitely. I'll tie you in intricate knots of silk, Em, your legs and arms bound for my pleasure. Then I'll have my wicked way with you all night long."

"Oh..." she breathed as a warm flush of arousal bloomed within her.

A cocky glint entered his eyes. "You want me, don't you?"

"Luke..."

"Right here, right now. You want me to take you. Possess you. Make you come."

Her eyes widened as she glanced furtively about. "There are people *everywhere*."

He gave a negligent flick of his wrist. "They're not paying any attention to us, angel. Come with me. We're going for a walk."

With a firm grip on her hand, he tugged her behind the house, to the garden. Some of the bulb flowers her mother had planted years ago still bloomed tenaciously, providing lovely splashes of color against the manicured bushes and grass.

He pressed her against the back wall of the house. And then he went down onto his knees, flipped up her skirts, and worshiped her sex with his mouth until she forgot about the people on the other side of the house. Until she forgot about everything but Luke and the pleasure he gave her.

Holding her firmly against the wall, he pushed his fingers inside her, stroking, as his tongue swirled over her most sensitive spot.

Her hips began to jerk against him, and little cries escaped from her throat. When she came, it was with a slamming intensity that racked her body from her toes to the top of her head. Such pleasure. Such peace.

When it was over, her knees began to buckle, but Luke caught her in his arms. Once more pressing her back against the wall, he commanded, "Wrap your legs around me."

She complied, and he settled his cock at her entrance and pushed into her with a single hard thrust. She bit his shoulder to prevent the scream.

Holding her pinned against the wall, he moved inside her in heavy, rough strokes, staring at her with piercing blue eyes, his hands tight over the backs of her thighs, the material of her dress bunched between them.

"Luke," she moaned. "Luke."

He grew impossibly harder, his thrusts impossibly stronger. His body was so solid, so perfectly strong against her.

"I love you, angel," he gritted out. And then he held her pinned, still, as he emptied into her. She wrapped her arms around him, opening herself, taking every bit of him she possibly could. She wanted nothing less than all of this man—and he'd given it to her.

Finally he relaxed, lowering her gently to the ground and slipping out of her body.

Her skirts fell back around her ankles, and as he pressed his forehead to hers, she fixed the falls of his trousers.

She cupped his face in her hands and brought him to her lips for a soft kiss. When she pulled away, she said with a smile, "To London?"

"To London," he agreed.

Hand in hand, they walked back around to the other side of the house, where Bertram bounded up to them holding the pair of his shoes that he'd thought he'd lost, Jane hurried over to discuss some aspect of closing up the house, and their father, leaning heavily on his cane, asked

Luke about the horses he'd selected for this part of the journey.

Luke and Emma shared a secret, private smile, and then they turned to their motley band of a family with twin grins, happiness and fulfillment surging through them both.

Please read on for a preview of
The Scoundrel's Seduction . . .

Chapter One

꧁꧂

"Everything in place?" Samson Hawkins eyed the chamber of his pistol, then lowered it to his lap. He glanced over at Laurent, who studied him with a troubled expression on his face.

"Aye, sir."

Sam's lips firmed, and he looked away, ignoring the impulse to mutter something comforting to the lad. Laurent had chosen this life for himself. It wasn't a life for the weak but for the hard and pitiless. Sam never forgot that, and neither should Laurent, if he wished to live.

He glanced out the carriage window and scanned the dark back wall of the opulent Mayfair town house until his gaze paused at a second-story window. The window appeared innocuous enough, with the glow of the lamps inside the room casting golden light through the indigo silk curtains.

Dunthorpe was in that room right now, by himself. Perhaps reading, perhaps drinking. Perhaps involved in more nefarious pursuits, such as treachery and treason. Waiting for Sam—or, more correctly, for Sam's alias.

Waiting for death, though he didn't know it yet.

Sam drew in a long breath, and his fingers tightened around the grip of his pistol.

"Watch for my signal. It should come after the first shot. I'll be down thirty seconds after I give it. As soon as I am inside, double-check the streets and ensure everything's ready to go." He tucked his pistol into an inner pocket of his coat.

Laurent nodded.

He met Laurent's gaze evenly. "Good. When all's said and done, it shouldn't take more than five minutes. If a quarter of an hour passes and I haven't returned, you and Carter know what to do."

"Aye."

Sam's fingers curled over the door handle, but Laurent grabbed his forearm, holding him back. "Hawk?"

He glanced back at the boy, arching his brows expectantly.

"Good luck. I know...I know how much you despise this—"

Sam's teeth clenched hard. The boy had no idea...

"But it's the right thing to do. We must keep the Regent safe."

"I know, lad," Sam said quietly. Nevertheless, no matter how dastardly his target, killing would never be something Sam enjoyed. There was something about snuffing out a human life that made him feel unclean. As low of a creature as the scum he eliminated from the world.

And he knew better than anyone that Dunthorpe required elimination. The man had brought about too much death and misery already, and if he remained living, he would be the cause of much, much more.

Sam slipped out of the carriage. In measured, unhurried strides, he walked around the corner to the front of the town house. It was late, and the streets weren't as busy as at midday, but this was London—a city that never completely slept. He took thorough stock of the people who passed him—a woman flanked by her two small children, the three of them huddled against the chill. A man hurrying down the street. A rubbish wagon, a closed carriage, and three men on horseback. None of them paid him any heed.

He walked up the four steps and stopped on the town house's landing. Then, as if he were here on civilized business, he knocked on the door.

A manservant answered. The butler, Sam knew. Name was Richards.

"May I help you?"

"Denis Martin," Sam said, layering on a thick French accent. He'd learned French as a child and had spent so many years in France he could speak the language fluently and as flawlessly as a native. His Frenchman-speaking-English accent was also perfect. No one perceived his Englishness when he used it. "His lordship is expecting me."

"Of course, sir." Richards's expression didn't change, but there was a slight flicker of something in his eyes. The French weren't the most popular of people in England right now, and evidently this man didn't approve of a French frog visiting his master.

The butler stepped aside to allow Sam into the entry

hall. Sam kept his hat low over his brow and his face turned away and in shadows.

In the end, the problem of Richards was the most difficult element of this mission. After completing his investigation into Dunthorpe's household, Sam was convinced the servant was innocent as to the dealings of his master. Sam's superiors had requested he "take care of" Richards as well, to eliminate the possibility of the butler identifying him as the man who'd assassinated his master. But his superiors knew that Sam had drawn solid lines between those acts he would and would not commit. He would steal, lie, torture, and assassinate in the interests of king and country. But he would not commit cold-blooded murder of an innocent British citizen, even to save his own hide.

So his superiors had eventually given in, but everyone was clear that if there were to be any repercussions of Richards's survival tonight, all Sam's colleagues and support would fade into the shadows, and Sam would be on his own.

Which was all well and good. Sam had managed situations like this before, and he would do so again.

"May I take your hat and coat, sir?" the butler questioned.

"Non. It is not necessary. My message is a quick one. I shall be in and out in a matter of moments."

"Very well. Right this way."

Sam followed the servant up a narrow set of stairs, then down a corridor lit sparsely with two gilded wall sconces set widely apart. They stopped at the elegant door at its end, and Richards knocked before opening the door to the gruff, "Yes?" from its other side.

Sam waited in a shadow between two of the sconces, his gaze lowered.

"Mr. Martin is here to see you, sir."

There was a pause, long enough to make the hairs on the back of Sam's neck crawl.

"Very well. Show him in."

Richards opened the door wider, moving aside to allow Sam to pass. Sam stepped into the drawing room.

Once inside, he raised his head. As always, he scanned his surroundings. He'd been in this room before, to conduct preliminary information gathering. Nothing had changed—the furniture crowding the place was ornate, with much carved oak and silk and velvet upholstering. The many-paned window hung on the opposite wall, large and square and covered by that indigo curtain. He pictured Laurent down there, waiting for him. Worrying about him.

Laurent wouldn't need to wait long. In minutes, Sam would be back in the carriage and they'd be fading into the night.

His gaze focused on his target. Viscount Dunthorpe was an older man, in his late forties, with a full head of gray hair and dark, penetrating eyes that let nothing slip past. He was well known for his biting cynicism and cold wit, and also as one of the most brilliant debaters in parliament.

He was also a traitor.

"Lord Dunthorpe." Keeping his French accent firmly in place, Sam held out his hand. "It is an honor to finally make your acquaintance."

His face impassive, the viscount took Sam's hand. The handshake was terse and businesslike. Dunthorpe turned to his servant. "That will be all, Richards. You may retire for the evening."

After the servant left, Dunthorpe gazed at Sam, his expression cold and calculating. Sam schooled his own features to absolute flatness. He needed to delay for approximately sixty seconds. That would give the servant time to get to his quarters in the attic.

"Do you have the schedule?" Dunthorpe asked.

"*Oui*, I do," Sam said gruffly.

Dunthorpe held out his hand, palm open. "Give it over," he commanded. He spoke as a man accustomed to authority.

Sam glanced meaningfully at the tea service he'd seen placed on a round table in the corner. "Will you invite me to tea, milord?"

Dunthorpe crossed his arms over his chest and gave Sam an arch look. "Indeed, I hadn't intended to do any such thing."

Sam rubbed his frigid hands together. He hadn't worn gloves for a reason. "It is very cold outside, milord. Brandy, then?"

Dunthorpe's eyes narrowed. "*French* brandy? What do you take me for, a common smuggler?"

No, this man dealt in much more serious crimes. Sam shook his head. "*Mais, non,*" he said gravely. "Of course not, milord."

Dunthorpe sneered. "You haven't even removed your hat. You don't look at all like a man interested in settling down for a nice cup of tea or a nip of brandy. You look like a man prepared to do your duty and then flee in the event I should decide you know too much."

Well, then. Already hurling threats. Sam supposed that

one had been meant to infuse some kind of fear into him, but it hadn't worked. He had dealt with men of Dunthorpe's ilk too often.

He'd given Richards enough time. By now the man was entering his chamber and in another few seconds, he would be donning his nightcap and preparing for bed.

"Alas. In that case I shall hand over the plans, monsieur." Sam reached into his coat. His fingers slid against the cold metal barrel of his pistol before he clasped the edge of the folded pages. He drew them out and gave them to Dunthorpe.

The man snatched the pages from Sam and opened them greedily. Sam's lip would have curled in disgust if he'd allowed it. The bastard held such enthusiasm for destroying everything the British held dear.

In truth, these papers contained a plethora of false statements that made Sam grind his teeth. Deceiving the populace was another thing that ranked rather low on his list of preferred activities, but it was what his superiors wanted—to show Dunthorpe, this traitor, as a hero of the people. These papers would serve as the "proof" that he had died defending the Regent, not embroiled in the midst of a profitable scheme to murder him.

The powers that be had decided it would be "too traumatic" should the populace hear the truth about their national hero, who'd served as an officer of the British Navy for eighteen years. The truth was, the only man Dunthorpe had ever served was himself. He'd only cared about his own gain. He'd been selling secrets to the French since he was a youth, and now he had organized this conspiracy, all for personal political and economic gain.

"What's this?"

Sam watched Dunthorpe skim the papers, his movements growing more frantic, his eyes widening at what he was reading—all the sordid details about the plot, with the slight twist eliminating Dunthorpe from the list of those at fault and instead pointing to him as the hero.

"You bastard. This isn't the schedule." Then he flicked the papers away. They fluttered to the ground as Dunthorpe lifted dark, furious eyes at him. "Who are you?" he growled.

Sam raised a brow. His heart wasn't even pounding hard. He might as well have been sitting in his desk chair at his own house reading the *Times*.

What did this say about him? If nothing else, it said that he was too far gone to ever feel truly human again.

He shrugged and said softly, using his own, English-accented voice, "I am a concerned citizen. For God, king, and country, my lord. We cannot let you destroy it."

He reached into his coat again, this time drawing out his weapon, cocking it at the same time. But Dunthorpe was faster than his aging appearance made him out to be. The man scrambled backward, hands fumbling with the drawer on the table behind him. He jerked it open and yanked out a gun as Sam advanced on him, aiming.

Sam possessed the advantage. He had plenty of time. His heart had still not increased in its tempo. He was perfectly calm.

He squeezed the trigger while Dunthorpe's gun was still pointed at the floor.

The resulting *boom* of gunfire echoed through Sam's skull, loud enough to rouse every Londoner in a half-mile radius. Dunthorpe lurched backward, and he slammed into the desk, his body flailing as if he were a rag doll, before crumpling to the carpeted floor.

For the first time all night, Sam's heart kicked against his ribs. *Now* he needed to hurry. Needed to vanish before the authorities were summoned, before Richards showed his face in this room. He still had no intention of killing the man.

He glanced at Dunthorpe's fallen body, saw that the shot had been clean, straight through the man's heart. He quickly bent down to check for a pulse. The viscount was already dead.

Rising, Sam strode to the window and shook the curtains to signal Laurent that he was on his way down. Then he turned and made for the door.

A noise stopped him in his tracks. A tiny, feminine whimper. One he wouldn't have heard had every one of his senses not been attuned.

He homed in on the source of the noise, turning to that little round table tucked into the corner. It was covered with a silk tablecloth whose edges brushed the carpeted floor.

In two long strides he was at the table. He ripped the tablecloth away, sending the china tea service that had lain upon it crashing to the floor. Hot tea splashed against his boots, steaming when it made contact with the cold leather.

It smelled damn good—strong and brisk. He wished Dunthorpe had offered him some.

A woman cowered beneath the table.

A small, blond, frail-looking woman, dressed in white and curled up into a tight ball, as if she might be able to make herself so tiny he wouldn't be able to see her.

Goddammit. A *woman*. The truth of the situation slammed through him, and Sam ground his teeth.

She glanced up at him, her midnight-blue eyes shining with terror.

"Please," she whispered. "Please."

Her slight French accent clicked everything into place. He knew who she was, of course. It was the surprise of seeing her so out of her element—cowering under a table—that had shocked him into not recognizing her immediately. Two months ago, he'd seen her on Dunthorpe's arm as they'd strolled into the Royal Opera House.

It was Lady Dunthorpe, Dunthorpe's beautiful, elegant, cultured French wife. She'd emigrated from France during the revolution, after her entire family had suffered the wrath of the guillotine. She'd been rescued, sent with relatives to England, and had married Dunthorpe at age seventeen, ten or eleven years ago. It was then that Dunthorpe's ties to the French had grown much stronger.

Because, of course, she'd been in league with him.

She wasn't supposed to be here tonight. She'd been visiting friends in Brighton and wasn't due back for another week. The house had been under surveillance for days, and no one had reported her entering or exiting the building.

Bloody. Hell.

"Get up," he told her brusquely.

Her eyes flicked toward Dunthorpe, who lay on the floor, blood seeping across his chest and turning his gray coat black.

He considered his options. Killing her with Dunthorpe's pistol was the first that came to mind. She was as guilty as he was.

But Sam had never killed a woman. Killing a woman would be crossing one of his lines, and they were all he had left—all he had to use as the threads by which he grasped on to the unraveling spool of his humanity.

Out of the question.

He could leave her here.

But she knew too much. Just from the short conversation he'd had with Dunthorpe, she would have learned enough to put everything at risk.

That left the only other option, one that was almost as unpalatable as the other two. He had to bring her with him.

"Get up," he repeated. His voice sounded harsh even to his own ears.

"I...don't...please, I..." she moaned, appearing to make a valiant effort to follow his command but failing, her limbs trembling too violently to support her.

He jammed his pistol back into his coat and crouched down beside her, aware that his time was already up. They needed to leave this place. *Now.*

"I'm not going to hurt you," he told her, and he prayed that it was true. "But I need you to come with me."

She made a little moaning sound of despair. With a sigh, Sam scooped her into his arms and rose. God, she was a little thing. Light as a feather. But she was stiff in his arms.

"I won't hurt you," he said again. Although he didn't blame her for not believing him. How could he? She'd just witnessed him kill her husband in cold blood.

He turned to the door, to the only escape from this

room, and froze, clutching Lady Dunthorpe's rigid, shaking body tightly against him.

Running footsteps resounded on the wooden floor of the outside corridor, and then the door flew open.

Damn it. He'd run out of time.

From the desk of Jennifer Haymore

Dear Reader,

When Mrs. Emma Curtis, the heroine of THE ROGUE'S PROPOSAL, came to see me, I'd just finished writing *The Duchess Hunt*, the story of the Duke of Trent and his new wife, Sarah, who'd crossed the deep chasm from maid to duchess, and I was feeling very satisfied in their happily ever after.

Mrs. Curtis, however, had no interest in romance.

"I need you to write my story," she told me. "It's urgent."

I encouraged her to sit down and tell me more.

"I'm on a mission of vengeance," she began. "You see, I need to find my husband's murderer—"

I lifted my hand right away to stop her. "Mrs. Curtis, I don't think this is going to work out. You see, I don't write thrillers or mysteries. I am a romance writer."

"I know, but I think you can help me. I really do."

"How's that?"

"You've met the Duke of Trent, haven't you? And his brother, Lord Lukas?" She leaned forward, dark eyes serious and intent. "You see, I'm searching for the same man they are."

My brows rose. "Really? You're looking for Roger Morton?"

"Yes! Roger Morton is the man who murdered my husband. Please—Lord Lukas is here in Bristol. If you could only arrange an introduction...I know his lordship could help me to find him."

She was right—I did know Lord Lukas. In fact...

I looked over the dark-haired woman sitting in front of me. Mrs. Curtis was a young, beautiful widow. She seemed intelligent and focused.

My mind started working furiously.

Mrs. Curtis and Lord Luke? Could it work?

Maybe...

Luke would require a *lot* of effort. He was a rake of the first order, brash, undisciplined, prone to all manner of excess. But something told me that maybe, just maybe, Mrs. Curtis would be a good influence on him... If I could join them on the mission to find Roger Morton, it just might work out.

(I am a *romance* writer, after all.)

"Are you *sure* you want to meet Lord Lukas?" I asked her. "Have you heard the rumors about him?"

Her lips firmed. "I have heard he is a rake." Her eyes met mine, steady and serious. "I can manage rakes."

There was a steel behind her voice. A steel I approved of. Yes. This could work.

My lips curved into a smile. "All right, Mrs. Curtis. I might be able to manage an introduction..."

And that was how I arranged the first meeting between Emma Curtis and Lord Lukas Hawkins, the second brother of the House of Trent. Their relationship proved to be a rocky one—I wasn't joking when I said Luke was a rake, and in fact, "rake" might be too mild a term. But Emma proved to be a worthy adversary for him, and they ended up traveling a dangerous and emotional but ultimately sweetly satisfying path in THE ROGUE'S PROPOSAL.

Come visit me at my website, www.jenniferhaymore .com, where you can share your thoughts about my books, sign up for some fun freebies and contests, and read more about THE ROGUE'S PROPOSAL and the House of Trent Series. I'd also love to see you on Twitter (@ jenniferhaymore) or on Facebook (www.facebook.com/ jenniferhaymore-author).

Sincerely,

Do you love historical fiction?

Want the chance to hear news about your favourite authors (and the chance to win free books)?

Mary Balogh
Charlotte Betts
Jessica Blair
Frances Brody
Gaelen Foley
Elizabeth Hoyt
Eloisa James
Lisa Kleypas
Stephanie Laurens
Claire Lorrimer
Sarah MacLean
Amanda Quick
Julia Quinn

Then visit the Piatkus website and blog
www.piatkus.co.uk | www.piatkusbooks.net

And follow us on Facebook and Twitter
www.facebook.com/piatkusfiction | www.twitter.com/piatkusbooks

piatkus